I0647815

DIVISIONS

by Kyell Gold

DIVISIONS

Copyright January 2013 by Kyell Gold

Published by Sofawolf Press, Inc.
St. Paul, Minnesota
http://www.sofawolf.com

ISBN 978-1-936689-27-9
Printed in the United States of America
Second trade paperback edition: March 2014
Third printing: November 2020

Cover and interior art by Blotch

For all of you
and, as always, for Kit

CONTENTS

Book 4

Book 5

Foreword

It has been about six years since I started writing this story, and in that time, Dev and Lee's saga has continued to grow beyond my expectations. I have you all to thank for that, for loving these characters as much as I have and supporting the books, for asking for more and telling me how much you care about them. Thank you all!

When I set out to write book three, I had a firm story structure in mind. I wrote that story, but the world has expanded so much that at the end of it I found I had over two hundred thousand words, which would strain the goodwill of even my wonderful publisher, Sofawolf Press. So I looked at the volume and found a place that lent itself to a break, near the middle. I shelved what will become book four, and set about making book three as complete a story as I could.

Lee and Dev both reach milestones at the end of this book, and a year or so is a good space to pause and breathe and collect ourselves before diving into the next chapter. At least, for me it is. The story is not finished by any means, but now when you come to the end you can rest assured that there *will* be a book four.

Coming back to Dev and Lee's world after years away was difficult, but when I immersed myself in it, I found that the characters remained alive and engaging to me. I hope you will find the same, will enjoy this next installment as much as I have, and will come back for book four. I'm already looking forward to tackling that one.

-Kyell Gold, January 2013

LEE'S GUIDE TO FOOTBALL

When I was seven, I had a bunch of classmates ask me whether I wanted the Devils or the Firebirds to win the championship. I didn't know what they were talking about. My dad liked football, but I liked stories, and I may have said a couple things I shouldn't have about people who liked to watch thugs run around on a field and hit each other. So while my mom was combing the playground sand out of my face and chest and tail, my dad started to explain football to me.

Even though I was still at that age where I wanted to be like my dad, I didn't have much interest in football. But with the championship coming up, he thought it was the perfect time to get me started. Whatever else he's done in his life—and I've run through the list more than once—he got me into football. So if you're one of those kids who likes chess and books, listen up, because reading this story you're in the middle of is like growing up in Nicholas Dempsey Middle School. You don't have to like football to get through it, as my dad told me, but it helps.

See, what I always hated about football was that I was bad at it. I'd only played one football game up to then, at camp. I didn't understand the rules. To me, it was just a stupid excuse for big kids to beat up little kids. What my dad told me is that football is actually like a chess game.

Hang on. Stay with me. Imagine you've got these eleven guys. Each one can move in a certain way. You want to advance your position (symbolized by the football) up the field, either by giving it to a piece and having him carry it forward, or by passing it to a piece down the field. The guys who line up right at the boundary are the offensive line—like a bulwark. Behind them stands the quarterback, and behind him the halfback (or running back) and fullback. They're the ones who will carry the ball if you choose to run it. Out to the edges are the speedy guys whose job is to run down the field and be ready if you choose to throw the ball: the wide receivers and tight end.

Your quarterback is like a queen (and believe me, more of them are than you'd think). He's the most powerful piece and he directs the offense. Wolves and lions make good quarterbacks, because they have this inbred pack mentality. The offensive line is like pawns: they only move a very short distance, and their job is to protect the queen. You get big, aggressive guys in there, like bears and boars, because they also have to move the defenders in such a way as to leave room for the running back to run through. This is harder than it sounds, but I'm not going to get into it. The tight end (yes, we've all heard the jokes) either helps block or runs a short way down the field to act as a receiver. Then you've got the running back and fullback, wolverines and horses most often, who are like the bishops: they have to move through the spaces cleared by the pawns. The knights would be the tight end and the slot receiver, who can either help defend or jump short distances down the field. And wide receivers are rooks, who take advantage of long open columns to run down the field. For all those last ones, you get deer, cheetahs, and foxes. And what you have to do with these pieces is design a strategy that will help you gain ground, program a series of moves in advance, and watch them go. Meanwhile, our opponent has his own eleven guys, and he's trying to figure out what your guys are going to do so he can stop them.

If you're defending, your aim is to stop the progress of the other team. This is the part of football I hated, by the way, because I could never tackle, and they could flatten me with one arm. The QB starts out with the ball, so you go after him. You look at the situation on the field, you look at the way the pieces are set up, and you set up your guys to hopefully disrupt what the offense is doing. Your defensive line, setting up across from the offensive line, is actually attacking, which is why the best ones tend to be large, fast predators, like big cats. Then you have a bunch of guys that stay behind the defensive line to mess with the wide receivers and tight end if they get back into that territory. The best ones there are medium-weight predators, like coyotes, bigger foxes, and cheetahs. And because it's such a big field, you have to decide things like do you assign one defender to each specific offensive player, or do the defenders just cover sections of the field, and so on.

And then, not to make things more complicated, but there's everything else, which is called "special teams." If a team doesn't move the ball well enough on offense, they end up kicking it, either to the other team (a punt) or through the goal, if they're close enough. Horses and rabbits, of course, usually do the kicking. On the other side, you need someone quick and slick to catch the kick and try to run it back, and while you get a couple rabbits who are good at this, the best ones have always been weasels and otters.

The thing that makes football more interesting than chess is that the pieces can actually think (well, some of them) and make decisions on the field. They know what they're supposed to do, but if they see something that'll block them, they can make an adjustment and change it. Sometimes they do really stupid things, which is fun, and sometimes they do amazing things, which is even more fun.

Also, I mean, it's guys in tight clothes. There are closeup shots of the quarterback sticking his paws under the center's tail (with some definite touching). There's muscles galore, occasional tail-grabbing, and after the plays, there's butt-patting. What's not to like?

Quick reference guide

This is an example of how the players might line up on the field.

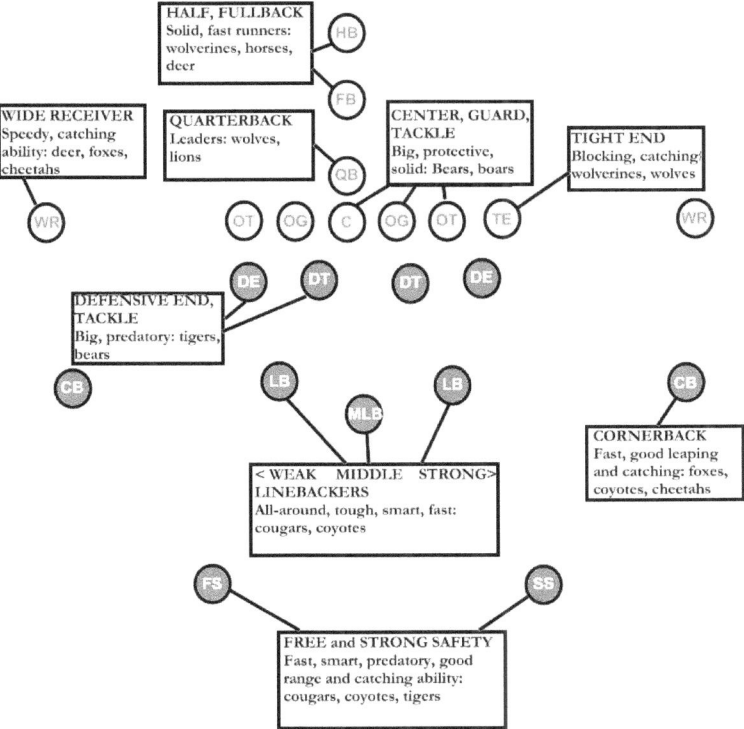

CHEVALI FIREBIRDS 2008 SCHEDULE

9/7, week 1: at Crystal City (L, 24-35)
9/14, week 2: Kerina (W, 31-24)
9/21, week 3: New Kestle (W, 24-10)
9/28, week 4: at Hilltown (L, 0-3)
10/5, week 5: at Aventira (W, 10-3)
10/12, week 6: Millenport (W, 21-0)
10/19: bye
10/26, week 8: Gateway (W, 10-9)
11/2, week 9: Highbourne (W, 20-17)
11/9, week 10: at New Kestle (W, 14-10)
11/16, week 11: at Hellentown (*)
11/23, week 12: at Port City (W, 35-18)

12/1 (Mon), week 13: Pelagia
12/8, week 14: at Yerba
12/15, week 15: Freestone
12/22, week 16: at Kerina
12/29, week 17: Hellentown

*documented in the bonus story "Heart" available online at:
http://kyellgold.com/stories/story_heart.html*

DEV'S GAME-DAY BRIEFING

Okay, with Lee telling you what all the players are supposed to do, I can walk you through how an actual game goes. The teams flip a coin at the beginning of the game. Winner gets to pick whether they want to kick off or receive. To receive means you start on offense and have the first chance to score. But sometimes teams want to kick off, because if you start the first half on defense, you start the second half on offense. Also if you stop the other team right away on the first drive, it gives you a lot of energy going into your offense. The coaches all figure this out. I just know I liked being first on the field.

When a team gets the ball, they line up like Lee described. They get four chances to move the ball ten yards; those are "downs." So there's first down, second down, third down, fourth down. I don't know why they're called that, they just are. Anyway, on first down usually you try to run the ball. That means the QB hands it to the RB and he tries to get ten yards up the field. Actually, if he gets four or five, that's pretty good, and then on second down you might try to run it again. If you can get three or four yards every time you run the ball, you can just run it all day long.

The thing is, though, if you don't get your ten yards in four tries, the other team gets the ball. So most of the time you only take three tries, and if you don't get ten yards, you punt. Punting is where the punter kicks the ball down the field and the other team gets to catch it and try to run back with it. Basically you do that so that they don't get the ball at the spot where you didn't get your ten yards. This is called "field position," as in having good field position (near the other team's goal) or bad field position (near your own).

The other thing you can do on fourth down, if you have good field position, is kick a field goal. If you've gotten close to the other team's goal, but not actually into it, you have your kicker try to kick the ball through the goalposts (the uprights, we call the arms on either side), and you get three points if he makes it.

Once you get your ten yards, you get a whole new set of downs. This keeps up until you punt, or get a field goal, or score a touchdown by getting into the other team's goal. Or—this is where I come in—until one of your players loses the ball and the other team gets it. It has to be a "live" ball, which is complicated and there are lots of rules around it but essentially it means that the play isn't over yet. So if your running back drops the ball and I pick it up, or your quarterback is a crappy passer and I get the pass before his receiver does, then that's a "change of possession" and the ball belongs to us. We can run it back as far as we can on that play, then our offense takes over on the next one.

That's why I love playing defense. We get to be in on the big plays, the game-changing ones that "turn the tide," "shift the momentum," whatever you want to call it. There's nothing like the feeling you get when you get your paws on the ball as a defender. Nothing.

Not to say there's nothing better. Just nothing like it.

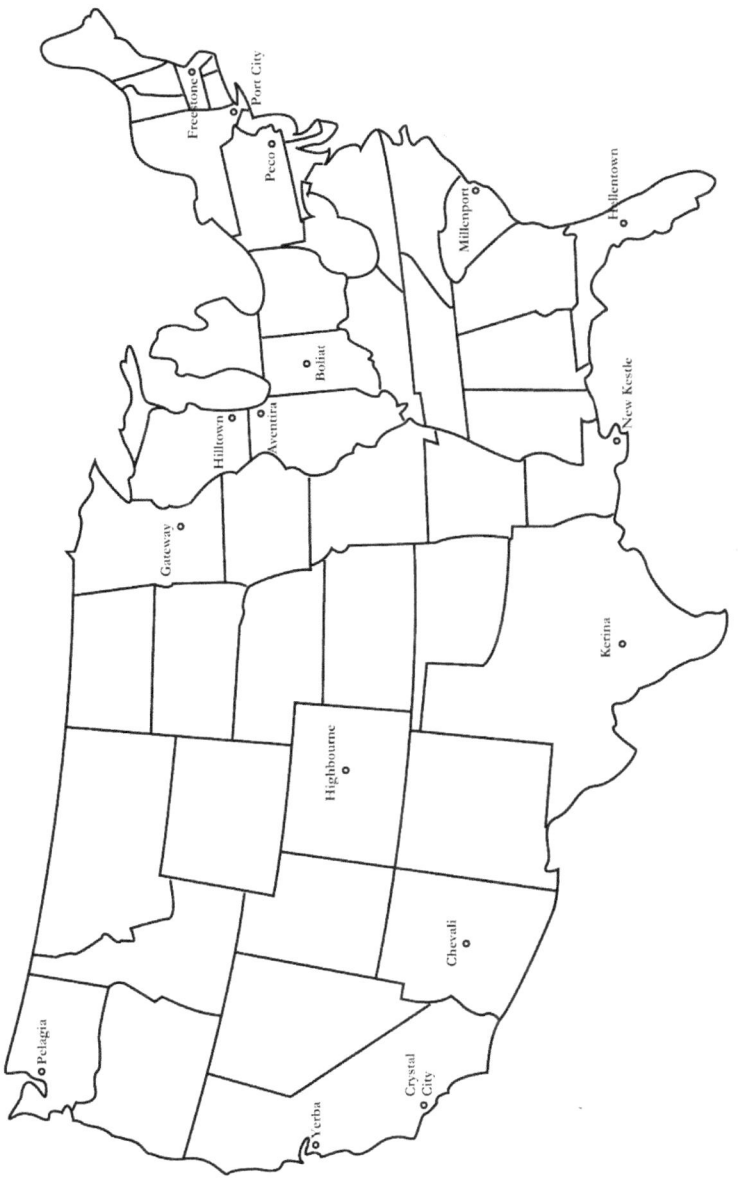

I'm not saying the Forester Universe cities are in the United States. But if they were, this is where they'd be.

Book 1

Chapter 1: Fracture (Lee)

From the other side of the menu, Father says, "I filed for divorce."

I lower the laminated page slowly. He looks gravely over the tops of his glasses at me, his paws resting on his own face-down menu. His ears are flat, but not down. "I asked if you want wine," I say.

He nods. "Yesterday. I thought you should know."

"So," I say. "That's a 'yes.'"

This has been coming for a while. A month or so ago, Father told me he and Mother weren't spending so much time together any more. She has new friends, a Mrs. Hedley and a poisonous anti-gay religious group called Families United. Mother was never a churchgoer, but she is a crusader. My aunt Carolyn has told me enough about their strict upbringing that if I look at her as a fictional character in an Edith Wharton novel, church sort of fits, if not hateful propaganda.

But I still want to know how they got to this point. Did he suggest it? Did she? I think it makes a difference. But I'm not quite sure how to ask that, so I keep quiet and flick my ears to the bland Christmas music, looking around the big dining room.

I'm spending Thanksgiving afternoon in a country club a few hours north of Hilltown, about midway between where my parents live and where I live until Saturday. Thanksgiving dinner is just me and my father instead of with both parents, instead of with my boyfriend, who is at his own family's place thirty minutes away in the small town of Lake Handerson. Father and I are going over there for leftovers tomorrow, not dinner tonight, but even though my activist brain reflexively yells at being shuffled to the side, really, it's fine with me. It's an enormous leap forward just to be invited there around a holiday, and it's hard enough for me to handle three tigers when just his parents are home. I don't need to confront ten.

Now, though, that would seem like a relief. I wouldn't have thought that the word "divorce" would hit me as hard as it has, but I can't focus on the menu at all. Fortunately, the Thanksgiving menu is much less about choice and more about what you're going to get, like it or not. When the waiter comes, I just say "two" to whatever my father orders.

Then the menus are gone, and I can't escape his gaze. "Nothing really changes for you," he says.

Nothing? I flare my nostrils, taking in the scent of fifty-year-old people and decorations under the bland kitchen smells of a Thanksgiving cooked to appeal to every species, rather than some of our fox-specific dishes. There's no sweet scent in the air from Mother's raspberry sauce, just the barely-sour cranberry. There'll be nothing crunchy in the stuffing, I'm sure; I've had bland stuffing before. It's not that the food won't be good. It just won't be what I'm used to.

When I look back at Father, ending my exaggerated sniff, he takes my meaning. "Holidays aren't about where we have them. They're about being together. So we come here instead of going home."

"Where's home?" I say, as he reaches for his drink.

The glass of water was halfway to the end of his muzzle. He lowers it and takes his glasses off, rubbing them on his napkin. "There's an apartment building close to work. I signed a lease yesterday. Anyway, you have your own home now."

The warmth of that remark doesn't stop my tail from curling under the chair. "You know, they always tell us gay boys not to come out to the families at dinner. Don't you have like a troubled marriage forum that tells you not to announce a divorce at Thanksgiving?"

"It seemed more logical than going through the holiday with it hanging over our heads." He replaces the glasses and drinks the water. "This isn't easy for me."

"No, I know." The tablecloth's fabric is rough under my paw pads, bunching as I rub it. My whiskers twitch as someone walks behind me: a mouse, from the scent. I look around at the other tables, seeking a distraction. "Hey, you think that whole family there just didn't feel like cooking? Or are they having their kitchen redone?"

"Wiley, I don't want you to look at this as something that's about you." My ears fold down. "Well, I *hadn't* been."

He leans forward, with his elbows on the table. "When your mother and I met, we were both ambitious. She wanted to get away from her family, I wanted to go somewhere different. For a while, we were pretty happy. But we…sometimes when people think they want the same thing, it's only because you can't see how different the things you want really are."

"Did you read that in 'Chicken Soup for the Estranged Soul'?" I snap my mouth shut. "Sorry. It just sounds like…" Like someone else talking out of my father's mouth. "Like one of those things that doesn't mean anything. What about 'Sometimes the things you want change'?"

"That too." He taps the side of his muzzle. "How's your football player? Devlin?"

"He's with his family." I say it without intending the comparison, but of course we both make it, and both cringe in different ways. "They've got the whole clan together."

"So you're not going to meet the extended family?"

"God, no." I laugh. "Even his brother didn't want to meet me. His parents were the ones who insisted."

"Sounds like Mikhail, what little I know of him. How's he doing?"

"Fine," I say. "I don't bring up the head wound."

"You talk to him that much?"

"Well." I look down. "No. But I don't bring it up, when I do."

Apart from getting to see Dev again—funny how we'd spend weeks apart, and now that I'm going to be living at his place, two days seems like forever—that's what is most on my mind about tomorrow's dinner. Mikhail ostensibly forgave me at the hospital, and Dev says he hasn't said anything bad about me, but that just makes me think that he probably hasn't said anything about me, period. But then, they did insist I come meet his brother. Maybe Mikhail is hoping Gregory can beat me up.

I'd hoped this dinner would be relaxing preparation for that meeting. Instead I'm trying not to think about my parents' marriage ending, which of course means that's all I can think about.

At least I'm distracting Father, if not myself. The corners of his mouth curve up. "That was one of the more surreal days of my life."

"Look at it this way," I say. "How many people can say they met their son's boyfriend's parents in the hospital after their son won a fight?"

"Oh, it's 'won' now, is it?" He raises an eyebrow.

"I didn't *lose*," I say. "And he ended up in the hospital. So."

The waiter brings our glasses of white wine, stalling the conversation. It's a good wine, but nothing special; about right for a country club full of middle-aged midwesterners. I barely taste it anyway.

"How are you doing?" I ask, unguardedly as I can allow myself.

He looks off to the side. "Change," he says finally, "even when it's only a change in the label you give something…it's still a change. It'll take some getting used to. I remember." He sips the wine. "I remember when we were first married, how strange it was to be called 'husband,' and 'wife.' How we laughed about it."

Even the activist in me knows this isn't the time to bring up gay marriage issues. I keep my mouth shut and nod. Now he's an ex-husband, a divorcé, single—a lot of labels that are new, or that haven't been applied in twenty-some years. And I have to learn to get to know him this way, too.

I had friends in high school and college who had three or four parents. Heck, Misha had six: an adoptive mother and father, a biological mother and step-father, and a biological father and step-mother. Through grade school and middle school, I'd been proud of having only two parents. By college, I'd come to view it as a curiosity, a relic, almost.

"Have you told anyone else? Aunt Carolyn didn't mention anything."

He shakes his head. "You had to be first. We both agreed on that. We didn't want you to hear it from anyone else. Of course, it is Thanksgiving. So I suspect it'll make the rounds of the family by tonight. Tomorrow at the latest."

That makes it sound like it was a mutual thing, but of course someone had to be first to suggest it. It was nice of Mother to agree, though. I imagine her saying that she doesn't think I would care one way or another, with that hurt tone that lurked behind her words every time she asked if I'd met a vixen in college, knowing what my answer would be. As if being gay were something I'd done to offend her. But divorce—that seems like a big step, and I see what Father means when he says it's not all about me. There has to be other stuff going on. Still, I can't help but feel that I'm a big part of it.

Even if the last time I talked to her was months ago, the image of Mother in my head telling Father she doesn't want to be with him is hard to summon up. It just doesn't work, somehow. They've always been together, unified even in their disapproval of me, up until…well, until I started dating Dev. Father talked more to me then, saw what I was going through and sympathized. I barely talked to Mother through all of the stuff with Dev's family over the last couple months. I'm not even sure she knows about it.

"I appreciate you telling me first," I say finally. "I'd hate to get a call from grandma telling me you were breaking up."

"She wouldn't call you," Father says.

"I know."

It's hard to make small talk with that leaden capital "D" dragging down the conversation, but I figure the best way to deal with it is to acknowledge it and move on. I don't know if it'd be proper to flaunt my relationship in his face, so I don't talk about moving in with Dev, although preparing for that has occupied most of the last month of my life. "There's this guy Emmanuel at Yerba, and Morty—my old boss, at the Dragons—gave me a good recommendation. He says they might have an opening and Emmanuel wants to talk to me."

"Sounds promising."

"I think so. I mean, I didn't play football, and that's a strike against me. But that whole thing about me and Dev came out now."

"I saw it."

"So Morty thinks that might work in my favor. Yerba, well, you know." I made him and Mother watch the Yerba Pride Parade when I was home one summer. Rather, I turned it on and watched, and Father stayed for some of it. Mother didn't. The next year, my at-the-time best friend Brian and I watched it at the FLAG (Forester U. Lesbians and Gays) club and swore we would go the following summer. But things…didn't work out that way.

He nods. "Why didn't you go to college there?"

I swirl my wine, staring at the patterns of the light on the surface. "After high school? I couldn't have. I knew I was gay, but I didn't know if I would like other gay people. Yerba might as well have been Oz. At Forester, I was close to home, so I had a safety net. Or something."

A smile touches his lips. There are a lot of things he could say there, to be honest, but he doesn't say any of them. Instead, he takes another sip of wine and asks, "So you're just going to wait for the end of the season?"

It feels like an indictment. My "yes" is hesitant and weak, so I follow it up. "Dev's got money, of course, and I'll…I guess I'll keep doing work, watching the games, breaking down players. The guys at Yerba aren't going to tell me what to look for, but I'll watch their players particularly. I'll try to figure out their weaknesses, and then see what players elsewhere might match them. College, too. Just…whatever I can do."

What I don't tell him is the other thing that's been nagging at my mind, that Brian called me when the article my reporter friend Hal wrote about me was published. It was just a profile, went into our relationship a little, but Brian's voicemail made it sound momentous. "Good to see the closet door open," he said, because when I'd been working for the Dragons, I'd had to keep my relationship with Dev a secret. And then he said, "I'm getting back into activism. If you remember what that's like, give me a call." The lure of activism wasn't strong when I was scouting, my life consumed with football and Dev, but with day after idle day stretching out in front of me, I've been thinking a lot about how I'm going to spend my time, and those words keep coming back. Brian always knew how to get under my fur that way. Not that I'd call *him*, but I feel like I want to call someone.

"Still going to travel?"

My father breaks my reverie. I shake my head. "Not to the college games. No point in going if it's not for business. There's a bowl game in Chevali, so maybe I'll go to that one."

"When do you head down there?"

"I'll head down after we leave Dev's place," I say. "Dev has to fly back Friday afternoon for practice, so I'll see him off and then hit the road. He plays Monday and I'll be moved in by Tuesday. I hope."

"Good luck." He sits back as the waiter brings the first course, a butternut squash soup that smells thickly of sage. It's only a few leaves, but for canids, a little goes a long way.

"I saw Aunt Carolyn last week," I say. She's Mother's sister, but actually talks more to Father. She didn't think much of Mother's attitude toward me; I can only imagine what she's thinking now.

My father picks sage leaves out of his soup delicately and places them to the side of his plate. "You mentioned. She doing well?"

"She's seeing some wolf from the gym down the street. I told her if he's under twenty-five, she's officially considered a cradle-robber."

"And?" He takes a spoonful of the soup, blows on it, sniffs it, and holds it.

"She laughed and wouldn't answer." I do the same with mine. It smells okay. I test it with my tongue. Squash seems fresh, anyway.

Father smiles and tips the spoon to his muzzle. "Long as she's happy."

Right. Relationships: not a great topic. "Um, and Dev won his game."

"I saw." He starts in on the soup now.

"He didn't do much. Not like the Hellentown game. But he didn't need to. Port City is terrible this year, even with Lightning Strike. They didn't even get him the ball."

"Isn't that because Chevali's defense is that good?"

"Not to hear Strike tell it. He said they needed to bench the quarterback because he was making bad decisions."

Father snorts. "Did you get to go to the game?"

"Oh yeah. I still have some connections from my time at the Dragons. They weren't great seats, but I got to see the game and get beer spilled on me."

"So you don't sit with the players' wives?"

I laugh. "Most of the wives don't go to road games, unless it's the playoffs. Some of the guys have a different girl in every town, from what Dev tells me."

He's halfway through his soup and I've barely started. So I ask him about some of the plays in the game, and about the Dragons game that weekend, while I finish my soup.

I'm just licking the spoon clean when my phone rings. I take it out. "Sorry," I say. "In case it's Dev." Father nods while I look at the number. "Oh. Aunt Carolyn." I frown. "Little early for her to call."

He holds up a paw as I move to put the phone away. "Go ahead and take it. She's probably worried."

"All right." So I pick it up and say hi.

"Happy Thanksgiving," she says, and then waits.

"I'm with Father," I say. "He just told me."

"Okay, good. Listen, if you need to talk to someone, just call me. I can't believe you were just here and we didn't know a thing about it. Damn that

Eileen. I gave her hell."

I smile at Father. "I can't imagine that did any good."

"It did me good. If I thought I could change her mind, I'd still be on the phone with her. Look, I'll let you and Bren get back to dinner. Just wanted to reach out."

"Thanks. I'm okay, really."

The waiter comes by to clear the plates and looks down his muzzle at me. "Sir, the club has a strict policy against cell phones in the public areas."

"Sorry." I say a quick good-bye and hang up.

"So you had a good time in Port City." Father picks up the conversation.

I nod. "Dev was out late celebrating. Last time they had eight wins was in the nineties."

"You didn't go out with him?"

"Not on the team-only things." I shrug. "Like I said. The wives don't go along. I don't want to get in the way."

"Did you get to know any of the players?"

I feel like I'm being interviewed, but I don't know what I'd ask him about other than the divorce, so in a way it's sort of a relief. "I've met some of his teammates back in Chevali. Gerrard Marvell is a nice guy, and Fisher Kingston's been a good friend to Dev. His wife's nice, too. Gena. And Charm is great."

"The kicker." Father nods. "The one with the 'guffaw.'"

"That's him." I chuckle. "So those guys are pretty cool. I haven't met most of the offensive players yet, but maybe once I'm down there…"

My cell phone goes off again. Father grimaces. "Relatives will probably be calling you all night."

"I'll shut my phone off." But when I pull the phone up, the number calling is Dev's. "Oh, hang on." I bring the phone to my ear. "Hey, handsome."

He laughs. "Hi, fox. How's Thanksgiving dinner?"

"It's fine. I'll tell you more later. What's up?"

The waiter sees me and starts across the room. I pretend not to notice. Dev says, "You know how you were supposed to come up here tomorrow?"

Ah, shit, they decided not to invite me. I can't say I'm surprised, but I am a little disappointed. The waiter stands at the side of our table and clears his throat. "Yeah?" I say.

"Could you come up tonight?"

"What? Why?"

The waiter points to the phone. Part of me is amused that he is so insistently polite in the face of my rudeness. I hold up a paw as Dev answers. "Uncle Roger's leaving first thing in the morning and he wants to meet you. Once he started in, Aunt Mariya and Aunt Ania did too. Then Auntie Za started in, and, yeah, that was that. So I said I'd call. It's okay if you can't make it up. They know you're with family."

"Let me ask my father and I'll call you back. Love you."

He rumbles and lowers his voice. "Love you too."

"So sorry," I tell the waiter, putting my phone away. "Last time, I promise. Look, I'm turning it off."

"If it happens again," he says in a low voice, but not low enough to keep the other diners from looking at us, "I am afraid I will have to ask you to leave."

"Really." I raise an eyebrow and look at my father. "What do you say? Want to get out of this place?"

●

As lovely and dramatic an exit as that would be, we do stay through dinner. But I call Dev and tell him to save us some pumpkin pie, and so about forty-five minutes later, after a stop at a liquor store to pick up a bottle of nice wine (my father is a traditionalist about being a guest), we're on the road north.

Father was worried about dressing up, but he was already in a nice shirt and slacks for the country club, and I tell him they won't care that I'm in jeans any more than the country club did. I have a nice shirt on too, after all.

"I'm guessing his family will be a bit different when they're not in the hospital," my father says. "Anyone else there you've met before?"

"Nope. I never got to meet any of his uncles or aunts, or even his brother." My left paw flexes around the steering wheel. The ligament at the base of my thumb still feels stiff where Dev's father grabbed and sprained it a couple months ago. We'd been arguing over whether I'd continue to see Dev; I won the argument, even though I ended up in the hospital dosed up on painkillers.

And when we drive into Lake Handerson, the first thing I recognize is the large white hospital building, lit up at night. I point it out to my father, and he gives a soft "heh," looking in the other direction. "And there's the jail you stayed in."

"I have to remember to write my review for the Michelin Guide. 'Lousy food, but at least the service was terrible.'"

"Please do me a favor and do not feel the need to embark on a comparison tour."

I shake my head. "My fightin' days are over, Father. Cross my heart."

His eyes gleam with reflected street light. "No matter what Mikhail says? Or any of his other relatives?"

"I will be on my best behavior. We already discussed this and I promised. Every time I want to make a smart remark I am to go to Dev and whisper it in his ear instead of saying it out loud."

"Sounds like a good system."

We pass a baseball field, lit up and empty. Thanksgiving night, there doesn't seem to be much reason for it to be on, but there it is. Most of the rest of the town is dark, all the inhabitants at home with family and turkey. One theater marquee shines down a street packed with cars; two blocks down, the street is empty, small flickering lights illuminating the signs of jewelry stores and pawnshops.

I remember the way to Dev's family's house, even without my father's navigation help. There are cars packed out on the street here, too. I point out the large maple tree in his yard as we get out of the car. "That's where Dev's father's friends waited while we argued. He called them over to beat me up."

My father looks across the car at me, holding the wine in the crook of one arm. "Should we have stopped for a shiv before going in here?"

"Ah, me and Ivan are cool now," I say. "He might be there too. Mikhail talks about him like he's family."

We walk up the drive, checking the maple tree first, but it's clear of everything but maple seeds and fallen leaves, a smell of fall I know from home. On the porch, I remember standing with Dev and hearing his father tell him not to come back, the words penetrating even the blinding pain of my thumb. But we did come back, we didn't give up, and here I am again.

The lights are on in every room on the lower floor. I glance up, but I'm not sure which window is Dev's room, or even if he's staying in there now. There's the babble of probably a dozen voices and the powerful smell of tigers all over the porch, and it's no trouble for me to sort Dev's scent out of the rest. That overcomes my hesitation; I bounce up to the door and ring the bell.

For a moment, I wonder if anyone's heard it over the noise. But after several seconds, the door opens, letting light and conversation and the smells of turkey, cranberry, pumpkin pie, stuffing, wax candles, and tiger drift out around us. Dev's mother, Duscha, smiles when she sees us.

"Thank you for changing your plans," she says. "Please, come in. Happy Thanksgiving. It's good to see you, Lee."

She holds her arms at her sides, tentatively out, and I choose to view that as an invitation for a hug. I step in, and she hugs firmly enough that I think I guessed right. "Good to see you, too." I don't add, *not at the hospital.* "Hope you two are well."

Would Mother hug me that warmly? The thought bothers me as I step back from Duscha, but I resolve to put that aside and just enjoy the company.

"I'm Brenly," Father says, holding out the bottle. "I brought this for you."

"Thank you so much. I remember you." Duscha is small for a tiger, but she is still taller than either of us. She takes the wine and beams down at us. "Please, come in." She closes the door behind us and gestures toward the stairs. "You may put your coats in Devlin's room. Lee, you remember where it is."

Oh, very well I do. I hold out my hand for my father's coat and look up to see Dev walking across the living room toward me, a huge smile on his face, almost pushing his relatives out of the way. And as he goes by, they turn in his wake to watch, a room full of tigers staring down at us. The conversation dies enough for me to hear the very soft music in the background, some kind of classic rock mix.

"Why don't I show you where we're putting the coats?" Dev says in his low rumble, and his smile, infectious, makes mine even wider.

"Sure," I say, and then, "Well, no. I should stay with Father."

Father smiles. "Go on, go on. I'll be fine. There's plenty of company here."

"All right." I beam, tail wagging, and fall in behind Dev. "Lead on."

My father clears his throat. "Don't be long," he says pointedly.

"We won't." I look around, but I don't see Mikhail.

Fortunately, Duscha takes my father by the arm. "I will introduce you to my brother," she says.

I feel a slight pang of guilt at leaving my father alone in a party of tigers, but it's not enough to resist being dragged upstairs by my boyfriend. We get to his room, he kicks the door closed behind us, and I've barely got the coats on the bed before he's wrapped me up, squeezing so hard I gasp. I wrap my arms around him in return and lift my muzzle to his.

"So how long you think we've got?" I ask in the husky female voice he likes sometimes.

"Not long enough." He presses his muzzle to mine, forcing my lips apart with his tongue, and I close my eyes for the kiss.

My whole body shivers against his, tail swishing, the warmth and his tongue and his body and his paws all sharp in my awareness. The scent of tiger overwhelms me, like coming home.

I'd been joking about having enough time to have a quickie, but I find myself just wanting to stay in his arms the whole night, clothes on or off. Sure, off is always preferable, but just standing together is more than we've had for two weeks and he doesn't show any more sign of wanting to break off the kiss than I do.

Finally, I feel a snagging tug at my shirt. I pull my muzzle back to smile up at him. "Hey, watch the claws," I say.

The snagging vanishes. He presses hard, clawless fingers into my back on either side of my spine. "I missed you," he says, nosing down across the bridge of my muzzle to lick between my ears.

I laugh and work my muzzle under his chin. "Missed you too, tiger." I sigh into his fur. "But I should go rescue my father."

"What's the matter with him? Problems with your mother again?"

I don't want to get into the whole divorce thing now. It's not just that I don't want to drop it on Dev. It's also that I don't want to talk about it. "Yeah. I'll tell you more later. So who's here that I should know about?"

"Let's see. My Uncle Roger…"

I giggle against him. "Someday I'll have to introduce your Uncle Roger to my Uncle Roger."

"I don't know about that."

I feel the rumble as he talks, the uncertainty in his shifting weight. My ears perk. "I thought he was the one who wanted to meet me."

"Yeah. Um." He rests his paws on my shoulders. "He and my dad argued about that. I think what he said was, 'I gotta see this fox.'"

The room cools. I step back as far as his paws will let me, about two inches. "So I'm a sideshow."

"Aunt Mariya and Auntie Za both actually want to meet you. Aunt Mariya says she has a gay friend back in Gateway. Or at least a gay hairdresser."

"Really? A hairdresser?" I shake my head. "I'm surprised she doesn't know any interior decorators or travel agents."

"She might. She didn't say."

He's half-smirking, so I don't know if he's serious or not. "All right. So one gawker and two Gayland tourists."

"Auntie Za's not…" He laughs. "Well, you'll just have to meet her."

"Will do. Anyone else?" I curl my tail around his leg. "What about your brother and…Marta, right?"

He reaches up to scratch behind his ear. "Gregory's here, yeah. I think he is, anyway. He's been…kinda weird this holiday." He shrugs when I give him a look. "Just…cold."

"On some kind of 'you're unnatural and going to Hell' kick?" I say it a little more flip than probably I should, and Dev looks away, ears going down. "Sorry." I step in and hug him again. "Let's go downstairs. We'll deal with 'em."

CHAPTER 2: FAMILY MEETING (DEV)

It's funny, weird—Lee has a word for it, I'm sure. As we head for the stairs, I feel more worried than when I'm stepping onto the football field. In a game, I know pretty much what's going to happen, how the eleven guys across the line are going to come at us, and Gerrard has twenty or thirty plays he can call that put us in a good position to deal with it. Worst case is we lose. Well, no. Worst case is one of our guys gets carted off the field on a stretcher. That happened to my buddy—mentor, really—Fisher almost two months ago, and to Corey a month before that (although I'm the one who replaced Corey in the starting lineup, so I guess it wasn't a worst case for everyone). But anyway, I know kind of the range of what's going to happen.

I'm walking down in front of my fox, and the range of what might happen is only limited by my imagination. Even that's not enough to predict things, because there's no way in hell I would've imagined that my dad would break Lee's thumb. Sprain it, whatever. So I'm nervous, going down these stairs and hearing the conversations of all my relatives, and I know my tail is twitching. I don't know how the team down there is gonna come at us.

And then Lee puts a paw on my shoulder and whispers, just for me, "Don't worry, tiger. We got this." That's all it takes. It's like Gerrard coming in with the playbook. Lee might have caused this tension, but he's also the reason I can deal with it.

We meet up with Aunt Ania first, and my formal thought-out introductions turn into simply, "This is Lee," when she turns.

Aunt Ania looks like my mom: same height, same stripes, just about, same build. But Mom is still on her first husband, and her older sister is twice divorced. "All the money and none of the dead weight," Ania likes to say. She wears flashy jewelry that my dad grumbles about, and her dresses are always out of the latest Vogue.

Under all that, she is definitely family. She greets us with a smile as bright as my mom's, and turns it full power on Lee. "What a pleasure to meet you," she says. "So you're the one turning my nephew's head."

"None of the running backs he's faced have managed to," Lee says.

Ania looks to me as she says, "How charming."

"Football humor," I say. "A 'swivelhead' is a guy who has to keep turning his head because the player he's supposed to be tackling is running past him."

"Oh, I see." She plainly doesn't. "So how did you two meet?"

He tells variations of this story three times in my hearing that night. "We went to the same college. I was a football fan, he was a player."

"And how did you start dating?" Aunt Mariya wants to know, later.

"Well, I had to talk him into it." Lee smiles, aware of Uncle Roger over her shoulder and the cup of buttered rum Roger's holding in his paw.

"I bet you did." Uncle Roger is not as big as me or father—not as tall, that is. He's as big around as both of us put together. "I bet you were real fuckin' persuasive. Foxes."

"I'll take that as a compliment," Lee lies with a long fox smile.

"Be polite, Roger, or he might put you in the hospital, too." Aunt Mariya doesn't sound like she'd mind all that much. She probably wouldn't, from what I've heard about their lives since my cousins went off to college.

"Where are David and Darlene?" I ask, to head off drunk-Roger trouble.

"College," Roger stifles a belch. "Hey, is Kingston going to be back this season?"

That's to me, about Fisher. "He wants to be, yeah."

"That bear's doing okay for him. What's his name, uh…" He scratches behind his ear.

"The cubs get Thanksgiving off, of course." Mariya sighs, maybe at her children, maybe at her husband's belch. "But Darlene is at her boyfriend's, and David and some friends are flying to Hyeong-Kin. Adventure holiday package."

"They better not come back with the clap," Roger mutters.

"Honestly, Roger." Mariya half-turns. "Why don't you get another rum and see if you can make a complete fool of yourself?"

"Great idea." Roger totters over to the kitchen.

Mariya beams at us again. "So you got together against all odds. How romantic. It's so nice to see a young couple in love."

Lee smiles. I look down at the floor. "The more I got to know Dev," he says, then and again, to Gregory, later, "the more I wanted to spend time with him."

Gregory, with Marta on his arm, is a little smaller than I am. An inch or two away in height, but he hasn't spent the last five years bulking up his frame. The difference is only really apparent when we stand side by side. In my head, he's still my big brother, so I get this uncomfortable awareness of his aging when I see him.

I used to look forward to being his height, to doing the things he did. Now, for the first time, I'm scared of the day when I'll be that thin, a little hunched over, and constantly flicking my eyes around the room like I'm worried some tackle is going to jump out of the china closet and knock me down. It wasn't this bad at Christmas, the last time I saw him in person, and he didn't look this bad on his commercial, though of course then he was in a suit and sitting behind a desk.

Marta responds to Lee first. "That's sweet," she says.

"Yeah. Course, back then he couldn't really keep a girl around." Gregory eyes me, slides his glance to Lee, then over my shoulder. "Yeah, football player on campus gets a lot of action, but this is the first time he brought someone to Thanksgiving in like five years."

"Well," Lee says, "for the last two, he hadn't been able to tell anyone who he was dating."

Gregory's face looks like he just ate a lime. "Personally, I'd be okay not knowing," he says.

"Oh, honey." Marta sounds slightly reproving, but doesn't take it any further.

I just shrug and grin. "Don't worry, we don't have a big wedding planned."

Lee arches an eyebrow at me. I showed him pictures of Gregory's wedding last year, which led to an argument about whether I'd take him to a family wedding. After making up, we used the white handkerchief that was Gregory and Marta's wedding favor to clean up.

This would be a great time to tell Gregory that, actually. If I were Lee. So I keep an eye on my fox as Gregory says, "I don't see how you could have any kind of wedding planned anyway."

"Oh, well," Lee says. "There are a few civilized places around."

"Legally…"

"Oh, boy," I say. Marta tugs at Gregory's arm.

"…the precedents have been—stop pulling—have been clearly set. This whole malarkey about it being an equal rights issue is just political posturing bullshit."

"That's an interesting take on things." Lee keeps his voice even.

Gregory points a finger at him. "And any court that finds in favor of this bullshit marriage law is not doing it on legal grounds. They're doing it to placate you people because you've finally started making enough noise that it bothers them."

I clear my throat. "You mean 'us people'?" I stand closer to Lee.

"Oh, come on, Dev." Gregory's attention is all on me now. "Don't pretend like this is anything more than…than posturing for attention from the national media. You planned this together, I bet, right?"

I kind of want to punch him, but I can't do that here, of course. Lee's whiskers twitch like he's thinking the same, but he responds smoothly. "None of this was planned, actually. It's just worked out okay so far."

"For you." Gregory snarls down at him. "I know Dev. I knew him all his life, he was always into girls, always! You people say you're born that way, so how come he never looked at a guy, not once, not until you came along?"

"Sounds like a Families United brochure." Lee keeps his tone light.

"United family," Gregory snorts. "Not since you showed up."

"Honey." Marta tries to pull him away, but he shrugs her off.

"You know how foxes are," he says. Cider from his breath spills over both of us.

I put my paw on Lee's shoulder. "Yeah, I do," I say. "I don't think you do."

"I argued a case against this fox once," Gregory shakes an unsteady finger at us, "and he tried every lowdown trick to get the case tossed out. But I held on and pinned him down and finally won."

"Sounds like a fun night out," Lee says.

"All right," I say, because Gregory's eyes are bugging out and I think he might take a swing at Lee in a minute.

"Those Family United people have the right idea," my brother yells.

Before Lee or I can say anything, my whiskers twitch at a presence behind me, and Lee stiffens. A deep, familiar voice rumbles. "Gregory. Stop it now."

Gregory's eyes slide sideways, and he hunches in more. "So you're on his side too now," he mumbles.

Dad steps around Lee, staring down at Gregory. "It is Thanksgiving."

"He's not family." Gregory stares stubbornly at Lee.

"He is a guest in our house. And he is important to your brother. You will behave respectfully."

I exhale. I'd talked to Dad about Lee, he said he was okay, but you never know with Dad. "Okay" could mean a big range of things. But he came over here to take Lee's side. Or at least, to take my side with him.

Gregory, too, sees where Dad is standing and with whom. "I was respecting the Lord," he hisses. "Is Devlin?"

Lee, to his credit, is standing up pretty well, despite the cold tones and tension in the large tigers all around him. My father puts a paw on Lee's shoulder. "His relationship with the Lord is his own business. I suggest you go to bed if you cannot maintain a polite conversation." He shifts his gaze to Marta. "How much has he had to drink?"

"I'm not drunk!" Gregory straightens. "And he put you in the hospital, for Chrissake, Dad."

"Don't take the name of the Lord in vain," I chime in.

Dad glares at me. "Devlin, there is no call to make this worse. Gregory, we have settled all that, and neither is that your business. Do we understand each other?"

"Yes." Gregory lowers his eyes just a fraction.

"Good. Lee, thank you for coming."

"It's good to see you again too, sir," he says. "Thank you for inviting us."

Dad reaches down to shake my fox's paw. I'm sure he's deliberately doing this in front of Gregory, and my brother watches with that sour curl to his lip as Lee's dark brown paw disappears into my father's orange and white one.

"Come. Your father is talking to my sister and she would like to meet you as well." Dad guides us across the room.

Behind us, Gregory calls, "You haven't even asked about my commercial!" I don't know if that's to me or to Dad, but we both ignore it.

I lower my voice as I follow Dad around an armchair, Lee trailing behind me. "Is he okay? Is he just having a bad day?"

Dad harrumphs. "Bad month. He says business has been down. You have not talked to him?"

"I've been a little busy with football. I thought things were going well. The commercial and all."

We circle Aunt Mariya, sitting at the coffee table with Mom, and walk over to my third aunt, Zarya—Auntie Za. She's sitting with Lee's father on the loveseat, but stands when she sees us. "Ah," she beams. "So this is Lee. I see the family resemblance."

Lee laughs, and before he can say anything, she's wrapping him up in a hug. "You are a lovely fox. So handsome! And your father, Brenly, I have just enjoyed the pleasure of meeting. He tells me that you have made my nephew very very happy. I am so delighted for this."

She steps back, leaving my fox a little breathless. "He's made me happy, too." Lee grins, his tail wagging.

I can't help but match his grin. Auntie Za is awesome. She notices the wagging and points. "And you wag your tail for him! So adorable, so wonderful. Look how lovely you look together. Hello, Devlin, come give your Auntie Za a kiss."

She hugs me and kisses me on both cheeks. "You are so big, so strong! You need it, to run into those other players on the field, yes."

"It helps." It's not just how cheery she is; it's how easily she's accepted Lee. Dad is still standing off to one side, but he's smiling—if only a little—and looking fairly relaxed. For Dad. Lee's father stands up, too, with a smile. Auntie Za does that to people. "How've you been?"

"I am leaving in one month—two days before Christmas, so sad I will miss it—to go back to Moskva for one year. There is counseling center there for abused wives, I am going to help them. Exciting, no?"

"Very exciting," Lee's dad says. "Are you a counselor?"

Auntie Za laughs. "Oh, my stripes, no. But I will work with counselors, and I hope to talk to some of the wives myself. Officially my job is working in kitchen, but they have asked for people with 'bright and cheery disposition,' and prefer native Siberian speakers, so I am accepted quickly." Her eyes catch the light of a nearby candle. "I am so excited!"

"It sounds really cool." Lee smiles. "Is domestic abuse a big problem there?"

"Always." Auntie Za's smile fades, the stripes over her eyebrows creasing downward. "Is terrible problem. Only now is truly being recognized. Counseling center is first of its kind."

"You never talked about helping domestic abuse victims before," I say. "I mean, it's great, just…I wouldn't have expected it."

She glances at my father. "When you reach my age, perhaps you will understand. I have been wondering lately if the things I do make a difference in the world. I love my life, you know, but I manage a restaurant. I go to parties. I have no family of my own, nothing to leave behind. So I want to do something that will…that will matter, that is making a difference. This center in Moskva, it is a wonderful thing. It makes a difference."

I catch the spark in Lee's eye, the wistful tone, when he says, "That's great. Making a difference in people's lives. My dad helps people plan their retirements, save money, make ends meet."

"Like Gregory," Dad says, and I follow his eyes across the room to where my brother, still angry, slumps against the wall next to his wife. "Fighting for people who need help."

The last two cases I can remember hearing about were on behalf of small businesses defending themselves against individuals. Property claims, tenant disputes, something like that. I know Gregory's specialty is corporate law, and I used to think that meant he would be fighting for people against big companies. I think he thought that too.

My sympathy is pretty low for him after the way he yelled at Lee, but I keep my mouth shut and let my dad use him as an example. Lee's the one who really did fight for people, once upon a time. He doesn't say anything, but his ears are down just enough that I know he's thinking about the stuff he did in college with his activist friends.

Me, I'm fighting for the people of Chevali who have never had a football champion in their town. That's kind of lame compared to what Lee did and what Auntie Za is going to do, so I keep my mouth shut about it.

"So Dev's brother is a lawyer," Lee's dad says to my dad.

"Yes. He has been with this company, this law firm, for two years now, and he continues to be assigned cases. This year he has been in charge of twelve cases by himself, and won nine of them." He sets his jaw. "This is good."

Lee's dad nods. "How's the auto shop doing?"

"Business is good…"

Auntie Za cuts across the conversation. "Oh, business. I want to know how this fox put you in the hospital, Misha." She turns to Lee. "Growing up, you know, I never won a fight with him, not once. Not even when I was five and he was three."

Lee flicks his ears. "It was luck," he said. "He tripped and hit his head."

Dad looks between his sister and Lee, and finally coughs. "This fox is clever. He makes me lose my temper."

"I'm not sure it's cleverness," I say. "He does that to a lot of people."

"That's for sure," his father says.

Lee looks around at all of us, but it's me he elbows in the side. "Aren't you supposed to defend me?"

I nudge him back, making him lose his balance. "When you need defending, sure."

Auntie Za laughs her boisterous laugh again. "So you are willing to fight for my nephew. Good, good. I can leave the country with peace in my heart now." She winks at her brother. "Now I know there is someone who can keep Misha in line."

"I wouldn't presume to do that," Lee says lightly. "I'm just happy to be here, meeting more of Dev's family. Do you have any embarrassing stories from when he was a cub? His mother already told me one."

"Well," I say loudly, "I think Mom needs some help clearing up some glasses. Lee, why don't you help me for a minute here?"

"Later," Auntie Za says to Lee with a wink, and how the heck am I going to keep him away from her until she leaves?

I pick up glasses and Lee follows me, doing the same until both our paws are full. We take them to the kitchen, where my mother scolds us and tells us to go back out and be social. But I'm a little weary of my family now, so I just lean against the wall outside the kitchen.

Lee leans back at my side, his tail brushing the backs of my legs. He's quiet, reflective, and then shakes his head as though dismissing some other thoughts and smiles up at me. "Your Auntie Za is awesome."

"She's pretty cool." We both look across the room. She's still talking to Lee's father there. "You ever miss that activist stuff?"

"Mmm. Sometimes." Lee rubs his whiskers back. "Especially when I see those, like, Families United people…that name's ironic."

"Ironic how?"

"Oh, nothing. They just…they're trying to prevent people like us from having families. And…" He sighs. "Some stuff about Mother. I'll tell you later."

I have a pretty good idea then what he wants to tell me, but I don't pursue it. "You could try to get involved again. Down in Chevali, I mean. There's a group that's contacted Ogleby about getting me to speak."

"I remember." He flicks his ears. "Why haven't you?"

"Me?" I wave a paw. "Timing never works out, I guess. Ogleby doesn't give me details."

We listen to the murmur of conversation in the room, and I think about how different my relationship with all my relatives is. I used to be the quiet one, the one who didn't really have many stories to tell next to Gregory's accomplishments, the one everyone asked, "What are you going to be doing when you're not playing football?" Now I'm the one with the stories, the football player. The football star.

The gay football star. With my boyfriend. I kind of want to put an arm around him, but I don't know how people would take it. Probably it would piss off Gregory, which almost gets me to do it right then, but he's not the only one in the room.

"You remember that Brian moved to Chevali, right?"

Lee's words break my reverie. "Of course," I say, but I hadn't put the pieces together. Brian's in Chevali. He was Lee's best friend in Lee's activist days. Probably Brian is involved in the gay rights scene there. "There's other activist groups, though, right? You don't have to be involved with him."

"Aww." Lee gives me a foxy smile. "You're not still jealous, are you? You know you won, right?"

"I didn't know it was a competition." I shrug and lean closer. "Anyway, I don't think you'd run off with him."

"Good."

"That doesn't mean you have to look him up. He's still an asshole."

He turns away from me, looks back toward the party. "He's just idealistic."

"Yeah," I say. His ears are splayed, so I work to keep the growl out of my voice. "An idealistic asshole."

"He might be a good connection. But if it bothers you," he says, and trails off as he watches his father smile at Auntie Za. It looks like his father's tail wags, too.

"Probably," I say, not saying that I'm bothered more by the reminder of his last visit to Brian, "but you know. You do a lot of shit that bothers me."

He flicks his tail against the back of my legs. "I like you bothered," he says. "Also hot."

"No sneaking around rooms this time," I mutter, even lower. "Gregory's staying in his room with Marta."

"Thanks for the invitation, but Father found a hotel room for us. The luxurious Quality Lodge."

I turn, but he's not looking at me. "It does sound better than our mildewy basement, but come on. I could put you up at the Hilton or something."

He shrugs. "It's okay. They're cheap and they don't surcharge for foxes."

"Does anyone really do that?"

"More expensive hotels do." Lee makes air quotes. "Euphemistically called the 'scent equalization surcharge.'"

"Even with the Orwell laws?"

"You're allowed to discriminate if you can show a compelling economic reason that non-discrimination would hurt you."

"Hmph." I lean over and daringly nuzzle one of his ears. "I think you smell terrific."

He flicks it and leans back against me. "I am glad none of your relatives commented on it."

"Nobody cares about smell in this day and age."

"Says the guy who doesn't smell musky all the time. I guess if they're expecting a fox, they're okay with it."

I nudge him. "We work with foxes and skunks and weasels, all of us. It's fine."

He grins. "Doesn't stop the occasional asshole from commenting on it. Or the hotel chains from charging us for it. Speaking of…want to come visit me in the hotel room?"

Across the room, his father joins my father and Auntie Za. From their gestures, I'd bet they're talking football. The two tigers dwarf Lee's father, but he doesn't seem uncomfortable. "What about your father?"

"He's a heavy sleeper, it'll be fine." A pair of sparkling blue fox eyes meets mine. "Kidding. I mostly meant just to sit and chat with me and him. Though I bet I could get him to go down to the bar for fifteen minutes."

"Mm-hmm." I curl my own tail against his. "And what could we do that he wouldn't smell when he got back?"

He licks his lips. "I'm sure we can think of something."

"You realize that in a few days, we'll be living together and we'll see each other all the time?"

"Doesn't mean I don't miss you now."

I exhale. "I miss you too. And tomorrow afternoon, I have to go back to football."

Mom comes out with another tray of small cookies. "You're welcome to stay longer if you like, Lee. After Devlin leaves."

"I thought I'd go with him to the airport. May I?" Lee reaches for one of the cookies, a small pile of coconut in a sugary glaze. They smell heavenly.

"Of course." She lifts the tray toward him. "So Devlin tells us you'll be moving in with him. I think that's lovely."

"I'm hoping to keep his apartment a little cleaner." Lee winks at me, chewing on the cookie. "This is really good, by the way."

Mom beams. "Thank you. Are you going to look for work in Chevali, or…?"

"I've got a couple interviews lined up, but nothing's really going to happen until after the season."

"I'm glad to hear you have options." Mom's eyes linger on him. I get the feeling that in this room of all our tall relatives, she likes having Lee to look down at. "Have you met everyone?"

"I don't know. Have I?" He turns blue eyes up to me.

There are a couple more distant cousins we haven't talked to, but I don't know them all that well anyway. "Kate and Peter," I say.

"Oh, you should go say hi!" Mom scans the room for them.

"We will, in a minute. We were just talking about my trip tomorrow and where Lee's staying tonight."

A cloud flickers across her expression. Lee sees it too. "Father got us a room a little ways down route 94," he says. "We're staying there and we thought we'd come back in the morning, if that's still okay."

"Oh, of course." Mom brightens, the weight of talking to us about what we are allowed to do under her roof lifted from her future.

Having set Mom's mind at ease, we walk around avoiding troublesome conversations as best we can and nibbling on cookies. I sneak into the kitchen to get Lee a piece of Mom's pumpkin pie, and then he takes it to his dad, so I have to get him another one.

While he's eating it, Mom takes me into the kitchen to get my "help with something." Once we're in there, though, she just glances past me to the living room and says, "Where's Lee's mother?"

"Oh," I say. "I think his father left her recently."

Mom puts a paw to her muzzle. "Oh, no."

"They've been having trouble. Lee won't tell me what's wrong, but it's not that hard to figure out."

"What kind of trouble?"

"His mother joined some kind of anti-gay religious group."

Mom stares at me. "His own *mother*?" She looks across the room; Lee's father is tucking into pumpkin pie and Lee's coming back.

"I met her once. She just seemed super-nervous."

I'm not sure she's even heard me. Her eyes are still on Lee. "I'll get him another slice."

"Dad doing okay?" I ask Lee when he reaches me, and he nods, just as Mom comes back out of the kitchen with a paper plate sagging in the middle from the weight of a double slice of pie. She hands it to Lee and his eyes widen as he takes it.

"Thank you very much." He smiles at Mom and wags his tail, picking up the plastic fork. "Father says it's the best pie he's had in years."

He knows it's homemade, of course, because I told him. Mom beams. "It's an old recipe," she says. "It never seems as good as my mother's, though."

"I can't imagine it being better than this." Lee grins, swallowing the first bite of pie. "See, Father's almost finished."

"And Dad's eyeing his plate." I grin. "Maybe he needs more pie."

"He has had enough for one night." Mom follows our looks. "He won't take more."

"Mikhail is in a good mood." Lee takes another bite, looking up at Mom.

She smiles. "He is pleased that Devlin's career is successful. Also he loves Thanksgiving. We did not grow up with it, but he says any country that allows him to close the shop to spend the day eating with family is a blessed country."

Lee laughs. "Next time I visit, I'll bring some food. I do really appreciate you allowing us to intrude here."

"It is no intrusion! We have plenty of food and it is a pleasure to see you and your father again." She hesitates as if about to say more.

Whether Lee senses the direction she was about to go, or just wanted to say more, I don't know. But in between mouthfuls of pie, he says, "I hope things turn around for Gregory."

"Yes," Mom says, and after some innocuous discussion about Gregory's practice and their cub Alex, Mom goes off to take care of her sister again.

Left alone, Lee and I stand quietly together, him still holding his plate, me with thumbs hooked in the pockets of my jeans.

The feeling is nice, the closeness of family combined with the presence of my fox. If someone had told me just a month ago that Lee would be here on Thanksgiving night, I would've assumed that he'd snuck in the back way to meet me for furtive sex in the basement or something. He really is pretty amazing, the way he can be so argumentative and yet still be charming when he wants to.

When he wants to, that's the key. Here, he doesn't seem to have an agenda, but it's always hard to tell. If anything, he's more worried about his father than about my family. And I wish there were something I could say to him about that to make him feel better.

CHAPTER 3: QUALITY TIME (LEE)

I've gotta say, I'm impressed with how mellow Mikhail is. He squeezed a little hard when he shook my paw, true, but we seem to have graduated from "furious rage" to "playful sparring." It's good to see him talking to my father, too.

Father's holding up well. I know if Dev and I split up, I'd be a mess, but I guess if you've been drifting apart for years, the impact gets spread out. I'm still trying to process it myself. Mostly I'm doing it by not thinking about it.

And there's a lot I'm not thinking about. I haven't seen or talked to Mother in a while. Now it's going to be even longer, I guess. I'm aware that it isn't fair of me to put all the blame for this split on her, but Father's the one I had dinner with, the one who reached out and stayed in touch with me and came around to support me. Mother's distant, and I know that to be completely fair, I should talk to her and get her side of the story.

Part of me wants to talk to her, but that's the same part that drove up here to pick a fight with Dev's father a few weeks back. It's probably wiser to keep that part quiet for the moment, not because of the strain it'd put on Mother, or on our relationship, but because of the stress it would cause Father. Divorce is one of the top three stressful things in a person's life, I remember reading somewhere, and the last thing he needs is for me and Mother to start yelling at each other.

When some of Dev's relatives leave, Father comes over and tells me we can stay as long as I want. "Actually," I say, "I'm ready to go. Would you mind if Dev comes over for a bit?"

He eyes my tiger, who gives him a winning smile. "I guess I can have a drink in the bar," he says. "Half an hour? Forty-five minutes?"

"Just to talk," I say, "and I really don't want to know how you came up with those numbers."

He affects a shrug. "I just wanted to be sure the estimate wasn't too short. I'm happy to leave you some private time."

"Thanks," I say. "Maybe a little."

So Dev follows us in his car. My father says he can drive my car if I want to ride with Dev, but I'll be seeing a lot of my tiger soon enough, and I'm still a little worried about Father. He's not being as edgy with his banter as he usually is, and I can see he's still thinking about things.

We turn into the hotel parking lot, and Father says, out of the blue, "What do you want me to do with the stuff in your room?"

I pause, my paw on the door handle. "I hadn't thought of that," I say. "Do you think Mother might do something to it?"

"I don't know what to think." His head droops a little. "But they're your things. You should have them."

I tap the steering wheel. "When are you moving your things out?"

For several seconds, he doesn't answer. His ears are down, but not flat, and search as I might in my recollection, I can't remember him looking this way before. It's a little frightening. "Hey," I say, "how much did you have to drink at Dev's place? The wine wasn't that strong."

He turns, fixes me with one eye. I want him to jibe back at me. But he just says, "We haven't worked out a date. I need to rent a truck, probably put some stuff in storage."

"Why don't I come up whenever you do that? I'll just move out my stuff at the same time."

He sits back in the passenger seat and exhales, and stays quiet. I breathe in, but his scent doesn't give me any further clues to his mood. Combined with mine, it makes me think of the family car, the one I always sat in the back of, with my parents in front. This car is sort of like the little brother of the one my father has, the compact version. I got it used when I got hired by the Dragons. Dev wanted to buy me a nicer car, but I refused. It meant more to have one I'd paid for myself. And even though the scents of the previous owners were wiped pretty clean, every now and then I'd get a hint of cougar, when the car rattled and shook something free. But I've had the car for over a year, and now all I can smell is fox.

Father finally says, "It might upset your mother."

"Well, sure," I say. "I wouldn't want to do that, seeing as how she's been so considerate to me—us."

"This divorce…" He stops. I let him collect his thoughts. "It was my idea."

"Did she argue?" The question slips out.

He shakes his head once, quickly. "We both knew it had to be done. She was tired of trying to bring me around to her point of view."

"What, the whole gay-hating thing in pro-family clothing?"

"There's no hatred," he says, but I don't let him finish.

"Bullshit." It's easier for me to talk about this stuff if I don't think about Mother being involved. "Hatred doesn't sell, so they sugar-coat it. They say they love us fags, they just want us to be able to live normal lives, but their definition of 'normal' is 'just like them.' They hate that we're different, or else there'd be no reason for them to spend so much time and energy trying to get us to change."

Now Father's ears are flat. "Not now, Wiley," he says.

"I just don't want to sugarcoat what she's doing."

"Wiley." His voice is sharper.

Dev pulls his car in next to us. I'm back to remembering that it's Mother we're talking about, and memories fog my righteous anger. "All right. Just tell me when you're going to be there and I'll show up. It'll be easier on you." He shifts, and I anticipate what he's going to say. "I don't really care if it's hard on Mother. This might have been your idea, but it's her fault."

"Wiley, it's not anyone's fault—"

"You're here with me. She's not. Who's the one who's invested in family?"

Dev's out of his car and standing a little ways apart from us, behind my father's window. His breath puffs white in front of his nose, but he stands patiently. My father raises an eyebrow, turning all the way toward me. "Now it's about being invested in family?"

I flick my ears back and look over his shoulder at Dev. "I was in college. You can't blame me for taking a little distance to find out who I was."

"No." Father looks back at me. "And maybe that's what your mother's doing."

"I didn't disown the two of you."

"And if it had been easy, if there'd been a legal way, would you have?"

"Of course not." I put my paw on the door handle. "Anyway, that's a pointless question. Asking me what I would have done years ago in a situation that didn't and doesn't exist? What am I supposed to say?"

He shrugs, opens his own door. Dev steps back. "I'm just asking you not to judge her too harshly."

We both exit the car and grab our bags from the trunk. I walk around to Dev. "Have trouble finding the place?"

He grins. "I made a stop."

Father shuts the car door and looks over to the both of us. "I'll check us in and then get a drink at the bar."

"Have you seen this place?" I say. "I think the only bar is the clerk's liquor cabinet."

He looks up at the bright yellow 'Q' and the 1970s font, at the carport roof missing some shingles, the weak glow of the yellow lamp in the window of the office. I'm wondering whether there even is a clerk there at almost eleven p.m. on Thanksgiving night, but the Quality Lodges advertise 24-hour service, and the door is open when I try it.

It takes us a good minute of ringing the bell before a beaver shuffles out of the back, yawning. Father's nose twitches with mine at the smell of pot, but we don't say anything. The beaver checks us in pretty quickly, but my father hesitates when we head for the room.

"Hey," he says to the clerk, "is there a bar around that'd be open?" The beaver blinks at him. "It's Thanksgiving," he says.

"Right." My father waits patiently.

"Um." The beaver scratches the side of his muzzle.

"You don't have to go to a bar," I say. "Just come to the room."

The beaver points out the office door. "Star Liquors is prolly open. Bout two miles down Garner. I think they were doin' a special on Wild Turkey today?"

"Can I take the car?" My father holds out a paw to me. "I promise not to be back too soon."

"No. This is ridiculous. Just come to the room." I turn my back and start walking. Dev follows me, and a moment later, my father sighs and walks after us.

The room is small, but it's got two beds and a bathroom and we don't need much more. Dev waits for me to claim one bed, and when I take the one nearer the window, he sits next to me. My father tosses his bag onto the other one and sits in the rolling chair at the desk. When he shifts, the wheels squeak.

Dev and I slip our coats off, and the pocket of his rustles as he tosses it behind us. For an awkward moment, we all sit in silence, my father looking out the window, Dev looking down at his paws which happen to be near where I've curled my tail on the bed. I take a breath. "Okay, we can all relax. I just wanted a little time to tell Dev what's going on."

Father stands and holds out his paw again. "Then give me the keys. I don't want to sit around and listen to that any more than I want to watch you…" He waves a paw, his meaning clear. "I'll go drive around for half an hour."

"Don't go to the liquor store."

He looks steadily down at me. "Don't tell me what to do." His fingers curl. "I'm not going to wreck your car."

"It's not the car I'm worried about."

He sighs. "Wiley?"

Dev reaches for his coat. "Maybe I should just go."

"No." Father glances his way, curls his fingers again. "Wiley, give me the keys. I appreciate what you're doing, but I want to give you two some private time."

I sigh, reach into my pocket, and hand him the car keys. It's clear he's not going to be comfortable staying, so I might as well let him go.

His tail stays curled beneath him as he walks to the door. "I'll be back in half an hour," he says. "I'll knock."

"It's okay," I say, but he's already on his way out, the door swinging closed behind him.

And Dev curls an arm around me. "They're splitting up," he says.

I nod, and lean back. "Yeah."

"Your mom's really getting into that religious group?" His paw presses in on my chest.

"Sounds like it." I close my eyes and breathe in his scent, let myself relax back into the warmth. "Father said they filed for divorce."

"Wow. Really?" He tenses.

My ears, pressed into his arm and chest, struggle to twitch one way or another against the soft fabric of his cotton shirt. "It's not a big surprise."

"I knew they had problems, but I thought maybe they were just separating…" He rubs my chest; under my shoulders, his chest sinks as he exhales. "It's funny, I never really think of your parents much—well, I didn't until a couple weeks ago. But now I have to think about you without a mom." His wide nose brushes the side of my left ear. "You okay, fox?"

"Pretty sure I am." I can see our reflections in the mirror, the stripes on his wrist where his shirt cuff has slid up, his small black ears and my large ones, my thoughtful expression and his concerned one. "I mean, I haven't talked to Mother in…a while. Maybe once or twice since Christmas."

"Still." His arm tightens around me.

"Ah, you know." I try to grin. "It's kind of like being traded. Look what happened to you. The Dragons said, 'We don't want him,' and you end up starting for the Firebirds. I'm just on a new team now."

"It's not quite the same." But he rumbles, almost like purring, and his fingers massage my chest, sliding down to my stomach. I tighten the muscles there reflexively and then relax.

"It's an analogy. I guess I'm trying to say, it's not the end of the world. I'm more worried about my father. I don't know what he's going to do."

Dev squeezes me again. "He's a smart guy. He'll figure something out."

I nod. "And meanwhile, we've got some changes to plan for too."

"Right. I'll drive down as soon as you leave tomorrow. Should be about three days if I take my time. I'll watch your game from a sports bar in the middle of nowhere."

"I'll know you're watching." His paw rubs around my stomach, and normally I know it'd be going lower, but he's hesitating.

"You better not slack off. After that Hellentown game, you've set a high standard." I put my paw over his. "You know, I know Father left us alone to…do whatever. But I don't know that I'm really in the mood, now?"

He laughs softly, his body shaking gently below me. "I've never known you not in the mood. That's why I'm a little worried about you."

"I could get in the mood, don't get me wrong." I squirm a bit against him. "But we don't have lube or anything—not that that usually stops us, but—what?"

He shifts, reaching for his coat, showing me the pocket that was rustling. From it, he pulls a small plastic bag, and inside I can see a box of condoms and a small bottle of lube.

"Aww." I turn around and crane my neck up to kiss him. "You're so sweet. You bought me lube!"

He kisses back, wrapping both arms around me. "I didn't know if we'd need it, but I wanted to be prepared."

"And the condoms?"

He grins. "So you don't make a mess on your fur. And so I don't, uh…" His ears flick. "Leave a mess in you."

I hug back tightly. "You're wonderful."

He rumbles and holds me. "I didn't know if I'd feel comfortable fucking you in the hotel room where your father's going to be sleeping in an hour, even if we stayed on your bed. But I thought, better have it and not need it than need it and not have it. Especially with you."

"We've done it in weirder places." I grin, tail wagging, and now I am in the mood a bit more, but not enough to override my common sense. Back in college, I would totally have fucked my boyfriend in the hotel room I was sharing with my parents, if I was sharing anything with my parents then. I would've said that they needed to accept my lifestyle or get out of my life. Now, that seems a little extreme, and I find myself imagining my father bringing back some vixen from the liquor store and curling up with her in the next bed and me and Dev going for a walk and… "But yeah, not tonight, I think. I'll keep the lube, though. Can I call you and jerk off on the road?"

"Mmm, no." He licks my nose. "No getting off until you're in my bed. And I'm on top of you. And—"

"Okay, you need to stop that." I push at his muzzle. "Because if you don't, I'm going to pull your pants down and then my father's going to come back and the room's going to smell like sex and I'll be uncomfortable all night. I'd rather be virtuously pent-up."

"Suit yourself," he says, but his big paw slips between my legs to see just how pent up I am. I squeak theatrically and squirm.

"You're embracing this whole 'gay' thing," I say, curling up at his side so

I can slide my fingers inside the buttons of his shirt.

"You forgetting that whole deal where I came out on national TV?"

"Yeah, well." I grin. "After Hal's piece, I got interviewed on radio."

"Radio." He snorts. "You sounded way too normal on that. Nobody can tell you're a…a queeny little fox."

I push my paw in farther and tickle him a bit, and he squirms more to oblige me than out of ticklishness. "Queeny? Since when do you say 'queeny'? Anyway, I'm in a shirt and jeans!"

"Uh-huh." He grins. "And you're in bed trying to tickle a big football player. That's pretty queeny."

"Well, how am I supposed to sound like that on the radio?" I reach a little lower and grope him, because he was groping me and it's only fair.

His squirming becomes more real. "Rrf. I don't know. You can look like a vixen, so…"

"That's totally a stereotype."

"Uh-oh." He fixes me with a golden eye. "Sounds like I'm in bed with Activist Fox again."

"Queer power!" I squeeze his erection through his pants, then my awareness of the line we're edging toward makes me let go. His tail whips around to curl across his body, and he follows, rolling his body in my direction.

I manage to sweep my tail out to the side, rolling onto my back as he lands on top of me, driving the breath half out of me. His muzzle lowers near mine. "Mmm, the only way to get rid of Activist Fox is to replace him with…" He kisses the front of my muzzle, licks down along my whiskers. His weight keeps me pinned, his arms slide down under my back to hold me tightly. "Boyfriend Fox."

"Mmm." I lick back. "No fair. Your boyfriend powers are too strong for me!"

"It's no use struggling." He squeezes and then drops his muzzle for a warm, open-mouthed kiss, and after that there aren't a whole lot of words for a while.

CHAPTER 4: ACCOMMODATIONS (DEV)

It's a minor miracle that we manage to keep our pants on, with all the kissing and wriggling around, but Lee seems pretty happy just to make out, and that's good enough for me. I can't get rid of the image in the back of my mind of what might happen if my parents split up, of the family Thanksgiving we just left being permanently in the past.

If it's that rough for me, it's gotta be worse for him. Kisses and my arms around him do seem to relax him, and he doesn't reach into my pants or grope me again, though he does mutter a couple promises about what our first night living together is going to be like. But thankfully, he doesn't mention his father, not during all the time I'm pressing him into the bed, holding his light frame against me, and not when I roll over and let him lie on top of me. My ribs are still bruised from the Gateway game a month ago, and all the smaller bruises since, but he's light enough that he doesn't hurt them. Not much. Not enough for me to make him move.

We're both in a half-doze when he shifts his muzzle, looks at the clock, and tenses all over. "Where's Father?" he says.

I feel my fur prickle. The clock reads 12:14. "What time did he leave?"

"We got here just before 11, didn't we? So he's been gone an hour." Lee jumps off the bed, so smoothly I barely feel him shift. He grabs his phone and brings it to his ear.

I roll onto my side, watching him, still trying to catch up to his change in mood. The last remnants of the sleepy half-aroused contentment take a little while to drift away from me.

He paces, perks up at a voice from the phone, then immediately scowls and puts it away. "Shit. He's not answering. Can we take your car?"

"And go where?" I sit up on the edge of the bed. Lee's already shoving his arms into his coat sleeves.

"That liquor store?"

I reach for my coat, more slowly. "And if he's not there?"

"Then we'll go somewhere else. I know what my car looks like. I can keep an eye out for it."

His tail is tight against his leg, so I pull my coat on. "Okay. Don't stress. I'm sure he just wanted to make sure he didn't walk in on us."

"As if we'd really have sex the day he tells me about the divorce," he mutters, patting his pocket to check for his room key.

I nudge him in the back as he opens the door. "He knows you. And anyway, we were pretty close."

"Mmf." He grumbles, holds the door for me, and lets it swing closed.

He's still tense in the car, ears flicking around, fingers tapping the armrest. He stares out the window, scanning the sidewalks and streets without saying anything. "I'm sure he's fine," I say, because I really believe it.

We stop at a red light. Lee turns to me and reaches over to squeeze my thigh. "Thanks," he says.

"Well, what do you expect me to say?" I try a grin.

"I mean, for doing this. I mean, you're probably right, he's probably fine. I just…" He bites his lip.

The light turns green. "I like that you're concerned about your family," I say. "And I don't mind doing this."

"I know you need to get up early."

I wave a paw, driving on down the road. "I can be a little tired. I can sleep on the plane, too. There's the liquor store."

Lee sits up, scanning the lot for his car as I slow and pull in. There are only three other cars, and by the time I've parked, he's slumped back into the seat.

I coax him out of the car and into the store, where we ask the ermine behind the counter if she's seen an older fox. "Oh, sure," she says. "We talked a bit."

Lee leans across the counter urgently. "Do you know where he went?"

The ermine nods. "He asked if there was a place a fellow could drink a bottle of wine alone. I said the White Pine bar would probably be pretty empty tonight."

"White Pine's open?" Back when I was in high school, that was the dive you went to if you wanted to drink with your fake ID and not get caught.

"Sure." She squints at me. "Hey, you're that football guy, right?"

Lee grabs my sleeve. "You know how to get there, right?"

"Yeah, and yeah," I say to both of them.

The ermine digs around under the counter. Lee's halfway to the door already. I move to follow him, but she's looking for something specific that I guess she wants me to see, so I wait a moment.

She digs out a newspaper, the Lakeside Gazette, and folds it around to a picture of me they must still have on file from high school, under the headline, "Local UFL Star Comes Out." She looks at the picture, then at me, and grins. "It is you!"

"That's me."

The ermine scans the headline and then looks at Lee. "So this guy's your boyfriend?"

"Yeah." Lee's ears are down, his tail tip flicking restlessly. He forces a smile, though. "And we're looking for my father. Sorry, but we do have to get going."

"Could you just sign this?" She holds the paper out to me and gives me one of the credit card signing pens by the register.

I wish the picture wasn't under the big "COMES OUT" headline. "Sure," I say, and scrawl my signature and "#57" across the bottom of the picture.

"Awesome." She gazes fondly at the paper. "I'm gonna frame this up on the wall, if that's okay."

It occurs to me that if she does, people will think I buy booze at this store. "Um—"

"Dev, please."

Right. We've got things to do. "Sure, fine." I raise a paw. "Thanks for the help."

It's been a while since I went to the White Pine, but it's not like there's a lot of roads out here. Lee's even more fidgety as I turn onto County Road 8. "It's two miles," I say. "Just relax."

There aren't many buildings. The only light out here is the circle of headlights along the road, showing gravel at the side, and that's bright enough that I can barely see the outlines of trees in what little moonlight and starlight there is. We pass the Greasy Gary's gas station and the Pine Mart convenience store, both dark and empty under the single street light. Then we plunge back into dark, empty country roads. "I hope he's there," Lee says. "Because if he went there to drink and then tried to drive back…"

"Your dad wouldn't do anything that stupid." Stupid being a relative term; I did it a couple times in high school, but I know the roads and I was never all *that* drunk. That I remember.

"Not sober," Lee says.

"Have you ever seen him drunk?"

"No." Lee leans against the door. "He's always been responsible."

Which is funny, considering Lee himself isn't always the most responsible guy in the world. I wonder how much of him comes from his mother, that passion and the willingness to go haring off on crusades. "Well, I'm sure he didn't get trashed and go driving around Lake Handerson. Anyway, we've passed like three cops just since we've been out. They'd pull him over if he was driving funny."

"Great." Lee's laugh is harsh. "Maybe I'll get to bail *him* out of jail. Chaz probably remembers me."

"It's only been two weeks. And that was pretty memorable."

He doesn't answer, just sits up staring ahead at the bar trying to see the cars. I slow and turn, but again, by the time I park, it's clear Lee's car isn't here.

We get out again, go in and talk to the bartender, but he says no other fox has been in, certainly not in the last hour. He recognizes me too, but not from the coming-out article, and I escape without signing anything or having Lee identified as my boyfriend.

In the car, Lee tries calling again, and again his father doesn't answer. He stares at his phone and then pulls up another number and stares at it for a solid minute. "Who else are you calling?" I ask. "Police? You got Chaz's number on speed dial?"

He shakes his head, and then taps the Call button and picks it up. "It's Wiley," he says, in a low, guarded tone I've rarely heard him use, ever. "I know it's late. I'm sorry. It's Father. I just wanted to know if he'd called."

I don't need to hear the female voice on the other end to know he's talking to his mother. His tone gets sharper. "Because he went to a liquor store and then disappeared." Pause. "No, I don't think that, but I was just thinking he might have called…no. Well, he's alone on Thanksgiving, so— Yes." Another pause. "Fine. Happy Thanksgiving." And he hangs up.

What do I say? "How's your mother" doesn't seem appropriate. So I just say nothing as we head back in the direction of the hotel. He stays glued to the window, staring out, ears flat against it, straining to hear through the glass.

We don't see any sign of his car all the way back to the Quality Lodge, where Lee gives up and stares down at his knees. But as I'm parking, I glance to the right and stop. "Hey," I say. "Isn't that your car?"

He sits bolt upright and looks, and shoves the door open. "Hold on!" I say, but he's closed it before I get any other words out. I park, and jump out to join him over by his car.

"It's okay," he says, and sniffs the air around the door, ears up and flicking around. "I think he was alone, but it's so cold, it's hard to tell. Don't think there was any alcohol on his breath."

"Maybe he's back at the room."

"Uh-huh." And we both run back inside.

At the room, Lee calls, "Dad?" as he opens the door. But nobody answers, and the room is empty. Lee checks the bathroom and comes out shaking his head.

I lean against the door, holding it open. "You're his son. You should kind of know how he thinks, right?"

Lee rubs the side of his muzzle, and then his ears perk up. He looks kind of disgusted and angry. "If he…" His eyes rest on the bench where his bag sits. He sighs and walks past me, out into the hall. "His bag's gone. I bet he got another room. Sit by himself, stay out of our way."

"Drink alone," I remember.

"Yeah."

I follow my fox back to the front desk, where the stoner clerk blinks as we ask him if the fox who was with us got another room. It takes him a while to answer, though I can't tell if he's struggling to decide whether to tell us or struggling to remember. Eventually, though, he says, "Yeah, about ten minutes ago. Maybe an hour?"

"I need the room number," Lee says.

"Uh…" There's another long pause.

"Come on, you saw us come in with him." Lee leans over the counter. "He's my father."

I put a paw on Lee's shoulder. "You know," I say, "if he's got a room here, then he's okay, and you'll see him in the morning. Maybe we should just let him sleep."

He turns to me, blue eyes challenging mine, and I know exactly what's going on in that pause. But he decides I'm right and waves to the clerk. "Thanks," he says, and lets me take him back to the room.

We don't bolt the door, in case his father comes back. Lee drops his coat on the office chair and sits on the bed, tail curled beside him. I sit next to him, naturally.

"You need your sleep," he says.

"Uh-huh." I wrap an arm around his back. "And you need a shoulder."

He doesn't lean into the embrace, but he doesn't pull away. "I'll be fine."

I pull him against me. "Listen," I say, "I know you'll be fine. But maybe you'll be just a little bit better if I'm here with you?"

"You've got to worry about football," he says. "Every game's important. You can't be at 95% because your boyfriend's parents are splitting up."

"You're important. And anyway, I'm not going to be at ninety-anything percent. The game's four days away and I can sleep on the plane." I'm sure most of the rest of the guys on the team are not spending their Thanksgivings exercising and resting up for the game. Except maybe Gerrard.

"What about your family?"

"I'll call. I'll go over in the morning and we'll have breakfast the way we planned."

"Your dad'll be upset."

I laugh. "That I spent the night here? Now you're just making things up. Dad won't care. I mean, as long as you don't call him a cocksucker again."

"I didn't call *him* a cocksucker. I called *you* one."

"Yeah, well, he doesn't like that either."

"No." He stays stiff for another few seconds. "If you're really sure…"

I squeeze again. "Fox, I'm sure. You need me, and I'm here."

"I don't—"

"Shut up, doc."

He grins, and then allows himself to relax against me. "I'm still not really sure I'm in the mood."

"Yeah, well." I lean over and rub my nose against his ear. "Even if that lasts until the morning, I'm okay with it." And then I whisper right into the soft fur of his ear, "*But I don't think it will.*"

He squirms, but just leans in closer. "You might be right," he says. "I just wish Father'd called or something."

"It does seem like something you'd do. You know, decide you know what's best and just sneak off and do it. Very foxy."

He laughs, a soft, sincere laugh. "It is, I suppose. All right. Well, look. What say we get under the covers and get our arms around each other and forget about my father for a little while?"

His eyes aren't quite sparkling, but at least he sounds a little more cheerful. So I kiss him on the nose and say, "Deal." The clothes hit the floor and we slide under the sheets, and I hold his body to mine, both of us on our sides facing each other.

We're both hard, and I'd be ready to go if he started something. But because he doesn't, I don't; I think that what he needs is just to be held, to have someone shut out the complications and frustrations of the world, and that I can do that is a joy to me. He presses his muzzle into my shoulder and wedges one arm between us, curling the other over my chest. My arm reaches all the way over his arm and chest to his opposite shoulder, and I keep him warm, and we fall asleep like that.

In the morning, I wake up around the same time he does. He's managed to turn himself around to a more familiar position, his back against my stomach, his rear against my erection. My arm's draped over his chest, and when I trail it down past his stomach, I find the tip of his hard cock ready as well.

Still, I just give it a little brush, like by accident, and then let it go. He shivers, presses back harder against me, and we snuggle pleasantly like that for a bit. "What time do you—do we have to be there?" he murmurs.

I glance at the clock. Ten after eight. "Mom said nine-thirty, so I could get on the road by quarter to eleven. If we're out of here at nine, that's plenty of time."

"Mmm." He reaches behind him, trails fingers up my erection. "Up for a little bonding time before we go?"

"I am if you are." I wriggle around until my tip is just beneath his tail.

"Mmmf. Go get your lube and condoms. I'll call my father again."

I give a playful thrust and then roll out of the bed. "Such sexy talk, you charmer."

He snorts and stretches a long foxy arm to the nightstand for his phone. As I dig in my coat pocket for the bag with the lube and condoms, he talks, so I guess his father answered.

"Yes, good morning. Thank you for finally picking up." Pause. "I guessed that, but it actually worried me more that you just disappeared."

I open the box of condoms and take out two. "Well, you've never gotten divorced before," Lee says, "so I'm not sure what to expect."

I'm not sure whether to go back to the bed or not. Lee says, "Right, Dev says we should leave here around nine." Pause. "Yes, but he wouldn't have if you hadn't disappeared, so…" He takes a breath. "So we'll meet you in the lobby then."

He clicks the phone off and drops it back on the nightstand, then looks over his shoulder back at me. "Well," he says, "we've got forty-five minutes."

I climb back into bed and drop the tube into his paw. A moment of pressing my nose into his shoulder fur and situating myself under his tail again gets me hard enough to put my condom on, and by the time he reaches back with a slick paw, he's hard enough for me to put his on, too.

And then we're together, really together, locked tight and moving on the same track, and I know he's not worried about his father because I'm not worried about anything else, just that wonderful motion, the closeness, the feel and the warmth and the smell of him, and I'm thinking, how lucky am I that I get to live with him now?

We make growling, panting, yelping sounds, tension and delight and straining together, and the end seems to come fast, but take a good long time. It's been four days—technically five, maybe—since the hotel in Port City, and I've missed him. And he's missed me.

"Mmmmf." I bury my nose between his ears and hold him tight, hanging on to the closeness. In three hours I'll be on a plane; in eight hours I'll be hitting people on a practice field. In eight hours he'll be in a car driving to Chevali. But for now, we're together, where we belong.

•

Clean and showered, we head to the lobby, where Lee's father is reading the paper. He puts it down and stands. "I'm sorry if I worried you," he says. "I just wanted to be alone." His eyes flick up to me. "And I thought you probably did too."

Lee opens his mouth, then shuts it, and takes a breath. I take the opportunity to dive in. "Thanks, Mr. Farrel," I say. "I mean, I know we'd have been happy to sit and talk with you. But if you wanted to be alone, then…"

"Yeah." Lee's tail swishes. "I was mostly worried about you."

"You needn't be." His father adjusts his glasses, looking up at the clock. "Shall we be going?"

He takes a step toward the door. Lee hesitates, then reaches out for his father's sleeve. "Father," he says. "You can talk to me. Not…now. I mean, whenever. This thing Mother's doing, it affects me, too. I'd rather not lose you both."

His father pauses, then takes off his glasses and rubs his eyes. He steps back and puts an arm around his son. "You're not going to lose me, Wiley."

"Mmkay." Lee hugs him back. "You want to have dinner tonight?"

"Aren't you supposed to be on the road to Chevali?"

I was going to ask that too, but his father beats me to it, with an eye turned toward me.

Lee grins, disengaging from the hug. "I can be a little bit late. You just gave me a night with Dev, so we sort of owe you anyway." He tilts his head, ears perking. "Want to come with me to Chevali?"

His father raises an eyebrow. "I can't take the time off work. But I will take you up on the dinner, if you're sure it won't make you late." He turns my way. "And if Dev doesn't mind."

"I don't." I rest a paw on Lee's shoulder. "And you should come visit us in Chevali sometime. You like burgers? I know a great burger place."

"We don't get good Sonoran food up here," his father says. "Maybe when I'm in the mood for that, I'll fly down."

The Sonoran restaurant we know best is the one where my dad tried to disown me while I got drunk. It was in the tabloids, sort of. Lee and I exchange glances, but I guess he hadn't read the story or anything, so he's not being funny. "Um, yeah, I'm sure I can dig up a place."

"And," Lee says, "if you want to be alone, tell me you want to be alone. Don't just sneak off somewhere like, uh." His ears fold down, and he looks kind of adorable as he picks at his claws. "Like I did in college."

His father does crack a smile, then. "I guess we both can learn from our mistakes."

"In my defense," Lee says, "I was twenty years younger than you were when I made them."

"All right, all right." His father checks the clock again. "Let's go, or we'll be late for breakfast. I don't want Dev to get in trouble."

Lee happens to be looking at me, so I meet his eyes and smile. "If I didn't want to get in trouble, I shouldn't have gone home with this fox years and years ago."

"Only two and a half," Lee says, but his tail swings behind him and his eyes have a bit of a sparkle.

"Two and a half years is a good long time," his father says. "I hope you have many more."

We walk outside, bundled up against the cold. The sun is out and the day is crystal clear, one of those days when all the world's edges are sharp. You can see your breath, and it feels like nothing's hiding, like everything is right there in front of you. I want to freeze things right now, even though Lee isn't completely happy and his father's still dealing with shit. Because in this moment, we all really understand each other.

Also, I just had a pretty nice morning with Lee. I'm sure that has something to do with it.

BOOK 2

Chapter 5: Moving In (Lee)

I can't say I'll miss the winters in Hilltown. I don't mind the cold; my fur grows out for it, so I stay pretty warm. But the slush and the ice, the wind and the sleet, all that drives you back indoors, and if you don't have someone to share it with, then it isn't fun at all.

At least Dev's plane isn't delayed. He's flying first class, but on a commercial flight, so he has to go through security and all, not like when we flew on the owner's private jet. So after breakfast, we get him to the airport, and then Father and I avoid the crowds of Black Friday shoppers and hole up in a sports bar. There's nothing on except basketball, but the Bikers are trying to defend their title and it's at least a pretty interesting background.

We don't have much to talk about anyway. He asks more about my plans, I don't ask him about Mother. The only time we come close to that is when he says, "Are you sure you want to come up to get your stuff? I could just get your things. How much is there?"

"A few books." I think back to my last Christmas visit. "High school yearbooks, and scrapbooks. Old DVDs I don't watch anymore. Some of my FLAG stuff from college. Clothes I don't wear anymore. Oh, my jean jacket, the blue denim with all the patches on it."

He wrinkles his muzzle. "I'd forgotten about that."

Freshman year, I bought that jacket at a Goodwill store and sewed pride patches all over it. I wore it to Christmas, and Mother and Father tried to make me take it off. That was the first time Mother really yelled at me over my gay pride activity. She said if I wanted to parade around campus 'like that,' it was my business, but I wasn't to dress 'like that' in front of family. "Maybe there's other stuff. I don't know, you've probably been in there more recently than I have."

"Your plush Hilltown Dragon."

I put a paw to my nose and laugh. "Hothead."

"I could just put all that in a couple boxes. It's no trouble."

It's tempting. The flight up is going to be a pain. "I think I'd rather be there. I kinda want to take the stuff myself. I mean…there might be some things I don't care about anymore."

"I think you always care." He tilts the beer into his muzzle. "Sometimes you just don't want to be reminded of it."

That phrase keeps echoing as I drive away from Hilltown, down through the cold towards the warmth of Chevali. It's snowing lightly, the flakes bright white in my headlights against the black night. Not many cars on the road once I get away from the city. But the roads are pretty clear still; we haven't had any accumulation yet this year.

It really is true that you can choose the things that matter to you and focus on them. For instance, everything I need to bring with me to Chevali is crammed into the back seat and trunk of my little car: books, clothes, movies, computer. But like the couple boxes of things left at my parents' house, I know that I have things in the back of my head that have never really gone away, no matter how much I ignore them. Like, I'm done with Brian. We were best friends, but then he ran away, and when I went to see him, he came on to me even knowing I was with Dev, not to mention his outing Dev to the media. Yeah, that ended up okay—for now—but he didn't mean it to, and it's the intention that matters, right?

But I'm heading to take up residence in his city, and we probably won't be able to avoid each other. Okay, that's an exaggeration. If I really want to avoid Brian, I won't go to the places I'm pretty sure he'll go: gay clubs, LGBT group meetings, perhaps football practices. But if I do that, I'll be letting him back into my life, letting him carve out negative spaces where I assume his presence. If I just do what I want, then when I do run into him, it'll be natural, and I can deal with him.

The problem is that I'm not sure what I want. I don't want to just sit at home cleaning the house and waiting for my boyfriend. Sure, that sounds nice for a while, but after you've read all the books and played all the games, then what? I can watch football and take notes, and I know I can still contribute to a team somewhere. If someone gives me a chance.

Morty's going to give me a good recommendation—besides the guy Emmanuel in Yerba, he said he'll give me a recommendation anywhere I want to apply. He's still head of scouting for the Dragons, which means he might be looking for work after the season too, the way the Dragons are headed this year. There were rumors the ownership was looking to clean house, and not just the coaching staff. Morty said if he catches on somewhere else, he'll bring me with him.

And that would mean leaving Dev again, going back to seeing him only on weekends when I can arrange a flight. If I get a job in Yerba, at least it's a little closer than Hilltown was; if I get a job with one of the schools down in Chevali, I wouldn't have to leave at all. But I don't really want a college job. I like working in the pros. It feels more real.

The road is lonely, even with my music. I try an audio book, but it just makes me even more sleepy. I have a headset, so I can call Dev, but he's got a couple intense days of practice and then a Monday night game, so

I don't want to bother him unless I really need to. I try Salim, the only college friend I'm really still in touch with, but he's too busy for more than a minute of clipped conversation. There are a couple guys from the Dragons I could call, like Alex, my former officemate, but I think those calls might just depress me.

Two days of driving through snow and wind, sun and clouds, of eating at cheap burger stands and soggy sandwich shops, get me near enough to Chevali that I can tune in one of their AM stations Monday night when the game starts. I listen to the first half, frustrated that I can't watch what Dev is doing on plays where the action doesn't go to him. He's doing well enough that the announcers mention "that great linebacking corps the Firebirds have developed," and then of course they have to say, "Miski's surprise announcement of his sexuality—the first openly gay player in the UFL or in any major sport—seems to really have energized this team and brought them together."

Of course that's how they look tonight. The Pelagia Manticores are a terrible team, last in the division, and they sound completely bewildered to be playing on Monday night, like the team thought they had a bye week or something. Chevali goes up 21-0 by halftime, even though Aston is still having trouble completing long passes. Doesn't matter; Pelagia can't stop Jaws, whether the wolverine runs up the middle or around the end. He's got almost a hundred yards at the half.

Dev doesn't have any sacks or interceptions, but Pelagia only has one first down, so the defense overall is doing great. I stop at a suburb outside of Chevali and get into a sports bar in time to see the second half.

Pelagia manages a field goal to avoid the shutout. That's how you can tell they've got a losing mentality: on the Chevali twenty-yard line, with only three yards to go on fourth down, they kick instead of going for the touchdown. The coach just wants to avoid being shut out; he's given up on winning the game. The players sense that kind of thing and they respond to it, consciously or not.

Chevali has no such issue. Early in the fourth quarter, Pike sacks the quarterback, who fumbles the ball. Brick picks it up and lumbers to the goal line, shaking off tacklers and diving in for a score which turns out to be the last of the game. The Firebirds kill seven minutes on a drive and then Aston throws a pass to the end zone which is tipped and intercepted. Doesn't matter; Pelagia goes three and out and Chevali runs out the clock.

I cheer with the others in the bar, but it's a muted kind of cheering, like if we'd won a race against a guy on crutches. I settle up and run out to the car.

At Dev's place, an hour and a half later, I let myself in with the spare key. He's still out celebrating, his text message says, but he'll be home soon, and I am so excited my tail is wagging into doors and walls and I can't sit still on the couch. I debate getting naked to welcome him home, but then I think he might want to talk before jumping in bed. Then I think, hell with it, and I strip.

So I'm sitting on the couch naked drinking one of his beers (a good local brew) when I hear the elevator clatter to this floor. I grin at the door, remaining on the couch, and that's what he sees when he walks in.

"I owe myself a hundred bucks," he says, closing the door. "Bet myself you'd be naked."

"That's a bet everybody wins." I put down the beer and get up to go hug him. He smells of tiger and shampoo and beer and liquor and he hugs back tightly enough to pop my spine.

"You get to see the game?" He presses his nose down into my ears.

"Second half. You looked pretty good. Didn't let up on them at all."

He murmurs, "Uh-uh," and sways me back and forth. I swish my tail in time and untuck his shirt so I can slide my paws under it, against the short fur and hard muscles of his lower back. He mouths my ear and I shiver, and he says, "Let me get these things off."

So I say, "No, let me get those things off," and we stumble to the bedroom as I unfasten and undo his clothing, shedding it all the way to the bed. By the time we get there, he's as naked as I am, and if we're both not quite ready, we're not far. He pushes me to the bed, falls on me face to face, and holds me tight.

"Welcome home," he purrs in my ear, paw reaching around to squeeze my rear, under my tail. His arousal rubs against mine.

I press my muzzle to his, kiss deeply. We've made love in his apartment before, but as I sink into the bedsheets—his bedsheets, our bedsheets—I remember that this is our bed now, that my paws running down his sides will happen every night, that this is where I live.

Instead of turning me over, he lifts my legs, and when he slides inside me, his golden eyes meet mine. We watch each other, gasping together, and press close to kiss when our climaxes come, arms tight around each other, locked and squirming with our shared pleasure.

I collapse back onto the pillow, close my eyes, and I am home.

●

In the morning, we get my boxes from the car. He has the day off because the team won, so we plan to go out to lunch, maybe see a movie, then grab a takeout dinner that we can eat here at the apartment. Our apartment.

The first thing I unpack is a picture of me and Dev that I have from our spring vacation, back when he was closeted and—and I guess I was, too. I had it up in my apartment, but in my bedroom so I didn't have to worry about visitors seeing it (though I never really had visitors). With Dev's approval, I put it in his bedroom—our bedroom—not because we're worried about people seeing it (though he never really has visitors either), but because we want it there to look at.

Then I pull out another picture, one I had done as a surprise for him, and I put that up next to it, on his chest of drawers. It's sort of hidden behind the door when the door is open, which I guess is a bonus. I look at it for a second and then take it down again. I'll put it up while he's away and he can discover it when he gets back. It'll be a little surprise, maybe stop our days from becoming routine too fast.

I don't have much else in the way of decorations, just a few knick-knacks that Dev doesn't really have a place for. So I leave them in a box and put the box in the part of his closet that he set aside for me, along with a Dragons poster and a Firebirds poster. There's wall space in the living room, but I want to make it a little classier: right now it's just a couch and chair, a coffee table, and an entertainment unit. Behind the couch is a small computer desk with Dev's computer on it, which reminds me to unpack mine.

Dev just has wired internet, so I'll have to get a router, or, better yet, a wireless router. I unplug his computer and set my laptop to checking e-mail in the living room. He doesn't have bookshelves, and I didn't bring mine—too big and unwieldy—so I shove the box of my books into the closet and then open up the boxes of clothes.

Half the dresser is set aside for my clothes. Dev says I can have half the closet, which is great, because I have a lot of shirts to hang up. Not that I needed to worry: his closet is three times the size of the one I used to have, and all he has in it is three suits, four shirts (still in their bag from the dry cleaner), and one wire hanger on the otherwise bare wooden rod on his side. "I'm gonna start a shopping list," I say.

"What?" Dev pokes his head around the bedroom door. "You're bringing a ton of stuff in here, what else do you need to buy?"

"Hangers, to start with. Then probably some stuff for the fridge. You don't eat in a lot and I want to start cooking. And some stuff for the bathroom. Also, do you have a vacuum?"

He shakes his head. "I keep meaning to get one…"

"It's winter, and my coat's going to grow out. So there'll be a lot of fur around."

Behind him, his tail flicks. "More fox to love." He winks.

"Uh-huh. You think it's cute now, but by December when you're picking fur out of your Szechuan takeout, you'll be happy for a vacuum."

"Heh. I'm gonna unpack the rest of your kitchen stuff and put it away. How much longer you have in here?"

I scan the list of eighty-eight e-mails and glance at the remaining clothes in the box. "Half an hour to get through the most urgent e-mails, half an hour to finish the rest of the clothes, I guess."

"Cool. Lunch at twelve-thirty, then."

"Great." I sit down as he disappears back to the kitchen, but I don't look at the e-mails right away. "Urgent," in my current situation, is an exaggeration, making myself feel important.

First I check out the coverage of the previous night's game. All the major sites have stories along the lines of "the Firebirds have arrived," and "they're winning the games they should, and a few they shouldn't." None of them mention Dev specifically in relation to that; they talk about the lock-down defense in general, Gerrard's leadership, and Coach Samuelson having the team playing together. They compare Chevali's linebackers to Crystal City's, also led by a coyote, and widely considered tops in the league, so that's pretty cool. Where they do mention Dev, it's to speculate whether the media attention around his coming out brought the team together, and talking about how the solidity of the team is one reason it hasn't been more controversial. They have quotes from a couple of the Pelagia players, who sound mostly annoyed that the media is asking them what it's like to play against a gay opponent. "I don't care who he [sleeps with], I just wish he was a half-step slower," their tight end says. The quarterback, a little more media-savvy, says, "Gay or straight or bi, they're playing at a really high level and it's a challenge to get anything by them."

That gives me a smile as I finally look through my e-mails. Bunch of spam, and then one from my father wishing me well. That one gets me staring into space for five minutes, thinking about him and my mother, and how dismissive she was when I called. "Harold can take care of himself," she said, using my father's middle name like she always does, and she sounded annoyed that I'd woken her up. She didn't even ask how I was doing. It's strange. For the last few years, I haven't wanted to go home. But I always thought that I could.

Then there's an e-mail from Alex, the rabbit from the Dragons. The e-mail's titled, "Thought you should know about this." I click.

It starts out with him hoping I'm doing okay, asking if I want to get together for lunch sometime. I guess I should tell him I'm living three days away now. He goes on: "Hey, you added this guy Vince King to the Dragons list a month ago and we just got this notification on him. College says he passed away on Saturday. Don't know the details, but you were interested in him and it's kind of an excuse to get in touch 'cause I felt shitty for not writing when I saw it, y'know?"

Aw, crap. Most of the good mood I had from moving in evaporates. I type out a quick, numb response. "Thanks for the heads-up. I'm in Chevali but I'll be back in Hilltown sometime this fall. Let's get together."

And then I have to go look at the Cobblestone College website. The athletic section has a page mourning the passing of Vince King, and a link to the article in the kid's local paper. That article just says that he was found dead in his family's home the day after Thanksgiving. The lack of detail smells weird to me. If it were a car accident, it would say "Car accident." If he had some kind of disease, it definitely would have mentioned a stay in the hospital. But nothing. No "heart attack," no "brain aneurysm," no "fell off a ladder." So it was the kind of death they wouldn't want publicized. Like a suicide. And a gay kid committing suicide, well, there's been a few of them lately.

I know he'd been having a hard time when he wrote to Dev, but…

Then I get a sinking feeling. I haven't checked Dev's e-mail since before the holiday. It had trickled off since he came out, and I figured I'd get back to it after the Pelagia game. I'm sure there's nothing there. Sure of it. But I'm still terrified, when I log in, to look, and my finger hesitates over the mouse click before I finally open the inbox.

God, what was his e-mail address? I scan the list, look through it again. Nothing from anyone with the name King, as far as I can tell. And I'm relieved that he didn't reach out while I wasn't looking, but I'm also disappointed. I wish he'd thought he had someone to talk to.

I do another web search for his name, filter it to prioritize recent results, and then I get a weird hit. "Praying for the soul of Vincent King," the page is titled, on a website with an all-too-familiar name: families-united.org. But when I click on the link, the page isn't found. Thank goodness for search engines; I can see a cached version that looks like it was stored last Sunday.

It asks the "faithful" to join the congregation (which one, it doesn't say) in prayer for the soul of the son of Paul and Vanessa King, who has been "tempted by the homosexual lifestyle" and who has been "receiving lies as truth from homosexuals seeking to lure him into a degenerate lifestyle."

It gets worse the more I read, but the thing is, most of it doesn't sound specific to Vince. It ends with a repeated exhortation to keep this young boy in the reader's prayers—doesn't even say "young bear." I snoop around the website and see a bunch of different prayers with a lot of the same terminology. Some of them have pictures, school pictures with the young fox, or ringtail, or rat, anywhere from high school juniors to college seniors, looking bright and smiling against that uniform school picture background. Pictures supplied by the parents, not the cubs. Many—most—of the pages are about poor boys tempted by homosexual degenerates, but I find two youngsters in danger from the evils of drugs.

When I click around the website, I find other charming essays posted. Things like how all homosexuals ideally want to fuck little boys. How the homosexual agenda includes a complete redefinition of marriage to include farm animals. How homosexuality is a disease that has a cure.

I sit and stare at the computer screen, wondering what could have happened to a twenty-year-old bear, and why my mother's anti-gay group is praying for his soul. I could call her, I guess, and ask her to nose around with the friends she's making. But that assumes I have any currency left with her. And right now, I would place more money on my ability to step into a Firebirds uniform and catch one of Aston's passes than I would on my chances of getting information out of Mother.

When I was twenty, I had friends and a social life and maybe a boyfriend, depending on when in that year you looked. I might not have known where I was going in life—I might still not know—but I knew that wherever it was, I was going to be able to get there. I never felt the crushing isolation or despair that I think about when I hear about kids who kill themselves.

That first year of school, though, when I came home with my pride pamphlets and my patched-up jacket and basically dared my parents to confront me…that was a more precarious time. When Mother yelled at me over Christmas, Father took me aside and told me to take the jacket off, to make Mother happy. At the time, I thought he was taking her side. Now, in hindsight, I'm not so sure. But he didn't tell me I was wrong or bad, not ever, and Mother didn't either. They didn't tell a bunch of strangers that there was something so fucking wrong with me that they had to put a call out onto the World Wide Web for prayer to cure me from being a sick pedophile. Even if they had, I had FLAG and Brian and a whole bunch of uppity gays and lesbians ready to tell me there was not a damn thing wrong with me. If I hadn't…if I'd just been scared, and alone, and then my parents turned on me…

And yeah, I'm speculating, but it's a feeling in my gut, the kind I'd get when I'd watch a kid play and I'd think, *that guy is going to be a star.* Those feelings weren't always right, but they were right more often than they were wrong.

"Hey, I think my silverware is nicer than yours," Dev calls from the kitchen.

It takes me a moment to reply, "I picked yours out for you."

He pokes his head in the bedroom again and sees me sitting at the desk in front of the computer, just staring at the screen. His paw lands on my shoulder and squeezes. "Everything okay?"

"Uh. Why?"

"Well, your ears are down and your tail's under the chair and your eyes look like you just watched your Dragons lose the big game." He bends down and kisses my ears. "Something in your e-mail?"

"This kid who wrote you a couple months ago." I click around until I find his picture. "Him. He died."

"Died?" Dev's claws prick my shoulder. "Shit. How?"

"I don't know. But he was gay, and he was 'found dead' the day after Thanksgiving, and there's this webpage up asking people to pray for his soul from this fucking anti-gay organization." I fold my paws in my lap and try not to think of Mother.

"You think…" He sounds confused. "You think they killed him?"

"No. I think…" I pause. "I think he killed himself. But I think they probably helped drive him to it."

He rubs my other shoulder as well, claws retracted now. "That'd suck, but…maybe it was just an accident."

I stare at the screen again. "I know it sounds crazy, but Dev, I have this feeling. I don't know how to explain it."

His paws knead my muscles. "Fox," he says, "let's get you moved in. I'll be at practice tomorrow and you can check the story out if you want. Hey, if you call Hal, I bet he'd help."

"That's a good idea." I lean back into his embrace, reach out with a paw, and hide the websites. "I'll call him in the morning."

Chapter 6: Exploratory Moves (Dev)

Tuesday's just a really nice day. I'm putting away things in the kitchen and then I think, is he really just in the other room? Or I take something out of the box that smells like him and put it in my cupboard and think, that belongs there.

That e-mail he got sucks, and I'm kinda mad at his friend for bringing down what was otherwise a pretty good day. So I work to take his mind off it at lunch, and then we go walk around a park and I take him shopping for all the things he wants. He perks up a little then, picking out some nice art—real art, not sports posters, but nature scenes of hills and oceans and one really nice winter landscape. "To remind us of winter," he says.

And he says I need an end table and a whole bunch of food, so by the time we get back we have to make three trips up in the elevator, between the paintings and the awkward little table and the five bags of groceries. "Are you sure I need all this food?" I say. "I'm never home."

"I will be." He gives me a smile, and I'm glad he's feeling better. "And I'm going to cook more for you."

I eye the steaks I'm putting into the freezer. "Should I leave some of these out?"

"I'm not cooking tonight. I'm worn out."

I hope he means just from the shopping, but I don't press. We order pizza and play UFL 2009, but in the middle of the first game, he gets distracted and I score an easy interception, returned for a touchdown. "Didn't have your head in the game," I say.

"No," he says. "Sorry." I wait for him to laugh, to tell me I won't get an easy score off him like that again, but he just goes back to the game. So I figure he's thinking about that e-mail, and I edge along the couch, closer to him, until he snuggles up against me. When the game's over, I suggest we snuggle up close in the bed, and he's grateful to quit playing. I know there's no urgency, that he's not going home tomorrow or the day after, that home is actually right where he is, under me in bed, but I still want him bad, and he wants me too.

After, he wants to shower, but I say I'm sleepy and I'll shower in the morning. He says he's not going to put his clean fur next to my sticky messy fur, so I get up and we shower together. And that's not so bad. Feels good to go to bed clean.

The next morning, we tease each other a little bit, and then he says that I should get to practice, that he'll still be there when I get home. I get dressed while he watches me, still naked, and I leave for the stadium with a huge grin on my muzzle.

The good mood persists in the locker room. The win over Pelagia on national television got a lot of coverage in the media. After we beat our division rival Hellentown in probably the best game I've ever played in, people started really taking us seriously. Best of all, the requests for interviews and comments from me about being gay have started to die down. The media's covering us as a team. Yeah, I still get questions in the after-game press conferences and stuff, but it's less than it used to be.

Coach gives us a quick speech in the locker room before we break up into individual units. He was a quarterback fifteen years ago, and players have gotten way bigger since then, but he's still an imposing wolf with a wolf's command of the room, a glare that can pin you to the wall, and a great deep speaking voice that I've never heard without some trace of a growl in it. He stands in the doorway of his office, from which he can see the whole room, with the other coaches flanking him. "One week at a time," he says. "I'm so proud of what you guys have done in the last month. We won a statement game at Hellentown, and then didn't let up. Port City, Pelagia, those weren't easy games, but you made 'em look easy. We control our own destiny." He's said this every week since the Hellentown game. "If we win out, we're in the playoffs."

He pauses to let that sink in. I know I'm still having some trouble believing it. "That's not an easy thing to do. Yerba has a good team, and Freestone isn't a gimme. Kerina isn't a good team, but division games on the road are always tough. Then…" He points at the calendar, where December 29th is circled in red. "We get Hellentown here, last day of the season. They're still just one game behind us, and you know they would love to show up here with a chance to take the division from us. But we control our destiny, and if we play the way I know we can play, we will exit that game as champions of the UFL South."

"Yeah!" Our cheer echoes throughout the locker room, so loud that no one voice is distinct in it. And then Charm's voice rings out, "Fifty G's, coming up!"

Charm, my roommate on the road, is a big stallion who talks as tall as he stands. We laugh, and Gerrard says that it's not about the money, and Ty says that's easy to say for the guy who already has all of it. We get a forty thousand dollar check if we make the playoffs; another fifty thousand if we win the division. That's nothing to turn up your nose at for most of us. Put together, it's about a third of what I'm making this year, not counting commercials. And we want to see that "UFL South Champion" banner flying over the stadium. The last time the Firebirds went to the championship, they went as a wild card. The team has never—never—won its division in its thirty-two year history, not when it was part of the UFL Central behind those great Kerina and Gateway teams, not when it was moved to the UFL South twelve years ago. Kerina has, I think, a million division titles; Hellentown has eight, including the last three; even New Kestle has six. Chevali, not a one.

Coach's rah-rah speeches have not changed much during the season; what's changed is our confidence and our belief in his words. And, I think, his own confidence in them. In the year I've been playing for him, I've seen him at the end of a lousy season and at the beginning of a new one. I think he always believed we could be good, but there's a big difference between believing and seeing, even for the most optimistic of us.

Just like how a couple months ago, I don't think I would've believed that I could have held a press conference where I told the world I'm gay. And I certainly wouldn't have believed that if I had, the team would be laughing, slapping each other on the back, including me in their jokes and rituals like they always did. Winning solves just about every problem, my coach in high school used to say, echoing every sports journalist ever. And maybe if we were slogging through another 4-12 season, there would be a lot more hostility, slurs and slams, whispers behind my back. But the other guys who start alongside me at linebacker, a coyote named Gerrard Marvell and a leopard named Carson Omba, all they care about is that I bring my game. Aston, our quarterback and the most high-profile player on the team, has gone out of his way a few times to assure me that he's cool with everything. Zillo, the coyote who backs up my position, thought I was a sissy until he had to go out in my place and try to block the same bruising running back who knocked me on my ass and cracked my ribs.

That's not to say that everyone's cool. Colin, this fox rookie who plays cornerback, has had it in for me since the first time I announced my sexuality to the team. Used to be real pally with Zillo until the coyote's change of heart—and I think they had it out a week or two later, when Zillo started hanging out with me more and he and Colin stopped talking altogether. For the fox, it's a morality issue, so Zillo's tainted by association; Colin wears a cross and takes his religion seriously. Of course, he was a big star in college and almost got in trouble for taking money illegally from alumni, so on the morality scale he doesn't have a leg to stand on. And then there's Corey Mitchell, but I think he mostly hates me 'cause

I took his starting spot when he got injured. I haven't even heard him mention the gay thing.

I have an eye out for Corey, because this is the first day he'd be allowed back in the facility. He was suspended by the league for a week for laying a vicious late hit on a New Kestle player, and the Firebirds added two more weeks to that. Corey's nowhere to be seen, though, when the linebackers assemble with our position coach, "Steez" Mikilios.

His ropy feline tail curls smoothly behind him, and his ears are up, so he's in a good mood. And he likes me, even though I'm not a cougar like him and Corey are. Species bias is okay to a point, but when it comes to football, like Gerrard says, it's all about the game. He's not above telling me where Corey is better than me, but it's been a couple weeks since he had to.

Gerrard and Carson and I have worked pretty hard to get on the same page, and Steez tells us where we need to improve. Gerrard could coach us himself, and has, when we do extra workouts, but when Steez is talking, the coyote defers to him, only adding in words when he really feels it necessary. We start out with an overview of the game, watching film and studying our own performances.

"Second half, good performance," Steez says. "Team has a big lead, easy to lose focus, but you all keep head in game. Tomorrow we fly to Yerba. Good team, balanced attack. We are writing new plays, you will learn them."

"No problem," I say, and Gerrard grins at me.

Steez curls his muzzle in a feral smile. "Good, Miski. You think is easy? Perhaps we write five more. You like that?"

The grins of my teammates turn to barks of annoyance. "Shut up!" "No, no!"

"Go easy on us, coach," Gerrard says. "We don't all have study partners like fifty-seven there."

I flick my ears and grin. It's a nice thing for him to say, an acknowledgment of my relationship with Lee and also of Lee's football smarts. And it gets Steez to say, "Study partner, no study partner, Miski learns plays fast. You all learn that fast, we win championship."

"Hey, can I borrow that fox of yours?" Zillo says, low, and then kinda gulps and his ears go flat. "I mean, uh, for studying!"

The other guys laugh, and Marais, a cougar who backs up Carson, says, "What's the matter, you can't get enough head on the road?"

"I get plenty," Zillo says. "Not as much as Marvell there, but who does?"

"True dat!" Marais slaps his paw.

Steez clears his throat. "New plays tomorrow morning. Today, station drills." We all groan. Station drills are draining, repetitive physical exercises: shuttle sprints, tackle dummies, blocking. There's a pass defense station that isn't too bad, because at least we get to jump after a football, but even that's tiring when you do it fifty times.

"Hey," Zillo says as we break for the drills, "I didn't mean nothing by that."

"Don't worry." I punch his shoulder. "I know what you meant. Actually, I bet Lee'd love to work with some other guys. He's not doing anything 'til the start of next season."

"Nah, it was just a joke. I mean, that'd be a little weird. Unless the team hires him as a coach or something." He scratches his muzzle. "That'd be weird too, huh? Like if your boyfriend was a coach."

"Yeah, ha ha." He already sort of is, or was; the last few weeks he hasn't had much to say about my play. I look around, imagine Lee in one of those Chevali Firebirds polos yelling at the football players to hustle. I bet he'd like it. I want to change the subject, though. "Hey, you know where Mitchell is?"

Zillo turns that long coyote muzzle of his back and forth, scanning the field. "Nah, I was just wondering that." The only cougar in our group is Marais, starting drills with Gerrard just ahead of us. "Maybe he got traded. Deadline's coming up."

I squint through the sunny morning, inhale the smell of fresh-cut grass on the air. Behind us is the secondary, with Colin and a couple other foxes, some cheetahs, a lanky marten. On the other half of this side of the field, the defensive linemen work the tackle dummies. I see Pike, the polar bear who took over defensive end when Fisher was injured, and Kodi, the black bear who's always hanging out with Pike. "Doesn't look like anyone else is missing on defense."

"Who would we get for Mitchell?"

I shrug. "He's still a starting linebacker in the league. Could maybe get another safety, someone on the offensive line?"

"We got a good group here, even without Mitchell. Hope they don't break it up."

It's our turn to go, but I pause a moment and give him my full attention. He's looking right back at me, with a little bit of a coyote grin on his muzzle. "Yeah," I say, and hold out my paw. He slaps it. "So let's go kill the drill."

Even though it's December, it's still fifty degrees out, and by the time we make it through our stations and break for lunch, everyone's panting and hot. We grab the thick beef burgers off the catering table, cram fries onto our plate, and take big glasses of Powerade back to the field, where we sit on benches and eat.

That's where we find out where Corey is. The defensive line is eating with us, my buddy Brick, the bear, next to me, and Pike, lazily chewing through his second burger, next to him, with Kodi on the other side. Pike's the one who says, "Hey, where the fuck is Mitchell?"

We all sort of look around, and then Gerrard answers. "Getting a physical," he says. "With Ford."

Ford is a fox, a starting wide receiver. That creates a buzz. "So he *is* getting traded," Zillo says. "Who're we getting?"

Gerrard shakes his head. "Haven't heard anything."

"Hope it's another wideout." "What about a left tackle?" When speculating about who's going to come to the team, it's always bad form to suggest that we're going to get a replacement for someone in the immediate vicinity. Unless you're doing it to needle them.

"Could use another defensive tackle," I say, nudging Brick. He came in the same time I did, and he's been starting all year. He's in no danger of being replaced, and we both know it. "The way you're putting away those burgers, I dunno. Might be cheaper to get another tiger."

"Fuck tigers," Brick says, punching me amiably. "Maybe we'll get another faggot on the team."

That remark stings a little bit, even though I know he doesn't mean it to. It builds up a little bit of separation between me and the team. But I have to swagger and play along. "I'd love one," I say, "if someone else would hurry up and come out already."

"Ain't gonna happen." Pike gulps down the rest of his second burger. "Only reason to do it is to get all the endorsement money, and our tiger here is top billing now."

"Actually," Brick says, "I bet they seen his commercial and just don't wanna dress in that Ultimate Fit crap."

"You're wearing that Ultimate Fit crap," I point out.

"Yeah, well, it was free." He grins. "And it ain't so bad under a uniform. Wouldn't wear it out on its own though."

"I hope nobody else does come out," Gerrard says. "Just distracts from the game."

I would love to just walk away, but I can't, not in the middle of a talk like this. I think about what Lee would say, and temper it as much as I can. "It does," I say, "but it shouldn't. And the only way to do that is for enough guys to come out so it's not a big thing any more."

"Ahh." Pike waves a huge white paw. "It's gonna be a big thing for years. Next guy to come out's gonna have to be like the MVP or something. Or do it off-season when nobody notices."

"I did it," I say mildly.

"Oh, yeah, I don't mean to put you down or nothin'. But I think like Marvell says here, people see it mostly as a distraction. No reason to put your team through that, right?"

I think about being able to bring Lee to Gerrard's house. I think about being able to talk about him with my teammates, and what a weight that is off my chest. I think about how excruciating this conversation would be if I were still closeted. "It's not about that. It's about being happy with your life," I say.

"If that's what you need to be a better player, do it," Gerrard says. "Just keep the distraction to a minimum."

At the end of the day, Coach gives us the info for the morning flight to Yerba and directions to the practice facilities we'll be using in case we want to do our own thing while there. Lee's flying in on a later flight and renting a car; he has a Friday appointment with the GM. It's not a formal interview, but the guy apparently was intrigued after Lee's old boss recommended him, and more interested once Hal's piece on Lee came out. We don't know how the whole thing with him dating a player at another franchise will work out, but Lee says people should be grown-ups about it, and I guess I go along with that.

"Hey, Dev, wanna go out for a beer?" Pike calls from his locker. "Fisher wants to see us off before we fly out."

"Nah," I wave. "Give him my best. I got dinner at home."

Another one of my friends, Ty Nakamura, happens to be walking by with Vonni DiCarlo, both foxes (Ty's a wideout, Vonni a cornerback). Ty punches my shoulder when he hears that. "Ah," he says, "that means the boyfriend is in town. Dev's gonna get some tonight!"

I grin, and push the fox back. I start to say more, and then I hesitate, and then I think, what the hell, these guys are my friends. So I say, "Actually, he moved in yesterday."

"Wow." Ty stops and shakes his head sadly, his tail drooping. "My friends, let's have a moment of silence."

Gerrard, next to me, snorts and keeps pulling on his shirt. Pike looks confused, furrowing his brow. "Isn't that a good thing?" Behind him, the two black bears, Kodi and Brick, watch the discussion. Brick looks bored, Kodi uncomfortable.

Ty raises his head. "Poor Dev's freedom is gone. No more nights out with the guys."

"Whoa." Pike lifts large white paws. "Since when? Nights out ain't got nothin' to do with having a live-in."

"He's lucky," Brick growls. "No fuckin' naggin' about engagements."

"Getting married isn't so bad." Vonni, in a short-sleeved blue collared shirt, holds up a paw with a gold ring.

Ty grins at Vonni and nudges my shoulder. "Hey, I'd be happy if my grandma would quit mentioning me getting married every time we talk. But sadly, I like me the vixens."

I bump back, grinning. "We're goin' to Yerba, you know. You might take a walk down Korsat Boulevard and see something you like."

"Korsat Boulevard?" Vonni squints at me.

"Uh, yeah." Lee's talked about it a bunch. I didn't realize everyone didn't know about it. "That's where, like…"

"The gay stuff all happens. Most famous gay neighborhood in the country," Ty fills in. "Gay bars and gay clubs all over. And any gal I pick up in Yerba, she's taking all her clothes off before I do anything. *All.*" His paws mime undressing.

Vonni sticks his paws in his pockets, hiding his ring. "Hey, what's the diff, Ty?" he says. "A mouth's a mouth, right?"

"Better than a girl, I heard." Pike grins; we all turn to look at him. "Hey, some of the old guys, they were in clubhouses where guys'd come around and blow whoever wanted it. Sometimes you can't get a girl to put anything in her muzzle, y'know?"

My ears get warm, thinking about the times I've had Lee in my muzzle. I turn to my locker and rub my head with a towel, but I can't stop hearing them. I wish Ty would stop saying "gay" all the time, too.

"It's different!" Ty turns around and taps his nose. "Smells different, you know?"

Vonni swings his hips back and forth. "They got pher-o-mones, you know? Make 'em smell like whatever you want. Even to us." He taps his nose the same as Ty did.

Kodi mumbles something to Pike and wanders out, while Ty is looking stricken. He stands up on the bench and spreads his arms. "No foolin' my nose!" he announces to the whole locker room. "Bring it on, I'll sniff it out."

"Sniff this," Pike says, lifting his sweaty clothing to the fox.

Ty waves it away, still talking to Vonni. "Maybe you oughta take that walk down Korsat," he says, hopping down. "Sniff out some gay action for yourself."

"I'm married," Vonni says, "so sure, I'll go with you."

Ty's tail flicks. Half the locker room is watching them. Pike, who was about to walk out after Kodi, stops to look, and even I turn around. I'm amused and fascinated, just thinking that I'm glad they're not talking about me anymore, and then Ty looks over his shoulder at me. "I'll go if Dev goes."

"Wait, what?"

Ty punches my shoulder. "Come on, what do you say?"

"Look," I say, "I don't really know—"

"Let him be, Ty," Vonni says. "You and me. Anyone else who wants to go, too. You don't have to be foxes," he adds generously to the rest of the locker room.

Ty kind of squints at me. "You think you'll get in trouble?"

I'm aware of Gerrard looking at me, Carson waiting behind him. "Not from Lee," I say.

"Oh, what, Coach over there?" Ty waves at Gerrard. "C'mon, we'll go Thursday night. Plenty of time."

"The thing is," I say, "I mean, I've never been there myself. I'd be as lost as all of you."

"So ask your boyfriend."

"Nah," Vonni says to Ty. "Then he'd have to admit he's going. There'd be questions and all."

"Aren't you gonna tell your wife you're going?"

Vonni laughs. "Hell no. She's got enough to worry about."

Pike shakes his head. "Still don't get why he can't just go out when he's on the road. You two should just hitch up your pants and go. I wanna hear what happens." He grins at Ty and Vonni, and lumbers out of the locker room. Brick follows him a moment later.

Vonni looks at Ty, and Ty looks at me. "Tell you what," I say. "I'll ask him to recommend some places for you to go. Depending how practice goes, maybe I'll go with you." I don't want to, but I also think it's kind of cool that they want to go, and I don't want to give them an excuse to back down.

Fortunately, they leave it there. And Lee is amused, at least, when I relate the whole exchange to him. "I've never been to Korsat either," he says, leaning against me on the couch. "But I can look up some stuff."

"Don't send them anywhere really skeezy." I run fingers through the fur between his ears. "They need to have a good experience of gay people."

"They need a good blow job." He turns and arches an eyebrow up at me. "Or a good fuck. Look what it did for you."

"Yeah, well." The portion of my dating life prior to meeting Lee is there in my memory, but it's misty, like the watercolor he hung in the living room. "So when are you coming out to Yerba?"

"I got tickets for Friday." He rests a paw on my knee and rubs gently. "My hotel's near yours but not too near, and I'll have a car."

"Sunday night I should have free." I think about our new plays and Gerrard's eyes on me. "Up 'til the game, I should practice, though."

"When you're not parading down Korsat Boulevard with your bi-curious friends."

"I think they're just curious."

"It's not a bad thing, being bi-curious. Means you're open-minded."

I shake my head and then stop. "I just thought it was cool that they asked. What's for dinner?"

"Oh." He rubs up against my paw and then gets up. "I got a roast chicken from the store, some salad, and potatoes. Mashed okay?"

"Great."

I look around while he goes into the kitchen to finish up dinner. He's also done some decorating, but not a whole lot. He had my Beatles poster framed—or just bought a cheap frame for it, maybe. I know he had other posters: Dragons, Firebirds, a male fox modeling a swimsuit. Those must still be in the closet, though.

Dinner is good, the mashed potatoes lumpy but tasty. I tease him about them, pick at the salad, devour half the chicken while he gnaws daintily on a leg. I help do the washing up, and then wander around the apartment while he sets up the video games.

There's more of his presence visible in the bedroom. For one thing, his scent is stronger there than anywhere but the living room couch. He's also got that picture of us up on the dresser, a picture of the Hilltown Dragons 1968 championship team up on the wall, next to that winter landscape, and on the nightstand by the bed…

I peer at it. "Hey," I say. "When did you have this done?"

He's leaning in the doorway of the bedroom. "Like it?"

The picture shows him reclining on his side, naked, with just about an inch of erection showing at the end of his sheath. His muzzle's curved in a sly smile, one paw cupping his sheath and balls, his tail draped artfully over one leg.

"I love it," I say. "But who took the picture? It looks professional."

He walks in, tail swishing behind him. "I just set up some lights in my apartment and a sheet behind. Looks good, though, huh? I took a whole set and this one came out best."

I turn and wrap him in a hug, linking my paws behind his back. "Oh, a whole set. Were there any 'after' pictures?"

"Uh-huh." He grins. "They're on my laptop. I'll show you."

"I'd rather get a re-enactment."

"We can arrange that too." He tilts his muzzle up, and we kiss, and rub up against each other.

"You're not going away in the morning." I grin down. "Still getting used to that."

"Mm-hmm." He squeezes my rear, his tail wagging, and we just hold each other, video games forgotten. I keep looking around at the changes in the apartment, the little touches combining his home with mine into ours. He's been careful about not moving too many of my things, and I'm determined not to have a sitcom moment where I get way too attached to some silly thing that he wants to throw out. Then I keep looking down at that picture, and I think it's pretty nice, but the real thing is even nicer.

"I sent Hal an e-mail," he says.

"About what?"

He steps back. "About Vince King?"

It takes me a second to place the name. "Oh, right." I scratch my muzzle. "Poor kid. So what'd Hal say?"

Lee shrugs. "He's going to look into it and get back to me. He thinks he might be able to talk to the local paper and get at least a little more of the story, if not something documented."

"Like he did when he wrote that story about me and my dad?" My claws flex out; I pull them in.

"Come on. He apologized for that, and anyway, the piece that ran last week was way better."

I grumble. The whole article seemed to me to be just a lot of fluff. It made me out to be some kind of heroic tough guy, Lee to be sensitive and smart, and our love to be some kind of passionate romance that defied all the odds. I guess it's just how you look at it. For my money, Lee's just a great guy that I'd do most anything to be with. Even if he is a fox, even if he does frustrate the hell out of me sometimes, even if I look at him in certain moments and see wheels turning behind those blue eyes, thoughts going places I can't imagine. I know I'm a pretty simple guy and he wants to be with me anyway, and sometimes I have no idea why.

"So anyway." Lee sits on the bed. "I'm trying not to think about King. I went out and found a frame for your poster at the store."

"It looks nice."

"And I talked to my father. He's doing okay. He won't settle on a time to get our stuff from the house."

I look down at the picture, at the posters. I imagine the two of us breaking up and Lee's things still being here. Would I want to hold onto them as tightly as I could, memories of the past? Or would I want to throw them out into the street? I guess it would depend on which of us broke up with the other, and that's not worth thinking about because it ain't gonna happen. "How's your mom doing?"

He scowls, and his ears lower. "That fucking hate group she's all in with? They put up a page for people to pray to cure Vince."

Vince, like he knew the guy personally. I sigh. "She didn't put the page up herself, though, right?"

"No…" And his muzzle lifts and his eyes get a shrewd gleam in them. "No, I don't think *she* did…"

I have no idea where this scheming could be going, so I head it off. "What's your schedule in Yerba? When are you talking to the Whalers guy about the job?"

He comes back to me, ears perking up a little. "Friday at two. Late lunch at a sushi place."

"Is he an otter?"

"Fox. But I guess everyone on the coast eats sushi. Hey, we'll be done by Friday night. Maybe I could go with you and your friends to Korsat Boulevard."

"If I go." If that's what he was scheming about, then I'm worried, but he looks just honestly enthusiastic. "If you go and I don't, that'd be weird. Anyway, I think they're planning to go Thursday."

"I've met a couple of them. Maybe they'll wait."

I lean over and growl at him, theatrically. "After you interview with another team, you want to drag my teammates out to a nightspot?"

"Hey," he says, curling his tail back around me and smiling a sly fox smile, "I won't start sabotaging your team until I'm officially hired by the Whalers."

"I guess we'll figure that out when it happens." We both go quiet, and I'm not sure what he's thinking, but I'm just thinking I'm happy to be with him, thinking about our future. Knowing there will be a future and that we'll be together in it is something new to me.

CHAPTER 7: DRESSING UP (LEE)

I give Dev a nice sendoff to the plane in the morning, teasing his erection until he's fully awake, then going down on him, then finally rolling over so he can jump on me and come under my tail. We lie there panting and (in my case) wagging, and then he kisses my ears and slips out and off. "Let's shower," he says, and drags me into the shower with him.

"I'll wash the sheets," I say as I soap him up.

He perks up. "Wow, there are all kinds of benefits to you living here that I hadn't thought about."

"Just don't start thinking of me as the maid." I grip his shaft and soap it extra hard, so he squirms.

"Does that mean you won't wear one of those cute outfits?" He grins down at me.

I just grin back and arch my eyebrows, and we finish up the shower. Then I kiss him and send him off to Yerba. "See you at the game," I say.

"Maybe for dinner that night," he says.

"I'll text you."

"Me too."

"Fly safe."

"You too."

"Shoo!" I push him out the door in his neatly tailored suit, with his two Firebirds-logo duffel bags over his shoulder, and I go back to the apartment—our apartment—for the day.

One thing about Chevali: it sure as hell beats Hilltown for winter. It's fifty degrees out at nine in the morning. Hilltown could go months without sniffing fifty. I'm sure in the summer I'll be much less happy, but on the other paw, Chevali probably doesn't have Hilltown's nasty humidity.

And I probably won't be here in the summer. I'll be in Yerba, or maybe somewhere else around the league. Who knows?

That's months away. I throw the sheets in the laundry and walk out to do some more shopping.

The thing I didn't tell Dev was that Hal agreed with me about Vince King's death. "Looks like suicide," he said when I called him and pointed him to the article. "You think he was bullied into it?"

"Maybe by his parents."

He was quiet for a while. "You and parents," he said. "Going to go put another one in the hospital?"

I have been trying not to think about that, but without Dev to distract me, it's hard. I don't know what I'll do if it does turn out to be suicide, except bring it to light. And after what Dev said about Mother, I think I might have to call her. I know that's not a good idea, but I can't stop thinking about that web page, the people talking about being gay like it's a drug addiction and praying for a cure. She might know who put up the page for Vince King. I wonder if she put up a page for me.

The last time I called, when I was worried about Father, she was colder than I'd expected considering the fox she'd been married to for twenty-five years was missing. Just remembering that pisses me off all over again, but if I'm going to get information from her, I have to put that aside.

She hadn't been working, and even though my father's moved out, she probably has enough family money to go without a job for a little while. She and Father used to talk about it as though it were a hoard of gold: "if we can do that without touching the family money," and "we'll put that in with the family money," and "the family money is doing well this year." So I take a chance and call her at home.

Her voice is suspicious when she picks up, that tone reserved for probable telemarketers and bad news. It doesn't improve when I identify myself. "What, has Harold wandered off again?" she says.

"No." I grit my teeth. "I just wanted to ask how you and those Families United people are getting along."

"I'm not going to stand here while you try to tell me lies about them." I guess that's fair, considering I've never talked to her about them before.

"Farthest thing from my mind," I say, blandly. "I just wanted to know who puts up those pages that ask people to pray for the souls of homosexual degenerates."

"Good-bye," she says.

"Wait, wait!" I listen for the click, but she hasn't hung up. "I just want to know if you put up a page for me."

The silence is so long that I think maybe she did hang up, and I just didn't hear it. Then she says, "My involvement with Families United is not about you." Before I can call her on that, she goes on. "It's about me finding a community of people who will listen to my worries and concerns."

"About me."

"Among other things." Her tone gets sharper. "Wiley, I tried to steer you away from the path you were on…"

"I didn't need steering. Just understanding."

She's quiet again. "I'm sorry I couldn't provide that to you."

"Yeah," I say. "So about those pages. You know who puts them up? I'd like to talk to them."

"I'm not going to give you permission to harass my friends," she says.

"So you do know who it is."

"All of Families United is one group of friends. We can call upon each other for support in anything."

"Sounds great. Do you all wear purple robes and drink Kool-Aid?"

"Good-bye, Wiley," and this time she does hang up.

Well, shit. That didn't help at all.

I'm on my way back with a small bag of groceries when Hal calls me. I flip open my phone and answer with, "Gumshoe results already?"

"They get up early on the east coast," he says. "Puritan work ethic."

"Also it's two hours earlier."

"Right. So look, want to get together for lunch, or are you consumed with domestic chores?"

I heft the grocery bag onto my wrist so I can open the door to Dev's—to our apartment building. "What, have you been faxed a top-secret file you can't tell me about over the phone?"

He snickers. "I haven't seen you since the Hellentown game and I thought you might like to see a friendly nose in your new hometown."

"Why, Mister Kinnel," I say in my breathy female voice, "are you flirtin' with me?"

He takes on an exaggerated private dick voice. "Our usual place," he says. "Wear that dress I like. And," he lowers his voice, "come alone."

"You want to meet me 'Between the Sheets,' is that it?" Between the Sheets is a sandwich shop that features "well-stuffed sandwiches" and lots of double entendres. The sandwiches are sloppy but good, and reasonably priced. When Hal thought I was Dev's ex-girlfriend, trying to get his story out of me, he met me there a couple times.

"You know it, shweetheart."

For kicks, and because it gets me to unpack the last of my non-book boxes, I do get out a nice blue dress that I wore a lot back when I was dating Dev at Forester and wanted to go to games without anyone knowing I was a boy. It's less formal than the dress I wore to Dev's coming-out press conference, the first one Hal saw me in, but that's kind of a "special occasions" sort of dress.

His eyes widen when I walk in, and his ears flick back under the fedora he's wearing. "I was kidding," he says.

I slide into the booth across from him. "Oh, were you? Nice hat, by the way."

He's wearing a pretty nice collared shirt, light green with dark blue stripes, and it goes well with the fedora, which I think he put on just to keep up the shamus effect. It looks a little dusty; he probably got it out of the back of his closet. Kind of cute, actually, even if he is ten or fifteen years older than me.

He takes the hat off and sets it on the seat beside him, letting his dust-colored fox's ears spring up. "See, now I'm going to spend the whole conversation tryin' to see where I should've guessed you aren't a girl."

"You're a fox. You should know better than to let another fox distract you."

"I'm a straight guy. We're susceptible to a whole other level of distraction."

I adjust the dress's shoulders and my fake chest, and Hal crosses his eyes theatrically. "Oh, come on," I say.

"It's been a while since my divorce," he grumbles.

"Haven't you been dating?"

"Matter of fact," he says, "got a date tomorrow night with a coyote."

He looks a little like a coyote himself, the swift fox does. Same desert-rock colored fur, but slightly smaller ears, and more orange in the edges, like the sides of his muzzle where it shades to ivory underneath. "Nice. How'd you meet?"

"Oh." He brushes his whiskers with a paw, very self-consciously. Like when my father talks about trying something new through the Internet. "Mutual friend."

I nod. "A friend named E. Harmony?"

He scowls at my grin. "Match dot com, okay? I have a good feelin' about it, though."

"All right, all right." I start to say more, but he holds up a paw.

"And look, if it's okay with you, I'll save the King file until after we eat. It's kind of heavy and I'd rather enjoy my lunch."

My grin fades. "So it was suicide."

He lifts his sandwich and takes a big bite out of it, and doesn't meet my eyes. So I do the same, and I try to savor the creamy tuna salad and the soft wheat bread while we make small talk about Chevali and what neighborhood I'm in and where are the good places to eat around there. I live here now, I have to remind myself. This is my neighborhood. It's a weird feeling, but I still have trouble concentrating because I'm worried about what he's going to tell me.

When the last glop of mayo is licked up and our napkins are lying crumpled on our empty plates, I brush the trappings of the lunch aside and lean forward. "Okay, so tell me."

His ears go back, and he takes a deep breath. "Vince King took one of his father's guns from the garage. He went up to his bedroom and shot himself in the head."

Even though I'd already guessed it, the cold reality of it bites hard. "Christ."

"Not much way to spin it as an accident. As a favor to the family, the sheriff kept the papers mostly out, but there's only so much you can hide. Both parents devout churchgoers. And on Friday morning, a couple people from the church paid a visit to the King family—only know that because they were interviewed by the police, briefly. Couldn't find out the names. Guy at the paper said the sheriff kept all that clamped down. But he did say that this group is pretty active in Nonsiquet. 'Specially around the Kings' church."

He reaches into his pocket and takes out a folded piece of paper. It's a printout of the front page of the Families United website. I glance down at the smiling raccoon family, the parents embracing the son, and then look back up. "I'm familiar with them."

"Thought you might be."

"So he just mentioned that group." I don't want to touch the paper. I don't even want to acknowledge that it's there.

"I mighta prompted him a bit. I'm sure there's other active groups, but the Nonsiquet Bowling League don't seem like it'd drive a kid to do something like that."

I shake my head. "Talk to the parents at all?"

"Nah. Been less'n a week. Seems a little soon."

Maybe. Maybe not. I nod. "Well, I appreciate the info."

He gestures at the paper. "You want that?" When I shake my head, he crumples it and tosses it atop his plate.

I take it from his plate and throw it into the garbage near us. He nods. "Guess you really are familiar with them."

"You seen some of the stuff they do?"

"Ayup."

I think of Dev's Auntie Za. "Hey, I know Equality Now has a chapter down here. Any other pro-gay organizations I could check out?"

He taps the side of his muzzle, thinking. "None that'd do anything on the level of Families. You want reach, pretty much they're the only game in town. You could also call up Fair and Legal—"

"I know them."

"—but they don't have a chapter down here. It'd be all remote."

"Also they mostly deal with legal briefs and cases. Not publicity and campaigns."

"Right. Sounds like Equality Now is more what you want to do." He pauses. "Speaking of…" I cup my ears forward. "A guy from them called me after that article I wrote about you. Wanted to reprint it in their newsletter."

"Really."

"Uh-huh. And I remembered some stuff you said, so when he said his name was Brian…"

"God dammit."

"Yup. Seemed real interested in how well I'd gotten to know you. Made a few unsavory insinuations, if you want to know the truth."

"Sounds like Brian. He believes everyone's secretly gay." Damn him.

"Wanted to know if I thought you and Miski were real serious, too. He put it like, 'did you just make it sound good for the article,' but then he asked a couple times."

"I didn't date him. For the record."

"Didn't ask." His whiskers twitch.

"We were just best friends, and then…" I sigh. "It's complicated."

"I saw him at the press conference, going on about the truth."

"Yeah, he has a blog where he wrote about Dev being gay. But before that, he got beat up by some football players at Forester. And he quit the college, moved down here, rather than stay and stand up."

Hal leans back against the bench. "Seems like that'd rub you the wrong way, yeah."

"Felt like he betrayed me. Or I betrayed him." And that's how I met Dev, trying to get revenge for what happened to Brian. I can't ever seem to escape him, so it doesn't really surprise me that he was talking to other people about me. He called me to brag about getting back into activism, for fuck's sake. "Then after he pulled that shit with Dev, Dev hates him."

"Can't blame him."

We part after agreeing to get together again for lunch soon. It is nice, as Hal said, to see a familiar nose in town, but it's not his I'm thinking about all the way home. I'm thinking about Brian, and how now I know he's working with Equality Now.

Well, so what? I don't have to work with him, right? It's a big national organization. I can certainly find someone else to talk to. But Dev is going to stress about it anyway. So I call him, and when his phone goes to voicemail, I say, "Hi, roommate-boyfriend. Listen, I want to do some work with this group called Equality Now. They do a lot of good work with publicity for gay rights and stuff, and I think I could help them. Thing is, Brian's a member. I don't have to work with him, and I'm going to try not to, but in any case I'm not going to call them until I hear back from you, but I do want to follow this up. Call me when you get a chance." After a second's pause, I add, "If you're not already down at Korsat Boulevard with your bi-curious buddies."

Then I go study up on my college football players. The interview Friday is with the general manager of Yerba, and I want to make a good impression, so I have to know his team inside and out, as well as the current class of players ready to come into the league. But I keep getting distracted, looking at the pictures and profiles of the players. This one doesn't mention a girlfriend, and he looks withdrawn; that one says he wants to be politically active. This one is a polar bear with a charming smile.

Jesus Fox, I still remember most of what Vince wrote. *I've been hiding who I am all through college, and it tears me up. I take out my frustration on the football field. I get drunk a lot because I keep trying to hook up with girls so nobody will know I'm gay.* I stare at the screen.

Before I went to the first FLAG meeting, I was scared. Mother and Father weren't all that religious, though, and they always taught me to express myself. I had no idea what to expect. All I knew was that all through my last two years of high school, I'd jerked off to the male models in magazines, not the female ones. I never drank, never tried to pick up girls; it was easier to be a loner in high school, especially since I wasn't on a team. I could pick my own social group.

I'd picked Forester, though, partly because it had an active gay student group. So I told myself I would have wasted all that if I didn't go. I walked in, sat with the four other new kids near the back. And there was Brian, just as young and wary as I was. When he stood up during introductions and said, "I've been waiting my whole life to be here," I knew I liked him. And when he leaned over to me ten minutes into the meeting and said, "I'm glad it's not just a bunch of queeny fags," I knew we were going to be great friends. I told him that's why I sat by the door, and his smile told me he knew we were going to be friends, too.

Vince King had parents who went to church every week and turned there for help. He went to Cobblestone College, pretty liberal—smart kid—but he was part of the football team from day one. You can't just walk into a Gay and Lesbian student group meeting when you're on the football team. He never had a Brian, never had anyone to confide in. And when he did, when his secret burst out of him and couldn't be contained any longer, the people he trusted told him he was sick. They told him they needed an army of closed-minded bigots to pray for his soul to save him from hell. They told him he couldn't have a normal life unless he gave up part of himself. And he had nobody to talk to, nobody to tell him he *was* normal. Nobody to tell him there was hope.

If I'd gone to talk to Vince King at the game I watched, would that have made a difference? I wrote back to his e-mail, but as me, not as Dev, and Dev was the one he'd written to. He might have seen Kinnel's article, or he might not. But if I'd introduced myself at the game, if I'd offered to help him out, would he have felt so alone? Would he have hesitated, picking up the gun, and picked up a phone instead?

I know I can't beat myself up over it, but that doesn't stop me from doing so. Maybe Hal's article will change things. Maybe I'll get more of a public face and I'll be able to do some good. I pace to the window and stare out at the city. Not so different from Hilltown, if you look past the details: glass office buildings, stone apartments and stores. But there's more red clay roofs near the edges, out in the suburbs, and beyond that, the hills are pale reddish-brown dotted with cacti like abandoned machine parts in someone's backyard, and the sun above them glows through a haze that reddens it, too. An older world, here, slower, more conservative. And now it's my world.

I turn back to the computer, which is also my world, but more familiar. Hours go by, and I succeed moderately well at forcing myself to focus on the college players and their abilities. Wish I had film of them to watch, but I remember most of them from when I was working for the Dragons, and I read up on the games they've played since then to get an idea if they've improved, declined, or stayed the same.

Dev calls around eight, right when I'm thinking I should either eat some leftover chicken or sweep up all the shed fur from pacing around the apartment. He gets right to it. "You really have to join his group?"

"They're a national organization, and not a bad one; they focus on political initiatives rather than legal challenges, and that's why they do more with publicity." I lean into the phone, sitting on the couch. "It's not about Brian. There's nobody else in the area, really."

"Did they do that prison commercial you showed me?"

"Yeah. It was a little over the top, but it got the message across about what it's like to be gay in today's society. And really, I promise I won't do anything with Brian alone."

He sighs. "I can't really tell you not to, can I?"

"You could."

"It's fine, fox." He exhales. "I gotta go. The guys are getting together for dinner."

"And then Korsat Boulevard?"

He laughs, shortly. "Not for me. But I gave them the places you looked up and Ty and Vonni say they're going to visit them. Couple other guys said they'll go Friday night if it's a good report."

"It'll be wilder Friday night."

"That's not necessarily a bad thing."

I wag my tail. "Imagine a bunch of hot football players dancing in a gay club on a Friday night. Hope it all goes well." A thought occurs to me. "Hey, if they do go Friday night, you and I could go along."

He pauses. "I don't think…"

"They look up to you," I say. "You could show them there's nothing weird about the scene."

"If you want an excuse to go to a gay club…"

"Or I could just go with them by myself."

That stops him. "You'd do that?"

"Well." I pretend to consider it. "No. I'd want to go with you. But come on, how weird would it look if a bunch of your teammates go and you don't?"

"It'd look like I care about football."

"I'm sure you can get Gerrard's permission."

He snorts. "Have a good dinner and a good flight."

"How was practice?"

"Oh, it was fine. New plays and all. But we're coming along well."

I grin. "Meaning Gerrard says you need to do an evening practice."

"We don't *need* to." He pauses. "But I want to."

Which is good. So I let him go off to dinner, heat up the leftover chicken, and eat it while cramming on college players, which is not nearly as fun as it sounds when I say it like that. I hope he'll let me take him out to Korsat, and going with his teammates would be even better. Might get us into the news, show people that football players can go to gay clubs with gay friends and not be gay. Might get my name out there, too.

Chapter 8: Interviewing (Lee)

Friday I get on a plane to Yerba first thing in the morning. We circle the city coming in, so I get a good first look at it. Where Chevali sprawls out in the midst of brown and tan rock and sand, Yerba is crammed into a peninsula between the ocean and the Bay, a cluster of concrete and glass jutting out of the deep blue like crystals. I even spot the football stadium, Bayshore Field, nestled in a little nook on the bay side of the peninsula.

Yerba's famous for its bridges and bread, fog and fags. The airport reflects none of that, though, except for the airport logo being a stylized bridge. No recruitment posters for the homosexual agenda, no gay proselytizers, not even any rainbow flags. It's almost like gay people are just normal. Also, no bakeries in the airport, which I find disappointing.

Driving, too, is like driving in any other big city. The weather is comparable to Chevali's, though a little less dry, so I roll the windows down and enjoy the breeze through my thick fur, which soon fills the car like snowflakes.

It settles as I leave the freeway, and by the time I pull up to the outdoor mall where my meeting is, I'm glad that the rental car agency doesn't have a cleaning fee. I brush myself off and walk into the restaurant, a little shop without a flashy sign just called Koto Sushi.

It smells of fish and rice, with tangs of soy sauce and rice vinegar. The chef and hostess are otters, and many of the diners are, too. I don't see any foxes seated in the crowded dining room. Maybe I'm early. I check my phone and the hostess asks me if I want a table for one.

"I'm here to meet someone," I say. "But I'm not sure he's here yet."

"Oh!" She smiles and half-bows, then gestures for me to follow her.

I weave through the tables somewhat less elegantly than she does. Her thick tail swishes below the hem of her kimono in exactly the right place to miss the chairs. I have to keep mine curled around my leg until we get to the bamboo screen at the back of the dining room.

It looks like the kind of screen that hides the entrance to the restrooms, and in fact we walk past a small hallway discreetly marked "Restrooms." Beyond that is a small room lit by paper lanterns of many different colors, with only four tables, and only one of them occupied.

The fox stands up as I walk in, extending a paw with a bright smile. "Farrel, right? Peter Emmanuel." He's dressed casually, in a polo shirt and slacks. The shirt is in the Whalers' maroon, with a gold-threaded logo embroidered over the chest. Unobtrusive and classy. He's probably around my father's age, maybe a little younger—early forties, late thirties—and about my height. The shirt stretches across his broad shoulders and a bit of a stomach paunch, but he's still clearly in good shape.

"Pleasure to meet you. Thanks for making the time to talk to me." I get a nice feeling of species familiarity as we both sit down. He's taller than I am, with darker ears—almost pure black, where mine are more chocolate brown. And like me, his winter coat is coming in, though his is very sleek. Professionally brushed, I'm sure.

He calls the waitress over with a flick of the paw. "Any friend of Morty's is worth at least a lunch. Want a beer?"

"Just water, thanks." Morty, my old boss at the Dragons, likes me. I thank goodness for that.

"Kiku, one more Sapporo in about ten minutes, with lunch."

She bows. "Hai. Two lunch?"

"Yes." He glances at me. "Anything you don't like?"

Not at a job interview meal I am hopefully getting for free. I shake my head. "It all sounds good."

"It is. This is the best sushi on the peninsula. You want to go into the city, there's a couple places, but this place gets their fish fresh every morning and the chef is amazing. I dread the day some other place steals him away." He drinks from the half-empty beer bottle. "Have you had good sushi before?"

I lift my nose again to sniff the air. "Never in a place that smelled like this. I guess I thought it was good at the time."

He laughs. "You are in for a treat. And it's on me, let's just get that out of the way. So look, Morty and I worked together for a few years back in Kerina. He still smoke?"

"Like a chimney."

He shakes his head and waves the air in front of his nose. "How'd you stand it?"

"I got really good at holding my breath." I grin.

He laughs. "Good. So tell me about your experience with football. Play in high school? College?"

I shake my head. "But I love the game. I've been watching it for fifteen years now, and I have this thing that when I love something, I need to figure out how it works. So I watched football and read articles and took it apart. And then in college I went to every game." Bit of an exaggeration. A couple I watched in the bar. "You start to see which players are doing well and which ones are just holding the team back. And you see which ones have potential."

"And that's what you saw in Miski."

I'm not sure how to handle that. He's looking evenly at me and I can't tell if he wants me to comment on the personal relationship or what. "Yes," I say finally. "He had potential and he was just wasting it."

"Uh-huh. Well, you were right about that. He's a solid starter. Who else did you scout? Let's talk about last year; I know you probably can't talk about this year yet."

"Right." So I list off some players I'd recommended to the Dragons, the ones they'd gotten and the ones they hadn't. Emmanuel gives quick nods to each name, ears flicking, checking them off in his head, I suspect, against a list he got from Morty. Four are doing well, two are okay, and one would be doing a lot better if they gave him a chance. "Like Dev," I say.

"Off the record," Emmanuel says, "Hilltown is shit at developing their players. Morty's doing great work scouting there and he turns up gems like, well, like Miski, and they can't figure out what the hell to do with them."

"Tell me about it," I say. "I had to watch them every week."

"So tell me about our players." He says it quickly, casually, but I don't miss the significance of it.

"You guys are a lot more fun to watch." I take a breath and launch into my prepared analysis of Yerba's rookies and the team's continuing needs. He nods throughout, but doesn't take notes or make another sign. Just the way I'd do it, playing it close to the vest. "If not for Crystal City, you'd be in the playoffs for sure."

He shrugs. "If we took care of business in the other games, we could nab the wild card spot. But I think your Firebirds or the Pilots are going to lock up one of those spots, whichever one doesn't end up winning the division. We need to beat Highbourne in two weeks to have a chance at the other. You know how it is—last year's beatdown in Peco just demoralized everyone."

I nod. "Not sure what the Dragons' excuse is."

"Years of losing become a habit. The staff here is pretty good about not letting that happen."

"Three playoff trips in seven years," I say.

He nods. "So what would you say is our top need? Who would you take in the first round?"

"Now," I say, "I can't share specific research I did for Hilltown this year."

"Of course." His whiskers twitch. "I meant, which position."

"Well, for the positions you need—linebacker and center—the top guys are pretty much public knowledge."

The waitress arrives just then with two edgeless, narrow bamboo trays upon which glisten six pieces of fish on small pedestals of rice. A green pyramid of wasabi makes my eyes water as it passes in front of my nose, and a yellowish pile of pickled ginger next to it smells mouth-wateringly sharp. Between two shallow bowls, she sets a small pot of soy sauce, and lastly, she replaces Emmanuel's Sapporo with a fresh one. "Anything else?" she asks.

"Good for now." Emmanuel pours a few drops of soy sauce into his dish and mixes in wasabi. I do the same.

"Anyway," I go on when the waitress leaves the room, "Where you're going to be in the first and second rounds, approximately, here's what I would look for with those picks." I give him three names and briefly explain their histories while we add more soy sauce to our mixtures. "This is all stuff you could get on the Internet. I checked."

He grins widely. "That's very interesting."

Even though he doesn't say good or bad, his vulpine body language tells me that I did pretty well. At least, I hope the smile and relaxed ears are more than just reacting to the arrival of the sushi. His tail flicks around and comes to rest beneath his chair. I relax my tail as well, and am pleased to find that I remember how to use chopsticks.

"Enjoy," he says.

"I will." I look down at the fish. I can tell the tuna by its deep red color, so I pick that first, dip it in the sauce, and delicately lift it to my muzzle as Emmanuel is doing the same with a paler fish.

He watches me start to chew, and I'm sure I look startled and pleased as the fish melts with hardly any pressure from my teeth, the fresh flavor spreading across my tongue with the sharp wasabi and the salt of the soy sauce. "Wow," I say.

"Fresh." He nods at me. "No substitute for it."

"I guess not. That's amazing." Immediately, I want to bring Dev here if we have time. He likes fish—usually cooked, but I bet he'd eat sushi if I told him how good it is.

While we eat our fish, and I try to savor each one, he tells me a little about Yerba and their organization. Good group, he says, smart and open to new ideas. They're probably losing a senior scout at the end of the year. "Won't say where he's going," he tells me with a sly smile and a wink, "but I'll tell you I'm hoping we can hire Morty over here soon after. We'll make a position for him. Senior scouting consultant or something. But we'll move the scouts up the ranks and there'll be room for a young, driven guy to come in. Even if he hasn't played the game. I think that'd be good for our guys."

Am I hired? "It sounds like a great family to be part of," I say.

"We can't do anything official 'til after the championship, of course." He takes a piece of ginger. I can smell it on his breath as he chews. "I'd like you to come up and meet the rest of the guys. Maybe come up during the championship game, if you don't have seats reserved. You could bring Miski with you, though we're not allowed to talk to him about next year or anything."

"You interested in him?" I hold up my paws, realizing my error before his expression goes stony. "Sorry. Forget I asked."

"Forgotten."

"But, so…" I try to figure out how to phrase this. "Me and him…that's okay?"

"It's a weird situation." Emmanuel leans back. "Never had anyone in a front office dating a player, much less on another team. I mean, front offices are mostly male. Far as we know, no other players are gay."

"Chances are someone is," I say.

"I said, as far as we know." He grins at me. "I'm sure some of them are. And a few of them might even be dating football players, maybe on other teams. Everyone moves around so much, Christ, it's hard to stop that from happening. And the sad truth is that if we found out about that, we'd have to fire them. Not because they're gay, but because of the undisclosed relationship."

"I'm familiar with that policy," I say, as dryly as I can.

"Right. But you're out in the open, so we can talk about it. Would you be willing to sign an NDA proscribing you from telling your boyfriend anything about the team operations?"

"Yes," I say, and then, "I'll discuss it with him, too, but I'm a professional. So is he. I never talked to him about the Dragons, and I never talked to the Firebirds about anyone I was scouting."

"Wouldn't have to give him inside info to help against the Dragons, would you?" Emmanuel grins. "Anyway, that's kind of a side benefit, far as I'm concerned."

"Me not telling him anything?"

"Us hiring a gay player's boyfriend. Shows we're open-minded." He sets down his chopsticks and looks around the room. "I don't know how this'll pan out. Might be nothing. But statistically there's gotta be something like, what, five percent of all athletes out there that are gay?"

"Something like that." I nod.

"So if we're the open-minded team…maybe that would give us an advantage in recruiting gay players."

Again, he's very casual, but his eyes are intently focused on me. This idea is obviously pretty important to him. Me, I'm thinking about Vince King again. "I know that would be a major thing for at least a few college athletes. Might save their lives in some cases."

"Right. Now, there'd be negative consequences too. There might be some guys who'd decide not to come here because we're too gay-friendly. But that's okay. Really, I know which way the world is going and I don't think that will hurt us long-term. And most of these guys will just go play anywhere."

"The pull for gay athletes is stronger than the push for most non-gay athletes."

"Exactly." He picks up his chopsticks again and takes another piece of fish, his next-to-last.

I put mine down. Things are going well. I'll take a chance. "So would you be open to…" I take a breath as he watches. "Sponsoring some public service initiatives? Outreach to gay college athletes?"

"Sponsoring? We could talk about it." He keeps his eyes on mine. "You know how busy scouts are, right?"

I nod. Back when I was working for the Dragons, it was film every day, travel on the weekends. I barely had time for a relationship, let alone a second job. "I know. I guess just…just sponsoring." I pick up my last piece of sushi and hold it while I talk.

He grins, showing his canines. "We're gonna work you hard. You thought the Dragons was a tough gig, wait 'til you join a winning team."

"I'll look forward to the championship and meeting the rest of the guys," I say.

His last piece of fish disappears between those gleaming fangs, and he sets his chopsticks down again. "I'm sure they'll like you. You going to want anything else? They do a pretty good mochi ice cream here."

"No, I'm fine." I set the rice and fish on my tongue and chew, and as with all the other pieces, the fish is soft and bursting with flavor. This one has a more fishy taste, with nutty overtones. Still delicious. Definitely going to have to bring Dev here.

Emmanuel pays, and as we get up, he asks about Dev's coming out, whether there was any friction from the team that didn't make it to the media.

"No," I say. "They were mostly supportive. A few weren't, but what are you gonna do?"

"That's great." Emmanuel holds the curtain aside to let me out. "We're waiting to see if anyone else follows his lead. Can't rush it, though, right? Everyone deals with it in their own time."

"Yeah. I'd kind of expected someone else to come out by now. I thought the first one would be tough, the next ones easier." I get to the restaurant door first and hold it for him.

He studies me through eyes narrowed against the sunlight. "You were pretty proud of him."

I feel the echo of the pride again and nod. "It was an amazing thing he did."

"Do you mind if I ask…" We let the door swing shut. I wait, watching him look hesitant for the first time. "Did you push him to come out?"

Memories jostle in my head. I grin. "That's a really long story," I say. "But the short answer is no, it was his decision."

He nods, thumbs hooked into his pockets, tail swishing behind him. "Good decision," he says. "Glad they're doing well." Then his grin comes back, all the way to his cheeks. "Hope losing this weekend won't keep them out of the playoffs."

I'm not sure what my best course of action is here, if I should be chippy and defend my boyfriend's team, or deferential. Deferential is a lot more work for me, so it loses out. "I'd say the same for you guys, except it looks like you're already out of the playoffs."

Emmanuel keeps the grin and sticks out his paw. "Good to meet you, Lee. Take care of that tiger. We'll be in touch."

"Thanks again for making the time," I say, and we walk out into the parking lot in approximately the same direction. I get into the rental and before I start driving, text Dev. *Had meeting with Yerba. Went pretty well.*

He's probably in practice, so he won't respond right away. I look up at the blue sky, clouds scattered across it, and picture living here next year. It'd be tough to move again so soon, to have a new place to get used to, but it'd be a great job. Maybe they'll trade for Dev, and he can come live here too.

I should really just enjoy living with him now, and not worry about the future. I think about tonight and what's on with his teammates. Welcoming atmosphere for gay players, Mister Emmanuel? I think I can manage that.

Chapter 9: Team Outing (Dev)

Thursday is work and work and more work. New plays to learn, drilling the coaches' thoughts into my muscles, translating the marks on paper into players and space and lines on the field. It goes well, but like Lee figures, Gerrard brings me and Carson back Thursday night to go through them again with some of the practice squad. By the time we break at nine-thirty, we're exhausted. Then we stay up another hour studying the Yerba offense.

Friday I want to hear about Ty and Vonni's trip to Korsat Boulevard, but they admit they never actually went. Pike laughs at them. "All right," he says. "Definitely we're gonna go tonight. I'll drag you there if I have to. Dev, come on, you too."

I shake my head. "Thanks, but I'll pass."

Charm, hanging out near my locker, laughs. "C'mon, Gramps. It's not a girlie bar."

"So you come along."

He lifts his massive hands. "I got a date or two, or I totally would."

"Or two?" Even Pike has to look up at Charm.

"I always have a backup. We'll see how many of 'em show up."

"Jeez." Pike grins and turns to Gerrard. "Come on, Coach, let the guy go out just for one night."

Gerrard, who's just pulled his jersey on, eyes the big bear. "He can do whatever he wants."

"Yeah, but he won't go if you say he can't. So tell him it's okay and then he'll come with us."

"Hey, look," I say. "It's got nothing to do with Gerrard. I want to be ready for the game, that's all." When Pike gives me a "yeah, right" look, I add, "And Lee's in town, and I was thinking I could sneak off to a dinner with him Friday night." Of course, he'd said he wanted to go out. I'm just not sure—but it'd be good, right? Him hanging out with me and the guys? Of course...of course, none of them are bringing wives along.

"There we are." Pike pats me on the shoulder. "Listen, that fox of yours might be cool and all, but you gotta get out and enjoy life while you can. It ain't like you're gonna be hookin' up out there...and if you did, so what?"

Gerrard shakes his head and lifts his paws. "There's no extra practice tonight. Dev, you want to go to Korsat, go."

"Yeah! Okay, me and Kodi will head up there with you guys after practice, right? Grab dinner, hit the street. You foxes," Pike turns to point at Ty and Vonni, "you're comin' along too."

They actually look relieved to have someone else taking charge. "Sure," Ty says. "Dev's comin', right?"

I sigh. I'll call Lee. "Yeah, I'll come."

It turns out to be Pike, Kodi, Ty, Vonni, and Jake, a bear from the practice squad who I think just wants to get in good with Pike now that the polar bear's starting. So it's foxes and bears and one tiger. Pike calls a stretch limo to take us up to Korsat and tells it to wait for us. So of course we attract a fair bit of attention as we get out on the corner in front of a big two-story café. The patrons on the patio gawk at us, some of them; others just go on about their conversations. A pair of meerkats on the balcony look down, and one leans over to the other.

I'm distracted from them by a fox in a tan sportcoat over a green t-shirt and jeans, sauntering up to me with his tail swishing back and forth behind him. His blue eyes sparkle with reflections of the café's neon as he walks up to me. "So," Lee says, "going to introduce me around?"

"Hey, Lee," Vonni says, stepping forward with paw outstretched.

I point. "You remember Pike and Kodi. That's Ty, that's Jake. Guys, this is Lee."

Everyone else holds out paws, and there's an amusing few seconds of shaking going on. Then Lee puts his arm around my waist. I tense, but only for a moment.

"It's okay here." Lee gestures at the other couples walking around, but as I look down at him, I see that his comment isn't for my benefit, even though he's looking back at me.

None of the other guys seems particularly disturbed. Ty leans forward, ears perked, and says, "So where we going?"

"Well." Lee gestures down the street. "Depends what you want. The Groom and Groom is supposed to be a good dance club. If you just want drinking, the White Unicorn has some killer cocktails, I'm told."

They all look at each other. "Drinking's good," Vonni says. "To start."

"Aw, come on." Ty nudges him. "Don't you wanna show off them dance moves?"

Vonni shakes his head. "I don't wanna shake my tail and have some guy think it's up for grabs."

Lee grins. "If you get grabbed, just ignore it. That means you're not interested."

"Yeah, but…" Vonni scratches behind his ear. "What if I get grabbed a lot?"

"That means they like you." Pike grins. "C'mon, let's drink."

We grab a big table at the Unicorn and their cocktails do look pretty fabulous, in a couple senses of the word. I get something called a Cinnamon Swish, and Lee orders a Tangerine Sparkle. The other guys order cocktails, except for Kodi, who orders a beer, and then they sit around and watch the rest of the patrons, who are also watching us.

"Six big guys sitting in a gay bar," Lee says. "Of course you attract attention."

But nobody really comes up to us. When our drinks come, served by a slender, attractive cheetah in shorts and an open short-sleeved collared shirt, Ty takes a sip of his and then says, "It looks so normal in here."

"Except that it's all guys," Vonni says.

"Yeah, but they're not doing anything."

Lee licks the rim of his glass. "If you want to see that, there are a couple other places..."

"No, no." Vonni laughs.

"Well, gay guys are just people, you know? We like to drink in a safe place and hang out together. We don't whip out our cocks at the least provocation."

"See, Pike?" Ty elbows him. "You ain't gay."

"Har har." Pike drinks from something cloudy and creamy. "Jury's still out on you, right?"

Ty grins. "I got no worries."

"Hey," Jake says as a new song comes on in the bar, "this is that new Copper Tube song. I love this shit."

"Copper Tube is cool," Vonni says, "but if you like them, you should listen to Trip R.C."

"Trip R.C. is awesome," Lee puts in.

Jake waves a paw. "Ah, you just like him 'cause he's a fox."

"I hired him to play at our wedding."

"No shit!" The bear leans forward, impressed. I gotta admit, I am too, kind of. "Your wife likes him too?"

Vonni grins around, a little smug. "Only thing I got to pick. Daria's mom picked out the place—St. Michael's in Freestone and then the Intercontinental for the reception—and the priest and the flowers and everything but I said, listen, if you want the best music, we are not getting the same band that played your parents' wedding. My agent made a couple calls, and..." He waves a paw. "Done."

"What'd it run ya?"

The fox shrugs. "Fifty K. Not bad."

Probably half what the rest of the wedding cost, I think, and not a bad way to show that he can hold his own with his wife's family. But we move away from the wedding and talk about music for an hour. Lee nudges me a couple times when people walk up near our table: a skunk, once, and then a reddish-brown stallion wearing a sleek blue satin shirt and khaki slacks. But we must give off some kind of vibe, because the skunk just wanders off, and the stallion gets a grin on his face and walks quickly back to his table.

Ty notices the stallion, too, and a few minutes later he nudges Vonni. "Hey, that guy's checking us out," he says.

Vonni looks over, and I can't help glancing that way myself. "Don't stare," he says to Ty, who is doing just that. "Then he'll think you're interested."

"Oh, fuck." Ty drops his eyes to the table and doesn't look up.

"See," Pike says, "Charm shoulda come along. That guy's totally his type."

I hear a very low sound, difficult to catch over the music in the bar, but it's enough to get me to look down at Lee and see that he's struggling not to laugh. He holds it back and then says, "Relax, guys. You're in a gay bar. People are gonna stare. But they'll be polite here. Someone's interested in you, he'll come up and ask if he can buy you a drink or something, and then you just say no."

"Or *yeeeeeeeeeeeeeeeeeeeees*," Vonni elbows Ty.

"Fuck you," the younger fox replies, and that does get him to look up from the table finally.

Lee laughs too, and he feels very natural sitting next to me. His eyes glint and he's chatting with the other guys, and I don't think about us being gay; it's more that we're just among friends. Once in a while, I admit, I look around the bar at some of the guys. The stallion's okay, but there's a leopard who's really pretty hot. *He would totally let me fuck him*, I think, sort of detachedly, and then I feel ashamed of it, and then feel guilty for being ashamed. I mean, here of all places, that's the kind of thing people are thinking.

It's not that I want to fuck the leopard. I mean, Lee's the only guy I've been with, and the only guy I want to be with. But I slept with probably a dozen girls before I met him, and so part of me kinda wonders what another guy would be like.

Lee isn't looking around the bar too much. He looks at me, but doesn't catch me looking around, which is good because I can only imagine what he'd say. His tail brushes mine and lingers there, which makes me flinch at first until I have to remind myself that we're in a gay bar. Or café, anyway.

I don't notice Kodi leaving, but his seat is empty when, a little later, the stallion comes over again. "Um, hi," he says.

Our conversation dies down. He looks around the table, and so do I. I see Ty looking apprehensive, Vonni grinning. Pike and Jake are just curious, and Lee's got a foxy grin on his muzzle, too. He's the one who talks. "Hey there," he says.

"Sorry to interrupt." The stallion fidgets and brushes a lock of his mane out of his eyes. "You guys are football players, right? I sorta recognize...you're Devlin Miski? And Ty Nakamura, and..." His gaze wavers over the bears.

"That's right," I say. "That's Pat Karritson."

"Pike." The polar bear raises a paw.

"And Jake Marrit."

The black bear raises his paw.

"I was wondering..." The stallion shifts from one foot to the other, and then produces a bar napkin. "Could I get your autographs?"

We all look at each other and then Ty breaks out in a big grin. "Shit, man," he says, "Sure." He holds out his paw.

The cocktail napkin makes the round of the table, while the stallion looks at Lee. "You're..." he taps his nose. "Hey, are you his, uh...his 'friend'?"

Lee grins back. "It's okay," he says. "These guys read the papers too."

"Oh, uh. Sorry, I didn't mean..." The stallion looks around the table.

Jake lifts his broad paw and passes the napkin to Pike. "Yeah, man. Graduated college and everything. I can read purty good."

Now the stallion cringes, looking desperately at the napkin like it's the starting flag at a race. I get it from Pike and take my time writing "Devlin Miski #57" so I can talk a bit more. "Hey, it's okay. We're football players, we're used to people thinking all we do is hit each other. We're just messing with you."

That relaxes him a little but not too much. He still grabs the napkin when I'm done, mumbles, "Thanks, guys," and skitters back toward his table. He drops the napkin there and holds his head in his broad hands while his friends look at the signatures.

"Football fans," Vonni says. "Cool."

"Gay guys like football too," Lee says. "It's not all sex and dancing and fashionable clothes."

"I was gonna say, I feel like I'm in either a clothes catalog or a tractor catalog here." Ty looks around at the stallion's table, then at another nearby table dressed all in checked flannel. "You coulda told us there was a dress code."

Lee grins back at the other fox. "If you want me to take you shopping, I will, but that's a whole other trip. Anyway, we can do that in Chevali."

"Yeah, maybe." Ty finishes his cocktail.

"Girls like a guy who looks sharp, too," Lee says.

Ty shrugs. "Girls like football players."

"You won't be playing football forever."

"S'okay. I'll be married before then. Soon's I get my first free agent contract."

Vonni and the bears look around the bar, but idly, not really at anything. "Where'd Kodi go?" I say to Pike.

"Ah, just said there wasn't much going on and he wanted to get some sleep. He got a cab back."

"We're not staying out that late."

"Yeah, I think he was just bored."

I grin. It hasn't exactly been an exciting night. "Are you bored?"

"I guess." He grins. "I go to bars to pick up girls. The drinks here are good, but there's no girls."

Lee flicks his ears that way. "So. You wanna go dancing?"

"Are there girls there?" Ty says.

"I'll tell you a secret." Lee leans across the table. "The gay dance clubs are pretty awesome, so a lot of single girls go there because they know they won't get hit on all the time."

Ty's ears perk up and his eyes widen. "No shit."

"Well, what are we hanging around here for?" Vonni scoots his chair back. "Hey, Dev, you got this? Toss around some of that Ultimate Fit money, huh?"

It bugs me a little—Vonni's salary is about three times mine. But it's only a hundred bucks, so it's not that big a deal. I toss the cash down onto the table and we walk out.

"Shouldn't you call your *wife?*" Ty says to Vonni on the way out, not because he wants him to call his wife, but because Vonni's tail is wagging as we head to the dance club.

"I can still look," Vonni says. "Don't get much of a chance to see all the single ladies."

Ty chimes in with, "All the single ladies," and they sing, off-key, a couple verses before breaking down laughing.

I grab Lee and pull him back, behind the others as they walk. None of them notice, and we keep walking behind them. "What the hell are you doing?"

He turns big blue eyes on me. "Trying to show your friends a good time."

"Taking them to a gay dance club? To get hit on?"

He scowls. "You've got the same prejudices they do."

"Hey," I say. "That's not fair."

He pokes me with a finger. "You think all gay guys want to do is fuck anything that moves."

"I do not," I hiss, because he said that kinda loud and Vonni's ears flicked back. "I just don't want…"

"What? To cause a scene? To have fun?"

"We have a curfew."

He rolls his eyes. "So go home before curfew. Nobody's going to grab your cock and hold you in the club." His eyes narrow and his smile widens. "'Less you want me to."

The guys are getting farther ahead of us, and Vonni turns to check on the two of us. "I know you, doc," I say. "There's something else going on."

His ears flatten. "It wouldn't be so bad for people to see that gay clubs aren't threatening. That straight guys can go in and have fun. Right?"

"Straight guys like football players."

"Uh-huh. Well." He trails a finger down my chest. "Mostly."

Ty's staring at us now, too. "That's all? You don't have…" I wave my paws forward, in the direction I imagine the club is.

"What?" He grins. "An army of fags waiting to jump your teammates' bones? No, stud. I haven't been to this club, but I promise, just straight girls." He glances ahead at Ty and lowers his voice. "Ty sounds like he could use some bone-jumping, though."

I sigh and hurry to catch up with the others, Lee padding quickly behind.

•

The air's chilly and the street is considerably more crowded than when we came in. People, mostly guys, jostle and laugh all around us. I see a couple holding paws, then another, and for a moment my paw itches to take Lee's. It'd be okay here; nobody would look twice at us. But then I pull it back to my side. We're still out in public, in front of the guys, and after all, they don't even hold their wives' paws when they're together. Well, Gerrard does, but the guys know what he gets up to on the road, so they don't hassle him about being whipped.

When Lee and I catch up to the others at a corner, Lee speaks up. "The club's in the next block. Might be crowded on a Friday night, but I think if you guys play your athlete card, you can get in ahead of the line. You okay with that?"

"Ty probably is." I glance up at the foxes, looking around at the neon and the crowds, and the shops. We cross the street and walk on, past a closed erotic bakery, and Vonni elbows Ty, pointing. The two of them snicker. I gotta admit, I don't know who'd want an enormous dong-shaped cake, but I guess there are some people. Not sure which species, judging by the shape of the cake, but it's not fox or tiger, at least. Vonni makes some remark about the cake to Ty and Ty says, "Shut up!" Lee looks in at the window, then up at me, and doesn't say anything. I can hear his thoughts loud and clear, though: he's thinking it's tacky, so I say as much in a low voice, and he chuckles, giving his tail a swing so it hits my legs.

The club is marked by a cluster of people on the sidewalk, the scents thick in the air. I can only barely make out the line to get in past the bouncer, a tall polar bear with a black leather vest and a clipboard edged with what look like blinking Christmas lights. Inside the open doors just beyond him, lights flash in all colors of the rainbow and a throbbing beat drives out. I'm not much for dancing, but it does get my feet tapping.

A few of the guys in line, then more than a few, turn and look at us. We're taller than most of the crowd, but not that much taller. One or two of us would probably not get a second glance, but all five of us together stand out. We're used to it, though, and the stallion asking for our autograph makes me feel like people are just staring the way they always do.

Lee brings us near the entrance, at the head of the line, and holds up a paw. "Wait here," he says, and slinks over to the bouncer. I step forward enough to hear what he says over the music.

"Hey," he says to the bear, and anticipates the guy's dismissal with a sharp finger pointing back at us. "You got a bunch of pro football players wondering if they can make it in."

"Huh." The bear stares at us.

"The tiger, that's Devlin Miski," Lee says. "First publicly out pro football player."

Now the bear's eyes widen. I feel a flush in my ears, but I stand straight. The guys at the front of the line heard it too. A couple of them say my name and reach out. "For real?" The bear looks beyond me. "Those other guys coming out too?"

"Nah." Lee laughs. "I told them we queers know how to put on a party."

We queers. I glance at the other guys, my tail curling, but none of them seems to have noticed. They're all full of themselves, expecting to get into the club past the line, preening at the attention from the crowd.

The bouncer nods. "Lemme get the manager." He talks quickly into a walkie-talkie at his shoulder and then looks back down at Lee. "He'll be here in a minute."

"Thanks."

"I don't need his permission to let people in." As if to demonstrate, he lets the next three guys in: a white-tailed deer and two pronghorns. One of them hangs back, looking at me, until his friends drag him in. "He just likes to know when celebrities show up."

Lee flashes me a bright smile and his tail wags. "Cool."

It really is only a minute or so later that a weasel comes up to the bouncer, just about his height, wearing a sharp white shirt and pretty tight jeans with a big brass belt buckle. "Hey," he says to Lee. "Educated guess— you Wiley Farrel?"

Lee gives him the same bright smile. "You read the papers."

"Yup. Jay Vista. I'm the manager." He gestures back to the polar bear, the open door, the lights and music and the crowd of people who are now all openly staring at us. "You boys want to come in for a dance?"

"Listen," Ty says, "Dev's, you know, but the rest of us, we're just curious…"

"Not that kind of curious," Jake butts in. "Just like 'look around' curious."

Jay grins wide. "It's cool, boys. You want to get your dicks sucked on the dance floor, you're about four blocks too far north and two hours too early."

Lee murmurs something to him that I don't catch, and he laughs, but doesn't answer it. "Nah, this is a safe club. You might get hit on—hell, you're gonna get hit on if you stand out here another five minutes. Just don't let it bother you. We're all friendly. Anyway, between you and me, you fellas won't be the only straight guys in there. So come on in."

Jay pauses by the bouncer and puts a paw up on the guy's massive arm as we file past. "Stevie, you go ahead and mention to anyone you want that we got some pro football players checking out the club tonight. Don't say who or what team."

"Got it, boss."

"Football players," Lee says to the people waiting in line, jerking his thumb at us, and goes in ahead of me.

"No shit," the guys grumble, watching me and Jake trail the others in.

Pike grabs us all once we get in. "Limo's leaving at eleven-thirty," he yells over the thudding music. "We gotta be back and checked in at midnight. Meet back there?"

We give him thumbs-ups. He and Jake go off to where there's a little crowd of bears, while Ty and Vonni stick with me and Lee. Lee takes my paw and drags me out, and the other foxes follow us, I guess still wanting a guide in the club. Lee's eyes occasionally go their way, and then he grins back at me, but mostly he just seems to be having a good time, swinging his tail around and doing some fancy dance steps. I just kinda sway back and forth, making sure to move my feet because someone told me once that that was the key to dancing.

Vonni isn't much more graceful than I am. But Ty, after the first fifteen minutes, really lets go and shows off some moves. Lee expresses his admiration with hand gestures and I try to convey back that I had no idea Ty could dance like that. Vonni looks impressed too, and when Ty sees us staring, he smirks and shows off even more.

I'm almost disappointed that we're not being hit on more. One ringtail does come up to me and Lee, but when Lee signals that we're together, he takes off again. Ty and Vonni just keep dancing, and I have no idea what's been going on with them until we all take a break by the bar.

"That wolf was totally checking you out," Vonni says to Ty.

"He was into you," Ty says back. "He just danced next to me for a while so he could stare at you."

"Like hell. He was sniffin' your shirt, dude, that ain't right."

"Oh, you guys got hit on too?"

They both turn to me. "Bunch of times," Vonni says. "Guys kept comin' up."

"We just ignored 'em." Ty grins. "Couple of 'em can dance, though."

"What did that one whisper to you?" Vonni asks.

"He said he didn't care if we were together, he'd blow me anyway." Ty looks out at the dance floor as if looking for the guy again. "I said, if you're a girl, let's go. Hey, what are we drinking?"

We order a round of rum and cokes, which Lee declines as he runs off to use the bathroom. It strikes me how weird this is, that they're talking very casually about being hit on, and it doesn't seem to bother them. But it bothers me, a little; they just seem very amused at the spectacle of all these weird people. Only I'm one of the weird people, too.

I'm not, though. I mean, yeah, I'm with Lee, and he is a guy with a cock and everything. And theoretically I'd be open to trying out any of these guys in the club, but they're not attractive to me. Well, one or two are, I guess. But it's not like when I was in college, going to bars and looking for the prettiest gal to take home. I'm just in love, and the person I love happens to be a guy. So I'm gay, at least on the outside. But I'm not gay like most of these guys are, where I want to strut around and show how awesome it is that I like cock. And yet, there's no middle ground. I see how it looks weird to people brought up the way I was; I see why they want to show people that it's not weird, or maybe it is but it's okay. I just want to be allowed to live my life, preferably with my fox.

I can't quite untangle that mess in my head, so I stay quiet until Lee comes back and drags me back to the dance floor.

Dancing is less complicated than thinking, and I shove all that mess aside while I try not to embarrass myself. Lee (of course) notices something and manages to ask me what's wrong, over the music. Ty and Vonni are still close, but not right next to us; still, I just shake my head. "Not sure. Feels weird," I say.

He saw me glance at them. "Worried about what they think?"

I shake my head again. "This is like going to the theater for them," I say.

At first, I don't think he's heard me properly, because he kind of laughs. Then he dances up close to me and slides an arm around my waist and says, "Don't you worry, hon. I took care of it."

I glare down at him. "You better not mean what I think you mean."

His arm tightens a little, and his tail swishes back and forth. "Oh, I probably don't. But don't worry about it. It's gonna be fine."

"Doc," I say, "don't fuck up our number three wideout."

He looks over at the foxes. "Which one is that, again?"

"Vonni's a corner—" He knows that. "Don't fuck up either of them. Whatever you did—"

"Relax," he says, but his ears go back and his eyes narrow, that stubborn expression I know from fights in the past. Then he looks past me, and tugs me away from Ty and Vonni. "It's probably not what you think, and he's been asking for it all night. It was just a spur of the moment thing anyway."

"Oh God." I twist while dancing and try to see what he was looking at, but I can't see anything but a bobbing mass of heads and shapes. "Did you—what did you—"

"I'm sure he'll tell you about it tomorrow," Lee says. "I promise you, I know what I'm doing."

"God dammit." I turn around, intending to drag Ty out of the club, but he's already watching as Vonni talks to an attractive young leopard in a slinky, shimmering silver dress. She—she?—is visibly excited, making "ohmyGAWD" gestures, wide-eyed, leaning right into the fox's personal space. He doesn't seem to mind at all. Maybe that's because her breasts are trembling like they're about to pop out of the low-cut top.

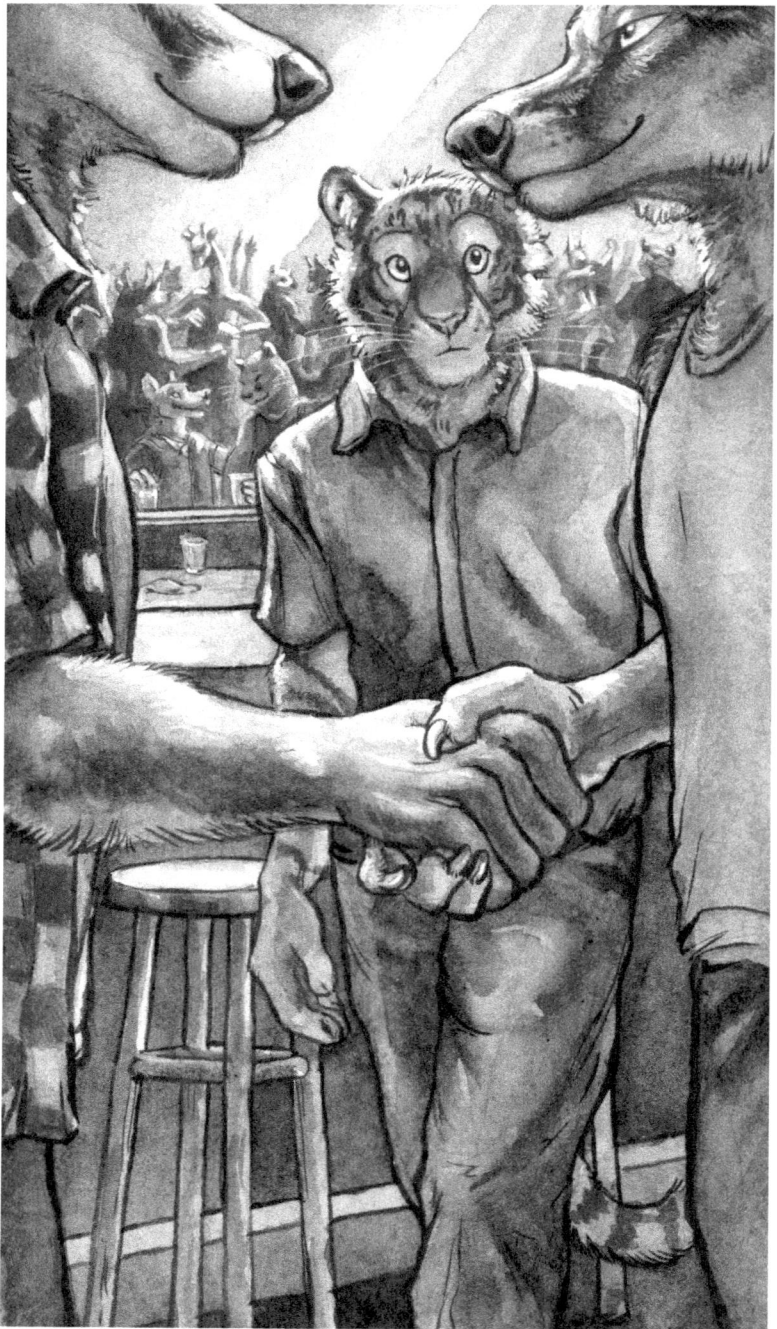

"You got her to hit on Vonni? Lion Christ, Lee, he's married!"

Lee's ears flatten. "I just said 'the fox who can dance.'" We watch Vonni put his arm around the leopard as Ty spins away from them. "Um. He's not acting married."

I turn away, not wanting to see where this ends up. "Is she really a—a she?" I say.

"Oh, stud," Lee says. "Would I do that to one of your teammates?" He gives me big blue innocent eyes. "Sides, those breasts looked pretty real, right?"

"Fuck," I say, and turn around, pulling away from him. I search the dance floor, but both foxes are gone from where they were. I see Ty farther along the bar and make my way down to him.

He's talking to a big wolf, almost as tall as he is, and they shake paws. As I come up, the wolf goes away and Ty sticks his paw in his pocket. "What's goin' on?"

"Where's Vonni?"

His grin is wide and a little bit knowing. "Oh, he went off with that leopard femme. Hey, White Siberian, please," he calls to the bartender.

"Was she, uh…? I mean really?"

Ty shrugs as though he's already thought about that. "Who cares? We gotta be at the limo in twenty minutes anyway. Not like they're gonna have time to go anywhere and do anything. Maybe they make out for a bit or she jacks him off or something."

"What if he finds out it's a guy and freaks out?"

Ty laughs and picks up his drink when the bartender puts it down. "Dude, if Vonni was gonna freak out he wouldn't have gone off with her. Anyway, he's married. He'll probably just feel her up and that's that." He spreads an arm, gesturing at the club and almost hitting Lee, who's come up to stand near us. "Must make him feel alive again, after bein' married."

"Who was that wolf?" I don't want to be the one who brought Vonni to a club where he cheated on his new wife.

"Ah." Ty sips his drink. "Just a fan. I signed a napkin for him."

I didn't see the napkin, but I could've missed it. "Glad you're having fun."

"Yeah," he says. "This ain't like I imagined it. It's fun. The guys here are pretty cool. I got my tail grabbed once."

"Really?"

He takes another drink. "No biggie. I shook my head and the guy took off."

"You're pretty okay with this," Lee says.

Ty grins. "I always stood up for Dev. Wideouts talked a bit when he first came out, and I said, hey, this guy's a standup guy, leave him alone."

I'm a little surprised, because he never told me that. Then again, he is a little drunk and in showoff mode for Lee, leaning back against the bar with his chest out and his muzzle up even though he has to look down it to talk to my fox. "Thanks," I say.

He waves a black paw. "If you weren't a good guy, I wouldn'ta done it." He finishes his drink and checks his watch. "I'm gonna dance for another fifteen, then we gotta go. You guys coming?"

I start to demur, but Lee drags me out behind Ty and we dance close. I keep looking around for Vonni, but I don't spot him. The funny thing that happens, which Lee has to point out a few minutes later, is a fox and coyote dancing near us, not slow dancing, just matching each other's moves, both grinning. That's a big fox, I think and it takes me a minute to realize that it's Ty.

At twenty after eleven, Lee says, "We gotta get you back," and I nod. Vonni's still nowhere to be seen. I make my way to Ty, who's still dancing with the coyote, and tap him on the shoulder. He nods, slaps paws with the coyote, and they lean in to say something, then he follows me and Lee out the front door, messing with his phone.

Pike and Jake are outside chatting with the bouncer, while a small crowd of guys watches and whispers among themselves. They shake paws when they see us come out and wave to the big leather-vested polar bear.

"Nice guy," Pike says. "Got family up north too, but I don't think I know any of 'em. Where's Vonni?"

"No idea," I say.

"He hooked up," Ty says.

The bears both grin. "What, with a guy?" Pike asks.

"Nah. Well, maybe. Leopard in a dress. Sure's hell didn't look like a guy."

"Text him, tell him to get his tail out here."

"Did already." Ty holds up his phone. "No answer."

"Maybe one of us should go back and look for him," I say.

Pike waves a paw. "He's a grownup. Hey, Steve!" he calls to the bouncer.

The other white bear looks up from his clipboard. "Yeah?"

"If our friend the fox comes out, put him in a cab, would ya?"

The bouncer shoots us a thumbs up. "There," Pike says, and starts on down the street. "Problem solved."

"Let's wait another five minutes," I say, but then Ty's phone beeps and he holds it up, reading a text message.

"He says to head on back, he'll grab a cab in half an hour."

"He'll miss check-in," I say.

We all look at each other. "He won't tell us where he is, that's his lookout," Pike says. When I hesitate, he says, "Look, Dev, what are you gonna do, search every room in that club? He told us to go back, we should go back."

I don't like it, but when Lee puts a paw on my arm and says, "He'll be fine. Trust me," I let it go and follow Pike back to the limo.

We make it back to the hotel at twenty to midnight, plenty of time for bed check. I let the other guys go in so I can say good-bye to Lee out front. The revolving door's barely slid to a halt before Lee says, "Really, don't worry about Vonni."

I grip both his shoulders. "How can you be so sure he's fine? You know that leopard personally?"

"Nah," he says, stepping forward so I have to loosen my grip, "but she was a tourist, all starstruck. Did you see the dress?"

"Yes. You're sure she was a girl?"

"Well, she was coming out of the ladies' room."

I shake my head. "Didn't you use the ladies' room when you cross-dressed?"

He lifts his muzzle. "I did it for authenticity. I don't think she was that devoted to her performance."

"Did you pay her to hook up with Vonni?"

"First of all, I wanted her to hook up with Ty. And second, pay her? With whose money?" He laughs. "I just happened to mention a little too loudly on my cell phone that my friend the pro football player was getting bored with the gay club but I didn't know any good straight places to take him. And she stopped and said, 'Pro football player?'"

I shake my head. "Christ, Lee."

"Hey, it worked."

I study his eyes, which seem wide and guileless. Seem. "So what's the angle?"

He shrugs. "Maybe Vonni doesn't know if he hooked up with a guy or a girl. Maybe he thinks about it some."

I know he meant well. I know he just got a buddy of mine laid, or blown, or something, even if that buddy is married. That's not Lee's fault. But still. "Look, if you're going to do your activism stuff again, fine, go join Brian's Equality Now, whatever, just don't use my teammates as your personal playpen."

He gets a stubborn set to his jaw, and now he steps back. "They asked to come out to Korsat Boulevard," he says, "and I didn't do anything to the other guys, though if you ask me, Ty wanted it more than Vonni. Ty was the one who kept talking about hooking up, and wanting to be scoped out, and come on, he's more than a little bi-curious. You don't see it?"

When I came out, Ty came up to me, and all he wanted to know was whether I was the one on top. I can picture him being with a guy as long as he was the top, I guess. "You still shouldn't…"

"Shouldn't what?" He folds his arms. "If Vonni were really freaked out, he would've come out to the limo. He wouldn't have texted that he was going to be late."

"There!" I point at him. "You're going to make him late. He'll get in trouble."

Lee grins. "Then he had a really good time." He reaches out and puts one paw on my stomach. "You want to get in trouble, too?"

I shake my head, not to say no, but to clear it. "Not tonight. But that's not the point."

"We're okay for Sunday?" He's still smiling, and I feel like I'm not getting through to him.

"Yeah, but—"

"Good. Let me know how it goes with Ty."

"You mean Vonni."

He leans up and kisses my nose. "Him too. I'll see you Sunday."

He waits. If I don't kiss him back, there'll be an argument. All the stuff he said makes sense, so I'm not sure why I'm still upset. So I kiss him back and say, "See you then."

"Snag a pick for me," he says, and walks on down the street, tail swishing behind him. I stand there and watch him go. I want to follow him, to stay out late and get in trouble, but he'll be at dinner Sunday night and he'll be at home Monday night when I get there, and Tuesday night and all the nights after that for a little while. So I wait until he rounds the corner, and then I head back into the hotel. Vonni still isn't back. I check in and then hang around until about five minutes before midnight, but the only other person to come through the lobby in that time is coming down from the rooms, a slender female coyote probably not more than nineteen.

She stops near me, arranging her fur and bringing out a little spray canister. She needs it, too—sex hangs around her in a cloud. I lean back, but just before I do, I catch another familiar scent. I mean, shit, the only guy whose musk I really know just took off down the street, but when you've worked out next to a guy and smelled his body odor and fur for weeks, the musky smell isn't that dissimilar. And of all the guys I've been working with, the one whose scent I know best apart from my roommate's is my leader on the defensive line. Gerrard.

The girl coyote gives me a little saucy wink and a flirty bounce to her hips and then puts her spray away, now smelling of rose petal. Lee might be able to catch the smell of sex below that, but I sure can't.

Shit. If Gerrard is cheating on his wife with another coyote, that's a big deal. It means maybe cubs, maybe disease. But, I remind myself, it's not my big deal. I don't have any responsibilities to his wife, nice as she might be. I'm mostly responsible for Vonni tonight, and it looks like he's not going to make curfew.

Both of them, though, married and cheating on the road. Of course I know that shit goes on, but now I'm feeling guilty in a different way about the guy I was scoping out at the café. Thank God I was too distracted to do that at the club. That big wolf Ty was talking to…interesting in a "I wonder what it'd be like" kind of way, but not even tempting me to cheat on Lee. What must it feel like, to need sex so badly that you'd get it from anyone? Or is it that Vonni and Gerrard, both stars ever since college, are just used to getting whatever they want?

Not my problem to solve. I wait one last second for Vonni, and then head upstairs.

Charm's snoring away when I open our door. I strip and sink into my own bed. Damn, it's a good thing we've only got one more night out here. I try not to think about Gerrard. I hope Vonni's okay.

And I think about the first time I went home with a guy dressed as a lady, and what it led to, and I call myself a big hypocrite. What if someone had stopped me from taking Lee home that night?

Well, I wouldn't be losing sleep in a hotel room in Yerba, that's for damn sure.

CHAPTER 10: RUMORS (LEE)

I have a whole Saturday to spend in Yerba by myself, so I check out some museums, do some shopping—they have fabulous stores here—and wait in vain for Vonni to give me a thank-you call for the hookup last night. That leopard jumped on my line about the football player like it was a half-off sale at McCauley and Fern. I'm sure she jumped on his cock with the same energy. And if he was married, well, he's no different than lots of other players. At least she wasn't a fox.

I do check the news to see if the football players at a gay club made any headlines, but even on the sports sites, there's not even a mention. I guess I could call Hal, but there's no real story there, more just a gossip piece. It'd be perfect for Brian's blog, but that would require me talking to him. I want to put that off as long as possible, though I can see it approaching as I get more determined to work with Equality Now in the month and a half I have left until I will (hopefully) take the Yerba job.

What is all over the 'net is that the Firebirds are looking to trade Mitchell to the Devils for star disgruntled wideout Lightning Strike (he changed his name to that, legally—not the "star disgruntled wideout" part, although he might as well have), with a few bench players and cash considerations thrown in. The cheetah, of course, has words to say about it in the media.

"I would love to join the Firebirds," he says, "or any other team that takes winning seriously. Of course, if nothing can be worked out before Monday," which is the trading deadline, "I will continue to give my all to the Port City Devils and hope that we can at least finish the season respectably."

The thing about Strike is, he's a loudmouth, but he's not always wrong. He's being shopped around because basically he called out the offensive line for not giving his quarterback time to throw to him on the deep routes, he called out the quarterback for underthrowing him, he called out the coaches for not calling his number more often. He's a me-first wideout, the kind the Firebirds currently don't have.

He's also a spectacular talent, the kind the Firebirds currently don't have.

And he talks about Dev, too. "I'd be happy for the chance to play with a gay teammate," he's quoted as saying. It's unclear whether anyone asked. "I've played with gay athletes in the past, but none that were open about who they were. I admire and respect Miski, and with cats like us on both sides of the ball, the Firebirds would be a force to be reckoned with."

Bets are on as to what color he'd dye his fur for his first game in a Chevali uniform, if the trade happens. Traditionally he goes with the team colors, so maybe he'd be gold with red spots. But that might be too close to his natural colors, so maybe he'd be red with gold spots. Or he might dye an actual Firebirds logo into his arm. He did that with the Pilots three years ago when he went over there in a mega-deal.

He hasn't won a title, and in Chevali, I'm sure he sees a team with a rising defense that needs a wideout to contend for a championship. I'm sure John Corcoran, the Firebirds' owner, sees that too, and is opening up his purse to get there. But I wonder, now, about the bond the team has forged in putting together a winning season, and whether this addition would screw that up. Teams have fallen apart from adding the wrong guy.

Teams have also won championships by adding the right guy.

You could make a case that Dev was the right guy for their defense. Not as much raw talent as Mitchell has, but a lot more willing to mesh with the unit. His coming out helped bring the team together, and even though that's faded now, it's still an experience they all went through. A strong linebacking team can give the front line confidence, and Gerrard is doing a great job being the key on that defense.

But adding Strike…I dunno. Personally, I'd replace that boar they have on the left side, the one who keeps letting defenders in to chase Aston around the backfield. But I'm no longer employed by a UFL team, so what do I know?

I call my father in the early afternoon, and he hasn't heard about the trade yet. We discuss it briefly; he's more optimistic than I am about the possibility it'll work out, and points out that, more importantly, it keeps Strike from going back to the division rival Pilots or another one of the Firebirds' potential playoff opponents.

"How's Yerba?" he asks when we've finished talking football.

"Good. Warm, for winter."

"We've been below thirty for a week."

I close my eyes to bask in the sun. "Awesome. I can't wait to come back home." Only after I say that do I remember that "home" isn't Hilltown any more. I don't correct myself out loud. "How are you doing?"

"Getting by. Got the new apartment mostly set up." He's quiet a moment. I imagine him sitting by a window looking out at the cold city, only because I don't know what his apartment looks like, I picture him at my window, his paw resting against the glass, spectacles halfway down the bridge of his muzzle. "I'm thinking about getting a fish."

"Whoa," I say. "Sure you're ready to jump into that kind of commitment already?"

"This place doesn't allow birds," he says. "So."

"Remember the lizard I had when I was eight?"

"Which one? There were three."

"There were?" I think back. "The one that died when his heater malfunctioned in the winter."

"It didn't malfunction," Father says. "It worked perfectly once I reminded you to turn it on."

"The point is, it wouldn't have died here. Or in Chevali for that matter."

"Are you thinking of getting a lizard, Wiley?"

I laugh. "I just got a live-in boyfriend. I think that's enough responsibility for one year."

"Don't forget to turn his heater on."

My mind makes that dirty, and then I squelch the rejoinder because I'm talking to my father. "Helped with that last night." I tell him briefly about our night out, leaving out the part where I set a girl on a married fox.

"Not worried about bad publicity?"

"Nobody's said anything about it. Pity. Wish people would notice that football players can go to gay clubs and it's not the end of the fucking world." I say that intentionally loudly, but the people out here in tech-heavy Yerba are all cocooned in their own little worlds with their phones and conversations. One small black bird, hopping around pecking for crumbs, tilts its head and looks at me. I wonder if it has a blog.

"Remember last time you tried to get something in the paper? You ended up in jail."

"Yeah, but it worked."

He sighs. "Whose parent are you trying to teach a lesson to now?"

I close my eyes and turn toward the sun to feel its warmth on my fur. "Mine."

His pause is longer than mine. "Your mother doesn't read sports sites. And if it's me, you can just tell me."

"That group of hers, Families United." I hate even saying the name. "They helped kill a college kid." I tell him briefly about Vince King.

He's silent for a good several seconds. "Well?" I say. "Horrible, right?"

"If that's what happened."

It's my turn to be quiet. "It seems pretty clear. I mean, circumstantially."

"Wiley, don't get mixed up in that. Activism is one thing, but going around accusing people of what is essentially murder, that's hard. And if you go too far, they could sue you, don't forget that."

"Now why would you ever think I would go too far?" Before he can answer, I say, "You can't bring up jail twice in one conversation."

"Oh, let me see. The time you tried to memorize the encyclopedia for Academic Challenge, the time you wore your pride jacket to church on Christmas Eve, the time you sprang your boyfriend on us at dinner…"

"That was him, not me."

"I'm just saying there is precedent."

My past paints a picture of me that I don't know I want to acknowledge right now, so I go back to my main point. "If they were involved—"

"*If.*"

"—then they should pay the price for it. People should know."

"You really think that'll change the minds of anyone supporting them?"

I look around the small square where I'm sitting. In the café to my left, a pair of wolves sit shoulder to shoulder. Both female, I think. Nobody around seems to care. Then again, this is Yerba, so it's probably not the best place to judge. There's also an otter rollerblading by who is wearing nothing but a thong bikini bottom. Might be female too; his/her chest is fluffy enough that I can't tell from here. The majority of people look like me: t-shirt, polo shirt (I'm wearing the over-large Firebirds polo I got from the owner's plane on our way to the Hellentown game), jeans, slacks, light jackets. And while a few people look twice at the otter, nobody looks outraged. It makes me feel like I could kiss Dev right here in the square without anyone batting an eye.

"Not all of them," I say. "Not even most of them. But maybe it'll get people motivated to shut them down."

"What was that story from two years ago with them? The guys who beat up that one gay fox in Kerina were members?"

I exhale. "Their wives were members, and they had pamphlets on them when they were arrested. But the national group disowned them. So there wasn't much blowback."

"And you think this'll be different."

A breeze ruffles the fur between my ears. I stretch my legs out, extend my tail, and enjoy it. "It'll all add up. Enough of these things brought to the media form an impression in people's minds."

"War of attrition."

"Exactly. And there are a lot of people like me trying to do this."

"I find it hard to believe there are that many ex-pro-football scouts engaged in gay rights."

I'm glad to hear his sense of humor again. "It's an exclusive club. I got the key to the washroom just last week."

"Speaking of…did you already have your interview?"

"Oh, yeah." I tell him about Emmanuel and the job. "Sounds like I'm in as long as I don't do anything stupid to piss off the other scouts."

"Like start a gay rights campaign movement in the UFL?"

"I think as long as I don't post some naked pics of me and Dev, I'm okay." There was an actor, a black panther, who came out a couple years ago by posting naked pictures of him with his paw on his white-coated ermine boyfriend's sheath.

We chat a little more. Father's now living near my old neighborhood around Forester, so I know all the places to eat. I tell him to try Ketteridge's and Goose's, and for God's sake not to go back to P.J. McGovern's.

"We like P.J.'s," he says. "I like P.J.'s."

"Everything there is coated in butter or cheese or both. Seriously."

"And your diner is much better, I expect."

I grin. "They're honest about it."

"Do me a favor. Find a good place in Yerba. When you get the job there, I'll fly out and you can take me to dinner."

"Deal. I have a place in mind. Supposedly the chef is this amazing coyote who went and trained in Lutèce and he's won all sorts of awards here."

"Can you afford that?"

"Dev can. It's our Sunday night plan. Tonight I'm eating something from a street vendor's cart." I pause. "I can afford *that*. As long as he doesn't catch me."

Father laughs, shortly. "Are you doing okay? I can send money…"

"It was a joke. I'm fine. Dev's taking care of me. He's got plenty of money and he's not spending it on crazy things like some of his friends."

There's another short pause. "You know, if he wants someone to invest his money for him…that is my job."

It's my turn to be quiet. "You never offered before."

"Well, I didn't…know him very well, before."

And Mother would have to have known about it. "I appreciate it. I'll mention it and see what he says."

We're winding down the conversation when he says, "I'm still working out dates to move my things out of the house. Wiley, if you want to reconsider about coming home…"

"I don't."

"I mean. Please think about it. If you really want to, if it's important to you, then come on home. If you're just trying to stir up trouble, then maybe it would be best if you just let me clear out the house. We can have dinner and talk about it afterwards."

I reach up and rub the ear the phone is clipped to. "I'm pretty sure I want to do it. It's important to me."

"I just don't want you to start anything with this whole college student committing suicide thing."

"I won't if she doesn't."

He sighs. "Wiley."

"If she's starting to believe in these people who think nothing of making a kid feel so isolated and worthless that he believes his best option is suicide, then I think she should know about that, don't you? And if she already knows, she should know that I know."

"Don't go there intending to start a fight."

A coyote one table over has her ears perked in my direction. I lower my voice. "I'm not. But I won't back down if she starts something."

"No," he says. "I guess you won't."

After the phone call, I feel restless, so I walk around the city some more. I go into a sports bar to watch some of the final college games of the season. The TV is better than nothing, though I keep itching to switch to a different view. Whenever I try to focus on one player in particular, I get to see about half of one play before the camera goes somewhere else.

The bar is festooned with Whalers gear, maroon and gold pennants, the iconic otter with eyepatch and harpoon all over. On the side is a board showing the Whalers' schedule to date. They're 6-6, with wins over Millenport, Gateway, Aventira, New Kestle, Boliat—impressive, that one— and Kerina. All except the Boliat game are games they should have won. On the flip side of the schedule, you can see where Yerba started off with a playoff hangover, losing their first three. Granted, it was a brutal start: on the road at Hellentown and Highbourne, then home against division-leading Crystal City, but they should have pulled at least one win out of that. That they've clawed their way back to .500 is pretty impressive. Even though Chevali is 9-3, this won't be an easy game.

Sitting in the bar reminds me of watching games with Brian in the bars near Forester U., and that makes me think again of joining up with Equality Now in Chevali. My college protests were a long time ago and small-time compared to the national campaigns they're doing, and having experience with this size organization would definitely serve me better with Emmanuel and Yerba, if I have to convince them to start an outreach program there.

But Brian. I don't know if I can deal with him. And if I know him, he won't make it easy for me to join Equality Now and *not* deal with him. Not to mention the tension with Dev. His claws came out just at Brian's name. I'll have to be really careful, keep him informed every step of the way, and that'll chafe at me, I know. I sigh. The things you do for love. I'm strong enough, and I have to do this. Vince would've been on the list of players I recommended to Emmanuel. Now he'll never get that chance. Somewhere—many somewheres—there's a gay kid starting for his college team who's still scared, who deserves better than to end up with a hole in his head.

"Firebirds fan, eh?" An otter a little ways down the bar distracts me from those morbid thoughts. We talk about the season so far and pass a pretty enjoyable couple hours until my phone buzzes. I don't tell the otter that it's my Chevali Firebirds boyfriend calling; I just tell him I need to head outside to take it.

"So," I ask as soon as the door swings shut behind me, "what happened with Vonni?"

"Oh," he snorts, "got fined a thousand bucks for missing curfew. Charm laughed at him, said it's easy enough to sneak out after curfew, no excuse for missing it."

"I mean—"

"I'll tell you later."

He's probably just making me wait to hear because I was right and he doesn't want to admit it. "Tomorrow night?"

"Yeah. Hey, you hear about this thing with Lightning Strike?"

"I was going to ask you that. Is it final?"

"Sounds like it. They're not reporting it yet, but the coaches on offense told the guys there to be ready Monday or Tuesday."

"Wow. Good luck with that."

"I know, right? Still, I won't have to worry about him much."

I grin. "He's worried about you. Already said a couple things to the media about playing with you."

"Really? Shit." There's some noise as Dev fumbles his phone around. "You think maybe he's…?"

"Gay? Probably not. Too showy. I think he's just attention-seeking."

"I guess you'd know better than I would."

"You'll find out pretty soon. Maybe you can introduce me." I swish my tail, leaning against the wall outside the bar.

"Maybe."

We sit quietly on the phone for a few seconds. "Everything else okay? You ready for the game?"

"Pretty ready," he says. "Ready as we can be."

"Good." I turn my head. Inside the bar, I can see the college game wrapping up, another one starting on one of the other TVs. "You know what to do. Go do it. I'll be watching."

"Thanks, fox. Love you."

"Love you too."

I hold the phone in my paw, tail wagging in the mild evening air. The sky is a gorgeous purple-blue on one side, streaked with gold and pink and orange on the other. The last rays of the sun light up the tops of the buildings against the violet backdrop, with pink-tinged clouds framing them. The air's definitely gotten a little chillier, too. I hug my arms around myself and enjoy the view for a little longer before going inside to catch up on the games and order myself some dinner.

Chapter 11: Missteps (Dev)

Sunday. Game day. Sunday mornings are the best, because you're a week removed from getting beat up the last game, and you're all excited to go play in this one. Charm and I get up, rib each other through breakfast, and head down to the stadium with the team. We go through our morning stretches and then head off to sit with our units for a couple hours. Because we're on the West Coast, we're playing a late game, so we have time to watch the early ones before we kick off. The coaches don't try to cram plays on us at this point in the week; if we don't know 'em, we don't know 'em. Gerrard does, sometimes, but he'll do it while watching the other games. He'll point out some play on defense and say, "See, look how they execute that." Carson stays quiet, but me and Zillo, we'll say, "Hey, c'mon, we're trying to watch the game."

Honestly, I don't really watch much the morning before one of our games. I'm too keyed up, thinking about what I'm going to have to do, running through plays in my head. So mostly I don't want Gerrard putting more pressure on me.

But one of the games puts a lot of pressure on all of us. The Hellentown Pilots win again, their third straight since we beat them in Hellentown to take the division lead. So they're nine and four now, only half a game behind us. We watch the final go up in Freestone, 30-13, and the room goes quiet before Charm says, "Keepin' it interesting."

"Gotta win today," I say, and Pace and Vonni, near me, agree animatedly.

Then we get ready and dressed. Aston walks around the locker room shoulder-punching all the starters, with his chant of "Game time! Game time!" A bunch of the guys kneel in a prayer circle. Charm takes out a photo from his locker, which I happen to know is of the Penthouse Miss October 2006, and kisses it for luck. Vonni and Pace come over in their tight Ultimate Fit clothes and ask me if they have the Ultimate Fit and I tell them they do. Vonni takes out a picture of his wife and kisses that. Charm asks if he can kiss her too, and Vonni tells him to fuck off. I wonder if Vonni's thinking about the leopard, or if that even matters to him.

Me, I have my own pre-game ritual. When we walk out onto the field, I turn my head and look up into the stands, into the section where I know my fox is sitting. Back in college, I used to be able to see him. These days, I have to settle for just identifying where he is.

Here in Yerba, he got pretty good seats: high up in the lower level, around the near 20-yard line. I still don't see him, but I know he sees me looking, and that's what matters.

The introduction of the players is interesting here. I get a bunch of cheers from some of the higher sections, and look up to see rainbow flags with "#57" on them, signs that say "FRISKY FOR MISKI," and a lot of standing, cheering guys. I give them a wave and then get to my sideline.

Things seem to happen in slow motion until the action starts. Even the introductions take forever, the singing of the national anthem sounds like the joke one they did on that cartoon show a few years ago, and the coin hangs in mid-air longer than a punt. But finally, the toss is over, we win and choose to receive, and our offense takes the field.

It's a big, chilly, windy stadium, and the wind makes field goals and extra points tough. Today the wind is gusting around, but no more than usual. Long passes might be tricky, but we don't throw a lot of those anyway.

Aston looks pretty good to start with. Lots of short passes, lots of handoffs to Jaws. We get about to mid-field and then the drive stalls and we have to punt. But Gerrard and Carson and I have been watching their linebackers, and Gerrard points out, quietly, where there are some flaws in their plays, how we can do better. Steez talks with him and radios information upstairs to the offensive coordinator when he thinks it'll be useful.

Then Yerba has the ball, in their maroon uniforms with gold trim, and we go out there in our road whites, red numbers with gold edging. I'm jumpy, my tail is lashing, and I'm fidgety until we're standing there on the other side of the twenty and the Yerba team is huddled across from us. I look up at Lee's section, and I'm calm. I know I can do this.

We get off to a good start. They run on the first two downs, and all I do there is run into the pile of guys trying to bring down the running back. On third down they bring in a mule deer at running back, and this guy rarely carries, so we're alert for a pass. And sure enough, they throw to the sideline, Carson's side. We're ready for it; he brings down the runner short of the first down, and Yerba punts. We head back to the sideline feeling pretty good.

That feeling lasts all of two minutes. On second down, Aston's pass is tipped at the line of scrimmage. One of the Yerba linebackers, a cougar, plucks the ball out of the air and sprints to the end zone. Aston looks stunned; only Jaws gets close to the guy before he scores.

Our special teams unit salvages a small amount of our dignity by blocking the extra point, a rabbit named Cliff leaping to get a paw on it as it sails over him. Those guys come back to the sideline to cheers as if they'd just scored a touchdown themselves.

Then our offense has to go out again, and they go back to the grinding ground game. Aston tries a long pass, which flutters long past the arms of Zaïd, the cheetah it's aimed at. He does get a short pass to Rodolf, our top wideout today, which the white-tailed deer takes down to the nineteen before stumbling and losing his momentum. Then Jaws runs the ball three times in a row, getting to the corner of the end zone on the last try, and after we make the extra point, we're up 7-6 and not feeling so bad about things anymore.

But they play conservative, getting three yards here, four yards there. Not much opportunity for us on defense to make a big play, take the momentum back. They drive down the field and power their way into the end zone, and this time the extra point sails through cleanly. 13-7.

That's how we go in at halftime. My ribs hurt again, though at least it's less than last week. Not even worth mentioning to the trainer. The foot I hurt while filming the commercial got twisted out there, too, but I just have to walk that off. In the locker room, Coach gives us a good encouraging speech about how good we are and how we just have to realize it.

On the defensive side, we nod and huddle around our coaches, trying to work out game plans for the second half, but you can see some grumbling on offense, especially the wideouts. Rodolf and especially Zaïd openly wonder which one of them will be losing playing time when Strike shows up, and the coaches just say they'll make that decision over the course of the week. "Bullshit," Ty mutters to me as we head back out onto the field. "They know. They just won't tell us 'cause they don't want anyone to quit. Want 'em to think they're fighting for a spot."

"Least you shouldn't worry," I say. "You're a slot receiver. Anyway, isn't Strike just going to get Ford's touches? Why does someone have to lose one?"

Ty laughs, a sharp bark. "Rodo says when you bring in someone like Strike, he won't be happy with just what Ford was getting. Someone's going to drop some numbers."

"I don't see Strike playing in the slot," I say.

"I could be a number one," he says, flexing his paws. "Don't know if I'll get the chance here, now."

"Stick around…" I start to say, and he laughs.

"Sticking around ain't part of the business. Why wait five years here when there might be an opening in Port City? You know, now that they're down to zero quality receivers."

"Port City stinks," I say.

"Won't always." Ty grins. "Anyway, it's a crapshoot. Might as well get your paycheck, right?"

"Didn't you already buy your mom a house?"

He shrugs. "Ain't bought myself one."

That's still on my mind as we take the field, on defense, but as I line up, I drive it out of my head and get back to the game. On first down, we're set up for a run, but they aren't, and Gerrard is just yelling at us to get back when they snap, and the quarterback heaves the ball down the field. Gerrard and Carson and I break off from the pass rush when we see the ball go up, and hustle downfield, but we have to stand and watch as their fox makes an acrobatic grab and tumbles to the ground at the six-yard line. And Vonni, trailing him, pulls up short and doesn't touch him to make sure the play's over—a player who falls down can get up unless an opposing player touches him while he's down. We're yelling at him as he turns to us, but he doesn't get what we're saying as the Whalers' fox scrambles to his feet and lunges to the end zone.

Fuck. Vonni gestures to the refs, saying he touched the fox on the way down, the refs are walking away from him, and there's nothing we can do about it. The Whalers all jump around celebrating as we walk off. They kick the extra point and it's 20-7 and we can really feel it slipping away from us.

The defensive coordinator walks around talking to all the defensive groups. "We've made a couple mistakes," he says, "but we can turn this game right back around. We just need to hold them, make a big play if we can, and trust in our guys to put points on the board."

So we watch Yerba's defense, hoping our guys can put points up against them. They could use another good linebacker, I think, watching their #52 flail at a pass that gives us a first down. And if Lee does get a job here, and they make me an offer…I look up at the "FRISKY FOR MISKI" sign again. It'd be nice to live and work in a city where I could maybe walk around with Lee, paw in paw. Where we could go out to eat together without worrying about what some homophobic jackass might do. Not that Lee worries about it all that much.

Gerrard nudges me and points out another play, and I snap my attention back to our offense. They're really rolling on this drive, staying on the field for a good six minutes, giving us a chance to catch our breath. Not that we really needed it, only being on the field for one play, but Steez points out that we'll be fresher than they will in the fourth quarter. And when Jaws powers through their line for a score and Charm adds the extra point, we get some hope and energy back.

We jog out to take our positions. Gerrard reminds us of what we're expecting from them, and I run through the play positioning in my head. I know where I need to be and where I need to go. They don't go deep again on first down, going back to the power runs, but we're ready for them. Gerrard spots the holes in the line and throws his body in there, clogging the lanes and holding them to two and one yards on the first two downs.

The mule deer comes in again at their RB slot, so we shift to pass defense. I keep an eye on the deer, remembering Corey trying to tackle the New Kestle deer by his antlers, which effectively spelled the end of his career with Chevali. So I resolve to go low in the unlikely event that I have to tackle him. But when they snap, the deer does break to my side; it's a screen pass, I feel it. I know where the ball's going to be almost before the quarterback cocks his arm to throw.

Into the gap I leap, paws high. I can see the ball landing in them, and there's nobody between me and the end zone. Defensive touchdown, tie the game or maybe put us ahead, and plus I'd impress the Yerba guys watching. I remember the feel of the interception at Aventira, and it's so close here—

I feel the air of the ball's passage against my paws—and nothing else. I land and spin around to see the deer cradling the football, charging ahead. Gerrard and Pace, the jaguar who plays safety, charge forward to meet him as I'm chasing him from behind, but he's still well ahead of the first down marker before Pace slams into him and my arms close around his legs and we bring him down.

The deer gets up and pauses, looking at me. "Good gamble," he says, trotting back to the line.

I stare. "What the hell did that mean?"

Gerrard gestures me back to the line. "He's just trying to get you to take more chances. We have to focus on stopping the play, not on showy interceptions."

"I had that," I growl. "Nine times out of ten, I have that."

Nobody says anything about it, back in the huddle. Everyone would've done the same thing in my place. We get back into formation and go back to work.

We can bottle up their runners, but we have less luck against their short, quick passes. When Norton, the cheetah at the other corner position, leaps for an interception and misses, allowing a first down, I feel somewhat vindicated, but I don't feel any better. At least we manage to hold them to a field goal attempt, and then our special teams unit blocks that, too, and they come away with no points.

So we feel pretty good, going into the fourth quarter down 20-14 but coming back. Our offense keeps driving down the field, to midfield, to their thirty, and then I'm huddled with Gerrard and Carson, Steez and Zillo and Marais, talking about tweaks to our plays, when I hear a huge cheer from the crowd.

We all look up and see a wolf in a Whalers uniform sprinting past our sideline with the football, Jaws and Ty and Rodolf in pursuit. Rodolf is the one who catches the wolf, after Ty herds him back toward the sideline, and they all go down in a tangle at our fifteen-yard line.

"Suit up, boys," Gerrard says as they replay the fumble and the Whalers' recovery on the big screen. We all shove our helmets on and trot out grimly to defend a short field.

The crowd is going nuts, louder than they've been all afternoon. I line up and stare ahead at the line. On a short field, I can always feel the weight of our end zone at my back, like it's a living thing and I need to stop these guys from getting to it. I'm so intent that it's only when Gerrard's helmet bumps mine that I realize he's yelling something at me.

"Sweep strong!" he yells into my ear, pointing, and then goes back to position. Carson has the same tense alertness I'm feeling, both our tails flicking from side to side waiting for the snap. If they run a sweep to the strong side—Carson's side—then my responsibility is to come across the field and make sure they don't double back. Carson meets the runner and Gerrard is his backup, in front of the play.

But I get blocked at the line by one of their wideouts, and later, on replay, I'll see the same happen to Carson. And meanwhile, the quarterback fakes the handoff to the runner and keeps the ball himself, darting through our line for six before Pace finally gets to him. They hurry back and snap without giving us time to set up, showing the sweep right again, and this time we're second-guessing so I spy the quarterback and Gerrard does the same but they actually do run the sweep and the wolverine running back dodges Carson and Pace and drags Vonni into the end zone.

We stalk back to the sideline, frustrated. Their kicker is all jitters at this point and misses the extra point, or maybe we block it again, I dunno, I don't even bother to watch. It's 26-14 and time is winding down.

"If we had a quick-strike offense," Zillo mutters, next to me.

"Next week," I say.

He doesn't take his eyes from the field, but his ears flick my way. "You think that Strike guy is…you know…?"

"What?"

He avoids looking at me. "Well, he dresses all flashy, and…"

"Oh. Lee says no," I say. "I guess he'd know better than I would."

"Mmm." The coyote's impassive.

On my other side, Gerrard snorts. "Doesn't matter if he sleeps with fish," he says. "Long as he can play."

Charm, behind us, booms, "Hey, you being discriminating against people who sleep with fish, Coach?"

Gerrard ignores him. I turn around and lift my fist, which he taps with his. "You're pretty relaxed."

He shrugs. "This point in the game, they ain't gonna have me kick anything. If we're close, we're going for it."

"I guess so." We all stare out at the field, where Jaws is getting momentum together for another run. "Think we can get two scores?"

"Think you can grab an onside kick?" Charm elbows me.

"He's not going out for the onside," Gerrard says. "Zillo's going."

This is a change from a couple weeks ago, not that we've had to onside kick in several weeks. Lots of guys play special teams (the guys on the field for punts or kicks) and some other role, and I had been on the return team until I got promoted to starter. They kept me on the "chase" squad—the guys they put in to execute or defend an onside kick—until a few weeks ago, when Corey got himself suspended.

"You should be out there," Charm says. "They need a guy who can really go after balls."

Zillo makes a choking noise that sounds like he's trying to strangle a laugh. I grin and say, "If the football was shaped like a boob, you'd be out there on every play."

"Fuckin' A," he says. "If the football was shaped like a boob, I'd never leave the fuckin' stadium."

That breaks the tension a little, and it helps even more when Aston tosses a short pass to Ty and the fox darts past defenders to fall into the end zone. We cheer and jump and get ready for the onside kick. Zillo runs out with the rest of the chase squad, and the rabbit who is better at punts and onside kicks goes out to try to give it back to our offense. Charm has tried onside kicks two or three times, and he just can't get the hang of kicking it into the ground so it jumps and hops. "I like to *score*," he says, often.

In this case, even though the kick is executed well, it skitters just beyond the reach of our guys and a cougar in maroon wraps his arms around it. Zillo comes back and slams his helmet to the ground as Gerrard and Carson and I are putting ours on. I pat him on the shoulder and say, "Nothing you could do," but he doesn't respond, and I have to run out to keep them from getting a first down.

They run and run and run, every time ticking the clock down a little more and making us use timeouts so it doesn't keep going and run out the game. But we stack the line and they don't get their first down, so they have to kick back to us.

On our side, we have to throw and throw and throw, and all the receivers run down the sidelines so they can run out of bounds and stop the clock after a catch. The Yerba defenders know that's where they have to run, and they follow there, leaping to break up the passes. On fourth and ten, Aston chucks it down the middle of the field in desperation, where it's grabbed by a coyote in maroon and that's the end of the game. We lose, 26-21. So much for impressing the Yerba staff. So much for cruising to win the division. I look up to where Lee is sitting, wondering what he's thinking. I could've done a lot better.

We congratulate the Yerba players, but most of our guys just want to head back to the locker room, so after a couple paws shaken, I start to trot back. Out of the corner of my eye, I see the Yerba mule deer, the one who said, "Good gamble," watching me, but when I stop, he turns and trots back to his own locker room. So I just turn back and do the same.

"This is a tough loss," Coach tells us. "Tomorrow's a travel day, but at Tuesday's practice, we'll have a new player on offense, and management— we think he'll really help us put up more points, put less pressure on our defense."

"We can handle the pressure," Gerrard says.

Samuelson gives him a thin, lupine smile. "Of course you can," he says, "but it's better to be out there with a 14-point lead than a seven-point lead, wouldn't you say? So I want all of you to make him feel welcome. We believe in him and we wouldn't have brought him to the team without interviews, without the assurance that he'll be part of the team and not a distraction."

"How can he not be a distraction?" They're the first words Zillo's said since the onside kick.

Coach goes on. "We're still nine and four, and we're in good shape to win this division. That banner can still fly over our field. I am proud of you guys and the job you've done, and now we just have to start preparing for Freestone. We've got three games left, and they're all winnable—but I don't want you guys looking ahead to the game with Hellentown. We've got the talent to win out." He pauses. "But we've got to win it. It's not going to come to us."

Despite the pep talk, we feel kind of lousy still, and it doesn't help when Gerrard says, ostensibly to me, but loud enough that everyone can hear it,

"And next week we're going to be more focused."

Lots of expressions around me go sour. Guys go quiet. Gerrard goes on, "It's no problem to go out and have fun as long as you don't let it affect the game."

I feel like he's talking to me, like I let the team down. I'm not going to say anything, though my stomach twists for a moment. Vonni, though, doesn't have any such reservation.

"What the hell's that supposed to mean?" he says, stalking over half-dressed, his chest and shoulder fur all askew.

Gerrard turns and faces him. "Means exactly what I said. Coach lets us go have fun and he expects us to be able to handle it."

"Like remembering to touch a guy when he goes down," Carson adds.

"Oh, fuck you both," Vonni says. "I touched him, the ref just didn't see it."

"Neither did the replay," Gerrard says.

"You know, I didn't see you guys putting any pressure on the quarterback all day. How many more picks did you get than us? Oh, right. Zero." He holds up a paw, thumb and forefinger circled to make an 'O.'

"We ran our routes," Gerrard starts, but Ty comes over to chime in.

"Hey, there were a bunch of us out. Don't pick on Von. He had as good a game as any of us did."

"Apparently some of you handled the night out better than others," Gerrard says.

Vonni gets up closer, in his face. "Fuck you, old timer. I'm tellin' you, that had nothing to do with it. And you should know."

Gerrard leans forward until their noses are almost touching. "I can handle myself," he says. "You want to back off."

They glare, and Vonni's tail is all bristled out, and then I catch Charm's eye and in a flash I think about what he would do and I step forward almost before I have a plan. I put a paw on each of their shoulders. "Save it for Freestone," I say. "Come on, we had some bad breaks."

I apply gentle pressure, and Vonni backs up slowly. Gerrard looks at me and nods, and then says, "But if there's any clubs you know in Freestone, go Sunday night."

That makes Vonni lay his ears back again. "Don't fucking start picking on Dev," he says. "Blame me, but this ain't on him."

"Hey," I say. "He's not blaming me. Look, it's cool."

"Dev did his job today," Gerrard says. "Mostly."

"We both got turned around in the fourth," I say. "It wasn't just me."

"I'm just saying," the tall coyote says, loudly, "that we should stop worrying about trades, stop thinking about what happened a couple nights before, and just play the game."

I can't say anything about thinking about being traded to Yerba, because that's not even something that's been discussed. I wasn't thinking about it seriously. Gerrard's talking about the trade for Lightning Strike, and how our receivers were bitching about that and maybe letting it affect them on the field, whether they were trying too hard to impress or just not thinking about the play. But I see Vonni ready to go off again, even with Ty kind of holding him back, and so I say, "Yeah. That's what we're all paid to do. We're professionals."

"Then let's act like it," Gerrard snaps.

He turns back to his locker. Vonni's still glaring at him, so I step forward to help Ty calm the other fox down. His ears are still back and his paws are almost fists. "Self-righteous motherfucker," he growls as we walk him back to his locker.

"Yeah, but he's our self-righteous motherfucker," I say, borrowing a page from Charm.

Vonni looks at me. "I wasn't thinking about her, I swear. I thought I touched the guy."

"I know. Everyone's just pissed off," I say. "Just a bunch of us had an off day at the same time. Including me. I shouldn't have jumped for that interception."

"Ah," he waves a paw, "you had a good shot at it." His ears come up, and he takes a breath. "It happens. Okay, I'm cool."

We finish dressing, we talk to the media. There are still a couple questions for me about how it felt to play in Yerba: did any of the players give me shit about being gay, did I see the signs and did I feel more welcome here, and would I consider playing here next year? I give the standard answer to that. "I'm just focused on finishing this year in Chevali, getting our team to the playoffs, and bringing home a championship."

When you say boring platitudes to the media, they leave you alone pretty quickly. Fisher taught me that, among lots of other things. I used to wonder why athletes all said the same things, and then when I came out and just wanted the fucking reporters to leave me alone, I figured it out. Whenever I get asked about being the UFL's—hell, the country's only out professional athlete, I just say, "Everyone has been respectful. It's business as usual." Now they don't really bother me anymore, and I can focus on football games.

But I'm annoyed at Gerrard's accusations. Even if they weren't meant for me, I had been thinking about going to Yerba, and maybe that lack of

Divisions

focus stopped me from making the one play that would've saved our game. That's the thing about football. If I, if anyone on the team, slips and misses one play, that play could cost us a game, and a game could cost us a season. There are 60 to 70 plays for one team in a game, and three or four players involved in every play, and any one of those might be crucial. It's not like life, where you can see the big moments coming and prepare for them. In football, you have to be prepared for a big moment every single fucking second.

•

It's easier to confess to Lee over the fancy dinner he drags me to than it is to talk to the guys in the locker room. "I got distracted thinking about playing at Yerba."

"Lots of guys on your side screwed up," he says.

"Thanks." I look away from him, up at the impressionist paintings on the walls, the dark ebony dishware cabinet, the ancient-looking doorway ten feet from us. Of course, the back wall with the door to the restrooms isn't much farther; this is a small place, only about ten tables in the one room.

"You did good," he says. "Come on, you know it. That screen pass was a gamble."

"That's what the deer said." I scratch my chin, remembering.

"The Whalers guy who caught it?" Lee asks. I nod. "Well, he was right. Make it and you guys win the game. You can't say it lost you the game, though. They didn't even score on that drive."

"But it kept the offense off the field."

"Yeah." He lifts his glass of wine—white, chardonnay, of course—and sips delicately. "Aston wasn't exactly cutting it up out there. I still think you guys need a left guard more than you need a Lightning Strike, but I'll be interested to see what Aston can do with a receiver who really lets him stretch the field."

"Our wideouts do a good job," I say, but he hears the lack of passion in my voice and answers only with a flick of the ears. "Well, he's coming, for better or worse."

"He'll make you better." Lee grins. "I'd also like to see what Aston could do with more time to set for his throws, but I think it'll be good for you guys all the same. The media says you should win the division now, this loss notwithstanding."

"Hellentown beat Freestone." I poke at the green salad, swirling lettuce around in the sharp-scented tan dressing.

"And you get to do that next week. You still own the tiebreaker." Lee picks up a forkful of his salad. "Just win out and you're in. Heck, just win two of three and you've got a pretty good chance anyway."

"What if we don't?"

"You know," he says, "this salad cost twenty dollars and you're not enjoying it at all."

I look down at my mess of a plate. "Sorry," I say, and take a bite. It really is good, crisp lettuce and sharp, sweet vinaigrette, with pine nuts and a pungent, crumbly cheese. When I stop worrying about football and let myself enjoy it, I feel a lot more like I got my money's worth.

"So," Lee says, "You going to tell me what happened with Vonni?"

"Oh!" I look up from the salad fast enough that dressing drips down my chin. I dab at my fur with a napkin. "Yeah, so. He didn't make it back for curfew, but he shows up the next morning. And we're all teasing him, like, man, out all night." I wasn't teasing him because I was still worried he was going to be freaked out over what happened. "And he says no, he got back around twelve-thirty. So Pike asked him what happened with the girl, and he says, all I had to do was show her my Firebirds ID and she was ripping at my pants like I promised to marry her."

"Marry her." Lee squints. "He's already married."

"That's what he said." I spread my paws.

Lee shakes his head and takes another drink of wine. "Straight guys," he mutters. "Honestly. So then what?"

I lean forward, 'cause this is a classy place, and tell him the rest in a whisper. "He says she just opened her mouth and went to town."

"And she was definitely a she?"

I shake my head. "Okay, I hate to admit you were right, but here's the other part. Ty said that, said something like, hey, a muzzle's a muzzle, you sure it wasn't a guy in a dress? And Vonni says, who cares, if you got blown like I did, you wouldn't give a shit either."

Lee laughs, a low, easy laugh that draws a smile out of me despite myself. "I'm glad he's at least that open-minded about it. If not particularly worried about word getting back to his wife."

"Nobody's worried about that," I say without thinking.

"Well. Good thing I came along for your road game."

I look at his muzzle, up to his eyes, and his smile is fading. I'm not sure whether or not he's serious. I know I should be jokey, but I can't quite muster the energy. "You don't really think you have to worry, do you?"

"I dunno," he said. "I saw the way you were looking at that wolf Ty was talking to."

"I wasn't—" I take a breath and rest my palms flat on my legs until I've retracted my claws all the way. "I was curious. I never went to a gay club before."

"Neither had your teammates. Seems like they all had a good time. I thought you did, too."

I sit back and take another bite of salad. "I just don't want you doing anything like that again."

"All right." He lifts his wine glass, his smile gone. "Next time your teammates want to go to a nightclub in a gay district, I won't come along."

I sigh. "That's not what I meant."

"No, you're right. I was treating them like friends of yours rather than being sensitive to their careers. So I should just stay out of their lives."

When he gets like this, the best thing to do is just let it blow over. So I finish up the salad and change the subject to his family. He tells me his dad offered to look after my finances, which I think would be good considering the guy I have now doesn't really ever talk to me at all about them. I tell him some other things from the game, about what Coach said, and he agrees about us having a winnable schedule.

We get our main courses: steak for me, with potatoes and these crispy green beans that are amazing—although they're nothing compared to the steak itself, which is mouth-wateringly tender and juicy, and seasoned just enough. Lee has half a rotisserie chicken, a puree of parsnips, and a weird-looking broccoli that he lets me try. It's also great. We've switched to red wine for dinner, a pinot noir recommended by the waiter that costs fifteen dollars a glass. That's as much as the most expensive bottle of wine I have in my apartment. Of course, I only have three, and I had none before Lee moved in.

About halfway through the meal, my phone rings, and I check the number out of habit. Mom and Dad have taken to calling me on game weekends, though after today's game I don't really want to talk to them. But it isn't them. I stare at the phone and then let it go to voicemail.

"Ogleby," I say to Lee, and he nods.

"He's better about calling you just once a week?"

"Has been. I wonder what this is about, though." The phone beeps with a voicemail message.

"Go ahead and listen," Lee says, taking another bite of chicken. "As long as you don't start having a conversation, I don't think they'll kick you out."

I eye the mink at the host stand as I lift my phone to my ear. Her eyes travel past me in a bored survey of the room, but she doesn't give any sign of caring what I'm doing. And then Ogleby's squeaky ferret voice fills my ear.

"Dev, honey, I just heard the news, can you believe it? You and Lightning Strike on the same team! I put in a call to his agent, but you know, he's pretty busy and might not get back to me but there's definite interest, did you hear what he said about you, how he's looking forward to playing with you? This could be huge, this could be bigger than Ultimate Fit, this could be, like…" He stops for as long as I've ever heard him stop (barring the time I came out in front of him on national TV). "Elite."

I arch an eyebrow at Lee. "Ogleby thinks me and Lightning Strike could get an Elite commercial."

He flicks his ears. "They're his brand. If anyone could get you in there, he could. More commercials would be good. Make gay athletes more of a mainstream thing, get people used to seeing you."

"It'd be another distraction from football."

He tilts his head. "True. But if you manage it right, it doesn't have to be a critical one. You got through that Ultimate Fit commercial okay."

"God."

"Just tell Ogleby that the club's media rep needs to make all the arrangements. That way they'll know what your schedule is and won't interfere with it."

I put the phone down. Ogleby's message is still going on, gushing about something or another, but I've gotten the gist of it. "Will they do that?"

"Uh-huh. Pretty sure. Worth asking, anyway."

"Why wouldn't Ogleby know that?"

Lee splays his ears and grins, looking rather adorable. "I wouldn't be surprised," he says, "if you're the first client of Ogleby's who's actually landed a commercial."

He has a good point.

CHAPTER 12: REFLECTION (LEE)

After that oh-my-God amazing dinner, I drag Dev out for a walk back to my hotel. I chose the restaurant specifically because it was the nicest one in walking distance, so that we could have a little stroll. Personally, I feel way full, but I know Dev probably didn't get enough to eat, because he not only ate all of his rich chocolate cake (except the bite he gave me) and all the raspberries around it and the last few bites of the pear tart I couldn't finish, but when he asked for the check, he also asked if they could refill the bread basket one more time.

So I'm enjoying the walk, and as we're walking, I reach over to take his paw in mine. He tenses at first, so I say, "Relax," and he gives me a look. "Seriously," I say. "Nobody's going to care, not here." Also not in Chevali, not in the downtown where he lives. Probably not. You can never tell. But that's the world we're working towards, and though I know better than to get into a discussion of how important it is to be open, at least I can lead by example.

"Feels weird," he rumbles, but he enfolds my paw in his huge one, and we walk along that way for a couple blocks. It feels weird to me, too, having to match my shorter stride to his long one, but we get used to it pretty quickly. And Yerba is totally cool with it, like I said. A couple people glance our way, but nobody looks twice.

The city is a little chillier tonight. There's a kind of fog that hangs around the buildings. You can just see it at the tops, where their light disperses like our breath in the air, and you can feel it in your fur when the wind blows moisture into your ears. I keep mine folded back, but despite all that, it's probably my favorite ten minutes in this beautiful city, job interview included.

Dev's quiet, maybe still thinking about the game, and if I let him, he'd probably go right back to the team. But I don't want the night to end. So when we get back to my hotel, I insist Dev walk me to my room and then I tug him inside. "You don't have a curfew tonight, do you?"

He steps in, lets the door swing closed. "Not unless you count having to be on an airplane at nine a.m."

The clock reads 9:15. "Just under twelve hours." I grin and slide my paws around his hips. "Plenty of time."

"Mmm." He hugs me back and pulls me to him. "What did you have in mind?"

His paws slide down to squeeze my rear, leaving me little doubt what he has in mind. "Oh," I say, "I was thinking I might show you what Vonni was missing if he got blown by a girl and not a guy."

"We're going back out to Korsat Boulevard?" He grins and looks down, and I rest my paws over his tail.

"Could if you want. Those bathrooms have seen a lot worse than a fox with a tiger cock in his mouth."

"Seems like a long way to go." He rumbles and shifts against me, and I can feel the effect my words and body are having on him in the warmth against my stomach. But there's no hurry tonight. I knew he'd be down after the loss; I don't think he got quite as much out of the dinner as I did. So I'm hoping a nice long play session will take his mind off things. Besides, I want to take advantage of the nice hotel room, and also it's been days since I saw him off Wednesday morning and I'm horny as fuck.

"We've always got this bathroom." I wave toward the marbled floor, the brass fixtures, the very roomy shower. "If you really want to do it in a bathroom. There's also this pretty swanky bed."

"Dunno." His paw slides up and down my back, over the base of my tail, and down as my tail pushes back up against his pressure. "Seems like there's too many pillows on that bed. No room for anything else."

I glance back at the bed, with its pile of brown and gold decorative pillows. Beyond it, the lights of the city wink over the water, already lightly hazy. "You could sweep the pillows dramatically onto the floor."

"Mmm." He slides his paw down my tail a few more times. "Then what?"

"Then you could throw me onto the bed. Romantically."

"Roughly?"

"Roughly and romantically?"

His paws curl around my waist, untucking my shirt slowly. I keep mine around his tail, pressing my stomach into the hardness that's growing at his waist. "Little hard for you to suck my cock when you've been thrown onto the bed."

"Depends where you're standing." I swish my tail behind me, pushing my muzzle up under his chin and twisting so I can see his golden left eye out of my left eye.

He looks down, and then turns me so my back is to the bed and he can see it. "I think I'm still too tall. Unless you were on paws and knees on the bed."

I grind the edge of my hip against his erection, and mine is getting pretty hard, too. "I can be wherever you want me to be." It's not just him who needs his mind taken off things, really. Between my interview and all the other stuff spinning around in my head, it's nice to just think about Dev and sex.

He chuckles and lifts his head, and then brings his paws up behind my ears, holding my head and rubbing gently at the base of them, which makes me close my eyes and press even closer, just that warm pressure right *there*, over and over. It's not the kind of pressure that makes me harder; in fact, I turn and just stand right against him as he rubs, not grinding at all. It's the closeness, the intimate touch in a place that most people don't think of as intimate—everyone I know has seen my ears, front and back, but very few get to touch them—that reminds me I'm with someone I trust, whose delicate fingers can go wherever they like on me.

There are places like that on Dev, too, that I can think of when I'm not having my ears rubbed like this. My tail swings free behind me and I just press up against him until he places his thumbs under my cheek ruffs and lifts my muzzle to his.

We kiss, warm and sweet and then more passionate, tongues sliding together and curling around each other. I reach for his belt, for his pants, for his zipper, and when all those are loosened, I push his pants and underwear and everything down to the floor, all the while holding the kiss, and he keeps his paws on my cheeks and just purrs his approval. My fingers find the broad curves of his hip bones, the tight muscles of his rear that twitch and move with minute shifts of his weight, the solid curve of his lower back, the tight muscles under the softer fur of his abdomen, and there, the thick ridge of his cock, the sheath below it. My fingers slide up and down the sides, tease the moisture at the tip, and then he lets my muzzle go.

Our noses touch, with smiles. I kiss his muzzle and say, "Someone needs to be cleaned up," and drop to my knees. Only I have to kneel straight up; I can't sit back on my heels, and even then I have to pull his cock down and he has to bend his knees, but neither of us seems to mind.

I wash my tongue up the side, along the familiar warm surface, taste the musk of his pre at the tip. He shudders, dropping his paws to my shoulders, as I curl my tongue around his balls and wash slowly up his sheath back along his shaft, back to the tip. Another few strokes of the tongue and he rubs up behind my ears again. The pressure is nice, but now I've got something else to distract me. Another few licks, and I take his tip between my lips.

He sucks in a breath. His paws tighten. I have to be careful; chances are he's as pent up as I am, and I could bring him to the edge quicker than usual. Not that it'd be bad for him to come on my tongue, and we'd still have tomorrow morning, but I want him in me when he finishes.

Still, I can't say I don't enjoy having that full length of his sliding along my tongue, the taste of his pleasure filling my muzzle. And I like the shudders, the jerking thrusts he makes with his hips as I suck on him, the shivers in his bended knees. I like that I can do that to this huge tiger, this professional athlete, that these fine-tuned muscles are, for this precious moment, at my command.

Back and forth and up and down I go, settling into the flow, while his fingers squeeze and his legs shake, and his breath comes in pants and gasps. His hips tremble and then jerk, pushing his length into my mouth, and just as I'm thinking I'd better settle down if I want him to finish anywhere else, he pushes my head back and looks down at me.

I get up slowly, starting to pull my shirt off, and his paws rush to help me, tugging at buttons and sleeves, while I grin and pant and the cool air of the hotel runs over my tongue and the taste of him stays with me. As the shirt falls away, he unbuckles my belt and then leaves me to finish the job, walking in two quick strides back to the door to shut off the lights.

"Nobody can see in," I say. "At least, not without a telescope. But I'm glad you're so protective of who gets to see my—"

My pants drop to my ankles and Dev grins, spinning me around to face the window. He pushes me to the bed as I kick my pants free of my feet, stumbling to keep pace, and on the bed he keeps me on my knees. Without the lights on in the room, my reflection in the window is ghostly, insubstantial. Behind me, Dev's is just as transparent as he settles himself against my back. He's kept his shirt on, wrinkled near the waist where it hangs free instead of being tucked in, cuffs framing his paws as he reaches around my chest to spread his large orange and white fingers across my white chest ruff and stomach. His erection slides between my legs, not up inside me yet, the tip tickling the back of my sac as he pushes his hips all the way up to my rear.

In the window, I watch his paws trace their way down my ribcage, watch them frame my stomach as I suck it in to look better in my reflection. Even though his thumbs press in on my back, his fingers almost meet at my navel.

And just below that, the reddish length of my own erection hangs, though he ignores it for the moment, just sliding paws down my hips, down my thighs, while his muzzle rubs my right ear and his tongue just brushes it. "I want us to see them," he says.

"You like it here in Yerba, hu-uhhh." My question becomes a soft moan as his fingers tease around my sac and then up the creases on either side of my sheath, pressing in at the firmness there. I arch my back against him and tighten my thighs around his length. He wriggles gently, not really trying to get away, and lifts one arm to hold me across the chest while the other takes my shaft in soft leather pads. The paws that only hours ago were pushing and shoving other players around the field close around me and hold me.

Slowly, he pulls his paw up my length, finds the moisture at my tip as I found his, and rubs it around as I did. I close my eyes out of reflex and then open them again to watch him play with me in the window-mirror over the city backdrop. His paw moves faster, closer, and though I fight off the growing arousal, I can't help squirming against him. He purrs against my ear and his paw keeps going, and then he mouths my ear and I let out a squeak.

He chuckles softly, keeps his muzzle there, and strokes even as my leg starts to tremble and then shake, and finally he stops and crosses both paws over my chest, holding me on the bed, his warmth and strength supporting me. Out of my unmolested ear, I hear the swish of his tail across the bed, while my own trapped one tries to swish and only manages to jerk spasmodically.

"Got your lube?" he murmurs in a bass growl in my ear.

"Uh-huh," I pant. I can't bring myself to break away from him—I don't think I could if I wanted to, not until he let me go. These arms shove aside massive linemen; they're more than a match for one lightweight fox. So I just say, "Nightstand."

"Oh, hm." He noses my ear. "Been using it on yourself?"

"No." I clench my thighs around his cock. "Just…knew you'd be here tonight."

"Okay." He laughs again, softly, and his arms loosen. "Go get it."

I slide away, trailing one arm behind me to brush his erection as I go. He doesn't make a move to take his shirt off, just watches me with golden eyes as I bend over, tail wagging, and open the nightstand.

When I turn back around, he's kneeling up with one paw on his cock, grinning at me and stroking himself. I slick up my paw and tailhole good and quick, and clamber onto the bed, where I take over stroking his cock for him.

I get it slick fast and then keep playing with it until he bites his lip and grips my shoulder. "Ready?" I say with a smile, and he nods fast.

I know I'm sure as hell ready, so I place both paws on his shoulders. His eyes flick open. "Fox—"

Before he can finish, I jump up and try to wrap my legs around his waist. He flinches and hisses as my weight comes to bear on him, and his body leans to one side. I try to disengage, but his arms grip my sides and then my rear and hold me, and slowly he rights himself.

"Sorry," I whisper. "I forgot—did you hurt your ribs again?"

He shakes his head. "Not specifically, but…" He lifts his chest, holding me close to him. I bump my chin against his nose and cross my legs behind his back, taking some of the strain off his shoulders. He settles himself. "Just, everything hurts. A little."

"I can get down. I just thought—"

"It's okay, doc." He lifts his muzzle and kisses my nose. "I can take it."

"I know you *can*. I'm saying you don't have to."

He grins, and there's little trace of the pained grimace. "The best thing for the pain is you. So the question is, can you take it?"

I reach below myself and give his cock a couple more strokes, watching him as I shift my weight. He adjusts okay, doesn't look hurt. So I pull him into position right at my entrance and say, "I think you know the answer to that."

"Always nice to find it out again." He pulls me down onto him.

He's big, and the rough barbs always scrape a little on their way in. But after that first twinge, I don't mind at all. The bigness I like too. I'm pretty flexible in a lot of areas, and so I don't need a lot of prep to be able to take him in. Sometimes when he goes in fast it hurts for a second or two until I adjust; tonight he eases in gently and there's nothing but the shivering delight of being one with him again.

I work my way down onto him, his paws tight on my body, and when he's all the way inside me, our noses are almost level. We kiss again, then, joined at the hips and muzzles, our tongues licking around each other with increasing urgency. Without breaking the kiss, he lifts me up and pulls his hips back, and then thrusts back into me. Up and down, as our lips shift and press together, up and down as his tongue licks the roof of my muzzle and my teeth, up and down as my paws tighten around the back of his neck and my breath whistles out my nose.

He thrusts faster; I clench my rear and moan into his muzzle. His paws grip me harder and his breath comes faster, with moans of his own. I feel my own passion building, even without a paw on my cock, but he's definitely winning this race. His thrusts are less gentle, his kiss is suffocating, his whole body is shuddering with urgency. I squeeze with my legs and arms as he pumps up and down, and he responds by bringing one paw from my rear to my head, leaning back enough that I'm not going to fall off, and holds me tightly in the kiss, his tongue deep in my mouth, his hips jerking up and up and up.

And with a loud moan that starts in his stomach and vibrates through his chest up his throat and into my muzzle, he slams hard into my rear and squeezes me. Incoherent sounds fill the room; I echo them back to him, gasping, holding him as best I can as the passion and desire flood out of him and into me. His hips shudder up, jerk again, and finally he exhales and comes to rest deep inside me, his hips pressed against my rear.

Our lips part. I think I felt him wince. "You okay?" I whisper.

He nods, growls softly through harsh exhalations. "It's only when you take me by surprise," he says.

"Oh gosh." I wriggle around the hardness, clenching my legs behind his back. I'm nicely close, but not urgently close. "I guess I will have to tell you everything I'm going to do."

He mouths at my throat, making me shiver and turn my head to the side. "Mmm," he rumbles through my fur. "How about I tell you what you're going to do now?"

"What's that?" I grin, but my breath catches in my throat as he squeezes me against him and slides a paw between us.

"You're going to struggle and squirm and come in my paw." He works his huge paw between us and brushes up and down my cock with leathery fingers. I shiver and do squirm, even at that light touch, but his arm is iron across my back.

"That sounds…" I gasp as his paw curls tightly around my cock, thumb rubbing the sensitive tip. "Plau-ausible."

Slowly, he slides his paw up and down, golden eyes fixed on mine, and the heat of him inside me and the wonderful fire from each stroke of his paw surge through my groin, up my chest into a whine from my muzzle. And even though he knows I'm close—because he knows I'm close—he keeps going slowly, deliberately.

I'm pressed tightly against him, but he has enough room between my stomach and his to keep moving his paw up and down, and before long I'm pressing the side of my muzzle against his head and biting down at the collar of his shirt, twisting as if trying to get away when in reality that's the last thing I want to do. I want this exquisite, ecstatic torment to go on and on, but my body needs the release, and Dev can't stroke slowly enough to put it off for long, not with his shaft still hard and warm in my rear, not with his scent in my nose, not with every nerve at my groin on fire.

And it's not long before the squirms become shudders and the whines become moans and my arms and legs tighten around him, and I jerk and come in his paw, just as he'd predicted. Warmth spreads into my fur with every spasm of my hips, and his paw holds my cock tight, slicker and slicker, moving more easily but slowing down as my climax fades and my cock gets all sensitive and my throat makes higher, whining noises.

He stops and lets me pant against him, brings his sticky paw out and wraps it around me, pressing into my bare fur. I hold him and rub my fingers through the cotton fabric and murmur against his ear, "You ruined your shirt."

"You have a really nice back and butt," he murmurs back.

His paws rub along my spine, but he's also looking at the window over my shoulder, at my reflection and the city beyond. "It looks best with your cock in it," I say.

"Mm-hmm." He squeezes me and I squeeze back, both with my arms and my rear. He grrfs and shifts his hips. "It's a nice city. Being able to live like this."

"What, having sex in front of a window?" I nudge his ear teasingly.

"Going out. Holding paws. Not worrying."

"There are places in Chevali like that, too. And ideally we'd like to make the whole country turn out that way." He's quiet, so I rub up to his shoulders. "You're helping. Coming out—that was huge. It helped a lot of people." I force myself to stop there, not to think about what else he could be doing. With the urgency of sex gone, other thoughts are crowding in around the fringes of my mind, applying pressure where I don't want any now.

"So maybe a championship-winning gay player would help even more?"

"Bet on it." I slowly work myself backwards to let him slide out of me, and disengage my legs from around his waist. Keeping my arms around his neck, I rest my knees on his thighs and bring my nose level with his. "It'll be good for gay people and good for the people of Chevali and good for you. So." I kiss his nose. "I think you should do it."

"Also would give me more opportunities."

I nod. "That too. Though I hope you aren't looking for more foxes to fill your time if I have to move out."

He nuzzles me. "I have enough trouble managing one fox. You think I want to screw up my life with more?"

"'Screw up' or 'make more awesome'?"

He squints at me. "Are you trying to talk me into cheating on you?"

"No." I wag my tail, filling the air behind me with shed fur. My rear is still warm from him and I relish the feeling. "I'm trying to get you to appreciate foxes."

"I thought I appreciated this fox pretty well."

"Oh, you did. Let's shower and maybe you can appreciate him again in the morning."

So we do, and he does.

BOOK 3

Chapter 13: Lightning Strike (Dev)

I'm probably in a better mood than most of my teammates Monday morning when we get on the plane, all except Charm, who I guess used his Sunday night the same way I did. We sit together and swap tunes and he asks me in a low voice about our night out with Lee. I tell him the stories and he isn't impressed. "Buncha pro jocks go to a gay club and don't even get a blow job?"

"Vonni got a blow job."

"Sure, the married guy." He chuckles. "Never needed a wedding ring myself, but I hear they work great. Hell, any club we go to, we oughta be the center of attention. And it's not like I was there taking the attention off y'all."

It's obvious where everyone's attention is. Everyone but the wide receivers is sulking over the loss; they are preoccupied worrying about which one of them will lose playing time to Strike. Everyone growls and snaps at each other, and it's a relief to get home that afternoon. Lee comes in later in the evening, and we have a good night that doesn't even include sex, maybe because we're both worn out from Sunday night and travel. I ask him what he's going to do this week, and he tells me he's going to start talking to that activist group, so I tell him to just tell me when something happens, and I try to forget about it.

Tuesday morning when I arrive at the stadium, I have to navigate through a mass of news vans, and the first thought that goes through my head is *Lion Christ, did Lee get a bunch of media to come talk to me already?* Pretty, suited foxes and mice and deer and one kangaroo rush up to my truck as I drive up, and I brace myself.

They see it's me, and most of them pause and then fall back like a wave at the beach. I'm a little baffled—it's more attention than I got anytime except immediately after the press conference anyway—until a leopard and a goat hurry up to the truck, and the goat calls, "Devlin! What do you think about the trade for Lightning Strike?"

Oh. Right. I wave them away politely, call, "No comment," and drive into the players' lot. I am curious, though. Part of me wants to go out and wait for him with the reporters. I shake my head and laugh, and go in to change.

The locker room is buzzing when I walk in, all about the media outside. We hang around in uniform—no pads today—long after we're supposed to be out on the field. Even Carson stays with us, curious to see what all the fuss is about. The coaches have to come in and shoo us out. "You guys will meet Strike this afternoon," Samuelson growls, a real snarl on his muzzle, and we run out to practice.

When I say "we," of course, I'm excluding Gerrard, who is just doing his calisthenics calmly out on the field, waiting for us. "Did you catch a glimpse of him?" he asks in a bored tone when we all come out to sit with him.

"Not here yet." Carson answers when I don't. His tail switches across the grass.

"Good. Can we get moving, then?"

We run drills in the morning, up and down the field, and then go in for lunch. The afternoon's for private workout sessions in the weight room, but that flies out of all our minds when we sit down for lunch, because five minutes past noon, a loud, light voice calls out from the entrance to the cafeteria, "Hello, Firebirds!"

The whole room, sixty-odd players, turns and stares. There in the doorway is a cheetah in a Firebirds jersey with #11 on it. His teeth are white in a face that is otherwise the red of our logo. As he turns to survey the room, the backs of his ears come into view, red with a gold splotch across each of them. His arms, under the short sleeves of his jersey, are also red, with patterned bands of gold around the elbow and wrist and a trail of gold spots like the Milky Way connecting them. And when he raises his paws, he shows off the Firebirds logo on each paw pad. I don't know if they're stickers or a tattoo. Knowing him, probably a tattoo.

Beyond the cosmetic, though, he's fucking huge. Nearly seven feet tall, the media says, but they don't mention the muscles that bulge when he bends his arms, the broad shoulders, the legs that are so long they almost look like stilts. Huge, muscular stilts.

"In case you haven't met me already," the cheetah says, walking in with a big smile, "I'm Lightning Strike, and I'm here to win a championship."

He waves to Aston, who waves back; clearly they've met already. I look for the other wide receivers, all sitting together: Zaïd, Rodolf, Ty, and a couple others, huddled at one end of a table glowering at the red-and-gold cheetah advancing toward them. Only Rodolf really looks at ease; Ty has his ears splayed and Zaïd's mouth is twisted up like the burger he's holding in his right paw was made of sour lime and bitters.

But Strike just points a finger at them and says, "We're gonna take this league and make it our bitch, boys," continuing his stroll through the tables. It's weird how quiet the room is, everybody just focused on him. He's basking in it, putting on a show for us. And then he's walking toward us—toward me and Gerrard and Carson. I figure he knows Gerrard is the leader of the defense and he wants to get in good with that side of the ball, but when he gets close to us, he stops and stares right at me.

"Devlin Miski," he says.

Half the room is still watching him. The rest are watching me. I shift in my chair. "Hi," I say. "Um. Welcome to the Firebirds."

He shakes his head. "So courageous. I want you to know that I stand with you. You're my teammate now and that means I don't care who you want to fuck. You're family."

He holds out his arms. I don't know what to do.

"Hug him!" Charm yells helpfully from another table.

There's some snickering, but I don't think anyone dares laugh. Strike doesn't flinch or even look away from me for a minute. I don't know what else I can do. So I stand up and reach out and hug him.

He squeezes hard, too, like when some guys will take your paw and try to crush it to prove how strong they are. So I squeeze back just as hard. He's smiling when he releases me, claps me on both shoulders, and says, "Don't let anyone take you down. Gay or straight, we're all one team, and I am proud of my gay teammate."

Christ, he had to go there. I want to ask, *Are you* my *gay teammate?* But I don't have the nerve, not right there in front of the rest of the team. And I don't get the vibe from him, anyway. He seems more like a college kid holding a passionate sign about unfair labor practices halfway around the world. Maybe he thinks discrimination is wrong. Maybe he just wants to draw more attention to himself. I wish he'd do that without drawing attention to me. "Thanks," I say, sitting down.

"I know you guys are a championship defense," Strike says, looking at Gerrard, "and now you've got a championship offense to go with it."

He looks around, maybe expecting applause, but he's just insulted our offense and we can't cheer that. So after an awkward second, he just smiles, says he'll see us on the field, and walks off.

Gerrard doesn't look very happy at all, and it's not hard to see why, as he watches everyone else stare at Strike's red tail waving. It has four gold lines painted up it, ending in four arrow heads at the tip. Clearly the last thing anyone in the room is thinking about at that moment is football.

"Colorful," I say.

"We don't have to worry about him." Gerrard goes back to his meal. "We just have to keep our minds on the game."

Easier said than done. Even in the weight room after lunch, as I'm working out with Zillo and Gerrard and Carson are spotting each other, everyone's just talking about Strike. "He was painted that same way when we played him a few weeks ago," Zillo says. "He just made the Devils' orange into our gold. The red isn't even right."

"It's close enough." Honestly, I didn't notice whether it was the right shade or not. "Anyway, he'll probably change it again before game time."

"Hey, Norton!" Zillo waves over the cheetah, our other starting corner. "What did you guys jaw about on the field?"

Norton, of course, doesn't need to be told whom we're talking about. "Just, y'know." He waves a paw and goes back to his station, his black-spotted yellow tail waving behind him. "Cheetah stuff. Who's faster, whatever," he calls over his shoulder.

Zillo and I don't need to remind each other that Strike had Norton beat a couple times back when we played them. Made him look slow, though we'd never say that to him. Wasn't Strike's fault the quarterback only threw his way once, and then it was two feet over his head. "Guy's a beast," Zillo says, then looks at me with a flick of his big ears. "So, uh. You think he's…?"

"What? Gay?" Carson is looking my way, too, and so is Vonni, his large black ears swiveled to face me. Great. I shake my head and wonder how many times I'll be asked this question. "I don't get that vibe off him. I mean, come on. If he were, he'd be doing a lot more to hide it. He wouldn't be painting his fur and coming over to talk to me right away."

Zillo scratches the side of his muzzle and nods. "I guess if he was that open, he'd just come out with it now, right." When I don't say anything more, hoping the topic will just die down, he lies back on the bench. "Okay, move me up to two-ten?"

I shift plates on the bars and spot him while he presses two-ten. Then we put fifty more pounds on the plates for me to do my presses. I'm still sore from Sunday, but my ribs don't protest too much as I lift the bar ten times. It feels good to work out the muscles again after the game and a plane flight. All the ones I didn't use on Lee Sunday night need the work.

By the end of the afternoon, I'm exhausted. We all wind down at the same time, do our stretches, and hit the showers, getting dressed for a little time in the film room before we go. Gerrard cues up film from our loss at Yerba, and we're watching some of the plays from different angles when the door opens and closes. We don't think anything of it; coaches and players come and go during film time. But then Strike's voice fills the room. "See, that right there, that's where that fox knew he had a chance."

The fox on the screen is raising his hand, calling for the ball. The quarterback rifles it over a leaping Carson into the fox's grip. We turn; Strike is standing in the doorway behind us. He points at the screen. "That little stutter step froze the safety."

Indeed, Pace is caught between the fox, running deep, and their tight end, crossing in front of him. Steez flicks his ears, his voice mild, but firm. "Poor decision-making. He took too long."

"Nah, he's good." Strike walks around the corner, farther into the room. "Their play's designed to freeze him."

"He should have spotted Carson trailing the tight end." Gerrard points at the screen. "Then he could've released to cover the fox."

"It's a split-second decision." Strike shrugs. "I use that stutter a lot. But not always. Sometimes you stutter and then change direction."

We've seen that, of course, on our film of him. We didn't look at it so much before the Port City game, but Norton and Vonni did and they talked about how hard he is to guard, how he can change direction and then speed up apparently effortlessly. But...

"Not everyone can." Steez leans his head against his paw and glances at the screen. "These can't do that. They stutter and go. Sometimes."

Strike grins. "Well, sure, I mean, not everyone can, but you never know, right? What these guys do well is they're all on the same page. Really precise with their routes. They don't have the talent we got here, but they're exactly where they need to be. Look, this tight end—couple feet in and you pick him up, Miski, couple feet farther out and the other safety, the cougar, he drops off this outside route and takes him."

"That would leave the other wideout open," Gerrard says.

"Sure, but that wasn't where the play was going."

"Okay." Gerrard stands, his tail arched and a little bristled. "Thanks for the input, but this really is just for the defense. Don't you have a film review to go to?"

Strike just laughs. "Aw, it's not a problem. I don't mind sharing what I know." He taps his head. "Helps you guys get into the mind of a wide receiver."

"You know who'd really appreciate that?" Gerrard points outside. "The cornerbacks."

"That's what they said about you."

Steez sits up in his chair. "Mister Strike, your thoughts are appreciated. I have plays to review and would appreciate some quiet. Watch if you like, but no talking."

"Yeah, fine." The cheetah leans across a chair toward me. "I just need to talk to Miski. Can he come outside a second?"

Steez waves at me as Gerrard sits back down. "Make it quick!"

I'm annoyed; I almost wanted him to forbid me to talk to the cheetah. Instead, I'm following my red-and-gold teammate out the door in the back, listening to the film and the discussion and wanting to be part of that.

"Hey," Strike says, and extends a paw. "Just want to say, really, you're awesome, man. Stepping out there, making yourself a target…there aren't many of us willing to do that."

I shake his paw automatically, thinking, *wait, did he just…yeah, he did.* "Well," I say, "Um. Is that what you wanted to say to me?"

He frowns briefly. Maybe he wanted me to be more effusive, to tell him we are brothers, all that. But the frown clears and the genial smile comes back. "Nah. Hey, I wondered if my agent got in touch with you."

"With me? No. My flea said something about a commercial…" He's frowning again, but puzzled this time. "Oh. Flea. A friend of mine called her agent that."

"Ohhh." He nods. "'Cause of how they just jump around from one guy to another, right?"

"Um. Because they suck your blood and don't give anything back?"

He shakes his head. "No, dude, my agent is awesome. Listen, he scored me this beer commercial and I thought it'd be a good idea if you and me did it together. Like, the pitch could be, 'No matter what your taste, you'll like Strongwell Light.' What'cha think?"

It's my turn to frown. "Is that their slogan?"

He beams. "Nah, I made it up. Y'know, I coulda been in marketing. But this was the dream."

"Right. Um, I haven't heard from him…when did this happen?"

"Just like a couple hours ago. After lunch." He gestures to the cafeteria.

"Really? You were on a call instead of working out?"

"Dude, I was on a call while I was working out."

I'm trying to put together this image in my head and failing. "Which weight room were you in? I didn't hear you." I can't imagine Jaws and some of the O-line tolerating a guy working out while yapping on the phone.

"Oh, I close the door when I'm on a call. Don't want to be rude. But you should be hearing from—"

"Sorry." I hold up a paw. "Still not quite getting it. You closed the door…?"

He smiles. "To my weight room. They set it up yesterday, it's in an office just up from the locker room. Nothing fancy, you know. Treadmill, bench, barbells." He waggles a paw. "The Port City one was a lot nicer, but I know they threw this together real quick."

"Who spots for you?"

"I got my own spots." He laughs, then looks down at his arms when I don't join in the laughter. "Well, not now. Cheetah joke. My trainer spots for me."

"Really? One of the trainers?" I stare.

"Well, no. My personal trainer. Not one of the staff here. I need him, 'cause the other wideouts, they don't lift near enough. Can't spot the weights I use."

"Okay, um." Private weight room, personal trainer. I try to clear that out of my head; after all, this isn't exactly "making it quick," as Steez ordered. "So, call from my flea—my agent."

"Yeah." He grins. "I think you'll like the amount. Go ahead, check."

"My phone's in my locker. I'll check when practice is over."

He stares at me. "You've gotta keep your phone on you. What if something blows up and you're hours late to the party?"

"I don't think my life moves that fast," I say. I glance over at the film room again. "Anyway, it's against policy. Coach makes us put the phones away."

"Ahh, gotcha." He nods, completely missing my pointed remark. "Okay, well, let me know what you think. I want to make this happen, so if you aren't totally cool with it, I can take care of it. Dig?"

"Yeah, I, uh…dig." He holds out his paw again, so I shake it. "I gotta get back to the film. Oh, and thanks. I appreciate it."

"Not a problem." His smile widens. "Good to help each other out, right?"

"Sure," I say, though I can't for the life of me figure how I'm helping him out by being in a commercial with him.

"About time," Steez snaps as I rejoin the team, but I don't hear anything else about it.

When I pick up my phone after practice, sure enough, the box is full. The first message is just Ogleby saying "Oh my God" over and over, interspersed with "Dev *call me!*" His squeaks are even higher-pitched than normal. The messages that follow are variations on the same theme, except for the one that sounds like he's hyperventilating into the phone. And while I'm listening to the messages, the phone rings again. Ogleby, of course.

"Did you get my messages? Did you?" he squeaks when I pick up.

"Yes. Calm down. What's this about?"

I'm really just curious to see if he can explain it to me coherently, and he mostly does. He sputters out Lightning Strike's name, and "Strongwell Beer" and "commercial" and then he says a number.

"Wait, hang on. What was that?"

Panting ferret gasps come through the phone. "One. Million."

I'm standing in the locker room half-dressed, in workout shorts and no shirt, surrounded by millionaires, or at least hundred-thousandaires, in a room that smells of sweat and work. The number one million seems completely remote and separate from everything else I am. I mean, I made a hundred K from the Ultimate Fit guys, but at the time I thought that was the ceiling for me—some of it was because I was willing to film a commercial quickly, not necessarily because of what I was worth. Next to it, one million doesn't seem like that much, but it could lead to more, to enough that if I invest it well, Lee wouldn't have to work. And when I retire from football, neither will I.

Ogleby's squeaking in my ear. "Yeah, I'm here," I say.

"You gotta make this work, Dev. It's your big score, it might never happen again, you gotta do what it takes."

"Even if it means losing the division because I'm away working on this commercial?"

"Dev, sweetie, maybe you didn't hear me, I said they will pay you one million dollars just for this one day of work."

"Day?"

"Just one day, I promise! No future options like in that Ultimate Fit contract."

"Wait, what?"

"Oh, nothing."

I lean back against the locker. "Ogleby…"

"Okay, look, it turns out that they have an option to film two more commercials at their discretion in the next six months but I told them not until the season is over. And that is still a great rate you're commanding. That's what I'm telling all the other people who ask about commercials."

"What other people?"

"You don't want to know, they only want to pay like fifty grand."

"That's still—" I breathe in. "Okay, send me along the terms and I'll take a look at it."

"We need to sign this week is the thing, they want it out for the playoffs."

"So you better send it out today, huh?"

"I thought I could read it over the phone and—"

Deep breaths. Resist the urge to throw the phone across the room. "I think I want to read the whole thing."

"Okay, okay, Dev, but let me tell you, I went through this and it looks great. Their tagline is 'No matter what your taste, you'll love the taste of Strongwell' and you don't have to kiss the guy at all, just have your arm around him—"

"Wait. Stop. What guy?"

"The actor in the ad, there's a guy for you and a girl for Strike."

"Shit, Ogleby, they want me to hug another guy on camera? On national television?"

"For one million dollars!"

Less fifteen percent, of course. That's, what, a hundred and fifty K? Worth it to him, but he doesn't have a boyfriend to worry about. "I'm gonna have to ask Lee about it."

"Be sure to tell him about the million—"

"I will." And I hang up on him. I hold the phone in my paw, staring down, and then toss it into the locker.

Gerrard watches me. "More commercials?" he says. "Do I need to ask Coach to bar cameras from the stadium?"

"No," I snap. "I don't know. I haven't agreed to anything. It's Strike, he wants me to be in a commercial with him—"

Immediately I regret saying his name, because Gerrard lays his ears back. "Not even one full fucking day," he says. "I wonder if he's being this disruptive to the offense."

I can't say anything. Gerrard curses so rarely that I feel like my dad just scolded me. Carson's eyes are wide too, and Charm yells across two lockers, "Hey, settle down, Coach."

Gerrard's ears come up and he shakes his head. "You think you can take phone calls and worry about commercials and still be preparing your best for a game…if you think that, you shouldn't be in this locker room. That's all."

"I don't think that," I say. "Look, if I do this commercial, I'll schedule it. They're not just going to show up."

"All right." He looks at me seriously. "I trust you."

There's a nice serious moment that Charm ruins by slapping me on the shoulder and calling me "Coach Junior," which after a pause he modifies to "Coach Gramps."

I walk out with him through the pack of reporters, who mostly completely ignore us. Charm sees me looking at them, and elbows me. "Miss it?"

"What, that?" We clear the last reporter, a ferret who looks briefly at us and then returns to fixedly staring at the door. "It's kind of cool, actually. They never stalked me outside the stadium."

"I know a guy who can dye fur, if you want."

I laugh. "I'm good with my stripes, thanks."

"He can work small, too." Charm draws a little heart in the air with his fingers. "This leopard chick I went out with, she had a red heart on her ass."

"And nothing else?"

"Just me."

We laugh back to our trucks, and I pull out the phone to call Lee when I get in. Then I remember he's waiting at home, and put the phone down. At least I have that to look forward to, at the end of the day.

CHAPTER 14: HEALTH TIPS (DEV)

Ogleby sends the contract over, which is ridiculous because he's supposed to be vetting these things for me. I consider hiring a lawyer to look at it for a couple hours and then I think about that some more and I get that nasty feeling like I need to get a new agent. I'd resisted because Ogleby was pretty good to me. He represented me when nobody else really was interested, and he did negotiate a good rookie contract with the Dragons. Granted, the pay is pretty fixed for those things. But still, he's always looked out for me. He set me up with Caroll and got me some publicity—not as much as Brian's blog posts, sure, but he also got me that Ultimate Fit contract—with those riders I didn't know about…

Fuck. I print out the contract so I have something to hold and my claws punch through it as I grab it off Lee's printer. I don't want to be that guy, the one who dumps the first agent when he hits it big to sign with a more powerful one. But Lee's told me I've already had some sniffs from other agents in my e-mail and I've gotten calls on my phone, too, ones I've ignored, but names I've recognized. One of them was from Fisher's agent, and he was the most courteous, the one I almost returned. He didn't drop Fisher's name; I had to look it up. Plus, he's a tiger.

"Hey," I say. Lee's on his computer writing something, an e-mail maybe. He looks up. I wave the contract. "Can you take a look at this with me?" I've learned that Lee sees angles and possibilities that I don't. They're not always ones I want to take, but they're often ones I've never thought of.

"I'm not a lawyer," he says, but he comes over to look.

"How'd your day go?" I hand him the papers.

He skims the text. "Fine. Talked to some people at Equality Now."

I wait for him to say more. When he doesn't, I nudge him in the side, and he looks up. "And?" I say.

"I'm going to have to look up some of these things on the Internet," he says. "Why didn't Ogleby look through this?"

"I mean about Equality Now," I say.

"Oh," he says. "Well, I can stuff envelopes or cold-call people next summer."

He sits down at the computer and opens a browser, glancing at the contract. I stand behind him and put a paw on his shoulder. "That's…not very interesting, is it? But it's something."

"It's not how I want to spend the next month and a half. Okay, this part here just means you can't use the footage anywhere else. I think."

"So you can just relax for a month and a half. You deserve some time off."

He scrolls through a couple more pages, types in some terms. "This one seems like a standard clause too. Means they can use stills from the commercial in their advertising. That's fine."

"Thanks." I squeeze his shoulder. "So, are you okay?"

He doesn't look up, but he slumps, and that's enough of an answer. I wait for him to talk, though, and finally he says, "I only have a month and a half. After that, I think I'll be too busy to do anything. And I have to do something."

"Why?"

Now he looks up. "What if...what if your college coach found out you were gay and tried to kick you off the team? What if your parents found out that was why you were kicked off, and told you it was a disease? A..." His lips twist into a grimace. "A 'disease of the soul.'"

"Uh." I shake my head. "This is about that Vince King kid, right?"

"It's not just him. I can't stop looking at these college players and wondering how many of them are gay. How many of them are scared, how many of them feel like they're just holding their world together with string and mirrors, that at any moment it could all collapse on them? How many of them feel like they're abnormal?"

"You made it through childhood all right," I say, because I'm not sure what else to say to him.

"I was lucky." He leans his head against my hip, and I hug him by the shoulder. And then he goes back to the contract. "You should get a lawyer to look over this, really, but it looks good to me."

"Thanks," I say, and then, "you know, it'll be nice having you around through the season. And maybe I can go up to Yerba with you after and help you get set up there."

For a couple seconds, he just sits and stares at the computer, and then he says, "I'm thinking of calling Brian tomorrow."

The words sink in slowly. At first, I think he's talking about the guy from Yerba, and I start to say that I thought his name was Peter or Manuel or something and then I realize what he said. I take my paw from his shoulder. "Lion Christ, Lee, why?"

"Because he's doing that kind of work with them."

"How did he get in and you can't?"

He shrugs. "Maybe he didn't. Maybe he's just stuffing envelopes there.

But at least he's in, and he knows people. Maybe he can point me to the right person to talk to."

"Maybe he can fuck up your life one last time before you learn to leave him alone."

When he looks at me, it's with narrowed eyes. "I'll be careful."

"I'd feel better if you just left him the fuck alone."

His expression softens. "I need this," he says softly. "I need to try, at least. I can't just sit on my ass here and live my good life." He reaches out. "It is a good life. I know that. I'm not going to do anything to fuck it up."

His paw rests on my hip. I sigh, and drop my paw back onto his shoulder, and hold him close.

●

Strike corners me again Wednesday, going into the dining room. He steps up behind me as I'm grabbing two burgers, same as I do every day.

"So what'cha think of the commercial? My agent says he's waiting on yours. It's gonna be a great opportunity for you, and Strongwell can't wait to get going on it."

Carson, in front of me, turns his head to look back. "Strongwell tastes like rat piss," he says.

"We don't have to *drink* it," Strike says. "I don't drink any alcohol, in fact."

I grab an energy bar from the basket and a 32-oz. sports drink. Strike has a protein shake, and a huge spinach salad, which he taps as we move on. "No greens? Spinach is really good for you."

"The deer and rabbits look at me funny when I go over there," I say. Carson looks at us sideways; he's got the same thing on his plate as I do.

"I eat a good spinach salad twice a day, and a spinach omelette for breakfast most days." He takes an energy bar, looks at it, and then tosses it back. "These things are full of chemicals."

Carson mutters something about the cheetah's forearms which I think is a Popeye reference. I manage not to snicker. "More chemicals than in your protein shake?"

"This is organic." He points at the big green word "organic" on the label.

"Yeah, well, I was raised on chemicals," I say. "So it's okay."

Strike shakes his head. "You want to get two more years out of your career, give that stuff up."

"Fisher eats them," I say, while Carson moves on to sit down.

"Fisher?" Strike flicks his ears and creases his brow. "Oh, Kingston? Where is he? Don't see him around."

"Okay, but he's not playing because he got stabbed in the leg, not because he…" I wave at the salad. "Didn't eat spinach." I have no idea what happens to old players who don't eat their spinach.

"You heal faster with organics in your body. All those chemicals just slow you down." Strike grins. "You know I ran a faster 40 last year than I did out of college? You know how many people do that?"

"None?"

He jerks a thumb at his chest. "One."

He follows me over to the tables, so out of courtesy, I don't sit next to Gerrard and Carson. Both of them are so pointedly not looking up at me that it's clear they don't want to deal with Strike. So I sit next to Charm instead, because Charm doesn't give a shit.

"Hey, Coach Gramps!" He shovels another mouthful of salad into his face. "Hey, Speedy."

"It's Strike," the cheetah says, a little stiffly.

"Speedy Strike." Charm grins affably and swallows his salad. "How ya likin' it here in Chevali?"

"It's Lightning Strike. I changed my name for a reason."

"Charm calls everyone by a nickname," I say. "It's his thing."

Strike looks about to say something else, but then subsides and goes back to his spinach. "Least he eats right," he says. "So look, when do you think you're gonna know about the commercial? Strongwell can't wait to get in bed with the UFL's only gay player."

"They ain't the only ones, right?" Charm elbows me.

"Tomorrow," I say, ignoring Charm and choosing a definite answer to get Strike to stop talking about it. "Promise." Lee was going to send it around to a lawyer and then maybe I can go over it with Ogleby on the phone or something.

"Great!" The cheetah leans over to Charm. "You're a pretty good kicker, you know that?"

Charm nods, with a mouthful of greens. "Uh-huh."

Strike points his fork at Charm's plate. "Salad. That's what does it."

Charm swallows and shakes his head. "Tits," he says.

I choke on a mouthful of burger. Strike stares for a second and then laughs and slaps the table. "You got a sense of humor, I can see that."

"I mean it," Charm says. "Games I kick a good one or two, I get more tits in the parking lot after. If I miss…" He wiggles his paw. "So-so."

The cheetah's still laughing. "At least you save the sex for after the games."

Charm shrugs his big shoulders. "Before, after…whenever."

"They let girls in the hotel the night before?"

I sometimes forget that not all teams have coaches as casual about that shit as Samuelson is. "Home games we don't have to stay in a hotel. I did with the Dragons, but Coach thinks we're more relaxed if we can stay at home. Long as we get here on time."

"Huh. Still…you can't have sex before games." Strike leans in. "Totally kills your stamina and drive."

"He's a kicker," I put in. "He needs stamina like you need a good kicking leg." I can't help thinking of Gerrard, though, and his girl coyote from Yerba. Does she follow him around to all the road games, or does he have a different girl in each town?

"I kicked a fifty-yarder in high school," Strike says. He takes a gulp of his protein shake.

Of course he did. It's Charm's turn to laugh, but he doesn't do it maliciously. "Those are high-school yards," he says. "Everyone knows they're shorter."

There's a fraction of a second where I think Strike's going to explode. But he just shakes his head, shovels down the rest of his salad, and leaves.

"Thank you," I say, taking a big bite of my delicious, juicy, dripping burger.

Charm's smile doesn't waver. "Fuck 'im if he can't take a joke, right?"

I keep those words in mind for the rest of practice, but Strike doesn't bother me through the end of the day. The crowd of reporters still circles the locker room exit, but without the numbers they had yesterday. A good sign, I guess. Maybe by the end of the season they'll all be gone.

Chapter 15: Old Friends (Lee)

To put off the time when I call Brian, I check over Dev's commercial contract again one more time. I don't trust Ogleby to look at anything more than the dollar figure at the bottom, not after Dev told me he's still on the hook for two more Ultimate Fit ads because Ogleby didn't read *that* contract closely. That also kills a couple hours for me, because let's face it, when I don't have a job, I need to do something besides play video games. The college season is done until the bowls start next week, so I don't have those games to scout, and the UFL doesn't play 'til the weekend. Even when I was working in scouting, this was a slowish time, when we'd go over our lists and review the film of games, spending hours and days in the office until it smelled of stale corn chips and beer and guys. Not the hot kind of smelling like guys, either; more stale and old.

But I don't have lists and I don't have film. All I have is the mild winter Chevali air, and the contract, and seven hours 'til Dev gets home.

Five hours left by the time I stop and break for lunch. I decide to investigate a local taqueria, and so my muzzle and paws still smell like taco sauce when I get back to Dev's place. I wash and get rid of most of the smell, but it's one of those things that persists no matter how much masculine spice musk soap you use to cover it up. Neutra-Scent would do it, but Dev doesn't have any around.

I spend half an hour washing my paws and trying different soaps, and am considering running out to get a new kind of soap from the market when I realize that I'm just delaying the phone call I know I'm going to have to make.

He answers on the first ring. "Wiley Farrel," he says in that same voice, cheerful and sincere, with just a touch of why-it's-been-so-long-since-we-talked.

"Brian Dallas."

"I've been reading about your adventures. Have you moved down here yet?"

"Last week."

"Ah, and I was planning to send you a welcome basket. How do you like our fair city thus far? Isn't it dreadful?"

I look out the window at the dust-colored air and the pale blue sky. "I'm surprised you're still in this dreadful place."

"Oh, Wiley, I'm in a much better place. The Equality Now people are just lovely and I really feel like I have some kind of direction to my life now. Also I am cast in a production of 'Romeo and Juliet' as Mercutio. We start rehearsals in a couple weeks. You should come by."

I lean back on the couch and stretch my legs out. "Yes, I got your message about activism. Seems like Equality Now is the only game in town."

"Only one worth playing. Are you considering getting back into it? We would love to have you on the team here."

"Stuffing envelopes?"

"Oh, you start there, but I'm sure you could work your way up. One way or another."

"Uh-huh." The repartee, the guardedness, is familiar and a little invigorating. "Is that what you did, or are you still licking envelopes?"

"I'm not licking anything right now."

"No boyfriend, then?"

"Not at all. I'm free as a bird in the romantic sense."

My tail flicks back and forth. "Lucky for the Equality Now people. How did you get off envelope duty?"

"I did some before the election, but I've been working with Shamma on the newsletter for a few weeks now, and sitting in on some of the strategy sessions. Fascinating stuff. You know, it's a lot like sitting around the FLAG meetings, only with less textbooks."

"Fewer textbooks," I correct automatically.

He snickers. "And *fewer* pedantic distractions. Well, actually, there are some of those, too."

"And less drama?"

"Oh, there's just as much drama. Fags are fags, dear fox."

"So everyone's sleeping with everyone else?"

"Pretty much, at least as far as I can tell. Not me, though. I'm saving myself for that special someone."

He's waiting for me to say that I'm taken, after which he would tell me not to flatter myself. So I don't fall into that trap. "Wore out the Abercrombie catalog, did you?"

"Not yet." I can see his smirk. "Check out the hot wolf on page 69 if you do pick it up. He's kept me company on many a night."

I shake my head. "Much as I would love to hear more detail of your masturbatory fantasies, Brian, I actually wanted to ask for your help."

He coughs, theatrically, the way Brian does everything. "Oh my. Wiley Farrel, the self-made fox, heroic football scout and boyfriend of the famous gay football tiger? What could you possibly need the help of a poor fellow like me for?"

"You know, I like you less and less when you do that," I say.

"Forgive me. Nay, I am the very pink of courtesy."

"Shakespeare?"

"Mercutio, I told you. What can I do for you, Wiley?"

I take a breath. "I want to do something with Equality Now. Only I'm not having a lot of luck getting hold of anyone who can do something about it."

"Something. Like what, specifically?"

That's the question, isn't it? "I'm not quite sure."

"Well, with a brilliant plan like that…"

"I want to reach out to high school kids."

He's quiet for a moment. "You know, they put people in jail for that."

"Har har. Thy wit is a very bitter thing."

"*Bitter sweeting*, if you're trying to steal my lines."

I never played Mercutio, but that was one of Shakespeare's insults I remembered from college. "There was this kid, Brian. He was a gay college player, and he killed himself."

I tell him most of it, leaving out the part where my mother is cozying up to the group that, in my mind, made this happen. When I finish, he doesn't say anything. I worry that he thinks I'm being melodramatic, that I'm making this up, that he's going to say *so what do you care about this kid, you can't help him.* "Brian?"

"Christ on a stick, Wiley, that's fucking horrible."

He apologizes to someone away from the phone, and I sit up straight on the sofa. "Isn't it? I mean, they put up a web page telling people to pray his gay away."

"Like it was a cancer or a disease."

"Yes!" I stand up and stride to the window, as though the people who did this are out there. "There are a couple pages up on the site for praying away drug addiction, too."

"Those people are fucked up, Wiley. No," he says to the same person on his end, "get the fuck away from my desk if that bothers you." Back to me. "What do you want to do here?"

I smile and look out the window, over the rooftops and into the downtown of the city. Maybe even here there are cubs and kits who could be helped. Maybe especially here, in the conservative desert. "I want to put together some ads that will just fuck up Families United."

"You're sure they were actually there?"

In the reflection, my smile falters. "I'm working on that. Through another source." I'd gotten so caught up in this that for the moment…for a short time…I'd forgotten about Mother.

"All right. Well. I'll talk to some people here and I'll give you a call back."

"Thanks, Brian."

"Oh, Wiley. It's really good to talk to you again."

Glowing and full of energy, I think about the Families United situation and how it would be great to be sure before I go into Equality Now. Should I call my mother? I'm sure I can handle her. Maybe feeling like I have an ally in this Vince King crusade makes me a little more confident; maybe the reality that someone wants to do something about it sharpens the necessity of knowing for sure what Families United did and who the people were who did it.

I mentally prepare myself as I punch in the number. It rings and rings, but she doesn't answer. Then I get her voicemail. "You've reached Eileen Van Langston. Please leave a message."

She went back to her maiden name. Anger flares, but I put it down. It's not useful when dealing with her. I have to get the answers I want out of her, and there'll be time for anger later, maybe.

I still want to talk to someone. Dev's at practice, and my father's at work. Besides, if I call him I'll end up asking him if he knew Mother was going back to her maiden name. So I call Hal.

"Hey," he says. "More news about that bear?"

"Sort of. I'm signing on with Equality Now and hopefully we can get Dev to do some PSAs aimed at college kids."

"They're on board with that?"

"Well, I have a connection there. Trying to get some more information from my side, and working with him to get them involved."

"Connection, huh?"

I hear the question before he asks it. "Yeah, it's Brian."

"The guy who caused all this trouble."

"He…" I falter, remembering more things from the past year than I want to. "He's in a better place now. He wants to do something about those religious nutbags."

"He's not a fox, is he?"

I laugh. "Skunk. Spotted skunk."

"Well, no problem then."

"It's not that, but…he feels the same way I do about the King suicide. And he didn't even know him."

Hal taps on his keyboard, but otherwise it's quiet on his end. Must be at home writing. "Another activist soul. So you're full time with this Equality Now thing?"

"Not yet. Still working out details."

"Okay. Think you could meet me for drinks this afternoon, maybe lunch tomorrow?"

"Both?"

"Either."

I grin. "Sure, I can swing lunch tomorrow. What's the angle?"

He laughs. "Wouldn't buy that I just like talking to you, that I don't have that many friends around here, would you?"

"No."

"Okay, then, how about getting Miski's reaction to Strike?"

"I can give you that in a word: exasperated."

"Wouldn't you rather I buy you lunch in exchange for that word?"

I laugh. Truth is, I'm the one without a lot of friends, and I'm enjoying chatting with Hal. "Sure. Let's do it. Know a good pizza place around?"

•

By the time Dev's home, I'm running football players into each other. He slumps down on the couch and doesn't take a controller right away, but after I shut down my game and start a new one, two player, he does. "How was practice?" I ask.

"Draining." He stretches his arms then his legs. I scoot over to lean against him as he selects his team.

"Thought you'd be used to it by now."

"Starting games is different from sitting on a bench. You can see all the practice guys, they're hungry like we are and they're not injured. I started nine games and I just ache all over now. My toe's gotten mostly better." He flexes it. "But my ribs are still sore, my back hurts, my right leg hurts…" He shakes his head.

I rub the leg, which happens to be the one near me. "Poor guy," I say. "All you have is your fame and money."

He growls in his chest. "Not saying I want to give it up." He wraps his right arm around me, keeping the controller in his massive left paw, and squeezes me against him. "And you left out one other thing. I got my fox."

"Yeah." I lean into him, keeping an eye on the screen. "That doesn't mean you're going to trick me into not noticing you took the Fraters." Peco won the title last year against the Boliat Boxers with a blocked extra point in the fourth quarter, 21-20.

"So take Boliat," he says with a grin.

"I'm gonna take Port City," I say. "Then it'll be a bitter rivalry and I'll get more motivation, especially if it's at home."

He laughs. "The game doesn't know about rivalries."

"No, but we do." I flick my tail against the couch and settle in against him. Also, me picking Port City will let him kick my ass, putting him in a good mood to do other things to it later.

He does win, though I keep it close, and after that I make him a nice dinner of chicken in orange sauce with rice. "Y'ever cook naked?" he rumbles from the doorway of the kitchen.

"Um. Not when cooking anything over an open flame or that involves sauces." I raise an eyebrow at him. "I could microwave you a dinner if you like."

"Nah." He grins. "Just thinkin'."

"You can shred some lettuce while you're thinking. And if you want to do that naked, that should be safe."

He gets the lettuce from the fridge. "Nah. You're the housefox. You should be naked."

"Oh, is that how it works?"

He pats my butt. "Uh-huh."

I wag my tail and we finish dinner together, with me pretty sure I'm going to get some tiger tonight. So I don't think that's in danger when I tell him about the call with Brian.

He gets quiet when I mention the name and looks down at the table, and his claws come out as he stabs the last piece of chicken with his fork. But he notices just after I do and pulls the claws back in, then lifts the chicken to eat it in a quick bite. "So he's going to help you."

"Sounds like it. At least he's on the same page."

"I never said I wasn't," he says, taking my comment the wrong way. "I just have to focus on football."

"I know, I know. That's not what I mean. I mean, even if the rest of the group isn't that excited, he is. And he has a way of talking people into things."

"Except you, right?" Now he looks up, with a gleam in his eye that bounces between dangerous and playful.

"I told you, we want the same thing."

"Sure." He relaxes a little; his tail uncurls, but it flips back and forth over the floor. "So what's going to happen?"

"I hope I'll get to work on a campaign of some sort, maybe aiming at college students. Even if it's not exactly what I want, it'll keep me out of trouble and at the very least it'll do some good."

His eyes glint. "Anything that can do that is okay in my book. So what's involved in a campaign?"

I chew on some lettuce and think about how to frame it. "Could be a lot of things. Probably a TV spot, maybe some messaging to local news media, billboards, things like that. You could be on billboards."

"Whoa, wait. Me?" He frowns.

"It'd all be very tasteful. We wouldn't do anything you wouldn't agree to."

"Lee, I have to focus on football. I can't take time off."

I've barely asked him for anything. "I haven't even talked specifics. It might be like a one-hour photo shoot."

His ears are down, shoulders lowered, and his voice drops. "It's still a distraction I don't need during football season."

I bite my lip and then shove a mouthful of salad into my muzzle. So it's okay to be distracted for a million-dollar commercial, but not for something that might really help a lot of kids? But I swallow the salad and just say, "It might not be during the season at all. I haven't even talked about anything concrete yet. I won't push you to do anything you don't want to do."

His features slide into a smile. "I know you won't, fox," he says. "You're happy enough with the things I do want to do."

When we finish washing up, he settles into the couch and turns his gold eyes on me as I come out of the kitchen wiping my paws dry. "So Brian didn't want you to come over or anything?"

I sit down next to him. "No. I would've told you. And I wouldn't have gone." I rest my paw over his.

He shakes his head. I hurry to go on. "I can handle him. I'll only meet him in public and I'll make sure we stay focused on work."

His features relax into a smile. "Okay. Sorry. You said you're doing lunch with Kinnel? Why? What's he want?"

"My winning personality." That gets a smile from him. "Also, I think he's lonely."

Dev raises his eyebrows. "Do I have to worry about him, too?"

I plop myself down into his lap, angling at the last minute to try to avoid his right leg. "He's very straight. Also he's like ten years older than me. Don't worry about it. Am I allowed to have friends here or do I just have to stay in the apartment all day?"

His paw strokes between my ears. "You're allowed. He's a good guy. Is he still asking you for quotes from me?"

I lean into him. "He wants to know how you feel about Strike."

"Oh God."

My fingers rub his right leg. "That bad?"

"No, it's just…" He exhales. "I don't know how to sum it up. He's frustrating, but he's also…Lion Christ, I dunno. He keeps calling me his 'gay teammate.'"

I slide a paw over to squeeze his sheath. "The nerve of him."

"It's not that." He tightens his arm around me. "It's like, why does he have to call attention to it? I just want to play the games and have nobody give a shit what I do when I go home."

"I know the type," I say. "We had a couple at Forester. Go out of their way to show how liberal they are, how they totally don't care that this guy is gay, and in fact they'll stand near him for a picture to prove it. But still that's kind of all they talk about, so you know it's on their minds."

"He's not exactly like that. Still. I'm glad we only have to play with him for three more games."

"Hopefully five or six," I say with a poke.

He hugs me closer. "Yeah." His paws slide down my back. "But I don't want to talk about him any more."

I give my hips a little shimmy. "You sure that aching body is up to not talking?"

His muscles shift, his arms tighten around me like steel. Next thing I know, I'm up in the air and moving toward the bedroom. "Why don't I show you?" Dev says, his eyes bright and nose almost touching mine.

I kiss him. "Sounds like a lovely plan."

Chapter 16: Communicating Priorities (Lee)

I show up for lunch with Hal in a t-shirt and jeans, which he acknowledges with a grin and a twitch of his whiskers. We sit at the orange plastic table and munch on what is some pretty darn good greasy pizza, and we have a nice chat about his life and his friends and my life and my friends, which I have to say are much more interesting. His newspaper buddies don't really talk to him much; his wife doesn't talk to him; he has friends on the local basketball team and in the Firebirds front office, but being a freelance writer is tough.

He does say that the first date with the coyote went okay. I ask if he has another lined up and he says maybe, he'll see.

I realize I never told him that my parents got divorced, which makes him jot down a note to call my father. Good, I think. He could use the help. I oughta call him myself. And mother again. That separation in my mind makes me uneasy, tinges my conversation and shortens my answers for a little while.

"How's cohabitation?" Hal asks as we push the empty pizza plates away from us.

His ears are perked, and the way he says it, it looks like he's trying to get my mind off the divorce. So I smile and wipe my muzzle with a napkin. "Going well so far. He hasn't objected to my additions to the apartment."

"Nice to find someone you fit with like that." He pauses and then his ears flick, like he changed what he was going to say. "Going to look for a house?"

I look down at the table and trace drops of condensation around my root beer glass on the orange plastic table. "It looks like I'll be in Yerba next year."

"Oh?" His ears perk. "Congratulations. That's great."

"Provided I don't piss off the rest of the Whalers' scouting team."

He grins. "Hence the gay activism?"

"Me, I'm going to be behind the scenes."

"With that Brian guy."

I flatten my ears and frown. "I'm already getting it from Dev. Now you too?"

"Hey." He puts his paws out. "I'm all for mending fences. Just seems like this guy caused you more trouble than good, over the years."

"We were good friends for a while." I drink the root beer. "It'll be fine. I'm more worried about how I'm going to get Dev to take time off during the season without him getting a million dollar paycheck for it."

His ears cup forward. "Someone's paying him a million?"

I set down the glass coolly. "When it's public, maybe I'll tell you."

"Hmph." He looks genuinely hurt, but then, he likes to mess with me. "How much time would he need to take off?"

"I don't know. It's not like I've even talked to anyone or made firm plans. I just mentioned it and he closed down." I still don't want to tell him about Dev's ad, so I think up another question, a safe one. "So what are you working on now?"

That does jar him out of the sulk, mock or not. "What?"

I'm not sure what he thought I might mean. "Another article about football, something else about Dev?"

"Oh. Right." He nods. "Been wanting to do a follow-up on Miski's article. Little bit of interest from ESPN on the reaction, but they got their own guys. Also following up another story about injuries."

"Football injuries?" I grin. "What, is the 1920 Times buying stories again?"

He smirks and taps his nose. "There's a unit in a college outside Peco that's been studying the long-term effects of football injuries on quality of life. It's gotten a little play, but not a whole lot. I interviewed them and then last week I've been talking to the local school here, too. They do a lot of work on retirees in this climate and they have a good baseline to measure the effects of age and maybe isolate them from the injuries. Anyway." He waves a paw. "Just something that came up through a friend."

"Seems worthwhile. I'd volunteer Dev for it, but I don't know if he'd want to go. I'm amazed at how much he's getting beat up, though. I mean, you read about it in the papers, I know it's a brutal game, but…college wasn't this bad."

"Don't worry about it. Probably won't go anywhere. Nobody wants to see the bad side of their entertainment, right?" His muzzle dips, ears folding back to the sides. "Nobody wants to know that shit. But they ought to."

"Sure." I nod. "Families putting kids into football programs."

"College kids making decisions about their futures."

I shake my head. "Don't know about that one. College kids think they're invincible."

A long grin spreads up his muzzle. "You do, do you?"

"It's been a couple years." I sip the root beer. "But I remember what it's like. Still, if colleges were forced to provide full disclosure…"

"There could be legal ramifications as well. Another reason the UFL and fans aren't likely to be that interested in the story."

"But people ought to know."

He nods. "Like they ought to know about Miski and you."

"We're like football injuries?" I tilt my muzzle to the side.

"Only in that nobody wants to talk about you yet." He laughs. "That's changing though. Can you believe how nobody's talking about Miski being gay any more, even here?"

"Couple video segments on SportsCenter two weeks ago, but now it's all about Strike," I say.

"Flavor of the month." He drains the last of his Coke. "Look, if you want to get your boyfriend to take some time off for this ad, I think…if you want to hear my opinion…"

I nod. "Sure."

"Well, look. Can't you just show him how important it is to you? I know he's got all his football goin' on, but you guys really got it for each other. I think if you laid it on, told him it really mattered to you, you could get him to do just about anything."

I stare down at my paw, chocolate brown against the orange tabletop. The orange is not Dev's orange; it's artificially bright and cold and smooth. But still, when I stroke my fingers down it, I feel the toughness of his muscles. "Maybe," I say. "But then if I lay it all out like that, what happens if he still says no?"

"Yeah." Hal shakes his head. "I been there. Let me tell you, it's better to get it out in the open soon as possible. Don't wait ten years to put it all on the table. 'cause, you know, that don't change the result."

The table doesn't give under my fingers, but the condensation collected on it lets them slide smoothly back and forth. I sigh. "But maybe you never need to put it all out there like that."

"Don't you worry," he says, leaning across. "He's got a good heart, and so do you. I wrote a whole article about you, remember? You won't end up like me and Cim."

"Maybe we will, eventually," I say. "Maybe it's all just a matter of how many years you can squeeze out before it all goes south."

"My parents never split up." Hal pokes the table with a finger. "Lived together 'til Mom died."

"And were they happy?"

He falters at that, but recovers quickly, ears and whiskers flicking up. "Happy enough," he says quietly. "Ain't nobody one hundred percent happy in this world. You get to eighty percent and you count yourself damn lucky."

Eighty percent. That's not so bad. That's less than what I'd say I've got with Dev, even with the fighting and everything. And maybe when I actually get to talk with Brian, with the Equality Now people, they'll be reasonable about it. I try to push away the image of Dev sitting at the table, putting up walls against me as soon as I mentioned doing commercials. It was just a reflex, just him reminding me he has to focus on football. That's all. That's good. I should be proud of him.

Hal watches me think and then taps the table. He grins when I look up. "I guess I oughta let you get going."

"Sure." We get up together and I stick out my paw. He grasps it and holds it just a half-second longer than I expect. I wonder if there's more he wants to talk about, but if there is, he isn't ready to do it just yet. So I smile, and say, "If you want to get together again, just let me know."

He smiles back. "Sure will. And you know, if you need to talk…you do the same."

"Yeah," I say. "I will."

Chapter 17: Cracks (Dev)

Saturday we run through a bunch of drills and then some scrimmages, defense against the second-string offense while the offense takes on our second-string defense. It's good to run some practices that require a lot of thinking on my part so I don't have to think about what Lee's been telling me since he hooked up with that activist group.

The fact that he's going to be working closely with Brian bothers me, but he did tell me about it, and I have to trust him. It just makes me squirm. It feels like trouble waiting to happen, mostly because every experience I've ever had with Brian has made me want to punch him in the face. What's black and white and red all over? A skunk with a bloody nose, ha ha.

Then there's the part where I'm involved, filming commercials or doing billboard spots or God knows what. The commercial deal pending with the Strongwell people is scheduled tentatively for the week after the final game of the season, and that's already stressing me out. Of course, it's also stressing me because of my co-star in the commercial, who's decided that since we're doing a commercial together, we must be best friends. Or maybe it's that "stand beside a gay person" thing Lee was talking about. Or maybe it's because already most of the other players in the locker room won't talk to him. Whatever it is, it's annoying, and it means I've been eating most of my lunches with him and Charm.

I get an idea over lunch as he's talking about what he's going to wear in the commercials. He's still got the same Firebirds colors painted into his fur, and I'm almost used to it at this point. "Hey," I say. "You know, I have this friend who's helping with a bunch of gay rights spots. Maybe you could do one of those with me, too. It'd be like the Strongwell spot, only in reverse."

Strike stops, rubs his chin. "How much does it pay?"

"Um. You'd be doing it for free. To help gay kids."

His eyes widen. "For free? Look. My time is valuable and there's a lot of kids that need help out there. I founded the Lightning Strikes Twice Foundation to help out kids who been in trouble with the law once, so I think I'm doing my part for the kids, right?"

"Gay kids too?"

He taps his tray, rubs his fingers over his whiskers. "Some of them are gay, I guess. I don't ask. It's their business, you know? Unless they decide to tell you."

"Hey," Charm says. "Is that the color you're going to be tomorrow?"

We both turn and stare at him. Strike brushes the red stripe on his fur. "No, dude, I'm getting it redone tonight."

"What's it gonna be?"

The cheetah grins. I don't want to describe it as smug, but I can't think of a better word. "Oh, don't ruin the surprise."

Charm blinks. "I wasn't gonna tell the papers," he says. "Do you really think people care?"

The grin vanishes and Strike stands abruptly. He picks up his tray. "I have a website," he says, and then turns and leaves, though his food was only half done.

"Lion Christ," I mutter, "it's like I'm back in high school again."

Charm bumps my shoulder with enough force to knock me half into Strike's abandoned seat. I push him back, grinning. "Ah, the guy was being a dick about your commercial. Rather he be pissed at me about making fun of his fur than have you guys get in a fight."

"Thanks, Mister Charm," I say in an affected high-pitched voice. "I don't know what I'd do if you weren't here."

"Get in fights." He shrugs and chews a mouthful of greens, grinning around stalks of spinach and lettuce leaves. "This don't mean you're my bitch or something, does it?"

I laugh. "Lee would have something to say about that."

"Bet he would." He watches Strike stop to talk to Aston and the backup quarterback, another wolf named Ferrix. I follow his gaze and see the two wolves with their ears partly back, both leaning away from him. Strike seems oblivious to their body language, chatting happily, and then he says something to Ferrix with the air of a teacher giving a student a gold star. He pats Ferrix's shoulder as the wolf flinches, recoiling so much that it's visible even to me from halfway across the room, and then walks on.

Aston and Ferrix lean together to talk in low whispers. I'm about to say something to Charm when another clatter sounds beside me and I smell fox. I turn to see Ty picking up the steak sandwich he's slathered in horseradish to take a huge bite out of it. Zillo sits down across from us a moment later, says hi, and looks off to the side to make sure Strike is really gone.

"Hey," I say.

"Thought he'd never leave," Zillo mutters.

"That guy's an asshole," Ty says around his mouthful of steak. His tail's curled tight around the back of the chair.

"I dunno." Charm chews slowly. "He's kinda growing on me."

"He keeps trying to coach us. Marky tells him to just quiet down and run his routes, but he just won't fucking shut up." Ty looks across the room at nothing in particular, as far as I can tell. "I think Zaïd might actually take a shiv to him. This experiment is going to last all of like two weeks."

"A shiv?" I shake my head. "Does Zaïd have a shiv?"

"Probably, I dunno." Ty munches on his sandwich. "He keeps talking about his 'hood and all the guys he grew up with who are in jail. And you know what he said to me?" That "he" is Strike, obviously. "He said, 'You know, for a fox, you run pretty good.'"

"Wow."

"I know, right?"

"What lousy grammar," Charm says.

"No kidding," I say.

Ty stares at both of us and Zillo does too. Charm grins. "It should be, 'You run pretty good—for a *fox.*'"

Zillo laughs. For a second, I worry that Ty is going to lunge across me and punch Charm. But then the fox's muzzle breaks into a smile and he shakes his head. "Lippy fucker," he laughs. "I run pretty *awesome.*"

"For a fox," I add.

Ty takes another bite. "I'ma tell Zaïd you said that. He's gonna crack up."

"Tell him to just do his job. So they're keeping you in at slot, that means Rodo's down to fourth?"

"Well…" Ty gulps down a mouthful. "They're doin' a lot more trips, so I'd be the inside guy on the trips side and they'll put *him* on the end and iso Zaïd on the other side. So Rodo takes the middle position on the trips side. When they run that. If it's just a power run then they take me or Zaïd out 'cause we don't block as well."

Trips is a formation with three wideouts on the same side of the ball, so "trips right" would be three wideouts on the right side; "iso" means Zaïd would be the only receiver on the other side. "That's good," I say. "At least they're putting something in for all you guys. Sucks to learn a ton of new plays so fast, though."

Ty wiggles his paw. "It's not bad. Mostly it's the same shit. It's the blocking that's different—the O-line is pissed about that. Me, I just run and break, or else I block. Been doing that since I was eight." He describes a zig-zag with his paw. "Five steps and break, or ten steps and break, or just cross the middle and be the hot read."

"That leopard from Yerba told me you're not as hot a read as Vonni," Charm says.

The fox's ears flick back. He shakes his head. "I gotta get a wedding ring. Hey, Dev, any gay clubs in Chevali? If girls like that hang around 'em, I should go."

"I don't know." I look away, like I'm looking for someone elsewhere in the room. "Never actually went and looked."

"Really?"

"I've been with Lee since before I moved here. So you guys going to be okay with Strike on game day?"

"Doesn't he ever wanna go out and dance?"

Lee, he means, of course. I can't get away from being the go-to guy for gay lifestyle questions. "Never really thought of that. He was always just here on weekends and we didn't have a lot of time to go do stuff."

Ty points a finger at me like a gun. "If you find one where hot girls hang out, lemme know. I'm cool with dudes dancing with dudes. No matter what that asshole over there thinks."

I look in the direction he jerks his head and see Colin there. He's sitting with the backup quarterback.

"Aw," Zillo says, looking in the same direction. "Colin's not a bad guy."

"He was all buddy-buddy with me—fox pride and all that—until Yerba. Now he looks down his nose like I stepped in shit or something." Ty shrugs. "Vonni can't stand him. He keeps trying to get the guys to do prayer circles after practice."

"He's religious." Zillo shrugs. "I think he just wants to play football without people rubbing his face in the whole 'gay teammate' thing all the time."

"He won't say a word to Vonni," Ty says. "'Cause he knows Vonni likes you."

"Who's rubbing his face in it?" I say. "I just want to play football, too."

"Yeah." Charm chews another mouthful of salad. "That's all any of us wants to do. You got a problem with someone here, save it for after the games."

"He's been playing well." Zillo kind of looks away from us.

"He hasn't talked to you much since you started hanging out with me, either, has he?" I say.

"No, well…" Zillo sighs. "We both been pretty busy."

"See?" Ty glares in Colin's direction. "He's an asshole. Listen." He leans across to Zillo. "You come with us next time we go out to a gay club and I will hook you up with some sweet ass. Girl ass," he clarifies. "You're invited. You got it?"

"Yeah." Zillo shakes his head. "I dunno if I'm ready for that…"

"Hey," Ty says. "There's no question. You're coming. Right, Dev?"

"Sure." In the back of my head I am thinking, no way am I going to give Lee another chance to fake Ty out into having a gay experience, or whatever. I was freaking out already when it was just a girl. Next time I bet Lee does dig up someone in drag.

And again I get that feeling of being a hypocrite. Ty is pretty gay-friendly, almost curious even, so what if he just needs that push? What if he gets married and fifteen years from now ditches his wife and family to go off with a guy because he didn't have the guts to do it when he was younger, or didn't know?

That's not my problem. All I know is my own situation, and I can't put that on Ty. He's got to make his own decisions, and I think he's been around me enough to know that it'd be okay to be gay. So I put that out of my head. But I keep thinking about Strike, and how quickly the team's gone from a bunch of guys having fun to a bunch of guys complaining about the new guy. At least we're still sort of united, although if Zaïd quits on the team or Rodo gets upset at his reduced playing time, I don't know if that'll balance out.

When I tell Lee about my day that night, I leave out the bit about Ty and the gay club. He makes sympathetic noises about Strike, and asks if I need his help in going over plays.

"Nah," I say. "They're really focusing on getting the new stuff in for the offense. Our plays haven't changed all that much, to be honest."

"Oh, okay." He shrugs and goes back to the chicken he's sauteeing, which smells like wine and mushrooms.

"That smells awesome," I say, and that gets a smile out of him.

It tastes as good as it smells. "Where did you learn to cook?" I ask. "I'm seriously thinking about licking this plate clean."

He grins. "The Internet. And you can if you want, but I also have bread. That's how grownups do it."

"Really?" I rub the bread around in the sauce and then lick the side of the bread. "That doesn't seem to work as well."

That gets a laugh out of him, and it's a pleasant enough evening. We play some UFL 2009 and I'm winning (with the Firebirds, even), and then he mentions that he talked to Brian again about the activism stuff.

"It sounds like they want me to come in and talk about some of the things we could do," he says.

"Great." I focus on the game, hoping that none of those things involve me, knowing full well that they will.

"Before I go in, I need to know what you're willing to do."

I pause the game and drop the controller. "I'll support you."

He holds on to his controller, balancing it in one paw. "Support me by...coming in to film a PSA spot?"

Christ. I can't hesitate too long, or he'll know I'm thinking about an answer and not giving him my immediate response. But I know better than to give him my immediate response, because he would not react well to me saying I don't want to push the gay angle until after this season. So I start with a vague protest until my mind kicks in something more concrete. "It's a time commitment, and there's a lot on the line. The coaches are really riding us, and I mean Gerrard, too." Ah, here we go. My mind clicks in with a solution. Thanks, brain. "Anyway, aren't you the one who told me I need to focus on football? We have a chance to win the division, to go to the playoffs here."

He looks steadily at me. For a moment I'm convinced he can see through me, because he always does. But I'm not lying, just not giving him the number one reason. Focusing on football is a totally valid reason. "It wouldn't take that long," he says. "And..."

He's searching my eyes, and he looks nervous, uncertain. I don't know what's going on. I just hold my pose, and when he doesn't say anything, I say, "And?"

"It'd be something really good you could do."

"I can do it after the season," I say.

He nods, but his ears are a little askew, not up, and his eyes aren't completely on mine. So if he accepts this, I'm going to have to do something to make him happy after. Like an unspoken "thanks for dropping it."

But we're not quite there yet. "It's just that..." He hesitates. "Then I wouldn't be able to be involved."

"Why can't I do it in Yerba? Your group has offices there, right?" And, bonus, Brian wouldn't be around for it.

"Fine." He picks up the controller and quits the game. "We can talk about it later, I guess."

I look at the screen. I hadn't been ready to quit; I wanted to keep playing. But he doesn't, so I just shrug and get up. "Want to put in a movie?"

"You need to go to bed in an hour anyway."

I reach down a paw. "I could go to bed now."

He looks at me a moment and then takes my paw and stands. His tail swishes behind him. "If you really want to."

"Well," I say, "Strike says I shouldn't have sex the night before a game. But you know what?"

The faint trace of a smile lingers over his lips. "What?"

I bring my lips to his ears and slide my paws down his back. "Fuck him," I whisper.

He shivers. His body relaxes and he wraps his arms around me and his scent fills my nose as I bury it in the fur between his ears. And he murmurs into my throat, "No. Fuck me."

So we go to the bedroom, and I do just that. But there's something a little off about it. Even as I'm moving inside him, lying on my back thrusting up with my paws on his hips, I feel like he's distant. He's smiling down at me, and he's certainly erect and enjoying himself, but his body doesn't vibrate with that energy and excitement I've come to expect from him. Beyond a certain point, I don't notice; my hips arch and I push him down onto me, straining to get as far in as I can, and my body shakes and then shudders as I empty myself deep inside him, mouth open in gasping growls. A couple moments later, his back curves and his tail shivers, his muzzle hangs open, and he makes strained squeaking noises as his cock jerks in my paw and spurts warmth over my fingers. And then we just lie there, panting, and he collapses on top of me.

I want to ask if he's still thinking about the commercial, I want to clear things up and figure it out, but we're exhausted and happy now, so I just wrap my arms around him and hold him. We'll talk about it later. I'm sure we can work it out. For now I need to get my rest and be ready for the game.

Chapter 18: Pre-Fight (Lee)

Sunday morning, I'm on a bus on my way to the game when Brian calls. My first reaction is apprehension, that tightening in my gut that accompanied that number coming up on my phone in the past, along with a wash of minor disgust. Not fair, I tell myself. Sure, Brian did some crappy things, but the important thing is that he's helping me out now. With that in mind, I pick up.

"Sorry to interrupt on your way to the game," he says.

"Aren't you going?"

"Sadly, with the success of the team, tickets have gotten more exclusive. And I didn't get invited by anyone with connections to the players."

The bus pulls up at our stop and two dozen people in Firebirds gear lurch toward the door. "Hang on," I say, jostled by the crowd as we all hurry off, tails tucked around our bodies so they don't get caught—still, I accidentally step on the tail of the lion in front of me and say a quick sorry, and he says no problem, the way you do. Tails get stepped on in crowds.

"We're only just talking civilly again," I say as I step out into the brisk— oh, who am I kidding, it's warm—Sunday afternoon air. Green Christmas garlands wrapped around the lightposts along this street look out of place, even hung with red-and-gold Firebirds ornaments. Chevali around me bustles with excitement over the game, crowds in glowing red and gold. It still feels weird to me to be going to football when it's warm, to be smelling desert and dust behind the tens of thousands of people flooding into the stadium. It feels even weirder to see so many people enthusiastic about the Firebirds, to hear "win the division" and "playoffs" and "championship" in snatches of just about every conversation my ears pick up, but that gives my step a bounce. My tiger is part of the reason for that, and catching sight of a #57 jersey in the crowd, even just the one, makes my tail wag, despite the danger of it getting snagged.

"For which I am grateful," Brian says as I fish in my pocket for the ticket. "I know I haven't always behaved the best in the past."

"Are you calling from outside a church?" I ask.

"This isn't a confession, and I'm not asking for penance." There's a little of that familiar edge. "I talked to Marilee and Paula yesterday. Marilee's the Communications Director and Paula's the regional office head. They both love the idea of having a PSA starring Miski."

I stop about fifty feet from the entrance, in line behind two white-tailed deer, one with a Firebirds jacket and the other with a #14—Aston's jersey—that's clearly too big for her. Maybe she gets to wear it while her husband's antlers are in. "Yeah," I say, and find the guy wearing the #57 jersey again, a big stallion not too far from me. He's gesturing to his friend, who's wearing Gerrard's #55 "Thing is, we can't do that during the season."

"Why not? He filmed that terrible Ultimate Fit commercial."

"It wasn't that bad."

"Wiley."

I sigh, and edge forward with the line. "Okay, it was pretty bad. But he looked good in it."

"The point is, if he can film that, he can film this."

The ears of the couple in front of me flick back. I lower my voice and face away from them, trusting to the noise of the crowd to hide my words. "They're in the playoff hunt now. He's paranoid about taking time off."

"It won't be that much time."

"I know. I tried to talk to him…"

I shut up, but Brian picks up on it. "Oh, already. I see. So it's not that you're giving up without even trying. It's that you're giving up after trying once."

"I'm not 'giving up,'" I snap.

"All right, all right." He stays calm. "The important thing is we both agree something needs to get filmed, right? So if he can't take the time to do it himself, then maybe we can, you know, just film a spot with a picture of him. Maybe a voiceover, if he can take the time to record that."

I've seen commercials like that. The static picture, the voice behind it. I haven't seen any in about fifteen years, probably, and even then I thought, *how do I know that's really the guy? How do I know someone didn't just take his picture and slap it up there? I don't know what his voice sounds like.* "Or we could wait until after the season's over. That'd be good, too."

"Depends. You wanted to hit college kids, right? College players? Guess when they're watching the most TV."

I sigh. The line edges forward another few steps. "Playoffs. Championship."

"Bingo. Look, Tip, I sympathize, I do. Trust me. You know I know football. Not as well as you, but I know how it goes with those players. Continuity, superstition, belief, whatever you want to call it. If they believe they're going to fail, then they will."

"Right." The deer in front of me are back to ignoring me, now exchanging friendly jabs with a guy in a Freestone jersey.

"So if there's any way you can talk him into this. It's just a day. Don't they get a day off practice?"

I lower my voice again. "They're supposed to be in film on the days off. Unless they win."

"Well, there you go. They've got Kerina next week. They could win that with ten guys on the field on every play. He'll have off a week from Monday. We could get a script written, book some studio time quickly, get it done in one day."

I'm pretty close to the turnstiles where they're checking tickets, just five people back. "But the following week, they've got Hellentown. He needs to be completely focused for that."

Brian's silent. "Tip," he says finally, "there's never gonna be a good time during the season. But look, I get you. You're going to Kerina with him, aren't you?"

"I'm…I don't know. Probably. Well, not with, but…" I'm trying to be vague so the people listening don't get what I'm talking about. "Might fly in Friday or Saturday. But I can't talk to him then. He's going to be all focused, and…"

He laughs. "The Knights stink. I'm pretty sure you don't have to worry about that. But that's not what I meant. I was just wondering if you would want to have dinner one night if he's not around."

I think back to the dinners we had in college, great times talking politics and relationships and classwork. And football, of course. But it's Brian, who basically told me he'd lay off Dev if I jerked him off, the last time I visited him. "How about lunch?"

"We can start with lunch and work up to dinner, sure, Tip." He sounds amused. "Let me know what day works."

I'm going to have to tell Dev about this. "All right. I'm at the stadium now."

"Enjoy the game," he says.

My ticket gets me through the turnstiles and I'm alone in the 68,000-person stadium, one fox navigating a crowd. Brian and I used to go to football games together in college, or sit in the bar when we didn't feel like fighting the crowds, watching the people turn their heads with their noses up and the knowing expression on their faces when they saw us, the skunk and fox. Here in Chevali, I'm on my own, but at least the dry air doesn't carry scent as well, and I don't see any wrinkled noses.

Like when Father took me to Dragons games up in Hilltown, though there it was cold as well as dry, and the long coats we wore muffled our scents as well as our movement. Mother never came along with us to those games, and maybe that was the start of things unraveling. But no, thousands of families across the country exist in happiness with one parent loving sports and the other not.

I grab a hot dog for lunch at one of the stands, listening to the pre-game buzz around me, walking through past corridors in my mind. My father would not let me have hot dogs the first time we went to a game. Brian sneered whenever I got one, but it was comradely sneering because he always got the terrible pizza they served, which I could sneer right back at. And Dev, Dev loves hot dogs.

My seat is way up in the second deck of the stadium. Dev offered me a seat with the players' wives, but at home those all get snapped up quickly, and anyway, I'm not quite ready for them yet. I know Gena, Fisher's wife, and have met Gerrard's wife Angela, but I don't know if I know them well enough to sit with them for three hours.

It worked out okay anyway. I think I'm fine sitting by myself today. I keep thinking about what Brian said, and it makes a lot of sense, and then I think about what Dev said, and that makes a lot of sense too, and my head goes round and round and I don't know that there's an easy answer to it.

There should be, my mind tells me. I should side with Dev, no questions asked. We're living together, we're committed. But the knowledge that I'm going off to Yerba in a month and a half, his obstinacy in refusing to engage me at all…the fact that he doesn't really get what Vince King means to me…I know it's just stuff we can work out. I know in the grand scheme of things, what matters is our commitment to each other, and I'm pretty sure that hasn't wavered.

But it still bothers me enough that I call Father, with the game clock ticking down five minutes until kickoff. "I'm at the game," I say when he picks up, to explain the crowd noise.

"Where? I'm watching at the bar with Kev and Dave from work."

"Two-twenty, a third of the way up." I wave.

"I'll keep an eye out." He chuckles. "Is Dev ready?"

"I think so." I pause. "I wanted to ask you something. How much did you and Mother disagree, or argue about things?"

The crowd around me roars as the Firebirds jog out onto the field. I stick a finger in the other ear and yell, "I didn't catch that!"

"I didn't say anything," he says, faint over the people screaming next to me. "Do you really want to have this conversation now?"

"I was just wondering."

"We argued about as much as any couple argues." I think that's what he says, as best I can make it out. "We got along well until the last couple years, when we just didn't have much to talk about."

They had something to talk about: me. Maybe they had too much to talk about and that's why they stopped talking. "Okay," I say. "Thanks."

"Get to your game. I'll talk to you later."

"Bye!" I yell, and put the phone away.

To my left is a wolf in a Firebirds t-shirt. To my right is a family of ringtails bedecked in red and gold. It would be nice to have someone I know to talk to, but I have a feeling I'll be doing enough talking over the next week. Right now I just want to watch the game and cheer.

Chapter 19: Creating Separation (Dev)

Freestone isn't a bad team. They finished 8-8 last year and they've already got eight wins this year, which is good enough to lead the East. We're favored to win by three, if you look at the gambling line, but I've learned not to take any game for granted, especially after last week. The coaches have been drilling that into us over and over again, and Coach Samuelson says it one last time as we're all sitting in the locker room just before game time. "You might think you deserve to win this game," he says. "Well, that and four bucks will get you a beer at Mickey's. You need to prove you deserve it, and that means you need to go out and earn it. Play sloppy like we did last week and we'll lose another game like we did last week." He glares around the room, challenging us. "I know you're not going to play sloppy. Play the way I know you can play. Take care of business. Chevali hasn't had a double-digit win team in a couple decades. You guys are going to be the first, and it's going to be this week. So get out there and bring that tenth win home, and then we'll go out and get this city its first division title. 'Firebirds' on three—one, two—"

"Firebirds!" We scream it until the room echoes. In that moment, all of us are one, moving with the same energy, the same confidence. Coach believes in us and we will not let him down, not at home, not this week. I grab my helmet and then realize that the last echo was a different voice, not a reflection of ours, coming in late with his own "Firebirds!" cheer. I turn. The rest of the defense is pushing past me, until some people turn with me, and then everyone just kind of stops. The only movement is back at the entrance to the locker room, and that's where my eyes, along with everyone else's, are drawn.

Strike's standing there, leaning against the door in just his uniform pants. His chest has been bleached white, the better to show off the stylized firebird design across both pecs, its wings reaching up to his shoulders. It looks like something I might've seen on one of the old vans my dad occasionally got in his shop, complete with the flames running down his arms.

None of us can say anything for a good ten seconds. I actually grab my cell phone, thinking I need to get a picture of this. Then Coach Samuelson says, "Everyone's required to be in the locker room for the pre-game meeting."

"Sorry I missed it." Now Strike walks into the room, heading for his locker, keeping eye contact with Coach. At least he's that respectful. "I was doing my meditation."

"Don't miss next time. Now get out there." He says this last to all of us, and it snaps us out of our mesmerized state. I shake my head, toss my phone back in my locker, and trot out to the tunnel.

Freestone comes out on the field in their white road uniforms with green helmets and green trim. Gerrard gathers me and Carson together and reminds us of what we have to take care of—watch their screen passes and tight ends, which is more Carson's responsibility than mine, but I have to cover where he's not.

We join the rest of the defense, huddle up, and under Gerrard's direction, break on "Defense!" We won the toss and opted to defer, so Freestone gets the ball first and we have to run out and defend first thing.

They do try a run, which I help stop, and then a short pass to the tight end, which Carson takes down just short of the first down. They punt to us, and we trot back to the sidelines with at least a better feeling than we had after the Yerba game. Sometimes you just need the reassurance that yes, you can do this job.

There's a little buzz in the stadium as our offense takes the field. The firebird on Strike's chest is covered by his uniform, of course, the big white "11" outlined in gold against the red, but the flames down his arms are visible. I don't know how obvious it is to everyone else, but just watching him next to Zaïd, it's immediately apparent to me how much bigger and bulkier he is. He's as heavy as I am, though four inches taller, and Zaïd, one of the taller guys on the team, looks average next to him. No wonder Ty was grumpy.

The crowd settles down as the offense lines up at our 25 in a standard running formation. Aston fakes the handoff to the running back, gets good protection as he drops back three-four-five-six-seven steps. His muzzle's fixed toward the left sideline, all the way through his steps, as he cocks his arm back and heaves the ball to the left side.

The buzz grows again around us. Scanning the field, we see Strike already, somehow, at the Freestone 40, the grass blazing under his feet. He's two yards ahead of the hapless Freestone cornerback, and even though there's a safety racing to catch up, neither of them has a chance. The ball is underthrown, but Strike reaches up with those flaming arms and plucks it out of the air, then somehow cuts hard to his right without breaking stride and then…

We're all cheering, yelling, jumping up and down, and the crowd is too. And then there's a pause, just a half-second pause, because what Strike does next is insane. It looked like he'd been running all out, leaving the cornerback five yards off his tail. But when he catches the ball, he extends those legs and lowers his head and he is gone. He's got some other gear, and so do we and the crowd, our cheering reaching new heights. By the time Strike crosses the goal line, the cornerback who'd been chasing him is barely across the twenty.

"Holy shit," Gerrard says.

"You see it on TV," Pace says, shaking his head. "But…"

I elbow the jaguar. "Glad the Port City QB never got him the ball with room like that?"

"Well…" Vonni comes up behind us. "We jammed him at the line more. Got him off his routes. Those Freestone corners thought it was a run and just let him get behind them."

"'Let' him." Pace shakes his head. "Yeah, like there was gonna be anything they could do there."

I look up into the stands, to where Lee is sitting, and I grin. I don't know if he can see me or if he's even looking, but I hope he's feeling the same swagger for this team that I am.

Strike comes back to the sidelines, still holding the football. He has his paw up, high-fiving anyone who will raise their paw, and considering the number of people who were grumbling about him just twenty-four hours ago, there are a lot of them. He catches my eye, so I put my paw up too. Hell, the guy just put us up 7-0 after fifteen seconds of game time. It's not just obligation that raises my paw and smacks it against his.

Vonni steps back from high-fiving Strike and shakes a paw at the cornerback, number 22, trudging to the opposite sideline. The curl of that fox's long red tail around his leg shows how he feels at getting beaten on the first play of the game, as opposed to Vonni's jaunty arch. "Twenty-two shoulda bumped him."

"No species loyalty," I tease him, as the extra point sails through the uprights.

The fox grins at me. "Goodie and I are friends. He'd say the same if I got beat. Anyway, he knows it. Just look at him."

Charm kicks off to the Fighters, who try to return the ball and get all of three yards. Gerrard fits his helmet over his muzzle. "Back to work," he says, and Vonni, Pace, and I follow the defense back out to the field.

That first score puts Freestone into a little bit of a panic. Even when they run, you can feel their desperation, and when they do things like fight too hard for one more yard, or tense up at the line of scrimmage, those things eventually result in mistakes. On our side, we only screw up once, and it doesn't come until late in the fourth quarter.

We're up 13-3 and the game is almost over. Gerrard and I misread the offense and both hang down to cover the screen pass, but their QB fakes it beautifully and freezes us, lobbing it to their number one wideout. We can't do anything but turn and watch it fly right into his paws, and then we run down, because you never know, but Vonni tackles him at the nine yard line. Once they're there, they run it on four straight plays, converting on fourth and two to score the touchdown. But that's left only two minutes and four seconds on the clock.

"Don't feel bad," Gerrard tells me as we head back to the sidelines. "They ran that really well."

"One of us should've picked it up." It's the first time I think I've had the confidence to suggest that Gerrard might've screwed up, too. In the back of my head, I realize it in time to modify the statement, but instead I just wait and see what he'll say.

He nods, stopping on the sidelines with me and looking out at the field. "Just gotta put it behind you," he says. "Can't let it affect the next play. If you're always looking back at your mistakes, you can't look forward at the game."

My mind skitters elsewhere for a moment. "What if you keep making the same mistakes?"

He looks at me. "You're not. I told you, don't worry about it. They ran a good play and we bit on it. It's on film now. We learn from it and go forward."

Go forward, always forward. Good philosophy for football. Not sure about anything else. Like, I know I've done some dumb stuff on the field. I learned to stop doing it, and those mistakes, they're gone. When the game's over, the plays are saved on film. You get to see all the things you did wrong over and over again, but the score is final, the stats are inked, the game is done. Every game, you start over from 15:00 in the first quarter.

Oh, sure, your history matters. Teams look at things you did wrong and they play to those weaknesses, the way we know Freestone likes to run the screen pass but their tight end sometimes misses his blocks; the way we know their cornerbacks are sometimes tentative on running plays. Even so, it's only if you keep making the same mistakes that those things hurt you. And then it's your own damn fault, and you deserve to lose your job. Like Corey "Killer" Mitchell, letting his emotion and ego get in the way of his play. Strike might be an ass, but he doesn't bring it onto the field. It's the one thing we had drilled into our heads, getting ready to face Port City: he'll do whatever bizarre thing will get him attention off the field, but he knows that all of that rides on his success on the field.

At Port City, though, he didn't look anything like this. This is him showing off for a new team, keeping a smile on his muzzle even when the team went an entire series without throwing to him. And even though he was pretty quiet for the middle part of the game, compiling over a hundred yards without any other huge plays, he shows up big again at the end. Freestone tries an onside kick and Ty, out there with the chase team, swipes the ball away from a green-and-white clad tiger to give possession back to our offense. With two minutes to go and Freestone out of timeouts, we just need one first down, and it's Strike who gets it for us. Aston finds him on a short slant over the middle and he dodges one, two, three tacklers, zigging and zagging up twenty yards nearly to midfield, where he goes down under their safety, clinging to the ball with both paws.

Aston kneels three times, and the clock winds down to 00:00, and this game, too, is committed to film and paper, all our plays fixed and the slate wiped clean. We trot out to congratulate the Freestone guys and shake paws. Two of them, a jaguar and a coyote, pass me by with narrowed eyes, but they don't say anything, so if it's more than just frustration at losing, I can't tell. Most of the other guys are cordial, as much as a losing team ever is.

Coach gives the game ball to Strike, predictably—he scored the only touchdown—though he stresses again that this was a real team effort. Strike gets patted on the back, jostled around, and says, "I'm just glad to be in a place with a real winning mindset. That touchdown is just the first of many. We're going all the way to the championship."

"Don't mind him so much if he can do that once a game," Carson mutters to me as we dress.

Gerrard, between the two of us, nods. "He keeps his mind on the game during the game, at least."

"Glad he's on our team," I say. "Might've been a smart move."

"If we can keep our focus on defense, then he gives us a real chance to break open games on offense," Gerrard says. "Kerina, next week—they have no secondary. If he plays like this, he'll get a couple more scores and some confidence for the Hellentown game. That's where we'll really need him."

We watch the division race to see if Hellentown falters, but they get a close win over Gateway, keeping pace with us. Both of us play weak division opponents next week, so it's looking more and more like our game against them on the last day of the season will be where the division is won or lost.

The good news is that there's a pretty good chance that even 11-5 will be enough to get us into the playoffs. It's not assured, but the way the rest of the field sits, we feel like one more win will do it. A lot of the other playoff hopefuls right now are at 8-6, so if we lose two and some other team wins two, it gets complicated with tiebreakers. One win will keep us from having to think about that. Two wins will give us a division title and a whole week off to recover and rest up as one of the top two seeds in the playoffs.

But to get there, we need to take care of Kerina. Gerrard makes sure we don't forget that at our celebratory dinner after the game. We all laugh at him—Kerina's two and twelve—but he reminds us that one of those two wins came against Hellentown.

That's a week away, though, and even the prospect of losing to a terrible team doesn't dampen our excitement at our performance and at having Strike on the team. My ribs ache again and my toe is bothering me, but we're all at about eighty percent by this point in the season. If you're healthy enough to walk out of the game with only five or ten minutes in the trainers' room, you count yourself lucky and you get ready for the next game.

Lee's worried about my injuries, when I get home, but I tell him I'm fine after this game. "Fine," in this case, meaning that my ribs only hurt if I try to lift something heavy (like a fox), and my toe doesn't hurt if I walk on my heel, and my legs will be okay after a day off. He gives me a little shit about that one play we screwed up, and I tell him Gerrard and I both screwed it up. He says that's true, but Gerrard is his wife's responsibility, and I think about the coyote girl in Yerba and I don't say anything.

We talk a bit during dinner about Strike and other news around the league, but he doesn't really talk to me about his day until we're on the couch after dinner. The night game wraps up and I pull up UFL 2009 because I've already seen today's highlights about ten times, in the clubhouse and again during the game we just watched. We pick teams, and he's quiet while that happens and the game starts. Then he says he talked to Brian again.

I feel the annoyance register on my muzzle, and I'm sure he sees it, because he holds his paws up. "Just on the phone. They thought of a way they could film some spots on your day off. Monday, after a win."

"Tomorrow?" I growl. I run a play and his defense stuffs it. I already know how this argument ends: with me giving in to whatever he wants. I don't want to film a commercial, parade around like, *hey, it's okay to be gay!* Get the locker room snickering, get Gerrard telling me I obviously have better things to worry about than football. The guys are cool with me being gay because I don't try to make a big deal or set myself apart. Look at Strike: he does everything he can to be different, and half the team hates him. But Lee wants me to do this, and historically that means it's going to happen, and I'm already resenting him for it.

"Next week. Dev, this could really help a lot of people. Guys who maybe felt like you did in college. Scared, alone…"

"I was never scared," I growl. "And I was never alone. I had you."

"Not everyone can have a fox." He has to get that little bit of preening in. And of course, on the next play his defense stops me again.

"If I didn't have you," I point out, "I wouldn't have been scared or confused or anything. Not that I was."

He sighs. "There are some guys who realize what they are and don't have anyone to turn to."

"Like that Vince King, that bear."

He watches me as though I'm defusing a bomb. Or as though he is. "Yeah."

"Why does he mean that much to you?" He's quiet, and I realize right away how that sounded. "I don't mean he shouldn't, I mean, I really don't understand. Guys kill themselves all the time. I know, he wrote a letter, but it's not your fault, not at all. Is it the thing with your mom?"

His ears flatten. "Maybe it is. I don't know. I just feel…don't you feel like you coulda been him? I mean…" He chooses his defense. We run the play and watch as I get a first down. "What if you'd fucked me and then couldn't find me again? Or if you'd come by and I told you to get lost or I'd call the police? What if you ended up going around with this thing inside you, that you'd fucked a guy and liked it, and you didn't have anyone to talk to? What if we hadn't fallen in love?"

"Is that it?" I search his eyes. "Is it because you're feeling guilty about what you did to me all those years ago? You think I might've ended up like Vince King if you weren't careful?"

He slumps back. "No," he says. "But…I used to help people. Now I just help…"

"Me. And the Dragons, and, soon, the Whalers."

"You barely need my help any more. The Dragons, the Whalers, they can hire whoever they want." He opens his mouth to say something else, looks at me, and then closes it again.

"I'm okay with you doing all this stuff," I say, choosing my next play. He's already got his defense set. "But I really need to focus on football."

He looks annoyed, but those were his words, so he can't be that angry at me. "This is just one day."

I see the slight flick of his ears when he says that. I know my fox. "Just one day…during the week before the biggest game of the year."

"It'd be a day off anyway."

"You know Gerrard. You think we won't be practicing on Monday?"

"Right," he says. "I guess that is more important than the lives of a few gay kids. Who probably wouldn't even make it as football players."

The game beeps for a delay of game penalty because I didn't pick a play in time. I drop the controller. "God dammit, doc, you know I want to help those kids, I do. Why the fuck does it have to be next week?"

He curls his tail around himself. "Because interest in football drops. If you don't win the championship, and more, if you don't distinguish yourself so much that you're a national celebrity—"

"I thought I was. First gay player, hello."

"First one out." He looks steadily at me. "And yeah, you are. But already people are forgetting about that story. That's good!" He lifts a paw. "Really good. But the impact is just better while everyone's excited about football."

"Is that what Brian says?" I stare at the screen, where it takes me a moment to register that Lee has put the game on pause. "What if I'm so distracted by doing all this activist stuff that I don't excel, that I ruin my career?"

"Is that what you're worried about? Or are you just being stubborn because it's Brian?"

I cross my arms. "After that Ultimate Fit commercial, I almost fucked up my toe."

"Equality Now isn't going to make you run across an asphalt parking lot." He puts down his controller. "Look, if you don't want to do it, then..."

"I didn't say I don't *want* to. I just don't want to fuck up the team. Hell, that asshole cheetah is already doing a bang-up job of that. Gerrard would skin me if I made anything worse. And..." I hesitate. I didn't really tell him about the blow-up over the nightclub, because there wasn't time and he was all caught up with his family issue that, to be fair, was a little more serious. But now it feels harder to mention. And Colin hating me isn't a big division in the team. Just him and a couple other religious guys.

"If you think it'll fuck up the team," he says, "then just forget it."

"I just don't want to take the chance." I'm not quite sure what's happened. Did I win this argument? Is he backing down?

"If you think it'll fuck up the team, then it will." He shrugs. "Let's finish the game."

We finish the game. I win by two touchdowns, which makes me think he's stopped trying, or else he's thinking about something else and not focusing on the game. *See?* I want to say. *See what happens when you're distracted?*

"Good game," he says, and we turn the console off and get ready for bed. I'm trying to figure out some way I can take his mind off the Equality Now thing, not only now, but for the next month or so, but I have no good ideas.

Well, at least for tonight, I have one, but when I slide in next to him, and he gives me a kiss, he doesn't push for more. Hesitant, I don't either. Does he not want to have sex? I'm tired and actually not all that upset by the prospect.

When I don't make a move either, he turns over so he can press his back and rear against me. The annoyance of the PSA discussion fades, and as I drape an arm over his chest, part of me does wake up, wanting to thrust up against him and start something. But I am tired, and he'll still be there in the morning.

Monday dawns with a cloudy sky and threats of drizzles, so there's no real hurry to get out of bed. Overnight, my brain has come up with a possible solution to this PSA thing, so I feel better, and he doesn't object when I roll him on his stomach and work myself under his tail.

"Good morning to you, too," he pants as we both squirm and thrust against each other, but I'm close already, too far gone to answer. Soon enough, he's made a mess of the sheets, and then I've got my arms wrapped around him and my muzzle pressed against his neck, feeling his warmth and inhaling his scent. Beneath me, his warm, taut body relaxes, his tail twitching up between my stomach and his back. I'm reminded of how fragile he is, and yet how strong; he doesn't complain at my two hundred pounds flattening him against the mattress.

We shower, a habit that is becoming nicely routine, and then he takes the sheets down to the basement to wash them. I take the opportunity to call up Vince, the press liaison for the Firebirds.

"I'm kinda glad I don't have more to do with you now," is the first thing he says.

"Huh?"

"Mostly because that fucking cheetah has me runnin' around eight ways from Tuesday. But also because it means that it ain't a big deal." He's kind of like Ogleby, but coherent. Weasel, not ferret.

"I'm not a big deal?"

"You were a big deal. It blew over. People are used to it. Gay player, whatever."

I scratch the side of my muzzle. "So why hasn't someone else come out?"

"Someone will. Give it time." He pauses. "Hope to God it ain't another Firebird."

That'd be kind of cool, actually. But I feel enough support from the team that I'm not aching for it the way I used to. And this is the perfect opening for my idea, anyway. "Just in case…I was wondering, do we have a specific guy who's supposed to go out and build up support for the team in the gay community?"

"Community liaison? We've got Chuck, but…" Vince snorts. "Yeah, he's not gonna help with the gays. Why, you think he should?" His voice gets a little higher. "I can't do it, I'm workin' fourteen hours a day just keepin' a rein on that fucking cheetah."

"No, no. I have a friend…" I pause, then just go on. "A friend who's interested in doing that. Maybe."

"I don't think Corky's hiring. He just spent an assload of money."

"On the fucking cheetah."

"You know he had a reality show call and ask if he wanted them to follow the team around during the playoffs? We ain't even made the goddamn playoffs yet." He coughs. "Sorry, I'm sure he's a great guy and all, and man, he looked good yesterday, but he's a fucking pain in the ass. Anyway, I dunno, it's an idea, but look, level with me. Is your 'friend' really interested in doin' this? Or are you just trying to land him a job?"

"No, no, he's really interested! Just for, like, the rest of the season and playoffs."

"Okay. I'll talk to Corky, see if maybe we can take someone on for a couple months. Trial basis, see how it goes."

"Cool. He's done that before."

"Oh? Where?"

I'm not sure how much I should tell him, now, but I've gone too far to not tell him the whole truth, so I just let it out. "He used to work as a scout for the Dragons, but they started him as a free intern."

Vince doesn't respond right away. Then he says, "Oh, it's Lee?"

It's my turn to be silent, as shock paralyzes my brain. Finally, I scrape words together. "You—you know Lee?"

"Well, I know of him." He laughs. "Miski, I read every fuckin' word written about our team. Have to. It's my job. If they fuck somethin' up I gotta go back and deal with it. Yeah, so, your boyfriend. You sure this isn't just to get him a job?"

"Well…"

"Because that's cool. Just not real possible right now."

I hear the creak of the elevator. "He's trying to work with some local group, Equality Now—"

"Jesus."

"They want me to do a commercial, but they want it during the season—"

"Yeah, I know, they started buggin' me Friday. Also your agent did. So what, you want to get him a job doing that with the team?"

I shift the phone. The elevator stopped, but Lee's taking a long time. He should be up any minute now. "Yeah, but I don't want him to know it came from me. I figure if he's working with the team, he'll have to do what you guys say and you guys won't let me get too distracted from football."

"Got it. Okay." After a pause, there's a beep. "Set myself a reminder. I'll call Corky today, see what we can put together. I'll keep your name out of it."

"Thanks, Vince. I appreciate it."

"Yeah, no problem. Good game yesterday."

That's what we hang up on. Lee walks back in a few minutes later and I manage to look as innocent as he does when he's just pulled some tricky thing. We go to a movie that day and I feel rather proud of myself. Maybe the fox is rubbing off on me.

In other ways, I mean. Maybe if we live together, I'll have to be more like him. I kind of hope that means he might be more like me, too.

Chapter 20: Three Phone Calls (Lee)

I volunteer to do laundry as a way to get a little time to myself, collect my thoughts. Dev's not going to do the commercial. On some level, I always knew that. I can keep after him to try, we can try different approaches, but I would have to be at my most persuasive to get him to do it, and I'm not.

In fact, I didn't even try that hard. I didn't go all out, like Hal told me to. I saw the determination behind his golden eyes and I thought, if I take it to that extreme, then there's only two places it can go: he'll say no and I'll be crushed, or he'll say yes and he'll resent me. So I backed down.

Now I need to think of what to tell Brian, as I take our mingled clothes and toss them into the washer in the basement. He's invested in this campaign as much as I am, and having gotten him on my side, I can't just let him go.

But if I can get some info on Families United, maybe go back to them with a definite connection to the suicide…that could be something that could get out to the news. It might not help college students feel better about themselves (I feel a pang at that), but at least it could hamper some people from making them feel worse.

There are probably a lot of other places I could go to get that information. But there's only one person who has the answers to that question, plus a bunch of other ones I have. So I call Mother.

This time, she answers. And when I say hello, she says, "Wiley, I'm trying to get the house ready for Christmas. I am not in the mood to have this conversation."

"What conversation?" I ask.

"About Families." Edgy anxiety pervades her tone.

"What about just one family?"

Anxiety gives way to resignation. "Of course you can ask me questions if you're confused about the divorce. Have you talked to your father?"

"Yes. But I want to understand it from your side."

"Well, I appreciate that." She takes a breath. "After you left for college, I realized that I had created a lot of my life around being a mother, and that was no longer…my primary role in life. Your father has his work, and he…he had a closer relationship with you. So I went looking for myself somewhere else."

She waits for me to talk, but I don't. "And I found a friend of my own. She…she really helped me. You're probably too young to know what it's like to meet someone who really listens to you, who shows you your life in a different way."

"No, I'm not," I say.

"Well," she says, and then stops as she gets what I mean. "I am sorry that path took me away from your father, but he had followed his own path, and our paths didn't go the same direction." She coughs. "That's not very eloquent."

"I get what you mean," I say. "I guess me being gay kind of influenced where your path went, and the people you met."

"*You* wouldn't listen to my concerns," she says, sharper. "Celia does."

"I'm sure she tells you just what you want to hear." I lean on the washer, which is vibrating with the wash cycle.

"You could stand to listen a little better, Wiley. All I wanted was to help you."

"By changing me into what you wanted me to be."

"By making you happier!"

I curl my tail around my legs. "I *was* happy. You're the one who wasn't."

"Is this why you called?"

"No," I say, because I can't say that I don't know. "I called to find out if you're going to be sending anyone over to talk to me."

"Sending…who?"

"I don't know. Don't your friends have a kind of 'gay hit squad' they send to troubled families to tell the poor gay cubs how worthless they are?"

Shit. That's not how I'd intended to ask that question. She takes it predictably badly. "As long as you keep viewing us as enemies, you'll never get better."

"I am getting better!" I yell just as an old possum comes into the room with her laundry basket and heads for one of the other machines. She frowns at me. I resist the urge to give her the finger.

"You are just getting more lost," Mother says.

"Only to you," I say coldly, and snap the phone shut.

Jesus Fox. That probably could have gone worse, but I can't quite imagine how. I stalk out of the laundry room under the old possum's sour gaze and glare at the elevator as though it's the one responsible for my mood. I'd better take the stairs.

I stomp up the first two flights before I settle down. That attitude, that there's something wrong with me, something that needs fixing, that's what I can't stand. That's what I want to fight against, eradicate wherever I can. Finding it this close, inside my family, is like finding a nest of bees in your bedroom wall.

My fist smacks the big number 4 in the stairwell. I'm shaking when I stop. I knew it was there, of course, but I'd never faced it head on. I knew I'd neglected the relationship with Mother, and I knew her views on me being gay, but it was all abstract. We'd been silent toward each other, and she'd never outright told me she thought I was going to Hell, or needed to be fixed somehow.

Mentioning Christmas just made it worse. I can't help but picture the Christmas decorations in the house, and it makes me want to decorate Dev's apartment. Then I picture that and I don't want to decorate the apartment at all, because I don't want to admit that I miss it. I'll probably end up doing nothing, because that's easiest.

The crazy part is that I don't really want to go home. I haven't in a long time. I just always thought I *could*.

As I walk past the fifth floor, I try my best to put it all out of my head, because I'm starting to feel hemmed in. Dev won't let me take away from his football time, not that I want to. Mother's actively working against me. Brian's great to talk to—about one subject. I have to watch what I say otherwise, with him. I only really have Father and Hal to talk to, and both of them have their own lives and problems. Maybe Father will want to come down for Christmas.

I turn that thought over in my head. Do I want his company, or do I just want to show Mother that I win, that Father gets the bigger half of the wishbone in this break? No, I think, I really would like Father to be here. Plus, I'm worried about him. I'm not sure he has as much in his life as Mother thinks. Unless she was talking about him having me.

At the sixth floor, I take a breath before I open the door. I can't let this mess up my day with Dev. It's his reward for winning, this day off. I'm going to make sure he enjoys it.

•

We go out to a nice lunch, wander through an upscale shopping mall where I try to get him some nice clothes but end up finding more things for myself, and avoid the Christmas decorations. Dev doesn't say anything about them either; I remember that last year he was on the road for Christmas, so I guess he didn't see the point in decorating his place. Also he didn't have anyone to spend it with. I saw him the following weekend, and we had our Christmas sex then.

Late afternoon, with a couple hours to kill until dinner, he wants to see the latest big-budget explosions movie. We sit there and hold paws in the dark, and that plus the explosions works wonders to completely distract me from the morning's conversation, so much so that on our way out of the movie, I talk about the two leads, a wolf couple who rediscover their dissolving romance when horrible furless aliens attack the world. "I'd do Brian Barker," I say. "Like whoa."

"I liked them both," Dev says.

I grin and elbow him. "You don't have to say you liked either of 'em."

"I did, though." He shrugs. "I'd do either one."

"I guess the girl, whatever her name was, she was pretty cute too. I could see that." I flick my ears.

He grins and lowers his voice. "I don't think she has as nice a cock as the guy. Probably not your type."

"Oh, like she's yours," I shoot back, and he laughs. We walk on a little more, and I rub at my whiskers. "Do you miss it?"

"The movie? Not really. It was a little long."

"No, I mean…girls."

He wraps an arm around me in an affectionate bro-hug, okay in public. "Aw, if I do, I can just get you to put on a dress." We're passing a Mary Taylor store, and he points in the window. "You'd look good in that slinky black thing."

I snort and push him away, with about as much success as I'd have pushing away a brick wall. "I'm serious. Do you miss girls?"

"Nah. You know, it wasn't ever about the body with me. It was more the whole package. I mean, the body's important, but…" He thinks as we walk on, past a family of skunks trying to calm their baby in a stroller. "It's more like, y'know, it's gotta be someone I'm in love with."

"That's sweet." I know he's said that before, but I still like to hear it. "So you really think I'd look good in that dress?"

He looks at it again. "Ah, I was just pointing at it. You'd look good in anything though, so yeah."

"I'd have to have it trimmed to fit my chest. I can't even push it out as much as that mannequin is." The plastic generically feline mannequin has breasts the size of grapefruit, to be fair, and makes Dev squint at it.

"I don't think I'd like you with boobs," he says.

"Thanks," I say. "I've been working on keeping my chest down." But it's kinda nice to hear that he doesn't covet a big chest. I can give him a slim body and I can dress up in a dress, but I draw the line at estrogen injections.

He pokes my side and grins. "I like you in shirts or dresses, and out of 'em, too."

"Same here." I lead us on, out of the mall. "For the record, I'm not interested in getting that for my birthday."

"That's months away," he says. "I'd forget."

"Yeah, but you'd be running frantically through the mall looking for something to get me and you'd see the dress and then you'd remember. So don't get it." I pause. "Unless you really think I would look good in it."

"Come on," he says, laughing, and we head back to the truck.

The evening is good, with a couple UFL 2009 games and some pizza, and we're relaxing in front of the TV. It's easy for him to relax, just stretch out and have nothing to do, but I'm a little twitchy still. The talk with Mother makes me restless, makes my paws curl and twist on empty air, makes me keep shifting in frustration, until Dev clamps an arm around me and tells me to hold still. "I'll fidget if I want," I say, but I limit the fidgeting to my tail.

"If I have to pin you down," he says, and just then my phone rings. I jump, tail bristled out, and grab it. It's Brian, of course, and I still have nothing to tell him. I stand up anyway.

"This'll just take a minute," I tell Dev, and pick up the phone. "What?"

"Goodness, Tip, no need to snap. I'm just calling to see if we have a day for lunch."

"Thursday," I say.

"Yes, I can do Thursday," he says. "I'll see if Paula can make it. Normally she's pretty busy, but she's interested in this campaign too."

"I'd prefer not."

"Really? Why?"

I eye Dev, who's pretending to ignore me even though his ears are pointed squarely at me. "I'll talk to you tomorrow."

"Huh." His voice goes smoother. "Oh, right. It was Miski's day off. Are you guys fucking yet?"

"Keep it classy."

"Ha." He breathes into the phone. "Not yet, I guess. You wouldn't have picked up the phone for me in mid-fuck, would you? But maybe some clothes are off."

"I'll talk to you tomorrow."

"Will do. Give him a suck for me."

I hang up. Dev relaxes as I sit down beside him again. His arm tightens around my chest and his paw rubs slowly over my shirt. "Didn't sound like you were talking to Hal."

I shake my head. I don't want to ruin the mood, but I promised to be honest with him. "Brian," I say. "About the Equality Now stuff."

He tenses, and his voice gets cold. "That skunk," he says.

"He seems sincere," I say. "I mean, he's really into the activist stuff again." Thanks to me. Really?

"Is he still acting?"

"Yes. Playing in Romeo and Juliet. Mercutio."

"Which one is that?" Dev's words inch closer to my ear, a bass rumble that gives me shivers down my back.

"He's Romeo's best friend. You know the line, 'He jests at scars that never felt a wound'?"

"No."

"Romeo says that when Mercutio makes fun of him for being in love." Dev nuzzles my ear, which flicks back reflexively. "So are you Romeo?"

"Only if you're Juliet."

"Doesn't that end with both of them dead?"

"Well, yeah." I squirm back against him. "But they kill themselves for each other."

"I'd rather be, um."

I toss the phone across the couch and slide my paw up his thigh. "How about we just be Dev and Lee?"

His tongue washes up the side of my ear, then slips inside it. "That works," he says softly.

That warm touch sends a shiver through me. My paw moves farther up, finding the warmth at his groin and rubbing it to hardness, which doesn't take long. "Should we move to the bedroom?"

His paw finds the bottom of my t-shirt and slips under it, pressing against my stomach. Fingertips slide through the fur and barely extended claws brush my skin. "Oh, we've done it in the bedroom a lot," he murmurs, warm breath against the soft fur of my ear. "And the couch is pretty comfortable."

I get his pants open just as his paw pushes down inside mine. "It is," I breathe. I'm kind of wondering what's got him so urgently horny, and so aggressive. Is he trying to distract me from Brian's call, or did something I said on the call bother him? Then his paw closes around my hard shaft and I shelve the worry for later.

"Maybe we should keep lube by the couch, too," I murmur.

He laughs. "Go get it," he says, but his paw doesn't leave my cock, stroking warmly up and down, so I don't move. "Go on," he says, still stroking. "You want it, don't you?"

"Urrrh." I free his erection and slide my paw over it, too. "As much as I think you do."

He presses his nose closer. "So go." His paw squeezes.

I'm tempted to just stay here and see if he really will jerk me off all the way if I don't go get lube. But the downside of that is that if I do stay, I don't get him inside me. Of course, then he doesn't get to be inside me, either. I trail my paw up and down his shaft. He's sticky at the tip, aroused. "In a minute," I pant, squirming as he keeps stroking, faster and firmer now.

"In a minute," he pants against my ear, "you're not going to need it anymore."

"Uh-huh." I gasp as his thumb tweaks my tip, and my body shudders. "Saves me a trip, then."

He pauses in his stroking and then pulls me up over his thigh to sit in his lap. "Mmkay, then. If that's how it is." I only have a second to settle myself before he's stroking again, and now I can feel his hardness against my rear, his chest and arms all around me, and he's managed to push my pants down enough to get my cock out into the air. I look down at his paw on it, still moving, at the glistening tip. I rarely get to watch myself being jerked off when I'm not doing it. It's pretty hot.

I squirm and he holds me tightly. I pant and he strokes faster. I press back, whining to let him know I'm close as my back arches and body tenses, and he must know that this is where he needs to stop if he really wants to fuck me tonight, but his paw keeps going, and then it's too late, I'm thrusting up into his paw, spattering sticky warmth over his fingers and my shirt and stomach and gasping out moans at the waves of pleasure.

He purrs against me, holding me when the shudders die down and I sink back into his embrace. "So," I manage to pant, "want me to get that lube now?"

His chest bounces as he chuckles. "Thought you didn't like to be entered when you'd just come."

"I don't."

"What about in that adorable muzzle of yours?"

"Mmm." I let my tongue loll out. "That could work."

And once I've recovered, it works very well indeed, even if I have to wipe myself up with my shirt and he has to keep his paw lifted off the couch all through the blow job. But soon enough, my muzzle is as sticky as his paw, and then we go clean ourselves up and crawl into our nice clean bed.

"See, this way, we don't have to clean the sheets again," he purrs, squeezing me against him in the dark, both of us sleepy.

"There's still the morning," I murmur back, and my tail wags against him because this is what I thought it would be like, living together. The thought passes across my mind that he pretty much did what he wanted to me tonight and I wasn't much good at talking him into anything. But I wanted it, too, so that doesn't count, does it? I squelch those thoughts as best I can.

●

Tuesday while he's out at practice, I go out and do some Christmas shopping. It's the 17th already and though I don't have a lot of people to shop for, I want to get something for my dad, and for Dev, of course. I should pick up a few cards for Salim and Allen, and Hal, and yeah, I guess maybe Brian too. I wonder if there's a card that says, "Merry Christmas. I wish I didn't hate talking to you so much."

Of course, that one would be more appropriate for Mother. I think of her when I'm passing a gift store and spot a family of crystal foxes, really nicely done. It's just the thing she would've liked, and just the thing I might've gotten her a year ago. Gifts like that kept the uneasy peace between us, something I could get out of obligation and that she could pretend represented affection.

For Dev, I get a couple nice pieces of art I think would look good in the apartment, and a sporty blazer. I'd like to get him something for our sex life, but I have no idea where to find a store like that in Chevali. At least the pharmacies sell lube now, even if it's not the flavored/scented kind.

I thought about a new phone, too—there are those brand-new iPhones out that everyone is so hot over. But knowing Dev, I'm not sure whether it's worth investing six hundred dollars in a phone that could end its life the first time we yell at each other, or the first time his family pisses him off in 2009. In the end, I get him a good solid case for his current phone, so the next time he fires it at the wall, maybe it won't shatter.

All the malls here offer bland gift shops, unless I want something that's mainstream-edgy. There's a t-shirt that says, "I'm not gay but my boyfriend is," which I think would be really funny, but he would never wear it. I walk around all morning, grab lunch at a food court, and then find that I'm just looking for gifts rather than thinking about what makes the people special, so I give up and go home to get online.

That turns out to have some better options, and gives me the best gift I found all day. Forester University is selling off pieces of the turf in the stadium as they replace it with the new synthetic turf. The fifty dollars, steep for a four by four inch patch of ground, goes toward the athletic program. Even though Forester turned out a UFL star in Dev, they don't have a lot to cheer about, so I don't mind supporting the program. And Dev will like having a piece of the turf he ran on while I was watching him, back years ago.

While I'm shopping online, I find a local microbrewery that offers a tour package and I buy one of those for Dev as well, setting the date for sometime in late February when he's finally going to be able to relax. Last February he went a little stir-crazy and took a week off to try to learn snowboarding, only his contract doesn't allow him to do anything harder than a cub slope, so he got frustrated and sulked for the last three days. I'll be busy with Yerba—I hope—but maybe I can fly down for at least a day.

By the time Dev gets home, I'm done with the majority of my shopping and back to playing video games. He flops down next to me on the couch and picks up the controller. Tells me a little about Strike and how he's still kind of an asshole, but the team is excited to see what he can do next. There's optimism about the Hellentown game. "Don't look past Kerina," I say.

"Trust me, we're not." He stretches and grimaces. "We're going through our exercises and they're adding new plays. Only new play we need is Aston to Strike, if you ask me." He mimes a long pass and catch, sitting on the sofa.

"Against Kerina, maybe," I say. "Doesn't hurt to get in some new wrinkles you can also use for Hellentown, though. What do the new plays look like?"

"Wish we could just play that game this week, instead of flying out to Kerina and back. There's no upside to this game. We're supposed to win, so if we win, it's like, big deal. If we lose, it's an upset, and they're motivated 'cause it's a division game. Wish Hellentown would lose."

I don't ask him again about the new plays. "Well, you can't control what Hellentown does. You can only control what you do."

My game ends, and he gets in on some two-player action. While we're setting up, he says, "Flight out is at 8 am tomorrow. So I need to get out of here around 6:30."

"Okay. I'll set the alarm."

He leans over to kiss me. "I got you a ticket and a hotel room for Saturday and Sunday night. See you there?"

"I'd fly out Friday," I say, "but I'd be bored in Kerina."

Dev grins and bumps my shoulder. "I'm gonna be bored in Kerina." He starts up our game, and his tail thwaps the couch. "So just get there Saturday and cheer me up."

"That's my job," I say.

I do my job pretty well, to judge by the noises breathed hot between my ears that night. I want to ask him about the beer commercial, but I don't want to spoil the night, because I know I'd just end up asking him why he doesn't want to take time off for gay kids. I promised myself I'd let him bring it up, but of course that was the same thing as letting him not do it at all, because I knew he wouldn't bring it up.

In the morning, though, I put up a wall in my mind about the Equality PSA so I don't talk about it, and I ask him if he and Strike worked out a time for the beer commercial.

"Oh, yeah," he says. "Ogleby finally got all the paperwork done and Strike's agent set up the time with Strongwell. It's going to be the Monday afternoon after the Hellentown game. They're flying us out to Crystal City for the filming and then back here Monday night so we can get to practice Tuesday morning. Coach ok'd it and everything."

"Great." I smile, because it is good for him. And for me, I guess, though when I think about getting that million dollars, it feels just a little wrong. If I wanted to, I guess I could get him to donate some of it to Equality Now, but that doesn't feel as constructive as him actually filming a commercial, getting himself out there as a gay rights spokesperson. It's frustrating because he has so much potential and he's not using it.

I remember how I watched him play football and saw that same wasted potential. And before I can stop myself, I say, "Maybe when the beer commercial's done, you can think about doing the Equality Now spot?"

So much for putting up walls in my head. He gives me a narrow look and I can see the wheels turn in his mind: don't yell at the fox right before leaving for a weekend. "I thought you were going to let that go."

Before that phone call from Brian, I hear. "Yeah, well. I mean, the whole Vince King thing and the stuff with my mom kind of keeps coming back to me. Sorry."

He shakes his head. "The beer commercial—I know it's just money, but it's sort of about gay rights too. It shows me as a regular guy who drinks beer and that being gay is okay."

He sort of has a point. Sort of. I nod. "Yeah, I know. It's better than nothing."

"And you know, maybe we can donate some of the million. To good causes."

It's so close to what I was thinking, with such a different spin on it, that I have to smile. "That sounds like a good plan," I say.

"I want to do the spot, too," he says. "After the season." I believe he means at least part of that. So I kiss him and tell him to have a good flight, and then watch him walk out the door.

It's so hard, because he has the opportunity to do something really special, and yet taking too much time to do that might compromise his career and his whole life. And then I think again about the kids whose lives are already compromised for them. Not just King, again, but kids who spend their lives feeling miserable because there's nobody for them to look up to. Dev could change that, or at least start to, and while a beer commercial is a start, it isn't exactly "I have a dream."

While playing UFL 2009 against myself (Dragons against Firebirds), my phone rings. It's a local number I don't recognize, and the voice isn't familiar either, but she knows my name. "Hello, Mister Farrel," she says when I've answered. "This is Myrna Martin from the Chevali Firebirds. I'm the assistant to David Rodriguez. Is this a good time?"

Rodriguez is the general manager of the Firebirds. I sit up straighter on the couch. "Yes. What can I do for you?"

"We've been having internal discussions around Devlin Miski and have decided that it would be advantageous for the Firebirds to initiate some kind of effort to reach out to the gay community."

"Oh."

"Your name came up in our discussions. We are interested in your background in gay community outreach, and of course, it helps that you are familiar with the internal working of football organizations."

"Right. I was a scout, you know, not community outreach."

"Of course." She asks me some questions about the Dragons, and about my work with Forester. I answer mechanically, while my mind is spinning, trying to figure out what's going on. Am I interviewing for a job that I didn't apply for? Or is this just a one-time thing that they want me to help on, like a contract?

I ask her that, when she gets to the point where she asks if I have any questions, and she says, "We're still determining what this position is going to look like. It would run at least through the remainder of the regular season, and sometime in the summer we would re-evaluate."

"And it's only community outreach?"

"Correct. Is that something you'd be interested in?"

In the short term, maybe? But I don't want to say that because this is, after all, an opportunity to do some good stuff and work with Dev. "I have been looking for scouting work and that would be my first priority, but this sounds interesting, yeah."

"Wonderful. Let me discuss this with David, and we'll be in touch in the next few days. Is this the best number for you?"

"It is, thanks." And it's only after I hang up that I wonder, how did they get my number? If it was from Dev, why didn't he mention it?

So I call up Hal, and see if he wants to do dinner Thursday night, because he knows some of the guys in the Firebirds, and this seems like a little longer than a lunch topic. We settle on a bistro he knows downtown.

While I have the phone out, I call Father to bug him again about coming down here for Christmas. He still sounds reluctant to commit to that, as though maybe Mother will change and he can go home. I point out that he should be with some family on Christmas, and he points out that that sounds disingenuous coming from me, and I say that clearly people can change, and maybe everybody shouldn't be so goddamn sure that they know me that well. Then he says he doesn't want to intrude on me and Dev and I remind him that Dev is basically working through Christmas. I don't even know if he's planning to celebrate other than a little bit with me the night before. The conversation ends with him tentatively booking airline tickets to come down.

Chapter 21: Rehearsing (Lee)

Thursday, Brian calls to ask if coffee would be okay because he needs to meet earlier than lunch, and I say okay as long as it's not Starbucks, and he picks some pretentious hipster place called Café Monde that is clear on the other side of town. It would take me an hour and three changes to get there on the bus, so I check a map online and drive, which I have been trying to do less of here. It takes twenty minutes and then twenty more looking for the right street and a place to park, and by the time I get to the coffee shop ten minutes late, my fur is bristled. I don't take the time to smooth it down.

"All in a lather, Tip? Have the vanilla latte, it's splendid."

I have to say, Brian does look pretty good. I think he's put on a little weight, but he's wearing a nice collared shirt and a pair of white slacks, and he's holding a stack of pages that are folded back: a script, I guess. He puts it down when I walk in, and lifts the drink he's got. I can smell the black coffee from here, probably a dark roast.

Since I had to walk past two anarchist bookstores and a head shop on the way here from my parking spot, I am pretty smugly happy I was right about what kind of place it is. Sure enough, they have "fair trade" slapped up all over everything, communist tracts on the counter, and coffee blends called "People's Roast" and "Mocha Revolution."

As a minor act of rebellion, petty revenge for making me drive through Chevali, I get a spiced chai, and I wait for it at the counter while Brian smirks, unfolds his script, and goes back to reading it. He gives it his full attention; it's like I'm not even here. Like I said, a great actor. I study him while he reads.

He's kicked back in the wooden chair, one foot on the coffee table, the other on the floor. Last time I saw him, a couple months ago, I felt like he'd never left college. Now I feel more like he's brought college to this coffee shop with him. He looks a lot calmer, and I think maybe I did actually do him a favor, getting him back into activism. He was never happy after leaving FLAG, and Equality Now sounds just like a grown-up version of that.

They pass my chai over the counter. I take it and sniff—spicy indeed—and walk back to the chair opposite Brian.

He holds up a finger, turns a page, and reads a couple lines, then puts his script down. "Ah, the Bard," he says. "The words really mean something.

He heareth not, he stirreth not, he moveth not." His eyes glitter at me, and just above them, his notched ear flicks.

"I remember the play," I say, though I must admit I don't recall those specific lines. But if it's Mercutio, chances are it's mocking Romeo. The parallel doesn't escape me. He already knows, I'm sure, that Dev won't do the spot, so I just say it outright. "I don't think I can convince Dev to be in a commercial."

He just nods, and his smile doesn't crack. "It's okay," he says. "You and me, we can make this work."

I thought he'd be more upset. Part of me wanted him to be more upset. But part of me is also excited that I could do something without troubling Dev. "Did you find something out about Families United?"

He tilts his muzzle. "I thought you were working on that."

"I was." I stare down at the chai. "I still am."

"Well," he says. "This is better. This is actually something substantive. You're going to love this one, I promise."

I'm excited, but the way he says "love this one" makes me a little apprehensive. All this time on the phone I had been remembering Brian from college, the excited, idealistic Brian, because that's what he sounded like. In person, his scent is older, and even though he looks good, he still has the desperation of someone who doesn't belong in this time but is trying to force the time to belong to him. He's much more like the guy I visited a few months ago. The one who guilted me into a quick handjob.

Memories and shame flatten my ears. I try to drown them in spiced tea and for a moment, I can't smell anything, so it sort of works. "Okay, what is it?"

"Paula's been working on setting up a meeting in Potomac. It's my first time working with her directly on something." His eyes shine, or maybe glitter.

I raise my eyebrows. "I thought this was a local branch."

"It is, but you know, we're not exactly on the forefront of the civil rights movement down here in the desert. Paula overcompensates sometimes. Sweet rabbit. Tough as nails. Her husband owned a cattle ranch, you know, and died when a bull trampled him. Paula took over the ranch, and three years later brought her partner Brooke to live with her there. They still run it. You'd like her."

"So she gets into national politics."

He nods. "She went to Potomac to lobby for the beef industry when her husband was alive."

"Lucky us. I'll think of her next time I make steaks for Dev." I pause. "So there's a meeting in Potomac. Lobbyists?"

"Senators." He looks proud. "There are a couple football fans who are at least willing to sit down and talk about some legislation we're proposing for next session."

I put pieces together. "Whoa. You want Dev to go to Potomac? I thought this was just filming some spots, maybe some Q&A later."

"You think small, Tip. Well. In some respects." He lets that one hang there. I don't swing at it. "This is a real chance to make a difference on a national front. It's the kind of thing we dreamed about getting involved in back in FLAG, and here we are with the chance to do it. You and I could go to Potomac together and really make a change."

The chai is warm in my paws, the ginger and cinnamon and cardamom all filling my nose with spice. I see Brian's vision, him and me and senators. I know he wants Dev there, too, but he didn't say for sure that he does. To hold on to the dream, I postpone the moment when I have to address that. "What's the legislation?"

"You know that we have a lot of Sonoran immigrants here in Chevali, right? Did you know that some of them have same-sex partners, but they can't get the rights they could get if they walked down the street and married someone of the opposite gender?"

"Of course I know that. I'm not stupid."

"Well, this legislation wouldn't allow marriage, but it would allow same-sex relationships to qualify for citizenship for immigrants."

"In states that have formalized relationships. Which we don't currently here."

He shrugs and waves a paw. "It's been introduced twice into the legislature. Last year it failed by three votes. This year it should pass. This federal legislation will protect future relationships."

I sigh. "How serious is it? Is it just another thing people are putting up for show that they don't seriously expect to go anywhere?"

"I expect it to go somewhere." He leans forward. "I expect it to be a turning point."

To do something real, to make a difference for millions—well, hundreds. Thousands maybe, eventually. But a real, tangible difference. And I could still work with Dev to do the PSA spot later. "I'm sure I can get away to go to Potomac."

"That's great." He beams and sips his coffee. "I'll send you my travel info. And you'll be able to bring your boyfriend along?"

Here it comes. I bite my lip. "When is it?"

"Keep in mind, this is something real. Talking to people who can make a difference. These senators are football fans and they'll listen to a player. It's not just parading around in front of a TV, which I know your boyfriend is expert at."

"Pays better, too."

His eyes narrow, his smile grows. "*I will bite thee by the ear for that jest.*"

"Don't waste Shakespeare on that," I say. "So tell me when this meeting is, and I hope you're going to say February, because otherwise…"

He shakes his head before I finish. "Second week of January. Congress goes into session that week and they're already all full up of meetings with oil and finance lobbyists eager to get into the new session. By February they're already going to have made their decisions on our bill. It's one of the first ones up."

I sigh and sip the chai, which is now cool enough to drink. The ginger and cloves sear my tongue, making my eyes water. Brian watches me. "When did you start drinking chai?"

"Oh," I say, "just in the last couple years. It makes a nice change of pace." Not strictly true, though I've had a couple chais on the road and like them when they're not quite this harshly spiced. "I don't think January's going to work."

Brian looks steadily at me. "It's the playoffs," I say. "In case you hadn't noticed, if they win today at Kerina, they're pretty much in the playoffs, and to take him away from the team for a day…"

"I know," he says. "They might lose a game. All their hopes hinge on the play of an outside linebacker who until recently was taking kickoffs and warming the bench."

"Every piece counts."

"Exactly." He leans forward, and I can smell his skunk scent and the coffee on his breath. That, now, that takes me back to college. "Every piece. If one of these senators is swayed by that meeting, that could be a critical vote. It could change legislation that makes life easier for same-sex immigrants. This bill we're proposing—"

"How is Dev going to address that argument?" I say. "His grandparents came over from Siberia. I'm a citizen. He doesn't have anything to do with immigration."

"Doesn't matter. He's famous. He has that innocent…" Brian waves a paw. "He doesn't come across as a political gay."

"The way you do."

He smirks. "I'm not famous."

I sigh. "If he hadn't lost at Yerba." If I hadn't taken him out to the club, if I hadn't gotten that leopard for Ty who ended up with Vonni...

"Yes, well," Brian says. "I can certainly go back and explain to Paula that a football game set back the rights of gay immigrants a couple years. I don't see any problem with that. Do you?"

The chain of events makes perfect sense to me, but the result doesn't. "It's his future at stake," I say. "I can't ask him to sacrifice that—"

"Maybe."

"For a result that isn't any more certain! To parade him in front of some politicians."

My voice is getting louder. The ferret behind the counter stops and looks down at us. I take another sip of the chai, getting used to the sting. Or maybe my mouth's just going numb.

Brian shakes his head. "Tip, what happened?"

"Well, I thought I'd try their chai," I say. "But these hipster places always make it too strong."

He smiles, making it a sad one, and he reaches out to touch my paw. I draw it back. "Was it all just talking and meeting cute guys, back there in FLAG? You said I lost my way, a couple months ago. But I'm really working, doing good. This is important work. And what are you doing? Just killing time until you can get another football job?"

I almost tell him about the Yerba job then. "I'm taking care of my family," I say. "That's just as important, isn't it?"

"Tell that to Maria Cortes, who wants to stay here because she loves Harriet Vick."

"You've memorized the names."

"Or David Thornton, who just wants to live with his partner Rick. They even got a house together. David's a fox, like you. He's from Anglia and has lived here for ten years."

"You know," I say, "I'm sorry for those people. I really am." I'm as bad as Dev, reflexively arguing against Brian. Am I arguing what I feel, or just arguing because it's Brian?

"What about Vince King? Not immigration, but aren't you fighting for his cause? Why is he more important than all those people who are still alive, whose lives can be changed?"

"That's not fair. This has nothing to do with him." And now he has me on the defensive. I'm sure he's planned this.

He leans forward, but gently, and his voice is soft. "We can do this, Tip. I know you can talk Miski into taking just one day. Imagine the senators charmed by his...by his football presence, and then you explaining to them how important this is, Dev backing it up."

I shake my head. "If they're really football fans, they'll wonder what he's doing away from his team during the playoffs."

"That'll just impress on them how important it is. And it's just one day." He leans back and sips his coffee, finishing it, then puts it down and spreads his paws. "You have some time. We aren't finalizing the meeting until January first. You've got two weeks."

"One day can be huge. You don't know…" I can't even pull the "how much a championship would mean" card. It just doesn't feel right. I abandon logic. There's no argument I can make to this that satisfies me. "I'm sorry. I don't need two weeks. I just can't push him that hard."

Brian puts down his latte. "This isn't you. I know you."

"It's me."

He shakes his head as I take another drink of the chai. "There was nobody closer to you for three years. That Wiley Farrel was not someone who would compromise his principles for love."

"I'm not compromising." I put the chai down and stare at it. "You just don't understand—"

"Oh, what?" He almost sneers, and catches himself. "The depth of your love? Spare me the sappy seventies ballads, Tip."

"I'm not having this argument again," I say.

"Afraid of losing it? I don't recall that it was resolved."

"I just don't see any point to it. You're stubborn and you're not telling me what you really want."

He arches an eyebrow. "What is that?"

"You want me back." He starts to protest, but I keep going, keeping my voice to a low hiss. "Not as a boyfriend or whatever, but as a friend. That's why you're trying to split up me and Dev."

"Tip," he says, "I am not trying to split you up."

"You're making this conditional on something ridiculous because you know that'll drive me away from him."

He holds up a paw. "It's not ridiculous. It's taking a day out of his routine. There's nothing excessive about it."

"And you won't want him to spend time studying for the meeting? Reading up on the legislation and the politicians he's talking to? Thinking about what he's going to say, worrying about what he's going to say?"

For the first time, his expression slips, his eyes widen. He really does know what he's asking. "I still don't think it's too much."

"Maybe you don't know football as well as you think you do."

"Maybe not," he shoots back immediately. "But I know you."

"Oh, will you stop saying that? You clearly don't."

He eyes me carefully. "I don't know the new you. But I'll say this: I would never be able to love someone I had to break my principles for. And I know your principles. I would want someone I could share them with. Like you and I did."

He is trying to get me back. And he's using this political thing to do it, fucking with me and Dev, and I don't want to be talking to him anymore. I don't do it on purpose—at least, I think I don't—but I stand up fast and bang my leg into the coffee table, and my chai wobbles and tumbles over. The lid pops off and spiced tea splashes across his script, onto his pants and feet. He jumps up, bangs into the table himself, and his coffee cup falls onto the floor.

The ferret behind the counter, who's been unabashedly watching us for the last five minutes or so, I guess, runs over with napkins. "Oh gosh, sir! Do you want another chai?"

"No," I say. "I've had enough." And I walk out, leaving Brian there to mop up his script and clean off his feet.

•

The rest of the day I sit in the apartment replaying the conversation with Brian in my head. I go over it again and again, find myself unreasonable, find him infuriating, feel noble for defending Dev and hypocritical for defending Dev when really I want him to go do the meeting. Damn Brian for telling me I had two weeks. If I'd just said no and walked out, I wouldn't still be thinking about asking Dev to do it.

Infuriatingly, it's his comment about "another football job," a dart thrown in the dark, that eats at me. I want to go work with Peter Emmanuel in Yerba, to go back to scouting and evaluating players, helping to build a team. I miss the discussions we had over who's good and who's not, who could thrive in our system and who would be better off elsewhere. But I don't have to take the job. I could just live here, work for Equality Now, and help thousands more young gay people.

If you'd told me in college that I could work with a professional football team, I would have jumped at the chance. If you'd told me I could do nothing but activism for the rest of my life, I would have pumped my fist and signed right up. If you'd told me I would have to choose between them, I would have laughed and asked what would happen when I woke up.

It's a relief to go have dinner with Hal. He gets to the bistro before me, at a booth on the far side from the noisy bar, dressed in a white collared shirt with a tie and looking somewhat uneasy. I slide in across from him and grin. "If I'd known you were going to dress up, I would've," I gesture with a paw across my rumpled pink collared shirt, down to my jeans, "dressed up, too."

He grins. "Don't have a job to dress up for. Ties're just gathering dust in the closet." He brushes a finger down his tie, which is pretty nice, really: a purple diagonal stripe pattern, looks like silk.

"Can't think of a better place than a burger joint to wear it to." I give him a long grin, which he returns. This place is actually better than a burger joint; it's got a polished wood bar with brass fittings and huge ceiling fans turning lazily overhead more for decoration than cooling, though I imagine they can turn faster in the summer. They keep the air circulating, the meaty smells of steak and chicken, the tangy oily smells of salad dressing, rich fatty potatoes frying, which all make my mouth water. The walls are wide windows that look out over the pedestrian shopping street outside, which today glitters with Christmas lights. Everyone seems to be carrying bags bulging with boxes, and people are smiling a lot more. Our waitress, a lithe rat, has a sprig of holly over her name tag ("Joliette") and a bright smile when she takes our order. Hal recommends the microbrews from a local place, so I order those and a small steak with fries, then I think about Brian's story about Paula and change my order to chicken. He gets a roast chicken breast and vegetables. Then I think, fuck Brian, I want a steak, so I change back to the steak before our waitress leaves.

"So what's this thing with the Firebirds?" Hal leans across the table once we get our beers.

I tell him about the job offer, briefly. He brushes a finger over his whiskers. "Interestin'. Doesn't seem out of character, necessarily, but I'm a little surprised. You want me to check around?"

I hesitate. If they hadn't called me… "Yeah, I guess. I mostly just want to know how they got my number."

He nods, takes a drink, and licks the foam from his lips. "Wasn't from me, I promise you that."

"I didn't think so." I'd considered it, but you never know. I'm glad he volunteered the denial. "It sounds interesting, but it's not really what I want to do. I love scouting and being part of the game. This just sounds like it would be a lot of calculating how to reach people and setting up events."

He nods, his ears flicking around and then back. "That's my read on it too. Course, you don't need to do it forever. Sounds like they don't even know if they want it to be forever."

"Right." I lean one elbow on the table and rest my chin on my paw. "But would this screw up my chances to land the job in Yerba?"

"Ah." Hal waves my objections aside. "Nobody's gonna fault you for keepin' busy. And maybe Yerba'd be glad you had some community outreach experience too."

"Emmanuel specifically said I'd be kept too busy to do shit like that."

Hal laughs. "Maybe he thought that's what you wanted to do. It'd make more sense in Yerba than here, anyway. Only reason I can see for the Firebirds to set up a position is if they really want to do one big blowout thing. So probably it'd just be short term."

"Which is fine," I say, "and it sounds like something worthwhile. At least something to do. I can't Christmas shop all the time."

He grins. "Having trouble filling the days? Weren't you going to do something with that activist group? Lots of players' wives work with charities."

"Ha ha. Equality Now. Yeah, I talked to them a bit." I rub a finger up and down the beer glass. "I talked to one of them a bit."

His expression gets more serious. "Your old pal."

"Yeah. He—they want Dev to meet some politicians. Second week in January."

"Playoff time." He leans back. "Sounds like a no-go."

"That's what I thought, but I..." I stare down at my beer.

"Can't mess with the playoffs." His voice goes low and dangerous.

"I won't! Believe me! But..." I sigh, and my tail stirs restlessly against the back of the booth. "Maybe I really am a hypocrite. If I don't do this, I mean."

"You gotta do what's important to you," he says, flicking his ears back. His claws tap the back of his other paw. "But you know, you're not responsible for saving the world. Worry about your tiger."

"I am," I say, "but am I worrying too much about him? Am I giving up myself for him?"

"Y'always give up some of yourself for your partner. And she—he gives up some of himself for you, too. That's how it works." His gaze drops to his paw.

Now I lean forward. Over the beer, I catch a bit of his earthy scent, familiar, and there's no shade of fear or lust or anything obvious in it. "You been talking to Cim?"

He shakes his head. "Nah, but..." He licks foam from his lips again, slower.

"The date went well." I grin, watching his reaction. "You've had another one. With that coyote, right?"

"Going sorta okay." He taps the table and doesn't meet my eyes. "Hey, tell me something. Is it okay for a guy to have a gay pal for relationship advice? Or is it just girls get to do that?"

"It's okay for guys." I grin. "I don't know what I can tell you about girls, but I'll try."

"It's cool," he says. "My question isn't really about her anyway. It's about me."

My ears perk. "Okay, shoot."

"Well, it's…" He has to pause because our waitress brings our food then, and there's a couple minutes to sort out condiments and extras. I ask for horseradish for the steak and he asks for pepper for the chicken. The steak is a little tough, but pretty tasty. Hal swallows his first bite of chicken and keeps eating, but talks between bites in a lower voice.

"We had our second date, y'know, and she was snuggled all close in the movie theater, and…" He stops, takes another bite of chicken. I listen to the conversation of the people around me, talking about sports teams and the weather, about politics and about their jobs. Two booths away, someone is talking about the Firebirds and Strike, but I tune that conversation out as Hal takes a breath and starts again.

"This is weird, y'know. I don't know you that well, but…I don't know anyone else I can talk to about it."

"It's okay," I say. "I won't tell anyone else."

"Not worried about that." He takes another bite of chicken and chews, staring down at his plate.

I put on my husky female voice. "Come on, Hal," I say. "You can talk to me about your feelings."

"Oh, put a sock in it," he says, but he lifts his muzzle with a grin. "Just haven't been in a lot of relationships, you know. There was a gal in high school and then there was Cim. So I don't know if it's right that I'm sitting with this coyote and I got my arm around her and all I'm thinking is 'she's gonna ditch me.'"

"Oh." I chew a little more steak and take a couple fries.

"It's stupid, right? We're on a second date, we aren't even sure if we'll have a third. So what the hell?"

The last words he says pretty evenly, but his pain shows through because he just goes still for a second. Then he recovers and he's got his easy smile back on. "Am I still getting over Cim?"

I laugh. "I don't know. I got over guys pretty quick back in college, and I haven't broken up since then. But I think maybe you're just thinking about it too much."

"Maybe." He spears a piece of chicken on his fork and looks at it. "I went on another date a few months ago, though that was through craigslist." His ears go back and he looks away again. "Hey, I was desperate."

"I didn't say anything."

"Anyway. I thought the same thing. Kept running through that in my mind, we were gonna go out again and then get engaged and get married and—"

"On a first date?" I dip a fry in ketchup and eat it. "Jeez, you straight people."

"I didn't talk to her about it." He pauses, puts his ears up again, and meets my eyes. "Sorry. Just feel pretty shitty about it, and talking about it doesn't make me feel better."

Now I put my ears back a bit. "Look, it's something you can get past. Just because it happened on one date doesn't mean it'll happen on all of them. I had...well, you know Brian?" He nods. "I told you he and I used to be friends. It didn't go well, when I started seeing Dev. There was a lot of other stuff there, it wasn't jealousy, but—well, I tried to smooth things over with him, and it was just clear that we were not as close as we had been."

"So it was kind of like breaking up with a best friend." His whiskers come forward a bit.

"Yeah. And it made me wonder about friendships in general, because I thought he and I would always be friends. But when I'm with Dev now, I don't think about Brian." I give him a little smirk, and I leave out the part where I'm working hard not to think about Brian as I'm having steak, remembering his story about his boss Paula. "At all."

"Uh-huh." He keeps his eyes on mine. "And you didn't think at all that what happened with your best friend from college might happen with your boyfriend?"

In this case, I think the truth might actually help him the most, even if it's hard for me to say out loud. "I did think it, briefly. But then I let it go."

"And it hasn't come back?"

I shake my head firmly. "No."

He grins. "No offense, but you're younger. And you seem to be a bit more forward-looking than me. But I'll take it."

"So go on another date with her. You know, talk about her and let her be herself, and then stop imagining that she's Cim in a coyote skin."

"That's disgusting." But his grin widens. "I think I saw a movie like that once."

"One of those Cronenberg jobs?"

"That's the one. Let's talk about something else." He lifts a bite of chicken.

I raise an eyebrow. "Weak stomach?"

"I thought I'd spare yours."

I cut another piece of steak, dip it in horseradish, and eat it with a flourish. "I'm okay talking about Saw III if you want. Doesn't bother me."

"Yuck." He sticks his tongue out. "You watch that trash?"

"No. But I can talk about it."

He laughs. "Fair enough."

So we talk movies for a while, until we're done, and then he tries to pick up the check. I get my card out first. "Let me get this." When he starts to protest, I say, "My boyfriend can afford it."

That stops him. "Reckon he can. Okay." He puts his card away. "Thank him for me."

"Oh, I will."

He shakes his head. "Just with words will be fine."

I grin. "Aw. Okay, I'll do that and then I'll thank him for me."

He rolls his eyes. I pay, we get up, and he holds the door for me at the exit. "What are you guys doing for Christmas?"

"Not sure. I'm trying to talk my father into coming down."

"Oh, good. How's he been?"

I catch him up on the latest while we walk amidst busy shoppers—not frantic, it's not that close to Christmas yet. My tail wants to swish, but people keep brushing it, so I keep it close to my legs. "So what are you doing for Christmas?"

"Well, if I don't spend it with Polly—the coyote—then I guess I'll probably continue my tradition of the past couple years and watch the Christmas Mass at home with my good friend Mr. Daniels. Then go to a movie."

"If we're not doing anything else, maybe we can go to the movie with you." I flick an ear. "Long as it's not Saw III."

"How about My Best Friend's Boyfriend?"

I look sideways to see if he's kidding, but he looks pretty serious. "Why? Because of Amanda Mandy?"

"I got a thing for cute wolves." He doesn't look abashed; in fact, I can see his fangs over his lip when he grins.

"We'll see." We get to his car. "I'll give you a call."

"Can I give you a ride home?"

I shake my head. "I'm gonna do a little more shopping while I'm down here and then catch the bus."

"Okay. Thanks for lunch, and, uh." His smile turns a little embarrassed, which is actually adorable. "For talking."

"Don't stress about it," I say. "And it'll go away." I hope I know what I'm talking about.

His joke about the players' wives working with charities stung initially, because Dev and I can't actually get married, but it stuck with me for another reason. When he's gone, I take out my phone and find Gena's number. I have it from way back and I never even thought to call her when I moved here. If I wanted a friend, I could have done worse, and it wasn't that I thought she'd be busy with a recovering Fisher. I just never even thought of it.

I lean with my ears back against the brick of a storefront and call. She seems surprised to hear my voice, and even after I say, "It's Dev's Lee," she's a little distracted.

"Oh. Right. I'm sorry. How are you?"

"Good. I'm in town—I moved down here to Chevali. How are things with Fisher?"

"Oh," she says. "He's…he's impatient. He wants to get back on the field. Next week he gets to go back to the facility and practice."

"That's good," I say, and she's quiet, so I follow up. "Isn't it?"

"I suppose. Anyway, I don't mean to go on. It's nice to hear from you. How are you liking Chevali?"

"Well." I look around at the Christmas lights as the cool breeze ruffles my ears. Nobody's even wearing a coat, much less a scarf or anything to keep cold off their ears. There is, of course, no snow on the ground, no nip in the air, no tingle of cold on my nose or the tips of my ears. My winter coat feels warm, on the edge of uncomfortable. "It doesn't feel like Christmas. The decorations are nice, but the cacti kind of ruin it."

She laughs. "We do our best down here. Not what you're used to, I'm sure. How is Devlin? We get reports from the team, but…well, not as much now that Fisher isn't playing."

"He's good. The team's good. Bad game at Yerba, but they'll get over it."

"We watched. Well, I did. Fisher went into the garage halfway through the third."

"Otherwise things are okay. I have a couple leads on jobs." It seems polite at this point to ask, so I say, "Would you two have time free for dinner sometime? Maybe after Dev gets back from Kerina…although then Christmas is Wednesday, and then there's the Hellentown game. Maybe after that, though?"

"We'd love to, and yes, probably it wouldn't be until after Christmas, at this point. Unless we see you at Christmas."

"Oh, we wouldn't want to intrude on your family. My father's coming down, anyway."

"It's not our family. Gerrard and Angela had Christmas at their place last year for some of the team. I imagine you'll be invited."

"Oh. Dev didn't tell me." I start to wonder if he's hiding it from me again, but fortunately Gena corrects me immediately.

"He probably doesn't know. I don't think they've sent out the invitations yet. Angela has those two cubs to keep track of, and they're winding up school. They aren't the best at planning ahead, you might have noticed."

"Yes." I grin. "Coyotes."

"Well, species aside. She has a lot to keep track of."

"I'm sure." I remember the two cubs, how energetic they were. Probably at least the younger one is still at an age where Christmas is magical to him. Which would be neat to see. I never had a younger brother or sister to share Christmas with, so for the last ten years or so it's always been a sedate family affair, more and more strained. "Well, if we're invited, I guess we'll see you there."

"I'm sure you're invited." I hear a deep voice in the background. "I'm sorry, I've got to go get lunch."

"Go take care of it. And Merry Christmas, just in case."

"You too."

I hang up. Well, it's good that I'm downtown. It looks like I do have a bit more Christmas shopping to do.

Chapter 22: History (Dev)

Kerina's overwhelming from the air, a sprawing metropolis around three clusters of skyscrapers. Even Aventira, which is a bigger city, had only one big downtown. I know Crystal City is bigger, but I wasn't looking out the window when we landed there. There's no ocean or lake, just a huge expanse of tan semi-desert broken up by spots of green and clusters of black machinery surrounding the city. Lots of oil money here.

The airport is crowded and busy, the city no better. The team gets into a bus to go to the hotel, and the air feels hazy and dirty. Ty, sitting behind me, complains about the smell. "Crystal City's supposed to have shitty air," he says, "but this is worse. Rotten eggs."

"Smells more like sewage treatment," Gerrard says from the seat in front of me.

Charm, beside me, rubs his nose. "Just smells like shit to me. Hope the hotel isn't near the dump."

"Come on," I say. "Couple of the girls who live by the dump? That's a good time."

He laughs. "They give better blow jobs," he says. "Know why?" He opens his mouth and points. "No teeth."

I laugh, and so does Ty. Then from behind us, Strike's voice says, "You don't want to do that. There's always a risk of disease."

"Not from a blow job," Vonni says.

"Not if you're gettin' it," Zillo shoots back.

Strike goes on. "Really, this air is doing damage to our lungs with every breath."

"Sure," Charm says, "but what doesn't kill us makes us stronger, right?"

I elbow him. "You know Nietzsche?"

He frowns. "Was that the fox gal from Hellentown?"

Strike, behind us, says, "That's a fallacy. It might not kill us, but it can weaken us. We need to be on top of our game."

"Jesus, lighten up," Ty says. "It's the fucking Knights. We only need to be about halfway up our game."

General laughter and agreement greets this, but Strike says, "Never let off the pedal. Never stop playing your best."

That kind of kills the laughter. In front of us, Gerrard says, "Least he has his head in the game."

"When it's not up his ass," Carson murmurs.

Behind me, I hear someone—not sure who it is—say, "Not like we couldn't play better," and someone responds, "You including yourself in that?" and then, "Hell yeah, and you too." Then silence.

Ty leans forward between me and Charm and points his muzzle at Gerrard's ears. He says, loudly, "It's a game. We're supposed to have fun."

That gets a few "Amen!" responses. Then Gerrard feels compelled to turn around and say, "It's a job, and we oughta take it seriously," which also gets some positive responses and some yells of "Siddown, Coach."

Samuelson stands up at that point and says, "Calm down, fellas. We got a game to get ready for." That simmers people down, at least for a little. But there's still some grumbling around Strike, and, unusually, around Gerrard too.

Fortunately, the hotel is not far from the airport. We get out and look at Knight Field, the old historic stadium, and then the brand new stadium being built next to it. A huge sign says, "Future Home of TFC Bank Arena."

"Jeez," Ty says to me as we walk away. "Glad I get a chance to play in Knight Stadium."

The hotel front shines as brightly as the clean white stone running around the base of the new construction across the street, and inside it's all gleaming efficiency, clean floors and fresh-smelling white carpeting with regular black patterns, and badger bellboys in stark white uniforms. Seriously, all the bellboys are badgers, and the desk clerks are all skunks. I check the name again to see if there's some kind of black-and-white theme to the hotel, but no, it's just the "Royal Metro."

The training facilities at the stadium, by contrast, are old and worn. Even I can detect all kinds of old scents on the benches, and some of the weight plates have initials scratched into them. Zillo and I try to decipher some of them and decide that one is at least ten years old, because the most famous guy with those initials was a wolverine running back who retired then. And honestly, ten years was kind of the low end of my guesses as to how old this equipment all was.

It doesn't matter that much, though Strike complains about it every time I'm near him. Halfway through Thursday, he finds some antibacterial soap, and after that he smells of it every time he comes over to put his arm around my shoulders. He wants to talk about the commercial, but he doesn't have a whole lot to say, and after a little while I notice that he mostly comes over to me before and after practices, when there are reporters taking pictures.

I'm not sure why he wants to be seen with me, and it's a little bit unsettling. When I'd just come out to the team, and Gerrard and Carson and Charm and Fisher all made a point to hang out with me, it was supportive. But the guys are mostly okay with me now, so for Strike to come over and single me out just reminds everyone why I'm different, and why he's different, and associating the two of us, and I don't really want that. So whenever he comes over and puts his arm around my shoulder, I pretend to get a call on my phone, or hear someone calling me, and I spin away from the attention.

The linebacking drills, fortunately, exclude Strike from being present, because he has to go practice with the receiving corps. And with him gone, I can focus pretty well on what we're doing. All the linebackers and most of the defense find it easy to ignore Strike, except that we bring up how lucky we are not to have to deal with him in just about every conversation. I'm kind of annoyed at him, but when the other guys gush over that touchdown, how he just ran past everyone, that makes it easier for me to admire the player, even if I'm not a big fan of the person. Norton gets all quiet when we do that, so we try not to do it too often, but damn. Vonni, of course, gets in his jibes at the cheetah cornerback—"When you said cheetahs were fast, well, now I know what you mean!" and Norton is comfortable enough to respond to him with a crack back about foxes—but the rest of us try to stay calm about Strike when he's around.

As Lee guessed, some of the patterns we're putting in are practice for Hellentown, though the coaches don't say that specifically. Zillo and I talk after practice with Pace and Vonni, all of us wondering why we're being made to learn a lot of long pass patterns. Vonni points out that he's going to be running farther in practice than on any play in Sunday's actual game. Kerina's longest pass play of the year is forty yards, and that was with a ten-yard run after the catch. They have a rookie quarterback, and their best wideout is a deer more famous for his many dropped passes than for any caught ones.

Hellentown, though, they've got that lion, Andy Buck, and he can sling it. Broke the league record for touchdowns two years ago. We know we're preparing for him, but we don't say anything to the coaches because they obviously have reasons for doing it. I don't say anything to Gerrard because I'm sure he's figured it out. We do grouse a bit—"what do they think we are, stupid?" Vonni says, but he's a fox and so naturally hates it when people try to trick him.

Ty and Vonni try to get us to go out again Friday night. Pace and Charm are up for it, but I beg off. Gerrard and Carson are sticking around

with the guys from the practice squad, preparing both for Kerina and for Hellentown, and knowing that Lee's coming in Saturday, I want to get in as much work as I can. Gerrard doesn't say much about who we're preparing for, but when Baki says, "Come on, it's only Kerina," he stops and glares at the cheetah. I'm prepared to say something about Hellentown, but Gerrard goes in a different direction.

"That's Knight Field," Gerrard says. "You seen the 1978 Championship? The 1984 semifinal game? That place is full of history, and I've seen guys stare at the championship banners and forget about the game. The banners give a place a sense of history. You can't be too prepared for a game at Kerina."

He doesn't have to point out that we have no banners at our field. But Vonni is unimpressed. "History's history. They're not winning any championship banners this year, so what's the big deal?"

"Yeah," Ty says. "Things change."

"They don't always change much or for long," Gerrard says. "We grew up watching these guys."

"You did," Ty says. "They were good for about two years when I was eight, stunk ever since."

"You think they forgot their history because they're two and ten?" Gerrard gets a little more animated, as much as I've ever seen him. "They have a lot more stake in that history than you think, a lot of pride, and if you let them, they'll use it to get your head out of the game."

"I only get distracted thinking about the championship banners in our future," Ty says.

"I only get distracted by the cheerleaders," Charm says. "And practice don't help with that."

"C'mon, Zill-o-matic," Ty says. "We're takin' you out."

The coyote perks up. "Really? Awesome."

"You think you don't need practice?" Gerrard's voice is mild, but we can all hear the steel in it.

Zillo grins at his fellow coyote, then points at me. "Don't get hurt," he says. "All right, I'm ready." And he follows Ty and Charm and the others out the door.

Gerrard takes only a moment staring after them. "All right," he said. "You people who're serious about the game, let's go."

I take that to heart, and work out until late in the evening, then go home and collapse. On the way up, I pass a female coyote waiting in the lobby, slim and fashionable and so like the one in Yerba that I have to stop and make sure it's not. But no, the one in Yerba had no jewelry and this one has a gold hoop in her right ear and a stylish necklace with a turquoise pendant, and besides, she's shorter. I shake the uneasy need to ask who she's here for, because it's none of my business, and anyway, I'm exhausted. I'm so out of it that I don't even hear Charm come in (ten to midnight, according to his story the next day), but he's there snoring when I get up.

Saturday is a normal Saturday: lighter workouts in the morning, film study and team meetings in the afternoon. We're dismissed around dinnertime and I skip out on the team dinner. "Goin' off to eat alone?" Vonni says.

"Nope." I just grin at him, and he matches my grin a moment later.

"Have a good night, then."

"Don't let Strike find out," Charm yells after me.

"I won't if you won't," I shoot back, and he laughs.

Lee's hotel is fancy like mine, but different. Instead of stark white marble and black fixtures, badgers and skunks on the staff, his is purple armchairs and red wallpaper, bright modern art paintings, and foxes, jaguars, and okapis in sleek red uniforms. I take the elevator up to his floor, staring at the pattern of solid colored circles painted on the walls, and hesitate at his door. The arguments of the previous week, which we haven't mentioned on the phone the times we've talked, flutter back to my mind. If he starts in with the activist stuff, I tell myself, I'll just say a firm "no," and then I will distract him. I know how to do that. I've actually been able to get around him pretty well the past couple weeks.

That bothers me when I think of it that way, because I've never gotten the better of him for very long, and if it's happening that much, I start to suspect it's part of a plan of his. Maybe he wants me to think I can shut him down that quickly. Maybe he's trying to avoid having a discussion about it with me.

Lion Christ, I can't waste energy trying to outthink him. I take a breath and knock on his door.

The peephole goes dark as he looks through, and then he opens it, hiding behind it. "I saw a neat dinner place on the way over," I say as I walk in. The door closes behind me. "Barbecue's supposed to be the local, uh, special—"

He grins at me. He's wearing a Kerina Knights t-shirt, ash-grey with the black Knights logo large on his stomach and the word "KNIGHTS" in big block letters above it, across his chest. And below the edge of the shirt, there's just ivory fur, the bulge of his sheath pushing out the fabric of the shirt, his sac hanging below it. His hips, ivory in front and russet around the side, are just as bare down his thighs to the chocolate brown of his calves and feet. His tail swings enticingly behind him. "I'm not that hungry yet," he says.

My gaze flicks from the logo down to his sheath, and back up to his blue eyes. "What the hell…?"

He flicks his tail at me, turning to one side. "I thought you might like a little practice tackling the other team."

I swipe at him, but he dodges out of reach. "You…" I step forward and swipe and miss again.

"Gosh," he says, staying teasingly back a step, "looks like you need to work on your tackling." He rubs a paw across the Knights logo.

One paw unbuttoning my shirt, I advance on him, growling. He circles the bed, muzzle wide in a grin, and he's starting to show how much he's enjoying this. "I'll show you tackling," I say, and leap at him.

He's quick. I miss him a few more times, but eventually I get him on the bed, pinning him down while I yank the rest of my clothes off. I flip him onto his back to fuck him, so that when he comes, too, he spatters the Knights logo, streaks of white across the black.

"Hope you have that much energy tomorrow." He grins up at me teasingly, and his tail flicks between my thighs.

"Rrr." I play-growl down at him. The messy Knights logo makes me smile, fills my chest with a fierce joy and confidence. "If I do, you have to do this before every game, you know."

"The t-shirts are cheap." He smears his finger in the mess on his stomach. "Even if I have to get a new one every week."

I grab his paw and lick the messy finger, tasting salt and fox. "If one of them works, we can re-use it."

"Fair enough." He pulls himself up by my shoulders to kiss me. "Shower and then try your barbecue place?"

"Yup." I slide myself out of him, panting, and kiss him back, and we put that plan into action.

The barbecue is great: sweet and spicy sauce over flavorful pork, with onion rings and garlic toast. "Strike would have a fit if he saw me eating this."

"Good thing he's not here, then," Lee says. "Or wasn't up in the hotel room an hour ago."

"Yeah." I chuckle. "Maybe he should try sex before games."

"Does he have a girlfriend?"

I frown. "I don't know. He's never talked about one."

Lee nods, chewing on a rib and looking thoughtful. "You sure he's straight?"

"Uh, yeah. Pretty sure." He raises an eyebrow, and I brandish a rib at him. "You haven't been around him. He's all painted up, sure, but I promise you he never even looked at me funny."

"Do any of the guys?" He grins.

"Not anymore. Used to, in the shower. But not that kind of funny."

"Statistically." Lee pauses to tear the last bits of meat off his rib. He tosses the bone to the plate and licks his paw daintily. "Statistically, there should be one or two other gay guys on your team."

"Yeah, well. Statistically, um, we shouldn't have won ten games."

"What?"

I lick my own fingers. "Some guy on some paper wrote that we're a fraud, that if you look at advanced numbers like, I dunno, pass efficiency and pass defense times rush defense or something, that we should really be eight and six. That we're relying on flukes: turnovers, mistakes by the other team. Coach put the article up on the wall for us to read."

"That's bullshit."

"That's what Coach said." I hide a grin.

"Anyway, your team is over fifty people, and so yeah, it's possible that there's no other gay guys on your team. But it's probable that there's at least one. And it's impossible that there isn't another in the league. If there were another one…" He trails off. I'm not sure what he's getting at.

I think about Saito, the white wolf backup quarterback for Highbourne, and his comment that he wanted to double date with me sometime. I never told Lee about it, because I wasn't sure if he just meant he'd take out a girl with me and Lee, or if he meant he was gay, too. Either way, it was supportive, and it reminds me that I ought to drop him an e-mail just to say hi. After the playoffs. Highbourne looks good for a playoff spot, so we might end up playing them.

Anyway, I can feel the prickles of irritation at Lee's activist side working their way through the velvety haze of good sex and good food. To head them off, and head him off, I put on a warm smile and a purr. "Yeah," I say. "Well, they haven't come up to me. Maybe because they know I have a super fox boyfriend."

He grins and licks barbecue sauce from his muzzle. "If we weren't in Kerina right now, I'd kiss you for that."

"I'll just count one of the ones from an hour ago." I grin at him. The prickles subside. "I like the shirt idea, if I didn't say that."

"Oh, good. I found it in the airport and I thought it might be good motivation."

"Not like what was under it wasn't motivation enough."

His tail flicks behind him. I curl mine under the table toward him, but he doesn't notice. At least he doesn't bring up the question again about why there isn't another gay player on my team or in the league. It's uncomfortable enough for me right now and I'm happy that things have settled down to the point that me being gay is just something in my bio, like Gerrard having two kids or Charm attending one year at Linwood College.

Oh God, I hope they don't put it in my bio next year. I can just see it now. "Devlin Miski, 6'2", 200 lbs., Forester University, gay." Actually, they might put Lee's name in there—no, they don't list girlfriends for the other guys, only spouses.

"What'cha thinking about?" His blue eyes stare across the table at me.

I look past his head, at the menu on a huge board on the wall. "Cornbread," I say, "and maybe some apple pie."

•

The game itself, the next day, is one of those great games that is really fun. It feels the way all the media assume it does when they ask you how you like getting hundreds of thousands of dollars to play a game. I mean, there's a lot of hard hitting, and Brick turns his ankle and has to go out for a series, but he's back right after that. Strike shows off, making two incredible highlight-reel grabs and one amazing run where he breaks three tackles on his way to a touchdown. We only punt twice the whole game, and the only thing that really mars our day is when they block one of our extra points. Charm fumes about that, but not for long.

As for me, I have a really good game. I find Lee in the stands before the game—or at least, he tells me where he is and I think I see a flash of red fur up there—and I feel like I'm seeing everything, swatting down a pass in the first quarter, getting one and a half sacks, even keeping up with one of their wideouts when they try overloading the weak side. Vonni has to take the number one wideout, but the guy who's my responsibility also takes off up the field, and I haven't run with a wideout in over a year, but I plant my feet and sprint after him, and the old instincts come back. I turn and see the ball heading my way, so I leap and get a fingertip on it, enough to break up the pass. Good thing their number three wideout isn't faster, and their quarterback isn't better.

Still, we end with a convincing 34-14 win, and I look up at the banners as we leave the field. The past is the past—it makes for nice decoration, but that's all. The present is us: 11-4 and in the playoffs almost for sure. There's no champagne in the locker room, but there's a lot of cheering, a lot of backslapping, and some teasing of Gerrard about his "history" thing. The loudest cheers come when Coach Samuelson announces that our playoff shares, about forty thousand each, will be paid out at a dinner following the last game.

We don't know where we'll be. If we win the division at 12-4, we might get a week off. There's only three other teams that could reach twelve wins, and Hellentown is one of them, assuming they win this week. I turn my phone on and exchange text-kisses with Lee—for once, he doesn't have anything to criticize about my performance—and sit around the locker room with the team watching the Hellentown game. If they lose, our division-winning bonus is assured as well.

Unfortunately for us, Hellentown is at home against New Kestle, and thanks to my boneheaded predecessor, New Kestle is without their star running back. Even if they had him, it wouldn't have been much of a game. Hellentown has been on a tear since we beat them back in November, and the Pilots aren't going to let up at home against a division opponent. They trounce the Unicorns pretty soundly, including one breathtaking pass that starts as a short dump to their slot receiver, a nimble fox, and ends up being a touchdown as the fox jukes past four defenders who never touch him. We all go "oooh," and then, "oh!"

"Gonna have to pay attention to that one next week," Gerrard says to the entire room, and particularly to me.

"I remember him," I say, and flex my paws. "He didn't get past me last time."

"Every game is a new start." Gerrard scans the room, then talks lower, just to me and Carson. "We'll have to get that cheetah from the practice squad to play slot receiver. I don't think we have anyone else fast enough to be good practice."

"Baki? I think he'd do it."

"He'll do anything he has to." Gerrard says it absently.

"Strike could do it," I say, and they both glare at me so searingly that I say, "Kidding, kidding!"

"Guess it's a game next week," Aston calls from another part of the room. "Merry Christmas, everyone." He lifts a paw and takes off, as though he's not going to see us in four hours on the plane.

"What are you guys doing for Christmas?" Pike leans forward between me and Gerrard. Kodi's behind me, keeping quiet, Brick beside him.

"Angela's having a Christmas party at our place Christmas morning," Gerrard says. "Usual thing. Anyone who isn't with family can come."

"Can't fly home and back in a day." Pike grimaces, his muzzle twisting. "Hate missing it, but Mom and Dad will call."

"Same here," Kodi says softly.

"My girlfriend invited me to her parents' place," Zillo says. "But uh, I don't think we're really there yet."

"Come on over." Gerrard looks at me. "Your family's up north too, right?"

I nod. "Lee's here and his father's coming down, but we'd like to come if that's okay."

"Sure." The coyote turns to Carson, who just nods. "Fisher's coming with Gena and their boys." He grins. "Vonni's bringing his wife, I think. Not many other married couples around. We're a young team. You guys are going to win a lot after me and Fisher are gone."

"Ah, cut it out." I bump his shoulder. "You're gonna be our linebackers coach when you retire."

"I see how it is." Steez, our current linebackers coach, calls from ten feet away. His ropy tail flicks behind him.

"We love you, Steez," Zillo and I say in more or less unison.

"Hah." He snorts and looks back to the screen as the game starts up again.

I text Lee, *Christmas at Gerrard's? Father welcome.*

He texts back a moment later, *Sure. Christmas Eve just us and Father?*

Yeah, I write back.

By the fourth quarter, the Hellentown game is pretty much over at 40-12. The Unicorns seem flat and uninspired and "just about ready to put a capstone on this disappointing season," in the words of the announcer.

We pile into the bus to go back to the hotel and pack up, which Charm and I do mostly in silence, except for the parts where he asks me how my night went, which is his way of trying to get me to ask him how his night went. "Twins," he says with a huge grin. "Wolf twins, and not those big stocky mountain wolves. Swamp wolves, all slinky and…" His hands describe curves down his sides and hips, and then come back up to cup two sets of breasts, as if he's juggling.

"Great." I can't help grinning.

"Oh, and there was a guy who says he knows you."

"You had a foursome with another guy?" This makes me stop and raise my eyebrows.

Charm puts his hands on his hips and glares at me. "If I had a foursome with another guy, I would ask you first, Gramps."

"Oh God, don't even." I laugh. "So who was this guy?"

"Just a fox. He was in the hotel and came up and asked where you were. Said he came all the way from Chevali."

"A fox? From Chevali? Oh, shit. Was he wearing like a scarf around his neck?"

Charm snaps his fingers. "Yeah! Like kind of a pink thing."

"Pampel-moose." I groan. I had one persistent gay groupie, fox named Argonne who sort of looks like a gay stereotype of Lee. He'd be perfectly at home in one of those gay clubs. "Fucking kid, I thought he'd given up."

"He said he didn't want to fight the crowds in Chevali around that cheetah."

"If you see him again, tell him to fuck off."

Charm salutes. "Already did, Gramps. I said you were with your boyfriend and he should take a hike."

I want to ask if Argonne said anything about meeting up with someone else on the team, like he did last time I saw him. I wonder if he met up with Ty. Couple of foxes—no, Lion Christ, I need to stop thinking that way. "So did he?"

"I didn't see him again." Charm shrugs.

I clear the groupie out of my mind and settle back into the seat. "Hope I don't either."

BOOK 4

Chapter 23: Holiday Cheer (Dev)

Christmas week is weird. We're supposed to get Monday off because we won, but the team votes to come in Monday afternoon for a light workout and film study in exchange for being off on Christmas Day, which is Wednesday. We know we're going to have to work even harder the rest of the week, but because we're not traveling, we have a little flexibility with the schedule. When I was with the team last year, we were on the road Christmas week and we had no time to do anything. I had a phone call with my parents and another with Lee, and that was my Christmas.

So this feels pretty good. I'm mostly worried about Lee, my mind going back and forth between whether he's going to bring up the activism stuff again (I have a reply ready: "after the Hellentown game") and whether he's going to be depressed that he isn't spending time with his mother. He seems to be okay, though; he went and bought some Christmas decorations, garlands for the door and windows, and a small silver tree, under a foot tall, to put on the small end table. We didn't get a full tree, but he did buy this Christmas tree video.

Lee's father comes in Tuesday and we'll have a Christmas Eve together. "Is he gonna sleep on the couch?" I ask Lee Monday night, when we're snuggled on the couch together watching "A Christmas Story." "Because, uh, I might have to get it cleaned."

"It doesn't smell that bad," he says. "But no, I think he's getting a hotel for Christmas Eve and Christmas night. Don't worry about it."

"If he even sits on the couch, though."

Lee puts a paw to my lips and smiles. "I said, it doesn't smell bad. Just watch the movie."

I crane my neck and see his picture, grinning naked at me from the bedroom. "We'll have to clean up some things."

He nudges me. "You're more worried than I am. Don't worry. We'll clean up and the place smells fine."

And indeed, when we've picked his father up at the airport and the older fox walks into my apartment, he doesn't wrinkle his nose. He looks around, points at the wintry landscape painting, and says, "I like that one."

My fox's tail arches and his muzzle lifts. "Thanks," he says. "The decorating here has been a joint effort."

"Meaning I give him money and he buys pretty things." I drape an arm over his shoulder.

He leans into me, and his father smiles. "It looks good. I'm glad things are going well."

"So are we." Lee's tail swings back to brush my legs.

"No tree?" His father looks at the pile of gifts under the television, at the tiny silver tree.

"Er, no." Lee hurries to the remotes. "But we have this…" He clicks some buttons and the video of a Christmas tree comes up on the TV. "With me just moving in, and Dev on the road, we didn't really have time to get a tree and bring it up here. So…this'll have to do."

"It's fine." His father smiles, and as far as I know foxes, I believe he really does mean it.

"Can I get you a beer?" I ask him, and he accepts. I don't have another chair in the living room, so I pull one of the stools out from the kitchen, and after a brief argument, Lee's father takes the stool and insists we sit on the couch. We do, though we don't snuggle up as close. I'm a little unsure how affectionate we can be in front of him, and I wouldn't pull Lee against me in front of my own father, so I just sit with my paws in my lap.

"So, Mister Farrel," I say, and he stops me.

"Call me Bren, or Brenly," he says. "Everyone does."

Lee's ears twitch; there's something there I think I'm missing, but I let it go. I'm definitely not up to calling him Dad yet, if that's what it is. Still feels awkward, though. "Uh, Bren. So you've been following the Dragons this year?"

"And the Firebirds." He smiles. His tail swishes back and forth. "You guys played a nice game yesterday."

"And the Dragons won, too."

He nods. "They have at least a little to build on for the future. Less than they did a couple months ago, of course."

Lee grins. "I'm not bitter. Well, maybe a little. Looking forward to Yerba."

I pat his thigh. "You'll do great there." Then I freeze, realizing that I've just been affectionate.

He doesn't seem to mind, and his father doesn't flinch or make a comment, so I guess that was okay. I leave my paw there, rub his leg, then withdraw it, and his tail flicks back against me.

"They know about the relationship?" His father gestures to us.

"Course." Lee nods. "I might have to sign a paper or maybe Dev might have to sign something saying he won't pass on anything he learned from me."

I react with mock-dismay. "Wait, anything?"

"About the Whalers." He nudges me and I nudge him back, playfully. It feels open and nice and relaxed, even with his dad there. His tail flicks against me again. "So should we open gifts tonight, or tomorrow morning before heading over?" He looks back and forth between me and his father.

"Tomorrow morning." I look defensively back at Lee. "Your gifts just arrived yesterday! I haven't wrapped them yet!"

"Yesterday!" He shakes his head.

"Uh-huh. And when did you get my gifts? They only appeared under the TV when I got back from Kerina."

"I just moved here." He pushes at me and grins, though his tail wags. "And I got them last week. I was just waiting for you to be gone to wrap them."

"You were hiding them in the apartment?" I lean forward to tease him into telling me the hiding place, and then remember that his father is watching us. Brenly has an amused grin on his muzzle as he takes a drink of his beer, but I sit back anyway. "I'm impressed."

Lee arches an eyebrow and smiles. "I have secrets. But tomorrow morning is okay. Would you like me and Father to go somewhere so you can wrap?"

"Nah. I'll just wrap them in the bedroom."

He keeps looking at me, his smile getting wider. "Well? Go wrap!"

"Okay, fine." I get up. "I was going to be social with your father and all, but…"

He shoos me off. "Go. We'll be fine here, and you can hear us from the bedroom anyway. Just leave the door open. I won't peek."

I stare back at him. "Oh, really?"

"I don't want to ruin surprises."

This is true. He loves surprises more than anyone I've ever met. It's just that usually he wants to be the one springing them on people. "All right. Fine."

He wags his tail as I disappear into the bedroom, taking the presents out from under the bed where I'd stuck them last week. I wonder if he found them and is just letting me surprise him, but they're all still in their boxes and they don't have any of his scent on them, so maybe not. "Where's the wrapping paper?" I yell.

"Closet!" he calls back. As if that helps. I had that big closet all neatly organized, and he had to go and actually fill it with stuff.

I suck at wrapping, but I manage to get the paper around the three boxes and taped in place. Meanwhile, he and his father talk about Kerina,

where it turns out his father spent six months once. "Second year out of college, took a job there. Hated it and quit."

"The job, or Kerina?" Lee asks.

"Both."

"What were you doing?"

"Data analysis. I was dating Eileen, but she had second thoughts about Hilltown, and I thought Kerina might be nice—big city like she grew up in, but without her family. But it turned out to be just…"

Lee lets him have a moment of silence. He seems to be okay talking about his wife. Ex-wife. When Lee does talk again, it's just to prompt him to continue the thought. "Big?"

"Too different, I think. I didn't like it, didn't feel comfortable there. I felt like there were groups of people all around who knew each other and that I would never latch on with any of them."

"That's weird." I hear Lee shift on the couch. "You always seem like you can get along with any group of people."

"It's a learned skill."

"Guess I learned it from you."

A short pause. "I'm glad." He clears his throat and lowers his voice, so I can only just hear him. "I talked to your mother."

"Oh?"

"She says you've been harassing her about her friends."

"I just asked a few questions! I wanted to know why she turned to them…"

"I know how your 'few questions' can go."

I stop crinkling the paper so I can hear Lee's response, but he doesn't say anything. I bet he's staring at the floor with his ears back. Finally he says, "In my defense, they harassed a kid to suicide."

"You don't know that," his father says, patiently, while I go back to wrapping because now I really am not sure I want to hear this. Does his father really not know that the only way to make absolutely sure Lee does something is to tell him not to?

"I know it. I just can't prove it."

"Leave that to someone else."

"Why do you care about that? They're the people she left you for."

Now I really try to crinkle louder with the paper, but somehow I always have to stop to tape, and I can't block out all the words. "…not that simple," his father says, and then, "I want you to talk to her tomorrow."

"Fine."

"And be civil."

I'm done the wrapping, but I wait. Lee doesn't say anything, so he must have nodded. I hope. I carry the presents out into the living room and find them there looking thoughtful, though not at each other. Lee's ears perk up when he sees my armful of presents. "I got you four," he says with a grin.

"It's quality, not quantity, isn't that what you always tell me?" I place the presents under the TV and sit back on the couch.

He just looks smug. "Remember last year when you gave me the same expensive tie you'd given me for my birthday?"

"You liked it! I wanted to give you a spare." I know he likes to tease me about it, but I really did forget, and I thought of him when I saw the tie—after he gave me a weird look when opening the box, I knew why.

"Right." His tail flicks on the couch; I curl mine over to brush it. His father glances between us. I worry, but he lets his gaze linger on our tails and then looks away, not upset, just accepting.

When his father's gone, I ask if he's okay, and he says he is, so I don't push. Well, I do, but in a different way, and later, and he likes it. We wait until midnight so that it can be real Christmas sex, and he whispers, "Merry Christmas" up at me when we're both finished, panting and happy and tired and twined together, and I tell him I like that present best of all.

•

Christmas morning, Lee makes coffee while we're waiting for his father to come up in the elevator. I sit on the couch and turn on the Christmas Tree DVD, watching the flickering. I miss seeing my family for Christmas, but it's not as bad as last year, as much because I have Lee with me as because, I guess, I'm getting used to it. I don't necessarily want to, but it's part of my life now. Hey, at least I'll always have Easter off.

Brenly's brought over his own coffee. "Starbucks was open," he says, and Lee sticks his tongue out when he sees the red-and-white holiday cup.

"Our coffee's way better."

Brenly sips. "I like Starbucks," he says mildly, but I see a little of Lee in the way his eyes crease when he says it.

"Let's do presents," I say, to forestall Lee from saying something else, and Lee goes to get two cups of coffee from the kitchen.

"Shall we gather around the TV?" Brenly perches up on his stool, still there from the night before.

The video pans around the Christmas tree, showing an array of shiny ornaments. I point to a cloud covered in glitter with a wolf angel on it. "This is my favorite part."

Brenly stares at the TV, staying quiet for a moment. I study his muzzle, so much like my fox's, with the same sharp angle from the eyes to the muzzle, the same little twist at the base of the big black ears (though there's grey on his), the same black marking up near the nose, a different mark than Ty has, or Vonni, or Colin, or any of the other foxes I know except his son. It's funny how much Lee is his father's son, even if he doesn't always want to admit it. I wonder if he'll need glasses later in life, too.

"We had that ornament, I think." His words startle me back to looking at the TV. One black-furred finger is pointing toward the rotating image, following a cherubic polar bear Santa. "Eileen always thought polar bears were very Christmassy."

"Do you have any polar bear friends?"

He shakes his head. "Up in Hilltown—well, you know. Species groups stick together. I'm sure your family knows some lynxes. We had a coyote friend, some wolf familes. Other foxes, of course."

I nod. "Gregory and I were babysat by a lynx a couple times."

"How is it with the team? Everyone gets along?"

"Pretty much, yeah. Species doesn't matter, just how you play."

Lee comes back out with two steaming mugs. "They're good guys," he says. "Most of them. But you'll get to meet them later."

"I know. Fisher Kingston." Brenly sips from his coffee again. "I know he's just a regular fellow, but I remember those two championships. It'll be a little strange."

"Will it be strange when Dev wins a championship?"

I flush, a little warm. Brenly smiles at me. "No, because I knew him before. Then it'll just be something I'm proud of." He pauses. "Like if you had actually graduated from college."

I frown, but Lee smiles. "What if I'd won a championship with the Dragons?"

"I only wanted a graduation, not miracles." Brenly smiles over his Starbucks cup. "Now, if you win a championship with Yerba…it is a shame that you two can't be on the same team somehow."

Lee doesn't say anything, so I speak up. "Lee's talking to the Firebirds about a community outreach job."

"Just a temporary thing," he says. "I'm not sure they even know what they want to do."

"But it'd be cool to work for the Firebirds, right?"

"If it's the right kind of work…maybe. I don't know that this is the right place for it, but…you know, let's just open presents."

I can't quite let it go. I mean, I feel like he just tossed aside one of my

Christmas presents. "Is there some reason you don't want to work for the Firebirds?"

"No," he says, "there's a reason I might not want to do that work for the Firebirds, but like I said, I don't want to get into it."

I start to say something, but he gives me a look, and I think, well, it's Christmas. So I give him the jersey I bought for him. It's an official away jersey of mine, but a limited edition because I know he already has the home version. I managed to get one tailored to fit him better than the standard sizes do.

He loves it, puts it on right away and lets it drape over his slender frame, and then pushes me to open his presents to me. They're all very sweet and thoughtful, from the Forester turf to the protective case for my phone. "I hope I won't need this," I say as I fit it on and watch him unwrap my last gift to him.

"Wow," he says, and drops the iPhone box to hug me. "That's amazing!" He even kisses me, there in front of his father, and I'm too startled to look for his father's reaction. When I do look around, Brenly's composed and smiling.

He got Lee a couple gift cards, to Amazon and, in a totally unplanned coincidence, to iTunes, as well as a travel scarf made by Neutra-Scent ("More subtle than the tissues, and I know you'll be traveling again soon"), and then a small, very light box that Lee hefts with a frown before opening.

"Oh," he says, and reaches in to pull out a small plush dragon with a leather jacket on. It's the Hilltown Dragons mascot, tag dangling from one horn.

"I know it's not your old one," his father says, "but as kind of a memento of your time there."

"I'll keep him with the old one," Lee says, "when I get it back." He holds the dragon up for me. "I slept with this guy for three years, back in middle school."

"When I was trying to get you interested in football, before I succeeded."

"You got me interested in male dragon mascots."

"You mean if I'd gotten you a female dragon, you'd have been straight?"

Lee raises an eyebrow. "Yeah," he says, "that's exactly how that works."

Brenly just smiles, and looks down again at the tabletop pool game Lee got for him. I grin to myself, watching him and his father spar. It's not like my family Christmas exactly, but it's not as far off as I might have thought.

Which reminds me to call home. I excuse myself and let Lee and his father talk. In the bedroom, I call home. "We miss you," is the first thing Mom says when she picks up the phone.

"I miss you guys too." I say Merry Christmas to her and Dad, and tell them I'm here with Lee and his father. Dad doesn't say much to that, just to pass his holiday wishes along, but Mom says she's glad I'm not alone. She asks how they are, and says to wish them a Merry Christmas. "I hope I can have Christmas with both of you next year," I say, though that would likely mean we're out of the playoffs. "Hey, did you hear anything from Auntie Za?"

Mom draws in a breath. "Oh, goodness. She said that the people in Moskva didn't want to celebrate Christmas because it was a domestic family thing and might be upsetting to the poor wives, and that nobody had actually asked the wives, and when she did that, everyone said they wanted to have a Christmas. So they are having spiced rum and snow and it sounds like she is doing wonderful things there. I cannot imagine leaving everyone behind, but she seems to be enjoying it." Then she puts a paw over the phone, her voice getting faint, but I can make out, "Your brother," and "Yes, you will," and "No, just him." Then she comes back on and says, brightly, "Oh, Gregory wants to say Merry Christmas to you." Before I can say anything, my brother's voice is on the line.

"Hey, Dev," he says. "Merry Christmas." It's flat and wholly unenthusiastic.

"Merry Christmas." I try to be a bit more positive. "How's the family?"

"Oh, Alexei is enjoying his first Christmas. You know kids. Marta's fine."

I let the pause go on for a little before I say, "How's the practice?"

"Still the same. They're going to put me on this fucking pro bono because I don't have anything else to do." He doesn't ask how the team is doing. Of course, why does he need to? He can just open ESPN.com. I don't want to just say good-bye, though, so I wait, and finally he says, "Saw you on TV."

"When?" Please, please not in the Ultimate Fit commercial…

"After the Yerba game. That was a tough one."

"Tougher to play than to watch."

"That's an obvious thing to say." At least he doesn't sound drunk. "Of course it's harder to play than to watch. Why would you feel the need to point that out?"

"Because I'm not a smart lawyer." I snap it out without thinking, and then remember that it's Christmas. But he started it.

"No. But I'm not a tough football player. So I guess that's sort of even."

"The practice'll pick up," I say, trying to be encouraging. "How's Marta's work?"

"I don't need her to work."

"I didn't say you did."

"She works because she wants to. And it's just from home, part-time."

I rub my forehead. "If it makes her happy, though…"

"It does. It makes her happy, and that's why she does it. We don't need the money."

"I didn't say you did." I sigh. "Look, I'm sorry, I didn't realize I was going to be arguing before a jury."

"Don't try to be a lawyer. Just be a football player. You're apparently good at that."

At which point I hear Mom in the background, and then on the phone. "Hi, Devlin, we're just about to sit down for breakfast. We love you and we miss you."

My dad echoes that in the background. "Love you guys, Mom. Merry Christmas."

I just sit on the bed for a bit. In the living room, Lee and his father are talking to someone on the phone, it sounds like. Lee laughs and makes a comment that doesn't really register with me. How up-and-down things are, that he's the one laughing with his family, and I'm the one feeling black after hanging up with mine.

I resented Gregory's success when I was struggling on the Dragons, but now that I'm the successful one, it feels different. I don't want to rub it in the way he did, but I can't just sit back and take it when he jibes at me.

And the problem is that he's better at jibing than I am. Like Lee, he's good with words, with taking them in whatever way he wishes, with making them mean whatever he likes. Unlike Lee, though, I can't just take him into the other room and fuck him when I want to make up. And unlike Lee, his words aren't tempered with or founded on love.

I sigh and walk out to the living room. "Oh," Lee says, "Dev just got back. Want to say Merry Christmas?" He wraps his paw around the small extended mike on his phone. "It's Aunt Carolyn."

"Oh, sure." I take the phone and say hello to Carolyn. She asks how the team is doing, because of course she doesn't follow football. "We're doing good. Probably going to the playoffs."

"Definitely," Lee says with a grin.

Carolyn bubbles in a way that reminds me of Auntie Za. "That's good!

Maybe you guys will get a parade like we had here a few years ago."

"Maybe." I smile at the thought, and then my mind turns to gay pride parades. I look at Lee and wonder if he'll try to get me to march in one of those. "You'll have to come if we do."

"Wouldn't miss it. You take care of my favorite nephew now, you hear?"

"How many nephews do you have?"

She laughs. "More than one. But don't tell any of the others I said that. So can I tell my friends on Cottage Hill anything?"

"About what?"

"Oh, I don't know. Life of a gay football player? When I'm at the salon, I like to have things to talk about."

I scratch my ear. "Ask them if they know any gay players on the Port City team. I'd like to know if…"

"If you're not the only one? Done. I'll find out for you."

The echoes of her laughter remain in my ear as I hang up the phone and give it back to Lee. How is it that Lee's aunt is more supportive than my whole family? Well, that's not fair. Mom was pretty good, and Dad is coming around. So really, it's just my brother.

How would Lee deal with a brother if he had one? I try to imagine that and fail. He's one of a kind, my fox.

"When are we supposed to be over at Gerrard's?" he asks.

I check the clock. "Not until after noon. We can leave here in about half an hour."

"Cool, I have time to set this up." He starts playing with his new phone, reading instructions on how to switch his service.

Brenly shifts, his tail swinging free behind him. "I don't have to go."

"Father." Lee leans forward, paws on his knees. "It's fine. We already asked. Well, Dev asked."

"Gerrard said you're welcome to come. There'll be—I guess some other family will be there too?" I think he said something about Angela's family, but I don't remember exactly.

"I just don't want to be the oldest there by a decade."

"Gerrard's like thirty-three," I say.

Lee glares at me, and I fold my ears back. "Um, and Fisher is around thirty-five?"

Brenly smiles with a little twist to his muzzle. "I'm forty-seven," he says. "So keep going."

"Well. It's Christmas," I say. "Do you want to spend it alone in a hotel room or with your son and some friends?"

Lee takes my paw and joins me in looking at his dad. Brenly looks at both of us and smiles. "Can I at least drive separately so I can leave if I want to?"

"Nope," Lee says. "Gerrard has a big house. You can find a place to hide if you need to. We all have cell phones."

"Did you get yours set up yet?" I ask him, at the same time as his father asks how Lee knows about Gerrard's house.

"I was there with Dev. I told you about it." He lets go of my paw and looks down at his phone. "Still working on it."

Brenly frowns, and then says, "Oh, that was Marvell's house? You said he was there, but I didn't know whose house it was. I thought it was your friend the stallion." He looks my way.

I laugh. "I've never been to Charm's house. I think I'd be horrified."

"Mirrors on the ceiling?" Lee says. "Pink champagne?"

"On ice, yeah. And probably discarded panties and bras all over." I shake my head at Brenly's amused smile. "Okay, probably not that bad. But Charm is single, and I don't think he spends much time at his place when he's not bringing girls back."

"All right." Brenly puts his paws up. "I admit I'm curious to see what a football player's house looks like."

"Father," Lee says, looking up from his phone to stare around him pointedly.

"This is an apartment." His father gets up, tail swinging behind him. "Are you done playing with your phone yet?"

"Not quite. Give me a few minutes."

So Brenly and I talk football for a bit while Lee finishes transferring his service to the new phone. I play with different places to put the piece of turf from Forester's field while I'm talking to Brenly. Mostly he wants to know about how Strike is changing the dynamic of the team, and I'm not quite sure how to answer that. I talk about how talented he is and how dedicated, and I mention the beer commercial, which I guess Lee didn't tell him about.

"So he's into equality?"

"Sort of. As long as it pays." I see Lee's ears flick, but he doesn't say anything. "I mean, he's kind of going out of his way to be friendly with me, but only really around this commercial."

"Do you get a preview of what he's going to be dyed as before the game?"

"No, he just shows up." I grin. "When he's done meditating."

"It's got to wear on the team."

"It did. Until that first touchdown run. Then it was like we were all back in high school watching him on TV. We were jumping up and down and it was crazy." I grin. "If he can do that just once a game, I mean…wow."

"Sounds like he was really a problem in Port City."

"When the team's not winning," Lee says without looking up from his phone, "he's a problem. When the team's winning, everything's okay."

"I don't know if it's all okay." I think about the way the other wideouts reacted, especially, and the arguments on the plane. "But it's easier to overlook things."

"That applies to a lot of things." Lee puts down his old phone. "Let me try calling you," he says to me, and calls up the touchpad on his phone's screen and dials.

The iPhone has an extendable mic for long-muzzled talkers, that slides out rather than unfolding on a hinge. It looks pretty sleek and kind of cool and I admit to being a little jealous of it. I thought he'd enjoy the cool new gadget, which I haven't gotten for myself because of my penchant for throwing phones across a room. I'd rather do that with a $200 phone than a $600 phone, to be honest. But I wanted Lee to have the best phone he could.

And he seems to be enjoying it. He keeps setting it up as I'm driving us over to Gerrard's. "Look, I can play games on this," he says from the back seat he insisted on taking. He's not playing with my tail, except to nudge it with his foot from time to time.

I glance back. He took off my jersey, thinking it'd be tacky to wear my jersey to a gathering of my teammates. At least, he said "tacky." But he looks really good in his simple yellow collared shirt, open to show his chest ruff. "Do they have football?" If they did, I might have to get one.

"Um, no. I don't think so." He plays around a little more.

Brenly watches the scenery go by from the front, his window half-open. "Lots of new development out here."

"A lot of people come down for the climate."

He sniffs the air and trails fingers out the window. "I can see why." He lifts his nose. "Eucalyptus?"

"And sage, I think," Lee says from the back.

"It just smells nice and herbal to me." I never bothered to sort out which smells are which, really, though I guess now that Lee's living with me, I'll have more of a chance to hear him do it.

When we pull into the front of Gerrard's house, with his impressive front lawn, Brenly's ears go up. "Now this is what I expected," he says.

"I'm only on my second year," I say. "Next year I'll be playing for a big contract."

"Hope they can afford to keep you here," Brenly says. "I mean, unless you want to come back to the Dragons. Which would be great, but they need too many other pieces. You'd have to be pretty patient." He trails his paw out the window again. "Also you'd have to rediscover winter."

"We played in Hilltown," I say. "Also Aventira."

"That's different from living there."

"I lived there, too."

"And would you go back?"

I think about the cold winds, the snow under my paws, snowball fights, and driving in slush. "I'll go wherever I have to. Wherever Ogleby gets the best deal."

Lee snorts at that. Brenly's ears flick back. "Ah, yes, Lee's mentioned your agent. Things going well with him?"

"He got me the beer commercial."

"With our help." Lee leans forward.

His father turns. "Why don't you be his agent?"

Lee barks a laugh. "Me?"

"Sure. Lots of athletes have relatives or family members as agents. I'm surprised you haven't already thought of it."

Lee's quiet a moment, his ears flicking at the edge of my peripheral vision. "I thought about it a little," he says. "But I don't think I have the experience. Also, you know, I'm going to work for another team. I think they would flag that as a conflict of interest."

"Well, I was talking hypothetically, or if you decide you don't want to go back to scouting. You've got common sense. And I have a little financial experience, and I know lawyers we could talk to for contract negotiations."

"What about the other stuff? Finding marketing opportunities, working out trades, dealing with the team?" Lee leans forward a little farther now.

"You have experience dealing with football teams. I wouldn't worry about that. And the marketing—those deals come to you, don't they?"

Lee's claws tap on the center armrest. "That's the thing. I don't know. I don't know how much Ogleby goes out and looks for that stuff and how much it just comes to him. I wouldn't want to screw up Dev's future because I didn't know how to find commercials."

"I'm pretty sure they just call him," I say, "but it's a moot point because I'm not firing him."

"Even to replace him with me?" Lee pushes his nose forward so I can see his smile.

"You do read my e-mail already," I say, "and you just said you wouldn't know how to act as my agent. So would you advise me to fire Ogleby?"

"I've been saying you should fire him for months." He retreats. "But if you're not going to hire me, which I'm not saying you should do, then at least you should get a competent agent."

"He's competent." I stop the truck in the driveway behind a truck I think is Pike's. "Look, at least if I'm going to get a big contract next year, I should keep him that long."

"It's your decision," Lee says, and sits back to open the rear door.

I get out too, staying ahead of the two foxes as we head on up to Gerrard's. What would it be like with Lee handling all my affairs? I mean, we've moved in together. I'm pretty much paying all his bills anyway. Wouldn't he like to have a chance to work for our money?

He's independent, though, and he's practically got the job at Yerba already. So what's the point in even discussing this? Would he like being my agent better? He'd still be around football, and he wouldn't have to worry about what he said around me. But no, I don't think he'd want that.

Then again, he seemed prickly earlier on the subject of where he would and would not work. I should talk to him about that. After Christmas.

Chapter 24: Holiday Chore (Lee)

The outside of Gerrard's house is decorated—professionally, I'm guessing—with hundreds of Christmas lights in brilliant cascades of different colors, with Christmas trees on the lawn, angels around them, and with coyotes in Santa outfits that I'm sure glow at night. Lights run around the edge of the garden, too, and in the windows, snowflake ornaments sparkle in the sunlight above corners dusted with fake snow. On the roof of the house, above the lights, perches a sleigh drawn by eight plastic four-footed reindeer.

We pull up next to one of five trucks; two smaller cars are parked to the side. Looks like the party's started. I let Dev knock at the door and stand behind him with Father.

Just like last time, Angela's the one who meets us. She smiles wider this time, says it's nice to see me again, and welcomes my father when I introduce him. "I appreciate you letting us share Christmas with you," he says, and she says it's their pleasure.

As soon as the door opened, I heard the screams of cubs, and when we enter the house, we hear them even more clearly. They're yelling about WonderWolf beating up Destructo. "Christmas toys?" I ask Angela.

She smiles, tight with tension. "Action figures. There's a little too much action, if you ask me."

I grin. "I like superheroes too."

"I remember. Well, if you feel up to playing with them, I'm sure they would love it."

"Maybe later." I hand her a bag with two wrapped presents in it. "We got something for you and Gerrard. Thanks for hosting."

"Oh, how lovely." She takes it, and looks around. I can see her starting to say that they didn't get us anything, so I cut it off.

"We really appreciate you having us over," I say. "That's a great Christmas present." The foyer here is decked out with ornaments and garlands of holly—not as professional as the outside decorations, but I like them better. Over the doorway to the living room, there's another coyote angel, and it's only here that I make the connection between angels and the name Angela. "Did you do the decorating in here? It's lovely."

She relaxes and beams. "Thank you so much. I really love Christmas and since we don't get to go visit my big family, I tell Gerrard to bring his big family over. Such a shame Carson doesn't celebrate Christmas, but well, we have enough people here who do." Her ears lower in what looks like disapproval that anyone could ignore Christmas. It reminds me, I realize with a twitch of unease, of Mother's devotion to Christmas and her disdain for my few Jewish friends.

As Angela leads us into the house, Dev whispers to me, "What'd we get them?"

He's not as quiet a whisperer as he thinks he is. Angela's ears flick back, then forward again politely. "Liquor for Gerrard—a Macallan 18—and a nice white wine for Angela." Hopefully those are good enough generic presents.

"So," Angela says at the threshold of the living room, "Fisher and Gena and their boys are here. And Vonni and his wife."

"I remember his wife." I'm glad other foxes are here. Hopefully that'll put Father more at ease.

And just then a tall fox pokes his head out of the living room, wearing a Santa hat. "Dev!" he calls, and then spots me. "Lee!" That brings him out of the room and over to us, paw extended. "Hey, Merry Christmas, guys!"

"Hi, Vonni." Dev half-hugs him. I settle for a clasped paw and then gesture behind me. "This is my father."

"Brenly," Father says, stepping forward.

Vonni's tail flicks, his smile still in place. He slaps his paw into Father's. "Good to meet you, Brenly," he says. "Welcome, Merry Christmas."

Angela takes us all into the next room. If anything, this room is understated compared to the others. There's only a Christmas tree in the corner with fake snow beneath it. It's small enough that I guess their main tree must be elsewhere. Sitting in front of the big screen TV, Gena and Fisher are watching the basketball game with a vixen—Vonni's wife, whose name I forget—while two adolescent tigers sit on the floor in front of them and play with handheld game units. Gena gets up and comes to hug me, and Fisher slaps Dev on the back. I introduce my father to everyone. Gena and Fisher introduce their boys: Bradley, the older one, and Fisher Jr., the younger. Both of them flick their ears and mumble, "Hi," and "Merry Christmas," without taking much attention from their games.

Despite my father's worries, he doesn't go all wide-eyed or embarrassed around Fisher, just asks when he'll be back on the field.

"Back for the playoffs, I hope," Fisher says in his deep rumble. He's not on crutches any more, but he's still favoring the leg that was gashed open by a Millenport boar over two months ago. "Leg's all healed, I'm just building up strength for it again. I could play this week if I had to."

"Let's hope you get another week of rest," Gena says.

"Bah." He waves a paw. "Don't need rest. I need to get out there and play. How many games you think I have left in me?"

Dev pats his shoulder and says, "We'd love to have you back out there," which he can say because Pike isn't around. Though heck, he'd probably say it in front of Pike, too.

The players lapse pretty quickly into talking football. Father seems happy to listen to them, while the wives listen with patient amusement. I go to get a cup of eggnog, and find myself near Vonni's wife, who smiles at me. Feeling slightly guilty about having gotten her husband a hookup on the road, I introduce myself again. Maybe I'll be able to figure out if she found out, or if she's okay with it, or something.

"I remember you," she says. "From the bye week."

"Right. I'm sorry, I didn't catch your name then."

"Daria."

I smile widely. "Pretty name. So how are you liking married life?"

She looks a little wary, as though the question is somehow loaded. "We've only been married six months."

"So...how do you like it?"

"Well." She examines her claws. "I had to move down here. He's gone most of the time during the season. And Christmas isn't right without snow, is it?"

"I'm from Hilltown myself," I say, trying to establish a rapport.

"I'm from Freestone." She sniffs.

Okay, so she's one of those East Coast people who think there's no worthwhile place in the country that isn't touching water. I can work with this. "My mother's family is from Freestone. They moved to Port City, but her father was brought up there on the shipyards."

"Oh." She looks a little warmer. "Do you have family there still?"

I shake my head. "Not since my grandfather passed away." That seems like the right euphemism to use with her, and indeed, it gets her ears to flatten and her eyes to soften.

"Where's your mother's family now?"

"They moved to Port City." I smile at her grimace. "I know, how could they? Freestone's so much nicer. I spent a lot of time there as a scout."

And that pretty much does it. She talks about the restaurants she misses there, the culture, the ocean. I try to ask what she likes to do around here, but all she can do is compare Chevali to Freestone. We talk about how terrible the shopping is here, and I'm just thinking how Hal would be disgusted with me, talking shopping with a vixen, when Vonni comes over.

"Hi, sweetie," he says, and then I catch a trace of that East Coast accent in his speech as well. "Hey, Lee. Your father knows a lot of old-time football."

I hadn't even seen them talking. "He's the one who got me interested in it."

"So, um." Vonni lowers his voice. "Where's your mom?"

I flatten my ears just enough to be proper. "Oh. They just got divorced. Like a month ago."

"Ouch." He looks across the room at my father. His wife lifts her nose just a little bit. Divorce, how crass, I read in her expression. Vonni doesn't notice. "So it's not just Dev keeping ya here."

I shake my head. "I'm glad we could come to this. You know, he doesn't really know anyone, but it's a big group and there's kids and it'll be a lot of distraction."

"Yeah. You guys used to big family Christmases?" He slides an arm around his wife.

I lift a paw to rub back my whiskers. "Usually it was just the three of us. But there was some stuff the last couple years…"

"Oh," Daria says. "Because of the…because you…" She gestures to Dev.

"Because I'm gay, yes."

She doesn't flinch, though her ears do flick back briefly. "I'm sorry."

I can't tell whether she means about the family troubles or about her hesitation in saying the word, so I give her the benefit of the doubt. "It's okay. Things kind of came to a head this year."

"But your father's here. So that's good."

I watch him sipping an apple cider, his dark brown ears perked to the conversation between Dev, Fisher, and Gerrard. "It is." And then, because I don't want to talk about my family anymore, "Did you get a chance to talk to your family today?"

"Oh, yes!" And she goes on about her family, while Vonni's ears settle lazily to the side and he eventually drifts off to join his teammates. "Actually," she says, "I have a cousin who's gay. But I guess if you haven't lived in Freestone for a while, you wouldn't know him."

"No. Probably not." I try not to smile. "How was his experience?"

"Oh, my, I never talk to him about—I mean—" Her ears go back and she gets flustered.

"I mean, how did the family react to him coming out?"

"Oh. Oh!" She shakes her head. Her ears come up and she smiles. "Well, I think it was all fine. I mean, he's found a nice fox to date who's a resident at Freestone Memorial, so Aunt Margaret's just pleased there'll be a doctor in the family."

"Are they getting married? We can, in Freestone."

"I don't know, I haven't talked to him in a while. He mentioned maybe adopting a cub. Mother was going to set him up with an agency." She tilts her muzzle. "Are you and Devlin going to get married?"

I look at Dev across the room and I grin. "Not for a while, if ever. God, can you imagine? I mean, with him on the road half the time." I watch her eyes.

They just sparkle brightly. There's no shadow behind them. "To tell the truth," she says, lowering her voice, "I enjoy the time to myself. I barely see him when he's with the team anyway, and when we do go out, half the time it's impossible to get anything done, with the people asking for autographs. I'm sure it's not as bad as with Devlin."

"You'd be surprised. There aren't a lot of tigers in Chevali—young ones, anyway—but mostly people leave him alone."

"Well, when you're out at more public events, you know…we are trying to get him involved in charity work."

"Oh?" I perk my ears. "Dev?"

"No, no. Vonni. Only when he's not working. Last spring he came to a benefit I threw for homeless children in Xenia."

"Xenia," I say. "I didn't realize homeless children were a problem there."

"Oh, yes," she says. "Evelyn Norton did a whole article about it in the Port City Review. She said they need help. So we organized a benefit for it. We like to—"

"Hey, everyone!" The booming voice is Pike, and behind him is Kodi. Everyone turns; Dev goes over to greet the big polar bear, and Fisher stands up too. Kodi gets some greetings, but it seems to be largely the overflow from Pike's rather than anyone seeking him out.

Pike does come over to me specifically to say Merry Christmas. "Forgot you'd had a cast on your paw 'til I saw you here. You didn't have it in Yerba, right? Paw all better?"

I flex it. "More or less. Still sore."

He laughs. "All the guys in this room would give their left nut to have nothing more'n a sore paw."

Daria turns her muzzle slightly away, and after a second, says, "I'm going to just go look for…" She wanders away without finishing the sentence.

"That's Vonni's wife, right?" Pike looks after her.

"Yeah. She's nice."

He snorts. "She's pretty, and she's well-connected, and he wants his kids to be able to go to a private school."

I raise my eyebrows. "She seems nice. And they seem happy together."

"Ah, maybe." Pike shrugs. "You prob'ly talked to her more in the last hour than I ever did. Hey," he says, lowering his voice, "you didn't say nothin' about…"

Sometimes people who haven't spent a lot of time around foxes forget that we have these big hyperbolic antennae for ears, and we are constantly flicking them around. Fortunately, Daria seems engaged in talking to Gena and her ears don't flick our way. "Yerba?" I whisper. "No. I'm not stupid."

His muzzle relaxes in relief. "Kay. I'm gonna grab some eggnog. You doin' okay? People being good?"

The concern surprises me a little. "Yeah, thanks."

Pike turns to Kodi, behind him. "You want some 'nog?" The black bear nods, so Pike gives him a thumbs up and lumbers off to the drink table.

I haven't ever talked much to Kodi, but it's just him and me, so I lift my glass of eggnog and say, "Merry Christmas."

"Merry Christmas." He says it automatically, but with a smile.

"Where's your family?"

He looks toward the TV, watching basketball for a moment. "Northwest," he says. "Between Pelagia and Yerba, small town on the coast called Laurel."

"There's a university near there, right?"

"Yeah." He brightens a little. "That's where I went. Twin Dolphin College."

"I think we scouted players from there. My region was the northeast, so I didn't get out there much."

"My team was the first to go to a bowl game in over a decade," Kodi says with a little more animation and pride. "Didn't win, but…" His smile is shy and cute, and right about then I get a weird vibe from him. Like, if I were just in a public place and I didn't know him, I might want to hit on him. And I'd suspect he might be interested.

Clearly, he's not hitting on me. I mean, he has more respect for Dev than that. And maybe I'm just projecting. Football teams are full of kids taken from their homes, from their families, and Christmas is an emotional time for a lot of them. So maybe Kodi just misses his family. Maybe he's just a sensitive guy.

But wow, I can't recall ever getting such a strong impression from someone and not having it immediately followed up by a touch or a word. I want to ask him a more direct question, but Dev would kill me if I did anything like, say, accusing one of his teammates of being gay. What if he's not, and it all bounces back on Dev—being the "gay player" and all? If I hadn't just endured stays in jail and the hospital in the last couple months because of my sharp tongue, I might go ahead anyway. As it is, I put a lid on my need-to-know.

I don't know how long I can keep the lid on, but fortunately, Pike comes back and joins the conversation. So I just talk to Kodi about Twin Dolphin, and about some of the northeastern colleges, and he does open up a bit. Pike talks about his school—he went to North State, of course, won two bowl games there—and then gets dragged off by Fisher to talk about the Hellentown game.

I want to bring the conversation around to Kodi's relationships, and I ask him at one point if he has a college girlfriend, but he just shakes his head. "Kind of a loner," he says, but his ears flick back when he says it and he clasps one paw with the other briefly. His scent has a touch of fear about it, too. "We moved around a lot. Mom's a bear, but Dad's an elk. Lots of people didn't understand me—us."

God, I am so sure. Fortunately, before I have a chance to confront him, my father comes over to talk with us. "Nice group," he says. "I can see why you work together as a team."

"Oh," Kodi says, "I'm just a backup."

"Still, you have to be ready to get in there and play." Father gestures. By this point, a leopard and bear have arrived to fill out the room. "It looks like you'd mesh with these guys really well."

"Maybe." Kodi looks over to where Pike is standing and shuffles in that direction. "I'm gonna try the cookies."

"They're great," my father calls after him, and then, to me. "She uses real butter. You can tell."

"I like ginger cookies," I say, still focusing on Kodi and not thinking that that's what Mother used to make.

"Carolyn probably has the recipe," Father says, and his ears are down. I hadn't thought that maybe he does miss our family Christmases more than I do.

"Sorry," I say, and Father puts a paw on my arm.

"Wiley." His tone is low, and despite the crowd in the room and the buzz of conversation, it feels very private. "You don't have to pretend either that your mother doesn't exist, nor that everything is okay." He smiles, a little. "I'm fine, and you are doing okay. Eventually this will heal, but I don't want you to give up your memories. You want ginger cookies, get ginger cookies. In fact…" He hesitates, and then trails off.

My tail swings back and forth, relaxing. I give him a chance to go on, but he doesn't. "I don't want ginger cookies. Not now."

"No, you should have them."

I laugh to defuse things. "It's okay. You don't have to force me to move on. I've moved on."

"Have you?"

I look away, toward the group of people around the cookie table. "I don't want to bring up sad emotions. It's Christmas."

"Ah, when you get older…" He releases my arm. "Nothing's purely about joy any more. There's sadness in everything. The Christmasses we had as a family are lovely memories, but I also remember Christmas with my parents, and those are gone too." He takes a drink, and the smell of cider hits me strongly. "So I'm just enjoying this one, standing in a room with Fisher Kingston and Gerrard Marvell—and my son—on Christmas."

"Okay—" I'm not about to bring up calling Mother if he isn't.

The doorbell rings again, and this time, when Angela hurries to answer it, there's a boisterous "Merry Christmas!"

I don't recognize the voice, but Vonni and Gerrard's ears shoot up and then go flat, almost in unison. The felines in the room snap their heads up, too, but their ears don't move as dramatically as big canid ears do.

"Oh, shit," Vonni says.

A moment later, a tall, muscular cheetah in a Santa suit with a bag slung over his shoulder bursts into the room. "Merry Christmas!" he calls out, and surveys the room. "To all my teammates and their families."

Even if I didn't recognize his build, there's no mistaking the red and green dye in his fur: red dots in the green fur on his head, red paws with somehow dyed-green pawpads that look—well, "hideous" is probably not a strong enough word. When he takes off his Santa hat, we see little Christmas trees painted on the backs of his ears, one red, one green. My jaw drops, and Father just stares.

"I can't stay long," Strike says, dropping his bag to the floor, "but I brought presents for everyone."

A few of the players manage a feeble "Merry Christmas." The wives just look stunned. Angela alone looks amused, though she stands in the living room doorway and keeps glancing out toward where, I assume, her cubs are playing. Only the tigers, Bradley and Fisher Jr., really seem pleased that Strike is there. They drop their games and jump up.

Strike sees them right away and says, "Aw, boys, I didn't know you were going to be here." He rubs his chin. "Tell you what—Marvell, you got some footballs around? I brought a couple for your boys, but…"

"I'll get them," Angela says, and disappears. A moment later, the yelling of her cubs, which has been present in the background of the conversations throughout the afternoon, subsides. Angela's voice, telling the cubs to behave themselves, filters back through the silence. All of us are just staring at Strike, not sure what he's got in the bag. Fisher reaches out to his sons, but Gena grabs his shoulder and pulls him back. He listens to her and steps back, but still folds his arms, flexing his paws into fists and glaring at the cheetah.

Dev makes his way to my side and whispers, "He's known us for a week. What could he possibly be getting us?"

"It's a nice gesture," I whisper back, not convinced.

The cubs appear, Jaren and Mike. Mike, the younger one, holds a football in his paws, but more like he's offering it as a sacrifice than if he's going to play with it. Jaren sees me and I think recognizes me from a couple months ago, but his eyes, like his brother's, are as as huge as if Strike really is Santa, and they can't look away from him for more than a second.

"Hi there!" Strike crouches down and produces a pen from somewhere, a thick black marker. "You guys want an autographed football?"

The two coyote cubs nod their heads, tails wagging. Now the teenaged tigers look more disgruntled, as though hoping they would get something different from what the two cubs are getting. But when Strike's signed the football and given it back to Mike, the teens are happy enough to get the brand new one he pulls from his bag. Fisher still has his arms folded and is glaring; Gena has a paw on his arm and whispers something to him that he shakes off, but at least he doesn't look like he's going to punch Strike.

"Now," the cheetah says, "for the rest of you. I know it's only been a week, but I'm really excited about this team, and I wanted to get you guys something nice." He reaches in and pulls out a bunch of boxes, all about four by three by three, all wrapped in silver with silver twine around them that catches the light and glitters. "I didn't know who all was going to be here, so I brought a lot of them." He hands out the boxes to everyone: Gerrard, Angela, Vonni, Daria, Fisher, Gena, and everyone else. When he comes to me and Dev, he hands me one box, and Father a box, and then says, "I got something special for you," to Dev.

"Oh, no," Dev murmurs under his breath. Some of the people in the room are opening their boxes already. I can tell just from holding mine what it is—the same iPhone Dev got me earlier today. So I'm not opening mine, and neither is Father, and half the people in the room are waiting to see what Strike got for Dev.

He pulls out a larger box with a flourish, wrapped in gaudy rainbow paper, tied with a bright red and gold bow. He tosses it to Dev, who catches it neatly, and then holds it. He looks at me. "Go ahead," I say.

"Merry Christmas!" Strike says. "I went to a special store for this. The guy said you'd love it."

The guy? I count only six colors on the rainbow paper and start to get an inkling of what store Strike might have gone to. I think Angela does, too, because she tells Jaren and Mike to run and put their football away upstairs. My embarrassment for Dev fights with my giddy desire to see just how horrible it is. I see my apprehension and anticipation reflected in other muzzles around the room. Now almost everyone is staring. Only my father is looking down, away from me and Dev and the package—and Kodi, over on the edge of the sofa, is picking at the wrapping paper on his box.

Dev claws the paper free, and there on the box…well, it takes me a minute to fully parse it. It's a picture of a polar bear in black leather wristcuffs and a leather collar, both studded with silver. He's not wearing anything else, but fortunately the picture is just from the belly button up.

We all just stare at it. Strike leans forward, eyes wide. "The guy said they're really easy to manage. They're the most popular item in his store."

The leather wristcuffs, I can see now, are connected to each other by thin black cords. I think there's a silver loop on the collar where more cords might be connected, but I don't get a chance to look closely, because Dev drops the box abruptly to his side and says, "Thanks."

"Is it the right size?" The cheetah looks honestly worried. Behind him, Vonni and the leopard—Pace?—look like they're about to die laughing; both of them run out to the foyer. Daria just looks confused. Fisher and Gena are fielding whispered questions from their boys, looking harried. Fisher's ears are flat down, actually, and he's snarling. Gena is trying to calm him as much as keep her boys from being too interested. If I turned my ears, I could probably hear their conversation, but I can't keep them from straining forward toward Strike.

"It's fine," Dev says, one paw flat on the box, covering as much of the picture as he can. He looks around the room. "Thank you."

Nobody seems to want to move. So I rip the paper off my box, as loudly as I can manage, look at the picture of the iPhone, and say, "Wow, a new phone! This is cool! Where did you get them?"

I get an instinctive thrill from all the eyes that turn to me, the moment before Strike relaxes and says, "I made a deal with the store. Reserved a whole bunch of them a month ago."

He smiles all huge. Beside me, Dev's shoulders relax and he shifts; his tail brushes mine in quiet thanks. But everyone else's expressions change from bemusement to calculation as people realize something. "So," Gerrard says, "you were going to give these to the Port City team?"

"Nah." Strike waves a paw—the green one—and points at the phones. "Those guys don't deserve these. I knew I was gonna get traded so I figured I'd grab something for the new team. Because I knew wherever I ended up was going to be a great team."

"Thanks," Vonni says, hefting his still-wrapped box. "Feels good to be appreciated."

Strike doesn't quite get the sarcasm, but he does sense the mood. "If you guys don't like 'em, I mean, when I was in Hellentown, I got watches. I could exchange 'em."

"No, the phones are fine," Fisher says, but he's still looking at Dev's paw. "The phones are appropriate."

The growl does tip off Strike that something's wrong, and he lays his ears back—both the green and red one. "Hey," he says, "Sorry, I mean, if you guys have some team thing, I didn't know about it." He looks at Dev and then rummages in his bag. "If you want a phone, fifty-seven, I can give you one too, it's no biggie."

"No, that's fine," Dev says. "Thanks."

"I just can't believe you would bring that in here. In front of the cubs." Fisher takes a step forward. "I think you better go."

"Hold on." Angela steps between them, and she's glaring at Fisher, not Strike. "He's welcome to stay as long as he likes. He meant well."

Everyone's looking at Dev, who's staring down at the box again. I brush his tail with mine, as subtly as I can, but he doesn't react. So I tap my foot against his, and finally, he looks up. "Yeah, Fish," he says. "It's okay." He bends to set the box on the floor, out of sight, and keeps talking in the uneasy silence. "I mean," he says, "the phones are cool. And…and thoughtful. Look, if we were all assholes, he didn't have to give us anything at all."

Looking at Strike, I can't imagine he wouldn't give his team something, whether because he really is filled with the Christmas spirit, or because he is pretty good at marketing himself. He is savvy enough to nod as people consider Dev's remark, which is the best thing he could have said.

Fisher's arms are at his sides, but at least one of his paws is curled into a fist again. Gena steps up to hold his shoulder, and then the fingers unclench. She looks harried, but not surprised. I guess when you're married to a football player, you live with a violent world. I wonder idly if he ever hit her—by accident, I'm sure. Dev hit me once, when I was drunk, but we both talked about it and made sure it wasn't going to happen again.

"Well, I think it's cool." Pace hefts his. "Got a camera and everything."

"So you can take pictures of all those wideouts running by you with the ball," Vonni snickers.

"Yeah, and then take pictures of you missing tackles on 'em." Pace grins at the fox, and Vonni shoots a finger-gun back at him with a big grin back. "Or of Dev getting flattened by that wolverine."

Dev laughs, but one paw goes to his side. "You know what I'd pay to see pics of? Corey tackling that stag."

"Go to the New Kestle locker room. I think they've got it up as wallpaper for next year." Pike joins in the conversation.

"Do they play Port City next year?" "I can get you that pic if you want. Or of the stag getting him." Vonni and Pace talk over each other.

And just like that, the conversation is back to normal. Strike talks to Angela for a little bit, and she's smiling, so I guess things are going okay. Dev is still absorbed with Pike, Vonni, and Pace, and Kodi is hanging around that group too, so I grab my father and go over to Strike, waiting until his conversation with Angela hits a lull. In the meantime, I try not to ogle him, but good lord, he's huge and muscular. He's got to be about two feet taller than me, probably weighs twice as much. You can see the grace in his movements that translates to his success on the field, from the balance on his feet to the whip-snap of his tail tip, unexpected, seemingly random.

Angela excuses herself to run out to the kitchen. Strike notices me and my father and turns to us, extending a red-dyed paw down to mine. His grip is firm and courteous. "You're with Dev, right?" His eyes go to my father. "Both of you?"

"No," I cough as my father's ears go back. "Just me. This is my father."

"Oh! Pleased to meet you, sir." Strike grins and shakes my father's paw as well, and it's one of the first times I can remember seeing my father genuinely not sure how to react.

"It's a pleasure," he settles on. "I thought you guys should have won that championship."

"So did I," Strike says.

"You did your part. But—"

I cut in before my father can ask why Strike called out his defense in the media. "How do you feel about the playoffs here?"

"Well, we're in, and that's half the battle. Port City, once we lost that second game to Peco, it was all over. But it's going to be us and the Pilots, the Rocs and the Sabretooths, the Boxers and the Frats. Sabres and Rocs are good, but I'd be most worried about the Boxers. Boliat's been there before, they're good every year, and they've got the same core. Sabres, too. Tough team, and feels like they're coming together. But so are we." He grins. "If they get me the ball, I'll take it to the house. That's all I can do. These guys all work on the other side of the ball and I'll tell you, I haven't worked with a better defensive unit ever."

People say that all the time, and I'm sure Strike is good at faking sincerity, but it sounds pretty real. Angela, coming back from the kitchen in the middle of the speech, smiles. Gerrard swivels one large tan ear in our direction, and Fisher and Gena both look over at the same time. That one comment, I think, generated more goodwill for him than a bag full of iPhones.

"We're certainly glad to have you here," Angela says, and I think it's clear she means the team rather than the house.

Strike lifts a red paw and pumps a fist. "Let's win a championship here."

If he was hoping for a big locker-room cheer, he's disappointed. Gerrard smiles, Fisher ignores him, and I'm not sure anyone else in the room heard him. "Oh, well," he says, lowering his arm and fixing his eyes on me. "You're helping too."

I grin. "Has Dev talked about me?"

"Well, no. But you know, a steady relationship of any sort really helps with a player's stability. I mean…" He jerks his head very slightly toward Gerrard and Fisher. "Look at the guys with stable families. Those are the ones we look up to. If Dev had to go around hiding, having sex in back alleys and cheap hotels, well, it'd be a big distraction and he might still be a backup."

"So I help mostly by relieving him of the stress of finding somewhere to get laid."

My father's eyes widen and his whiskers twitch, I think more at my tone than at what I'm saying. But Strike is so earnest, it's clear he's immune to sarcasm. It's pretty amazing. "Oh, I'm sure you're good at it, too. And I mean, the emotional support, obviously. But the male animal is primarily motivated by finding sex. When that drive is satisfied, then he can put energy toward other things."

"I imagine you keep your girlfriend busy," I say, trying not to be too snide about it.

"Don't have one." He puffs out his chest.

"Oh?" I can't resist, even though my father tries to stop me. "Boyfriend?"

"Jesus, no!" Strike frowns, then forces himself to smile. "I'm not wired that way. There's nothing wrong with it, it's just not for me. For people that are, totally. No, uh…" Now Gerrard's ear is swiveled toward Strike again, and he and Fisher have stopped talking. Dev, thankfully, is still engaged with Pace and Vonni, Pike and Kodi.

"It's okay," I say, because sarcasm becomes boring and self-indulgent when you're the only one who realizes you're doing it. I switch to broad hinting. "I'm used to it. Not everyone wants to think about it, or call attention to it, you know?"

"I'm really not like that," he says. "Don't think that. No, I practice tantric meditation, which relieves me of the need for sex. At least, during the season, I do. Girls are too much of a distraction. And boys, I guess, for Dev."

"Actually," I say, and then stop myself because my father reaches over and grips my wrist. "Actually, I'm glad to help however I can."

He peers across the room, then back at me. "Was it the right size?"

"Um." My mind races through possibilities. "Your present?"

"Yeah." His brow creases. "They didn't have a tiger one, so I just got the biggest."

I have to try hard not to laugh. "I'm sure it'll be—it'll be fine. Thanks. Um. Father, you want to get some cookies?"

"Very much," he says, and we go over to the table together.

"The male animal," I say in a low fox-whisper, "is primarily motivated by finding cookies."

Father laughs softly and shakes his head. "He's very sure of purpose."

"No, I'm worried about you now, you know." We've reached the table, and I take one of the sugar cookies.

"Because I'll have to spend all my energy finding sex?"

"Uh, yeah. That was a lot funnier and less weird in my head."

Father tilts his head and grins at me. "You don't want to talk about sex with me? After all those years of insisting I acknowledge what you like to do in bed?"

Sadly, Fisher and Gena and their cubs are all the way across the room, no convenient excuse for me to get out of this conversation. "That's different."

"Not so different." He takes a cookie as well. "If I start dating—"

"You're already thinking about dating?"

"Thinking about it. I didn't say I'm ready yet. But if I do, you'll eventually meet the person I'm dating. Which implies at least knowing a little of what I do in bed, right?"

"I already know—you know what, I don't care." I stuff the cookie into my mouth, barely tasting it. "It's Christmas, for crying out loud."

"Uh-huh." He bites off a piece of cookie. "So if I introduce you to my girlfriend the hyena…?"

"Jesus Fox, Father." I snap my head around, but nobody seems to have heard me swear on Christmas. "I'll be happy for you, okay? I can't promise to call her 'Mother,' but maybe, you know, 'Step-parent.' That all right?"

"Wait, you think I'd marry a hyena?"

I look at his eyes, which have a little sparkle, and I shake my head. "Now you're just messing with me. Of course you'd marry a hyena if you fell in love with one. You've got your cub already."

"Kind of liberating," he says.

Fisher comes over to the table. Hearing the last comment, he says, "I guess we're not talking about that Christmas present."

I choke back a laugh, because he sounds pretty deadly serious. "Uh, no. Come on, it wasn't that bad."

Fisher's deep voice makes my tail twitch, and not in the good way that Dev's does. "It was just goddamn inappropriate. If people want to do that, fine, but don't parade it out in public, and anyway, Dev never talks about that kind of stuff. Ever. Unless he started doing it in the last month or so."

"Nope." Dev joins us. Now we're surrounding the table, keeping everyone else from the eggnog and cookies. "I don't even know what store he could've gone to."

"I can find out."

"Yes," Dev says, staring at me, "I have the Internet too."

"I mean now." I take my new phone from my pocket. "I can just go look up the answers to things."

"Then see if there's an answer on there about how to deal with a talented, cocky kid," Fisher grumbles. But he's already opened his iPhone and is holding it in one paw.

"There isn't," Father says. "Believe me, I looked for years."

"Har har." I put the phone away.

Fisher's still staring at him. "You need to get this hooked up somehow, right?"

"Yeah, you can do it from your old phone," I tell him. "But I'm sure your cubs can figure it out."

That gets a smile out of him, finally. "Fucking technology," he says amiably. "Let me go ask Brad. But I'm still pissed for you." He points at Dev and then folds his arms.

"I can't remember when I've spent the holiday season with quite so many tigers," Father says.

"You get used to it." I smile and nudge my tiger, flicking my ears back to make sure there isn't anyone else close by. "You okay?"

"Yeah." Dev stares down at the cookies. "Just caught me off guard."

"It's one of those assumptions about gay people that just sucks. I think he means well, he just doesn't know all that much about us."

"So he should just not—just not do anything. Or ask. Fucking ask."

He says that last thing a bit too loud, and Daria's little "oh" is audible over where we are. "Hey, Dev," Vonni says. "Clean it up or Angela'll make you wash your mouth out with soap."

"People aren't comfortable asking a lot of the time," I say.

"Not everyone is your father," Father says.

I ignore that for now. "Sometimes you have to just tell him, look, there's nothing weird about my relationship. I'm with someone I love and what we do in our home isn't anyone's business."

"Just like anyone else," Fisher growls.

"Well, if you expand the definition of 'someone you love' to include tantric meditation," I say.

Dev looks startled, then angry. "What? No, don't bother. I don't want to have to explain my life to people. I just want to play football."

"Sometimes you have to do things you don't want to."

"Is that so?" His eyes gleam at me.

I stand my ground, aware of Fisher and my father, but not caring. "Yeah. To prevent shit like this."

Gena comes up behind Fisher. "Okay," she says. "I'm not a prude, but—"

"Our boys have heard worse," Fisher says.

"Jaren and Mike—"

"Are upstairs. Don't make this a big deal. For Christ's sake, there's worse being said on the TV right now." He gestures to the basketball game.

She pauses and then holds up her paws. "Fine. I'll just have Angela announce when her boys come down and then we can all start saying 'stuff' and 'freaking' again, okay?"

"Sounds good."

We're quiet until she goes back to talk to Angela. On the TV, the announcers yell about a dunk. Dev ducks his head. "All I want to do is play football," he says again.

"Yeah, well. That's what I want you to do too," I say. "And Fisher, and Gerrard, and everyone. But like it or not, you came out. You made your life public. And you have responsibilities now."

"What responsibilities? Nobody here is making funny faces at you, or holding their nose, or picking up things with napkins after you touched them."

"That was in a movie," I remind him. "I don't know anyone that's actually happened to."

"The point is, everyone here is okay with it. Can't we all just be okay and leave it alone? Why do people have to talk about it all the goddamn time?"

"Because you want to be able to bring me places?" I meet his eyes.

He looks away. "You don't come to the locker room during games."

"People like Vince King—"

"Oh, shit." He looks disgusted, and walks away from the table without letting me finish.

Fisher looks bewildered. "Who's Vince King?" he says into the silence.

I chew my lip, watching Dev's tail lash as he stops near Gerrard. "Someone I guess I've been talking about too much lately."

I excuse myself and leave my father and Fisher, so I can go stand moodily against the wall. I curl my tail around my leg and stare down at my half-empty cup until Father comes to stand near me.

"King was that bear who died, right?" I nod. "The one Eileen's group had something to do with."

They caused it. I can't bring myself to say the words, mostly because it's still Christmas, it's still cheery here around me. So I just nod again.

"And you're doing what you can to help kids, right?"

Am I? Most of what I'm trying to do consists of getting Dev to help. What can I do? I'm just a famous guy's boyfriend. "Sort of."

"Is that more important to you than the job in Yerba?"

The eggnog swirls back and forth in my cup. If it's important to me, why am I not able to make the sacrifice? If it's really that important, shouldn't I be able to call up Yerba and say, "No thanks, I'm going to work for gay rights"? Dev would support me, and I could go work with Brian…with Brian, who wants to be close to me again. Who wants me to push Dev to do the things I'm not willing to push him to do. Who is still waiting for an answer about Potomac, which I've managed not to think about because I know what it will be.

"It's complicated," I say. "I just think I can do what I want and also make room for the things that are important to me."

"That's the dream, right?" Father's tail swishes slowly back and forth. "But sometimes you have to make compromises."

"I thought my compromise was living apart from my boyfriend." I sigh. "I thought we had it kind of figured out. He's out, I'm out, people seem okay with it. The hiding part is over. Isn't it supposed to get easier?"

"I don't know." Father looks down at his cup. "I know we didn't make it easier on you. We didn't throw you out, or…or, you know, threaten your boyfriend…"

The thought of Father threatening Dev gives me an involuntary laugh. "No, you didn't."

"But we didn't exactly encourage you, fully embrace you."

"Mother was the one—"

"Wiley, listen. You can't blame her for everything. She and I had our disagreements, and ultimately I guess we weren't meant to end our lives together. But I took a long time to accept you, too. I'm sorry for that."

"Thanks." I know I didn't make things easier on them, but right now I'm just wondering if I'm always going to exist in this kind of pre-dawn state, with the prospect of sunlight just around the corner, just out of reach. There will be bright days, like today, but I'm still left with two paths to choose from, neither one completely fulfilling. I can live off Dev's income and do nothing but charity work like a football wife, have no responsibility for myself and no control over my life and nothing to do with football except when I'm his plus-one at parties, or I can take a job somewhere else in the country that is about football and is what I really want to do, and give up the activism, give up the feeling that I'm making a difference in anything except banners hanging in a stadium.

And Mother is one of the pressures on me, one of the people pushing me toward activism. She would be horrified to know that she and Brian were doing anything in concert. In fact, she would probably be horrified to be in the same room as Brian.

It's all too much thinking-about-the-future for Christmas, really, but I have trouble getting my mind out of those spirals sometimes. Father manages to do it for me, sort of, when he says, "It's about the time I told Eileen I'd call. You'll say 'Merry Christmas' to her?"

"Sure," I say. I want to add, "Happy Gay Christmas," but I know better than to cause trouble like that.

"And I think I'm going over there this weekend to pick up my stuff. You don't need to. I know Devlin has the game on Sunday…"

"I can go up Saturday, fly back Saturday night, if that would work."

He nods. "I think so."

I reflect that it means I'll miss the t-shirt ritual with Dev, and that was kind of a fun thing I was hoping I could do every week. Can't be helped. I want to make sure I get my things, all that history. And more, I want to see my mother in person.

Father walks off with his phone, and Angela comes back with a tray of cookies. "These are amazing," I say, taking one. It's ginger, sharp and spicy and still warm, reminding me of the chai I had in the coffee shop, which reminds me of Brian.

"Old family recipe." She flicks her ears toward me and smiles, one of those pitying smiles. "I was sorry to hear about your parents. So glad we could have your father here. I know it's not the same as a family Christmas."

"Lots of families here." I look over at Gena and Fisher and their cubs. "Why aren't Gena and Fisher at home?"

"Fisher," she says, and her voice tightens. "He misses the team so much."

"I'm glad to see them again." I take a bite of the ginger cookie, finish it in one more, and pick up a sugar cookie. "These remind me of home."

Angela watches me and smiles. "I'll send you home with a recipe or two." She turns back to the room. "I don't envy Gena. I hope Gerrard keeps on with football—he wants to coach, but of course, that would keep him away from the house even more. I already feel like a single mother."

"Why don't you envy Gena?" I'm trying to keep up with her talking, and feeling a little bad because she's talking so much. I think she doesn't get to talk to people a lot.

"Look at her and Fisher. He's bad-tempered, restless. She told me she's having such trouble in the house because he's tolerable around the boys, but he snaps and sulks all the time. When he retires…"

"He'll have to find something to do." I watch the curling and flicking of Fisher's tail, more active and, yes, restless than Dev's usually is. "Has he…" I stop, not sure if I want to go down this road.

She tilts her muzzle, and then lays her ears back. "Go on. I've probably been thinking about it too."

"I'm just wondering if she's mentioned—if you think he's hit her at all."

Angela looks their way again and lowers her voice. "She hasn't said anything. I wouldn't be surprised, though. Gerrard's…well, he's never hit me, but when we had a fight, he broke a lamp. That was years ago, though. We haven't…" She seems about to say something else, and then just shakes her head. "I don't know. Tigers seem more violent. I'm sure Devlin isn't, though. He's sweet."

She seems to be waiting for me to confirm or deny, so I just say, "He is. So how do you not get snappish and sulky? What else do you do? What did you study in college?"

"I didn't go to college." Her ears go down. "I had a job out of high school working in a restaurant near Moon University. Gerrard used to come in with the football team after games, and we started dating. I've been with him ever since."

"And you don't want to go back to being a waitress."

"I only really wanted to be a mother, and a wife." She looks at her husband, but not quite completely at him. Sort of through him. "I knew there'd be sacrifices."

"It sounds like the sacrifices are worth it." My own problems pale. I don't think I'll have to give up my career at all. "You have two lovely boys."

"I do." Her smile returns, but not full force. She lowers her voice. "Can I ask you a question?"

"Of course."

"It's a little…well, you don't have to answer it." She drops her head to look me in the eye. "Do you think Devlin, when they're on the road…I know some of the players have girls…"

"I don't think Dev messes around on the road," I say in a low voice, trying not to look at Vonni and Daria. "I know it's naïve of me. But I know him. I don't think he does."

She nods. She doesn't look happy. "I hope you're right."

I want to ask her about Gerrard, but looking at her expression, I don't have to.

Father comes over just then with his phone. "Sorry to interrupt," he says. "Family."

Angela nods and drifts off, and I'm stuck staring at the phone he's holding out. With a sigh, I grab it. "Merry Christmas," I say into the extended mic, and hand it back to Father without waiting for a reply.

He doesn't take it from me. From the speaker, Mother's voice rings out, but I don't focus on it, so I miss the words. I mouth, "I'm done," and shake my head.

He just shakes his head back and points at the phone.

I roll my eyes and put the phone to my ear, glaring at him. "…talk to me on Christmas." Her voice is trembling.

"I'm here, Mother."

"Wiley." She pauses, and when she talks again, her voice is more collected. "How is your Christmas?"

"It's fine. I'm here with my family. How's yours?"

She pauses. "I'm glad Harold came down there to see you. I didn't want him to be alone."

"You know everyone calls him Brenly," I say.

"I spent Christmas with the Romanos," she says as if I hadn't said anything. "Kailee is five now and she's just adorable."

"Not with Mrs. Hedley?" I say.

There's another pause, and then she says, "I just want Christmas to be nice, the way it used to be."

"Christmas isn't ever going to be the way it used to be. I've changed. You've changed."

"I haven't changed," she insists.

Father frowns and leans forward. I think in a moment he'll take the phone away. "Really? You're going with that? It's all on me?"

"You're the one who stopped coming home. You're the one who left. I tried to stop you, but in the end I had to just watch you go."

"Father managed," I say. "He's here. He likes me and my friends. Looks like you're the one who walked out on this family."

"Just for one day," and her voice gets sharper now, higher, "can we have peace on Earth? Good will toward all?"

"I don't know," I say. "Ask the King family."

"I don't know why you keep harping on that," she says. "I don't know anything about it."

"Maybe you should find out."

I hold out the phone to my father. He shakes his head at me, but takes it and puts it to his ear. "Eileen," he says, and then just listens. I try to find something else to do, but I can't help my curiosity.

"It's not your fault," he says. He faces me, but his eyes are far off. "No," and then, "Then you should tell him that." Now he focuses on me. "I think he will." He looks away again and shakes his head, slowly. "No, that's fine."

When he hangs up, he says, "She just wants Christmas to be Christmas. But she doesn't want all of this other stuff to come into it."

"I'm her gay son. She has to deal with that sometime."

He sighs. "You're not making it easier."

"Well, her joining an anti-gay religious group didn't make it easy on me."

"If you're going to be like this," he says, "maybe you shouldn't come up to get your things this week."

"Look," I say. "She's bought into this group, but she's afraid to confront me with it. You know some of the things they have out on their website? Charming stuff about how all gay people want to legalize…" I catch myself and drop my voice to a fox-whisper so only he picks it up. "Pedophilia. About how gay people are trying to remove the whole institution of marriage. About—"

He holds up a paw. "This is a nice Christmas, okay? Let's just enjoy the rest of it. We can talk about your mother later." When I glare back at him, he says, "Or much later."

I tamp down the fire in me, but it doesn't go out. "How much later is never?" I murmur under my breath, and my father pretends not to hear me.

Chapter 25: Restraint (Dev)

By the time we're ready to leave the party, I've almost completely forgotten Lee's comment about that damn Vince King guy. Strike, thank God, had to take off almost right away—more parties to ruin for people, no doubt. Pace leaves around four, and I'm getting hungry then. I grab Lee and ask if he's ready for dinner, and he says yes. His ears are mostly up, so I suppose he's saving up the conversation for us to have later, when there aren't all these people around and it's not Christmas.

His father exchanges a few words with Vonni and his wife, and Lee chats with Kodi as I'm saying good-bye to Fisher and Gerrard and those guys. "See you tomorrow," I say.

Fisher grumbles. "Next week." He cracks his knuckles. Maybe it's just because I haven't seen him in a while, but his fingers look swollen. No, he always had big paws. "Fuckin' playoffs. I got maybe one more year, two tops. We got to do it this time, boys."

"We will." I shake his paw, firmly, and everyone else crowds around him.

"Nice to have a party without everyone being in a cast," Vonni says, walking us to the door. "So, Brenly, I'll have my guy give you a call."

Brenly thanks him, and we walk out into the foyer, Angela behind us. As we stand around the door, the piney scent of the wreath filling the air, she holds out both paws, with a stack of little cloth bundles, red and green, each tied with a silver string at the top.

"Thank you for coming to our Christmas," she says. "Please, everyone take one."

I grab a green one, Lee a red. His father and the other foxes take theirs. It's light, and about the shape of a couple cookies, which I confirm from the smell. "Thanks," I say. "The cookies were delicious."

"So was the eggnog," Lee says. "Thanks for the cookie recipes."

Angela's tail wags, and she gives him a bright smile. "Let me know how they come out."

"Merry Christmas," Vonni says, and I notice Daria. Now I wonder what Lee said to her. Vonni came over to me when he saw them talking, freaked out 'cause he thought Lee might tell her about the leopard, hissing questions at me about whether Lee was hung up on fidelity and I had to tell him not to worry.

He said again that blowjobs don't count, but I don't think he's had that talk with Daria. In any case, it looks like Lee didn't say anything about the leopard, because the two foxes are holding paws as they leave.

In my truck, Lee leans forward from the back seat to ask his father, "Vonni's guy is going to call you? What guy?"

"Finance guy." Brenly looks very satisfied with himself. "Vonni and Gerrard both admitted they weren't doing a lot with their money, so I offered to take a look at their accounts free of charge."

"Gerrard seems like a guy who would have all his money organized." Lee rubs his muzzle, smoothing his whiskers back. "Nice job, though. Maybe you can be the official financial advisor to the Firebirds."

Brenly laughs. "Not a bad gig if I could get it."

"Gerrard wouldn't care about his money," I say. "He cares about football and that's it. I imagine he has it basically in a savings account."

Brenly's ears go back. "Not too far off, from what I understand. I guess Angela doesn't manage very much of his money."

"She's managing the family full-time," Lee says.

"Those cubs, that's a full-time job."

"Almost." Lee leans against my seat and sighs.

I reach up to caress his cheek fur. "Enjoy your time off before you have to go to make my job harder."

"Thanks." He rubs against my paw. "Is that if I take the job in Yerba, or if I don't?"

"What?"

"Oh, nothing."

Brenly coughs. "You have to take the job that's best for you. Don't base it on getting back at—"

"I know," Lee interrupts his father. "Enough life lessons for the day, okay? I'll make a choice. I just want to make sure it's the right one."

"Choices." Brenly stares ahead at the road. "You know, it's possible to overstate the importance of a choice. You can always start over. You've got a long life ahead of you."

"You're the one who warned me about getting stuck in a job."

"Right." He grins. "And you should worry about that. If you can save five or ten years of your career, you should definitely do it. But you also shouldn't think that this is the only choice you'll ever have to make, or that this choice will define the rest of your entire life. You have years to look ahead and figure out what you want to do, and what you want to do might change. You never know. What you have now, what you'll have five years from now, what you'll want ten years from now…you can guess, but you can't predict with any certainty."

The truck gets pretty quiet after that speech, and Brenly seems to realize that he's been pretty heavy, because he says, "Okay, so where are we going for dinner?"

"Just home. I have some ostrich steaks and a new recipe to try." Lee leans back into his seat.

"Ostrich?" I say.

"There's a farm south of Chevali. Supposed to be healthier than beef."

I squint up into the rear view mirror at him. "I like beef."

"I thought I'd try something different," he says, and before I can answer, he holds up his phone. "You guys have new phones to set up while I'm cooking."

I let him change the subject. I'm not really worried that he got some health-nut ideas from Strike. "Oh, so I'm getting your cast-off phone?"

"No, I'm keeping the one you got me, and you can have the one Strike got me." He nuzzles my ear. "Sound fair?"

"Sounds fine."

"By the way, what did you do with his gift to you? You didn't leave it there in the house, did you?"

I shake my head. "I asked Angela to throw it out, but she was worried the cubs might see it."

"It's not like it's—" He hesitates; I feel the motion of his whiskers toward his father. "It's not something that's inherently sexual."

"The box was pretty bad."

"I didn't think so," Brenly puts in. "But I don't think I would leave it around for the cubs anyway. It would create questions."

"I was asking questions about sex at that age."

Brenly laughs. "If I recall, your questions were more along the lines of 'Why does Adam Jensen like Callie Ferguson more than me?' Not so much 'Why is that bear tied up?'"

"Maybe if you'd brought home a set of cuffs—"

His father turns and catches my eye, grinning. "Who says we didn't?"

Lee's quiet for a second. I look up at the mirror; he's got his paw over his eyes. "Okay," he says, "I don't want to hear about how you tied up Mother."

"Interesting that you would assume she was the one tied up."

I cough. "They're in the back. I snuck out and tossed them in during the party. And I'm impressed you remember the names of Lee's grade school friends," I say just to forestall the rest of the conversation.

"Oh, Adam Jensen came over for a couple years. Slept over once or twice, as I recall. Which we wondered about, later."

Lee snorts, a warm puff against my shoulder. "He's straight. He didn't even want to play any interesting games like Lev Ponston did."

"I don't think I want to know about this," Brenly says.

"Who was Lev Ponston?" I ask.

"Summer camp buddy, after eighth grade, so, what, '98? Cougar. Wanted to see how we were different, you know, *down there*."

"Seriously." Brenly turns to Lee. "This 'no talking about stuff' works both ways."

"That's all that happened. We just looked."

"Uh-huh. You want me to start telling you stories from my childhood? I was in the Scouts, you know. Camped out."

I feel the flick of Lee's ears as they sweep back. "So, how did you like Dev's teammates?"

"Everyone was very nice. Not everyone really talked to me very much, but Vonni did, and Fisher was nice enough to spend some time."

"Fish is my best friend on the team," I say automatically, and then I wonder if that's really true anymore. He was, for a while, but he's been gone, and I'm close to Charm, too. I think maybe I'm putting too much weight on the species thing. I mean, I still like Fisher and all, but he didn't ask me too much about how things were going with Lee, with the publicity. We talked about it for maybe ten minutes and then he was off on how much it means to him to get back for the playoffs. Gerrard never asks me about Lee, but Gerrard only cares about football. (I think. I don't want to think about the coyote ladies in the hotels, not now.) Gena was the one who asked me how things were going, while Fisher listened, or pretended to.

No, that's not fair. He was listening, but he was distracted and he wanted to talk football. He's missed it, and I understand that. Having gotten the chance to start, finally, I'm sure I would be just as impatient if I were injured or if I couldn't play for whatever reason.

Lee, if anyone, would be able to ask if I really mean what I just said, but he just goes, "Mmm," and then, "Vonni's marriage seems to be doing pretty well. Far as I could tell. I mean, he loves his wife." He pauses, and when neither Brenly nor I chime in, he says, "She must be really good in bed."

"I bet there's some things she doesn't do." I grin back at Lee in the mirror and he raises his eyebrows, giving his lips a quick lick that his dad doesn't see.

"I thought she was nice," Brenly says.

"She was just kind of stuck up," Lee settles back a little. "And condescending about us being gay."

"Does that happen a lot?" Brenly turns to me. "How has the team been?"

"Generally good. There are a few guys who still don't like it. But it's not a problem. It's not really an issue at all."

"Except with Strike." The words come softly behind me.

"It's not an issue with him." I half-turn to the back seat. "I mean, maybe it is, but it's not my issue."

"Uh-huh." Lee isn't really looking at me, but I feel him accusing me of not taking my gayness seriously.

"Everyone already knows about me on the club," I say, maybe a little defensively. "He doesn't have to put a fucking spotlight on it the whole time."

"Spotlight kind of comes with the territory," Lee says.

Brenly maybe notices the tension. "So how do you feel about the Hellentown game? Lot on the line. It'd be nice if it wasn't quite as exciting as the last one."

"Right, you were there, weren't you?"

"Owner's box." He smiles. "Courtesy of your owner, which I hope Hal thanked him adequately for."

"You want to see Hal while you're in town?" Lee speaks up. "I think he wouldn't mind seeing you again."

"My plane's at eight—work tomorrow—but if he has time for a cup of coffee, I wouldn't mind saying hi."

"I'll give him a call." Lee taps around on his phone. A moment later, I hear him asking Hal if he's free, that his father's in town, and then, "Great. The Starbucks by the airport. See you then." He hangs up and then says, "I picked the Starbucks for you."

"Thanks," Brenly says. "I do want to squeeze in every Starbucks I can before we get back to Hilltown where they're so much harder to find."

It's really interesting listening to Lee and his father. I see so much of where Lee gets his mannerisms from, and I think, I couldn't use sarcasm that regularly if my life depended on it. And then I'll think some sarcastic remark and I'll realize that being with Lee for a couple years really has made a difference, in that and probably many other ways.

We don't have a lot of time back at the apartment. Brenly drives back to his hotel and Lee and I head to Starbucks to wait there for him and Hal.

I spend most of that drive quiet, thinking I should say something to him like "lay off the Vince King already." But I don't think he'd react well to that, and anyway, I already sort of said that with my reaction at the party. He reads me pretty well. Even if he doesn't agree, he knows how I feel, and that's enough. Well, knowing Lee, it's just enough to get him to goad me some more about it; I don't have the illusion that the argument is over. But we don't need to re-hash it.

"So," he says at one point, "you want to keep those cuffs?"

It breaks into my serious train of thought. I turn to see if he's smiling, but there's only a little turn up at the corners of his mouth. "Not particularly."

"I just thought you might like to try something a little different."

"If I'm going to tie you up, I don't want to do it with something Strike gave me," I say.

He leans back and grins. "Interesting that you would assume I'd be the one tied up."

"You think you could keep me down?" I put a growl into my voice.

"Well, no," he says. "That's the point of the cuffs."

"Maybe sometime," I say. "After the season."

Then he gets quiet, and I wonder if he's thinking of all the other things I promised for after the season. But it's too late to take the words back, so I just stay quiet too, until we get to the Starbucks.

Since our flight from Lake Handerson to Hellentown, when I was more occupied with Lee, I've only seen Hal a couple times in the press room after games. He takes me aside while Lee and Brenly are saying their good-byes and asks me for an off-the-record evaluation of Strike's contribution to the locker room, and so I give him the same sort of sanitized version I gave everyone else. It doesn't satisfy him, so I add the detail about the commercial and tell him when we're filming it. He asks about me and Lee, and I say things are going pretty well.

And then Brenly's heading off, so I say good-bye to him. Lee and Hal set a lunch date, we all wish each other Merry Christmas, and then Lee and I head home.

We stay quiet on the way home, too. When we get to the apartment, I ask if he wants to play football or watch a movie, and he picks a movie: Die Strong. It's a mindless action movie, and he doesn't talk much while we're watching it. So I think about practice and what I'm going to have to do tomorrow, and Friday, and Saturday, to be ready for Sunday.

When we go to bed, he's affectionate, and I might almost think there was nothing wrong, except that there isn't quite that lift to his smile that there is when nothing is wrong. He's still thinking about things, I guess. That's okay. He'll talk to me when he's figured it out.

And anyway, practice is going to be a beast. I hurry out Thursday morning, only taking a few minutes to hug my naked fox before I'm up, throwing on a t-shirt and jeans, and heading out the door.

BOOK 5

Chapter 26: Pointed Words (Dev)

I don't get to see Lee much at all for the rest of the week. I stay late every day; when I'm not watching extra film of the week 11 game, I'm running extra practices with Gerrard and Carson, and Zillo and Marais even join us.

It's not just the fifty thousand dollars we'd get if we win Sunday, sealing the division title. It's not just the week off, time to rest up while the other playoff teams beat themselves up. It's pride. It is, as Coach reminds us, the announcement that we have arrived, that we are the alphas, the king of the hill in this division. Beating Hellentown twice in one season—something Chevali has never done before—would not only announce our arrival, it would slam the door and make everyone take fucking notice of us.

Those are Coach's words, "take fucking notice of us," snarled through his wolf's muzzle, spit out as a challenge. I take it personally, because this has been my journey, to go from unheralded backup to defensive force people have to plan for.

It turns out I don't take it as personally as some people.

Friday morning I drop off Lee at the airport on his way to get his things out of his mother's house. He's apprehensive about it, ears flat, hackles up, tail twitching, and he keeps trailing off in the middle of sentences. "She's your mother," I say. "It's going to be fine."

"I'm only half worried about what *she's* going to say," he says.

"You think your father will start something? He doesn't seem like the type."

He eyes me sideways and grins, though his fur doesn't smooth down. "I don't know what to expect. I think…"

"Listen," I say, when he doesn't finish. "Just remember, she's more scared of you than you are of her."

"Thanks, Ranger Rick."

"I mean it." We pull up to the dropoff zone. "Just think before you talk."

"Yeah," he says. "I'm a champion at that." He leans over to kiss me. "I'll keep you updated."

It's only after I drive away that I think maybe I should have told him, "hell with her," or "stand up for yourself." I'm so used to him doing that anyway that I just don't think he needs my encouragement. But his tail was dragging as he walked in the door of the airport, and I wonder if he thinks

I don't support him. I decide I'll send him a supportive text when I stop at a red light.

Only yeah, that never happens. Because when I take my phone out, it's got three missed calls—I'd apparently muted it somehow without knowing—and there's a text from a number I don't recognize. It says, *Come talk to me before you say anything publicly.*

My fur prickles. Who the hell wants me to come talk to him, and why would I say anything publicly? I'm a couple miles from the stadium, so I turn on the radio. They're just covering the weather, and I never listen to the sports talk radio so I have no idea what station it is. Wait, they interviewed me a month or two ago. It was… "All Sports 990"? Or was it 1090? I flip around the AM dial, and at 990 AM I hear a sports-talk voice I recognize from the interview saying, "…clearly just a tactic to get the Firebirds riled up and thinking about stuff other than football."

"I don't know," his co-host says. "Sounds like it was just a stupid thing he said off the cuff."

I pull into the parking lot and sit in the truck listening. Eventually they get around to the "if you're just tuning in" part and they play the audio clip again. It's one of the linemen for the Hellentown Pilots saying, "Whatever he wants to do with his life is between him and Jesus. I'm just glad I don't have to be on the field at the same time, know what I mean?"

I turn the radio off and sit in the truck for a moment. I'd thought all this shit was behind me. My tail lashes against the seat, and my paws grip the steering wheel hard.

My phone, on the seat beside me, flashes with a call from another unfamiliar number. I swipe a finger across to ignore the call, and the text message comes up again. And then, I realize who it's from.

Coach has all of our cell phone numbers. We were supposed to program his in, and maybe it was in one of those phones I threw at a wall. He and Gerrard are the only ones who would send me that message, and Gerrard's number is stored in this phone; I remember transferring it over with Lee Christmas night.

So I get out of the truck, looking around warily for reporters, and thank God there aren't any. Probably haven't had time to get here yet. I leave the phone off and hurry through the locker room.

"Hey," a couple guys call out, but nobody says anything about the audio clip. I get to Coach's office and knock on the door, then let myself in when he answers.

"You heard this yet?" he asks, pointing to his laptop screen.

I sit down and nod. "The Hellentown guy? Is there more?"

He reads the quote again, just like I heard it on the radio. "Vince is on his way," he says, "and he'll handle the media, unless there's something you want to say. Personally," and he leans forward, eyes trapping mine, "I would let Vince handle it. You want to keep your mind on football. Give him a short statement if you want, or he can write something for you."

"I'll think of something." I want to call Lee and ask him what to say, but he's on a plane now, or maybe he's not, but he might not have heard about it and I'm afraid he'll want me to say something strident like "Homophobia has no place in professional football," which is probably what I really should say, but I don't want to start that argument and get all this attention back on me being gay. And if he tells me to say it and I don't, then he'll be upset. Whereas if I just say I did the best I could, at worst he'll be disappointed.

Of course, if I know what he wants me to do and I still don't do it, that's just as bad as if he tells me and I don't do it. That's my problem to deal with, though.

"Short statement," Coach says. "And then back to practice. Winning this game is your top priority."

"Yes, sir," I say, and at that implicit dismissal, I get up.

Gerrard and Charm look up as I come back into the locker room. "What's going on?" Charm asks, and a bunch of other people turn their heads at his booming question.

"Some guy on the Pilots made a shitty remark about me and Jesus," I say. "Vince is handling it."

"You and Jesus?" Charm shakes his head. "Dude, here I thought you already had a steady boyfriend."

I wish I could laugh appropriately at that, like a bunch of the guys in the locker room do. Colin, sitting alone in front of his locker, scowls, but looks away when he sees me looking at him. "Yeah," I say, "well, let's just ignore it and practice."

Gerrard looks pleased at that. Maybe that helps when Vince comes to yank me out of calisthenics twenty minutes later, because Gerrard barely gets that look of annoyance on his coyote muzzle that happens whenever someone disrespects the game or the preparations for it.

"Okay," Vince says, "here's what I recommend you say: 'I prefer not to bring personal beliefs into this game. I look forward to a good game Sunday that is all about football.' How's that sound?"

"Good," I say. Lee is definitely on a plane now. I can't call him to ask. Vince pats me on the shoulder and gets ready to go, and then, as if a fox is guiding it, my paw reaches out to stop him. "Except…"

He perks his ears, sharp little muzzle turned up to me. "What? Something else?"

I take a breath. "Can you also say…can you say something about how I think this game has room for all kinds of people, anyone who can play?"

He makes a clicking noise with his tongue while he thinks. "Not bad. Good, hit the inclusive angle. Still taking the high road. Yeah, we can work that in. Just don't let your goddamn agent call any press conferences."

I shake my head. "Where were you three months ago?"

"Hey," he says. "You're new, you got hit with this all at once. For my money, it worked out pretty good. Anything happen with Lee?"

Worked out pretty good? I'm still trying to figure out if I agree with that when it sinks in that he asked a question. "Um, he's up north getting some stuff from his mom's house. Why?"

"I mean about the job."

"Oh oh! They called him, but I don't know if he's going to take it."

"Ah well." Vince flashes me a shiny weasel grin. "We tried."

"Yeah, thanks for setting that up."

"No prob. And don't worry about this. It'll blow over. Just don't let it distract you."

Easier said than done. I run drills, I watch film, I study plays. I go through all the practices the coaches have set out for us, and I work with Zillo a lot, on Steez's orders. "Not as good as you," he says to me privately. "But he is next on list. Marais working with Gerrard, Zillo works with you."

"What about Carson?"

Steez grins. "If he would say more than two words, I would give him Zillo to work with. You talk, you make friends. Work with the coyote."

So I study with Zillo, talk to him, help him along. All the while, I'm thinking about that guy calling me out, implying, what, that I'm going to Hell? That I don't love Jesus the way he does? I hate being singled out, and during the practices where we're on the field with the defensive backs, I'm hyper-aware of Colin every time I see him. It starts to feel like he's the one who said that about me. Because I know he would, if he didn't think his teammates would murder him for it.

Zillo, pretty sharp, notices. "Hey," he says, "don't freak out about Colin. He's been good about being quiet." I mutter something noncommittal, and the coyote's ears flick down. "Yeah, I know, I'm sure he agrees. That's just how he was raised."

"He's not even trying to change."

"Well…he doesn't think he should have to. I mean, you get to be who you are."

"Yeah, but who I am doesn't constantly disrespect who he is."

He considers that. "All right. I guess you got a point there."

Because we're both tired of that subject, I make an effort to ignore Colin, and we talk about other stuff. Zillo has a girlfriend, a coyote he met online. "Funny, huh?" he says. "I mean, I get lots of girls, but I have to go through some anonymous Internet service to meet a good one."

"Life's like that," I say.

He hesitates for a moment and then goes ahead and asks, "How'd you meet Lee?"

A smoky bar, a fox in drag, a slight haze of beer. I cough. "Um, in college. Hey, let's look at these Hellentown plays again."

Lee calls that afternoon to let me know he got in okay, and to tell me he's heard this whole controversy. I call him back from the locker room once I'm dressed. "I liked your answer," he says. "You could have been a bit stronger."

"You were on a plane," I say.

"I know. I was going to say, you could have been, but it's probably best you didn't. Don't let it take your mind off football. Win that game Sunday."

I relax, leaning forward with elbows on my knees. "How's your dad?"

"Much the same as when you saw him two days ago."

"Thanks, doc."

I can almost see his grin. "We're good. I'm still worried about how tomorrow's going to go, but I had a couple glasses of wine this afternoon, so I'm not as worried as I might be. Haven't talked to Mother at all, but he says she knows we're coming."

"Good luck."

"Thanks, stud. Love you."

"Love you too."

I feel better having his approval. Maybe this thing will work out after all. He didn't press me to be some kind of spokesperson for the movement, to evolve my thinking or anything. I leave the phone muted, and I walk out of the facility.

There are a few reporters there, but fewer than I would have thought. "I've already released my official statement," I say, and wave them all aside. A leopard from one of the local stations persists, asking if that's all I have to say on the subject, and I say, "I'm focused on winning the game and the division on Sunday. That's all."

They fall back as I walk toward the parking lot fence, and then one shadow separates itself from the fence, dappled with sunlight—no, those are spots on his black muzzle, and on the peach-colored silk shirt. "No camera," he says, holding his paws up, and then I recognize Brian.

My fists clench. "What do you want?"

"Temper," he warns. "There's reporters just nearby." He inclines his head at the leopard, standing some fifteen feet away.

"I'm not going to hit you," I say. "Probably."

"I just wanted to know your thoughts on this homophobic comment. Is this the sort of thing you think is okay in the league?"

"I've made a statement—"

"Yes," he cuts in. "I've read your bland, media-friendly statement. I wanted something more personal."

"Sorry," I say, and start away.

"What does Wiley think of all this?"

I shake my head and reach for the gate into the parking lot, and Brian calls out, louder, "You know he's not telling you everything."

Just walk away. Just let it go. He doesn't know what he's talking about. "I think he's not telling you everything," I say.

"I've known him longer, you know. It's killing him, not being able to go all out for gay rights like he wants to."

The leopard listens to us, aware he shouldn't be and yet still a journalist, knowing there's a story here. I cover the distance to Briain in two strides, so quickly he flinches back, glances over to the reporters for support. His black and white tail flicks up, and this close, I get a sniff of his musk over the desert air, similar to my fox's, but sharper and more bitter. I show my open paws to prove I'm not going to deck him, and I hiss as low as I can, "I'm not stopping him."

He recovers a little, enough to smirk up at me. "You're not supporting him. You won't even take a day out of your schedule to do something that's really important to him."

"What, that PSA spot?" I snort. "He understands how important this game is, that's why I couldn't take Monday to do it."

"Oh," Brian says, "he hasn't even asked you yet. How preciously sad."

"What?" My fur prickles, and cold grips my chest.

"No, no, never mind. If you've already castrated him so he doesn't even want to ask, then it's certainly not my place." He steps back, keeping his eyes on me.

"There's no reason I should trust a single thing you say."

"Of course not. So you should just ask him." He puts a finger to the side of his muzzle. "He has at least mentioned the gay bear who killed himself, right? He hasn't kept that from you?"

"No," I say, "he's told me about Vince King." I feel strangely annoyed that he shared that with Brian.

"Real tragedy, wouldn't you agree?"

"Obviously. I guess this is why your career as a journalist didn't pan out. Are all your questions along the lines of 'is suicide a tragedy'?"

He narrows his eyes. "Wiley's been a bad influence on you. I guess it does go both ways."

"Get out of here," I say. "I'm done. And stay the hell away from Lee."

At that, he laughs. "You should tell him to stay away from me," he says. "I'm not the one who's been seeking him out."

Fuck him, he's right, but I don't care. "He can do whatever he wants. We only have trouble when you come around to stir it up."

He doesn't say anything, so I turn around, and of course it's only when I'm at the gate again with my paw on the latch that he calls, "Why are you so ashamed to be gay?"

Again, I know I should just ignore him, but that last one the leopard definitely heard. He's not even pretending to be anything other than a journalist now. So I focus on Brian and say, "I'm not ashamed. I'm a football player first, and my top priority is my job, which is winning games for the Firebirds."

"So your top priority isn't your boyfriend?"

God *damn* him. "He understands my priorities as well as I do. He doesn't want to be a distraction during the season or the playoffs. We've worked that all out."

"I guess you have." Brian steps back. "You might want to double-check with him, though." He raises a paw and walks off quickly.

The leopard stays, until I meet his eyes, and then he drops his head. I turn and stomp through the gate, gripping my keys like a weapon until I get to the truck.

All the way home, I think about calling Lee, asking him what Brian meant about taking a day out of my schedule. At least I have to tell him about Brian approaching me, and if I do that, there's really no way I can avoid telling him pretty much everything the bastard said. But Lee's got his mother to worry about, and do I really want to bother him?

I think he would want me to.

Chapter 27: House Divided (Lee)

After a month in Chevali, my ears tingle and my fur fluffs up from the cold when I step out into Hilltown's December wind. I leave a trail of shed fur on the pavement from my tail as I hurry into Father's car, which is remarkably clean until my cloud of fur settles on the upholstery and mats.

We go out for an early dinner, to a nice place that serves a very drinkable white wine, and that's where I hear about the thing this asshole Pilots player said about Dev, and Dev's response. "More Jesus freaks," I say to Father after leaving a message for Dev.

"It wasn't an appropriate thing to say in public, true."

"I can't believe people still actually talk about relationships with Jesus in this day and age. I feel like I should go nail a thesis to a church door."

Father gives me a look. "Don't bring anything to nail to your mother's front door, please."

"Oh, god, no." I rub my chin. "Although…I could print out that web page on Vince King…"

"Wiley."

"Kidding. Mostly." I cough.

Father shakes his head. "It sounds like Dev handled it well."

"Fairly well, I guess. I mean, if he wanted to, he could've used it as a springboard to talk about the intolerance that's still in the league. The people who want to marginalize him, not talk about his sexuality…"

"Um." Father rubs his whiskers and says, in an apologetic tone, "isn't that what he wants?"

This is, of course, the thing I keep trying not to think about too much. "Yes. But for a different reason."

"Right." And there's nothing I can say to that. Dev's entirely reasonable goal is just to be a good football player. He's worked so hard to get where he is that I know he wants to be recognized for his ability, and he didn't choose to come out. Okay, he did, but he was forced into that choice. Making his sexuality a cause could alienate him from his teammates, and he'd be crushed if he lost his job because of that. I want him to be successful, and while I think I would be at least a little more outspoken in his place, I don't know for sure. I certainly wasn't when I was working for the Dragons.

Still, I think if some moron lineman made a comment about my relationship with Jesus, I'd say something a little stronger than "I'm just focused on football." I guess that's my job, if anyone would ask me. Hal might, but he doesn't call, and Brian might, but he doesn't call either, and I'm not confident enough to call him to talk about it. Because he'll ask about Potomac and I will have to confess I haven't asked Dev yet.

There just wasn't a good time, not on Christmas night when I was still fuming about the call with Mother and his reaction to me talking about Vince King. Not on Thursday, when he got up early for practice, and not on Thursday night when I was going to be leaving the next day. And certainly not this morning on the way to the airport. By the time Thursday rolled around, anyway, he was deep into practice for Sunday, and I didn't want to distract him.

Hopefully that Pilots lineman won't have managed to do that, either. Part of me thinks he did it on purpose just to see if they can get Dev thinking about something other than the game, or maybe rile his teammates up. It was a quote from a sports morning show, and the hosts specifically asked the guy about playing against Dev, because this guy talks a lot about his church and religious charities and whatnot. I feel like taking out my new phone and checking whether he comes up on the Families United website, but I resist.

Dev calls a little later, after his practice, and we talk briefly. When I hang up, Father asks if this whole thing is going to blow over. I tell him I'll check this evening, but there's not a lot I can do about it in any case except remind Dev to play the game, which is what I just did. So we talk about football, about Aunt Carolyn and about Dev's family, about Father's work and the team in Yerba I will hopefully be working with, and then we head back to his new apartment.

It's a two-level deal with gleaming modern furnishings and a spiral stair up to the bedroom loft. I lie down on the blankets on the couch and look up at the railing defining the edge of my father's bedroom, and above it, the softly lit vaulted ceiling. Here on the couch, at least, there is some of my father's shed fur, and it smells like him enough that it reminds me of home.

Dev calls for the second time that day as I'm lying there, after Father goes to bed. He tells me Brian showed up after practice and badgered him, and I pinch my eyes shut with the paw that isn't holding the phone. Goddamn Brian. It only took him three weeks to go back to being a total asshole. I apologize to Dev for the harassment and he says I don't have to, and I tell him I love him and I'll take care of it. He says he doesn't blame me and I'm not sure that's true, and I'm not sure I deserve to be free of blame even if it is. He mentions Potomac and I tell him not to worry about it, that I'll tell him when I get back.

What I'm thinking about as I hang up isn't so much Brian, it's Dev and the patient restraint in his voice as he told me about the incident. If he had any inclination at all to do a spot for Equality Now, much less take a day trip to Potomac, it's gone, his resolve to concentrate on football now set in concrete. And the more I badger him, the worse it'll get.

In the morning, Father comes down to make coffee, and I go upstairs to use the shower. My parents' bedroom at home smelled of my mother and reflected her quirky-elaborate aesthetic: lots of knick-knacks and colorful decorations. Father's room here is more spartan. He has a couple pictures up on the wall, art pieces of colorful landscapes that are not quite realistic. It's only when I get out of the shower that I see the picture on his nightstand: it's a picture from the time he took me to my first Dragons game, almost twelve years ago now.

I stand there, fur damp, and stare at it. Father's downstairs with the smell of coffee and toast, the occasional beeps of his phone. The scent of him is strong here, and unlike how I'm used to smelling it at home—at what used to be home—it is alone. I walk quickly over to the picture and pick it up, quietly. The two of us are standing in front of the scoreboard. "Get the logo in," he'd told the usher who took the picture. There's no grey on his ears. I'm wide-eyed and grinning. Even though the Dragons lost, I had the best time ever. All the smells were new, the beer and pretzels and mustard and sausages and fried chicken and melted cheese like we never had at home.

I rub my thumb over the glass and hopefully leave a little of my scent behind as well before putting the picture back down. I walk downstairs and don't mention it, but it relaxes me in a way, seeing some familiar things in this unfamiliar place. It reminds me of Dev's apartment, of the way we make our homes follow us, appearing wherever we are. Father's made this his home, and so part of it is mine. I am not so sure that is still true of Mother's house.

On the way there in the rented van, Father makes it a point to say, "Your mother said she's looking forward to seeing you."

The second time he says it, I say, "It's fine. I promise I'll behave."

He nods, and I can't resist adding, "As long as she does."

"Wiley." He sighs and shakes his head. "You're her son, all right."

"And yours, too."

He pushes his glasses up on his muzzle, and grins. "Yes. Mine too."

When we make the turn onto the street and drive up to the house, not only is the driveway not empty, there are *two* cars in it. I recognize Mother's blue sport wagon, but the white minivan next to it is unfamiliar. Father stops the car and sits. "She said she wasn't going to be there."

"Mother said she wasn't, or…" I gesture toward the minivan.

"Both." He smacks a paw against the steering wheel. He's bristling, his ears are down. "You want to stay in the car?"

"No fucking way," I say.

With perhaps a bit too much enthusiasm. Because he looks at me and I can see the thoughts behind his eyes. I head them off. "Don't you even think of leaving me here. After this bullshit, I'm going to have it out with her one way or another."

"Don't make it more difficult than it has to be."

I point, stabbing at the windshield. "She just upped the stakes. Nobody asked her to bring a friend along."

"That's Mrs. Hedley's car." Father stares at it as though he can dematerialize it with the power of thought.

"I figured it was something like that." I open the door and step out into the freezing air. "Come on. You think they're going to gang up on us? I guess she could've brought a lynch mob in that minivan."

He sits for a moment, but when I slam my door, he gets out too. "I'd ask you not to do anything rash," he says in a puff of white breath, "but I rather think that's like asking the water not to boil over an open flame. So can you please just try and think before you talk?"

"I've been thinking for a good long time," I start, then fold my ears down, as much against his expression as against the cold. "I'll do my best. But if she starts something…"

"I'm not going to hold you back." He holds up a paw, and a glint of light off his wedding ring catches my eye. "But I hope she won't be unreasonable. I hope she's just…I hope it's just that she wants a friendly face around."

"I'm kind of pissed she doesn't think of us as friendly. Maybe she wants backup in case we try to take something she doesn't want us to. She doesn't trust us."

"Well." We walk up the path. "Would you?"

I don't answer, staring at the lightly frosted flagstones under my paws. So many times I'd walked up this path, and even when I was coming home with the pink triangle pin and the rainbow scarf and the pride-patched denim jacket, it never felt this ominous. It always, even last Christmas, felt like home.

The porch is silent. We walk up the stairs, past the gardening tools under their winter blanket, up to the screen door with "The Farrels" on it. Dad opens the screen door and then the main door, and I follow him in.

A rush of scent hits me, mostly Mother's. There are some unfamiliar ones, too, the strongest being a female otter. In the small entry hall, a stack of eight boxes (medium size) hides the map on the wall; a wide, thin box leans against the stack. The rest of the foyer looks very much the same, with the exception of the picture of Jesus Fox that now hangs where our family portrait (1998) had hung. That makes me wonder if the map on the wall is still a map, so I walk over to the pile of boxes and catch a strong scent of Father from them.

As the front door swings shut, I hear movement in the living room and Mother appears in the doorway. "Harold," she says. "Wiley." She looks at me and bites her lower lip, her fangs showing. She's dressed in a white blouse with a sweater over it and a long navy blue skirt, and I can't help but notice that her fingers are bare of any rings.

"We're just here to collect our things." Father leans to his left, trying to see into the living room. "This is all of them?"

"You may look through the boxes if you like." Mother watches him. She looks really nervous, for someone who wants everything to go smoothly. And even though she's watching him, she keeps her ears turned toward me. "If there's anything else you want, we can discuss it."

"I've got all the important things from my office. Are some of these from Wiley's room?" Father pulls down the top box and I give him a hand with it, getting it down to the ground. While he opens it, I pull down the next one, which is lighter.

Mother stands with arms folded, like a store clerk making sure we don't slip anything into our pockets. "One of them is. The others are from our bedroom, your office, and the basement." Father looks through the books and model cars in the first box, then moves on to the one I pulled down, full of old clothes.

I sniff at the boxes until I find one with my scent. It's taped shut.

"Can I borrow your keys?" I ask Father, and he holds them out. Mother lifts a paw and then lets it fall to her side.

"You don't have to open that," she says, without force.

"My X-ray specs are inside it," I say, and slash the tape with a key and pull open the flaps. In there are a few things—some clothes, some of my college books, some CDs. I rummage through and find notebooks from high school, an old jacket I ripped my senior year. No denim pride jacket, none of my pride books or posters I worked on in college. And my old plush dragon isn't there; in fact, nothing that dates from before my junior year of college is in the box.

Only in looking through the box do I remember the things that are missing. Those notebooks used to sit next to my eighth grade sculpture project; the CD's were held up by a debate trophy. Nothing is missing that I need in my daily life, but I'm not willing to lose the memories. I think of Dev's room, still set up with all the trappings of his adolescence. He doesn't think about that all the time, but when he wants it, it's always there. I thought of it as cute at the time, the preservation of a room as though a bright-eyed high schooler would come rushing back to it at any moment. Now, the dismantling and possible disappearance of mine feels far more threatening than I would have thought.

"Where's the rest of my stuff?" I look up at Mother.

She fidgets. "It's all there," she says.

"Mother. It's not all here. What happened to the rest of it?"

Her ears flatten and she glances back into the house. "I thought that was all you would need."

"You thought wrong." I let the flaps fall back and return the keys to Father. "Is the rest of it still in my room? I can grab most of it now."

Mother gets a really strange look on her face, kind of half scared and half angry, and she says, "I don't want you taking anything else."

Straight ahead of the foyer, the door to the kitchen is closed, but I can get to the back of the house and the stairs to my room through there. I charge forward without saying anything, and Mother grabs at my shirt—actually grabs at me—and then hurries after me. But I'm moving pretty quickly too, and I get through the other side of the kitchen and then run into a female otter, who grabs my arm.

I wrench it away, but it gives Mother time to catch up with me. She pushes her way forward, trying to stand between the two of us.

"You needn't bother going upstairs," the female otter says. She articulates every word primly, glowering at me from beneath a wide white hat. I've never seen an otter look less playful.

"Who the hell are you?" I ask, though I have a pretty good idea.

Her little ears flatten at the curse, and she gives a look all full of judgment at my mother. "Eileen, you don't have to let him go upstairs."

Mother is panting slightly, glaring at me. Fur fills the air around us, and not only mine. "Don't curse. All the things you're here for are in the front hall."

I stare through the dining room at the back stairs. "There's a lot more stuff I want."

Father walks up behind me. "What's going on, Eileen? Did you not pack everything up?"

Mother and the otter turn to look at him, and I dart between them, making it to the staircase quickly. Footsteps thump behind me, but I get to the top first, cross the hall, and slam into the closed door to my room. I wrench at the handle, but the door still won't open. There's a metallic clank with every shove. I notice, then, the hasp and padlock that definitely were not there at Christmas.

"What is this?" I turn, facing Mother, who's standing at the top of the stairs, panting harder now.

She won't look directly at me. Her ears are back. "You…you turned your back on that life. I want to preserve it."

"I turned my back? You turned your back on me! Those are my things!"

"Not now. You were my cub at the time, and you didn't take them with you."

I press my paw to my door. Father tries to work his way around her. "Wiley," he says. "It's just some childhood things. We can have this argument later."

I can't smooth my bristled fur down, but I breathe deeply. "All right," I say. "But what about my pride jacket and books and stuff? Do you really want to keep those too?"

"No," she says.

"Then let me in to get them."

She takes a deep breath, and even Father waits, knowing something is wrong before she opens her mouth. As it happens, the answer comes not from her, but from the high-pitched voice of the otter behind her, on the staircase. "Those things are gone."

"Gone?" I say. Mother still won't look at me. "Gone? Mother?"

"They were…burned."

I actually don't believe my ears. I must have misheard, I think. "I'm sorry. They were burned? Who burned them?"

"It was…" She folds her arms and takes a breath.

"Who? Jesus?"

"Wiley," Father says, warningly. He puts a paw on Mother's arm, but his ears are down too, and his tail is curled around his leg. "What do you mean, Eileen?"

"It's a practice they recommend, when a cub is lost…"

"Lost?" I yell, and Father puts his paw up again, the one with the wedding ring still on it.

The otter, Mrs. Headcase or whatever, pipes up. "If the cub has made it clear that he has no interest in saving his soul, the burning of his tainted possessions is a way for the parent to cleanse herself and move on."

Even Father looks shocked at that. "Really, Eileen?" he says.

"It helped," she says, and pulls away from him. "I felt more liberated afterwards."

"Great." I am surprised to hear the snarl in my voice, and Mother's wide eyes show that she is equally startled. "I'm glad burning my things made you feel better. Is that standard practice? Did Vince King's parents do that in front of him?"

"I think you should leave," Mother says, voice trembling.

"Did they? Did they burn his clothes before he went into the garage and put a shotgun to his head?"

"Don't let him manipulate you, Eileen," the otter says. "We're not allowed to talk about that."

"Not allowed? Why not? Because when something goes wrong and one of the people you torture blows his goddamn brains out, you just erase him from existence? The way you're trying to erase the parts of me you don't like?"

Mother takes a step toward me. "Don't you utter profanity in this house."

"I'll say whatever the *fuck* I want." I pound on the door again. "What the hell happened to you?" I look at the otter, behind her. "Is this some kind of cult where you have to be with an ordained brainwasher at all times?"

"Calm down," Father says, though it's not clear whom he's talking to.

"Leave this house now." Mother lowers her voice, but her paws are shaking and her ears are flat and tight against her head. Her eyes narrow and they don't leave my face.

"Not without my books! My posters, my old clothes, my—"

"None of that is yours!" the otter says shrilly behind her.

"Mother," I say, deliberately ignoring the otter. "I want my things."

She takes another step forward, and this time my father holds her back by one arm. She gestures with the other. "No. Mrs. Hedley's right. You have made it perfectly clear where your life is and what you intend to do with it, and that room," she points with an unsteady finger, "that room is part of the life you left behind."

"I'm not leaving anything behind!" I shout back. "You're the one who's changed, you're the one who's found religion and abandoned her family!"

Her jaw sets; her voice goes cold. "I left nobody," she says. "My family left me."

We stand there, the only sound our harsh breathing, until the otter says, delicately, "Do I need to call the authorities?"

She has her cell phone out. Mother stares at me another moment. Father turns to the otter and says, "Nobody needs to call the authorities."

This doesn't satisfy Mrs. Headwound. "Eileen?"

"I'm fine, Celia," Mother says after what she deems an appropriate silence, I guess. "They'll go."

"I'm not going anywhere—"

"If you'd prefer I have Celia call the police," Mother says, and lets the threat hang in the air. The otter, halfway down the stairs, pauses there.

"We'll leave." Father steps around her before she can finish and grabs my paw. I pull it away; he grabs it again.

"No!" I yell. "She's being a selfish bitch! She's only doing this to spite me!"

Mother folds her arms. "I'm sorry that you couldn't control your temper during this visit."

"What happened to all that shit you said on the phone? Wanting to get along, wanting a day of peace and harmony? Had you already burned my things then?" I resist Father's attempts to drag me down the stairs, but to be honest, he's not trying very hard.

"I meant it all. I'm still holding a place for you in my life."

"You're not holding a place for me. You're holding a place for your sanitized, straightened out, Stepford version of me. That fox cub is gone, Mother."

"Don't you think I don't know that," she says.

I start to walk around her, following Father. "I was willing to give you a chance," I say, maybe only lying a little bit. Okay, maybe a quarter. Half at most.

"You came here intending to fight," she says. "You never gave me a chance. Ever since you went away to that school, you haven't given me a chance."

"You never even tried to understand," I shoot back. "You think you know all about me just because I finally told you the truth about myself, and you're dead wrong, but you don't care, because you have a bunch of friends telling you you're right, you're the victim."

"I *am* the victim," she almost cries.

"All that shit about making up and being nice was just for what? To try to get me to go straight? I'm *gay*, Mother. I have a boyfriend. We have sex, a lot."

"All right," Father says, because Mother really is near tears now, and he pulls me the rest of the way down the stairs. Mother stays at the top, rubbing her eyes. Through my anger, I almost feel bad.

At the base of the staircase, Mrs. Headshot stands aside, looking perfect and self-righteous, standing ramrod-straight under her wide-brimmed hat.

I'm still fuming at Mother, and I'm angry that I made her cry, and I'm angry that she made me, and this fucking bitch of an otter is right there in front of me. "Were you the one who called the Kings? Did you put up that goddamn web page?"

She doesn't answer at first. Of course it's ridiculous; she lives out here, a thousand miles from the Kings; she wouldn't have flown out there on a day's notice. She might not even know them. But she might know the people who run the website. "You might as well have put the gun to his head and shot that poor kid yourself."

Her expression doesn't waver. "Everyone is given a chance at salvation."

I don't miss her pointed stare at me as she says that. Father's pulling me toward the kitchen, out of the house, but I glare back at this church-otter and say, "You want to ascend to heaven right now?"

"Wiley!" Father pushes me into the kitchen. "Get out and get into the car."

But the otter follows us. "I lost two sons to the homosexual agenda," she says. "I know the pain poor Eileen is going through."

"She hasn't lost anyone!" I yell. "She's pushing people away, just like you probably pushed your sons away. What's their names? I want to look them up and tell them they are fucking lucky to have gotten away from a crazy psycho mother like you."

She stays icy calm, following as Father drags me back through the kitchen. "I have no sons, not anymore." Behind her, Mother appears at the doorway. "I tried to save them and I failed. It's my hope that I can help other parents."

"You're the one who's lost." I wrench my arm away from Father. He puts a paw on my shoulder, but I say, "It's okay, I'm not going to do anything. I just have one more thing to say." I point at Mrs. Headfuck but I'm looking at Mother. "You say you lost your sons, but you know they're alive out there. How would you feel if your sanctimonious hate-filled preaching made your son put a gun to his head and pull the trigger? Because that's what you and your people did to that family."

Those would be great words to stomp out on. Mother actually looks like they affected her, so I turn around intending to do just that. But that otter says, "They *are* dead, as far as I'm concerned. I tell their story as a cautionary tale to other parents who think they can live with their sinful children. Eventually the sin takes over, if the children are not corrected in time."

Father sees my eyes go wide and my ears go flat, and he doesn't take chances this time. "Get in the car," he snaps, and shoves me at the front door. "And don't you dare come back in. I'll get the boxes out."

"Get them onto the porch," I say. "I'll carry them to the car. I promise I won't say another word."

And I keep that promise, but only because Father also tells the two women to stay in the kitchen—I'm sure Mrs. Nineteen-Fifty is only too glad to—and he shuts the door. He puts boxes out on the porch and I carry them to the van in silence, staring at the white fog of my breath and flexing my fingers so they don't get numb in the cold. I stack boxes on the cold metal floor, throwing them harder than I need to against the walls. Father comes out to help, to push the boxes into more orderly stacks, and we don't say a word.

He turns the heat up full blast and backs the van out. I blow on my fingers and rub my ears to warm them as fur flies around us. My lips are cold and I still don't trust myself to say anything. The radio plays some adult alternative song about the color blue, but to its tune I just hear my mother's words, over and over. *The life you left behind. My family left me.*

I force them out of my head. If she's going to consider me lost to her, then she's lost to me too, and that's just too bad. I haven't thought that much about her since the beginning of the year, not until my father brought her up.

"When I didn't graduate college," I say. "You were both pretty upset."

Father's ears come up. "I still think you made a mistake," he says. "Look where you are now."

"I'm going to be fine. I have a rich boyfriend."

"And a job in Yerba. But a college degree is never a bad thing to have in your back pocket."

"Jesus Fox, Father."

He pauses. "You are doing well for yourself."

"Thank you."

The music changes to a cover of "Jingle Bells" by some female singer, a bobcat, if I recall, with a throaty voice. "How are you so much better about my life? You started out kind of…" I wave my paws. "Distanced. Did you and Mother ever talk about it? How did you go in different directions?"

"We talked about it. I said there wasn't much more we could do. Your mother wanted to send you to a counselor to get you to finish college. Looking back, it was probably for more than that." He keeps his eyes on the road, but his ears toward me.

"Did she start going to church again then?"

"No, it was just, um. February of this year? It was good, you know. She hadn't been doing much around the house and she was getting involved in the community. That otter started coming over to visit, and they had a little group playing games. She was preachy as—well, you saw. But she was Eileen's friend, and I had an office to go to and friends to talk to, and she didn't. So I just went out, or hid in the basement."

"You didn't try to talk her out of it?"

"Wiley…" He shakes his head slowly. "Did she change because I wasn't talking to her? Or did I stop talking to her because she changed? How can you know these things? I tried. I was always there, I asked about her friends. But she started getting more and more dogmatic. And when she talked about you, she talked as though you'd chosen your life to wound her personally."

"I didn't."

"I know."

"I would now, though."

He sighs. "That's not constructive."

"No. But tell me you don't know how I feel."

There's a pause. The stupid "Jingle Bells" song goes off and a commercial comes on. Father says, "I do. But do you know how I'm feeling? I'm sad at what's been lost. Your mother is still the person I married."

"No, she's not. Didn't you hear her? Once you change, you leave your old life behind."

"I don't believe that, and I don't think she does either."

"She said it loudly enough." I squeeze my paws together in my lap.

He drives us down a ramp and onto the highway. Focusing on the merge, he's quiet until we settle into a lane of traffic. "You weren't exactly giving her a chance to be understanding."

"She locked my room. She *burned* my clothes and books!" The posters, the books, the plush toys, all the things I hadn't really wanted until an hour ago, imprisoned behind stupidity and anger. The denim jacket… gone.

Father spares me a quick glance. "That was over the line. I will have a talk with her about respecting property, if you want, and I'll try to get the rest of your things. But you didn't handle it well."

"What was I supposed to do, say, 'Okay, you're right, I'll just leave'?"

"If your only other option was to call her a 'scheming bitch,' then, yeah, I'd say that sounds about right. She's still your mother, and you're still her son."

"She's not your wife."

I regret that right away, even though he doesn't react. "Sorry," I say. "I mean…"

"No, you're right. She's not. But she is still your mother."

So as to keep the peace, I don't let out the voice in my head, the stubborn refrain singing, *No, no, no, she's not.*

It takes us an hour to find a place to eat, by which time I'm a little calmer. We get dinner at Pasta Roma, an Italian place that neither of us has been to before, a place with no associations from our past. Those places are harder to find than you'd think in the big city twenty minutes from where you grew up. And Pasta Roma has wine, a cheap house chianti that usually I wouldn't think of as drinkable. I've only gotten through a glass and a half of it when Dev calls.

He's on a break from practice. I can hear the other guys in the background, talking and laughing. Dev wants to know if I'm done moving my stuff, and when I laugh, he says, "That's one of the bitterest laughs I've ever heard from you. What happened?"

So I give him the whole story, abridged because Father's sitting there and his ears go down farther and farther with every detail I recall, and because the wolf couple one table over keeps flicking their ears to listen. "She burned your shit?" Dev says, and Father definitely hears that, because he sighs and stares down at his salad.

"Yeah," I say. "Look, I'm going to finish up dinner. I'll be back tomorrow morning but I wish I were coming back tonight."

"I do too," he says. "Look, I got calls from a couple reporters about the Pilots quote today, but I just put them off. I didn't hear from Brian again. And whatever this thing is that he wanted you to ask me about, don't worry about it."

"Yeah," I say. "Okay. Thanks. Love you."

"Love you too," he says.

Our pasta dishes arrive then, in a cloud of warmth and mouth-watering cheese and marinara sauce scent. Next to us, the wolves are back in their own conversation. I inhale the strong, rich tomato, with just enough garlic to sharpen the flavor without overwhelming it. When the waiter leaves, my father says, "I'm glad you have Dev, and some of his teammates."

"I am too." I'm hungry and a little buzzed, meaning I'd better get some food in me. I lift my fork and plunge it into the pasta, and say, "Thanks," before taking the first hot bite.

"Christmas was nice. His teammates seem like good guys."

"They are. I guess you'll get to know them better, if you're managing their money."

We make small talk until the waiter takes our plates away. Then Father says, in a low voice, "I'm sorry this is so hard on you."

"It's not your fault."

"I mean…" He takes a breath. "You've made this worse, for sure. But you didn't do anything to deserve it, not to start with. If you were dating a female tiger, well, Eileen would still have issues, because you remember the thing with her sister who ran off with that fennec."

"I thought that would make her more understanding."

Father swirls his wine and breathes in the aroma from the glass. "Sometimes it does. Sometimes you think you're not going to be like your parents. And then you run into a hitch and you panic because not being like your parents didn't work."

"I'm a hitch, now?"

He raises an eyebrow. "I didn't mean it that way."

"I mean, I think that's underselling it. I'm way more than a hitch. I'm a huge tree falling across the path. I'm a burned-out bridge."

That gets a little bit of a smile. "I don't think the bridge is completely burned out yet. But the point is, we taught you to be yourself, and you went and did that in a way we weren't expecting."

"You handled it well enough. Aunt Carolyn handled it. Jesus, even Dev's backwards auto mechanic father handled it."

"Carolyn rebelled against her parents so thoroughly that I'm not sure she could do anything else now." He drops his gaze back to his wine and takes a drink, the red staining his white muzzle until he wipes it clean. "I thought your mother had left that behind too."

"I guess sometimes we can't leave behind the things our parents teach us," I say, and lift my glass to him. "Thanks for at least teaching me some things I want to keep."

It's only later, when I'm trying to sleep on his couch, that I start to process the whole day. I get angry again, shaking and clenching my fists, and I want to call Dev just to vent. But Father's still sleeping upstairs and Dev's probably asleep too. So I just stare up at the ceiling and I vow that I'm going to do whatever it takes to discredit those Families United fuckers. I'll leave the job in Yerba, I'll work with Brian, whatever it takes. This is my goal now, this is my passion…

And I think about Dev, him and Brian. Ice replaces the fire in me, and I close my eyes. I can't do that to Dev. If I become a crusader, the pressure on him won't stop. Even if I cut Brian completely out of the loop, it won't matter. Everyone I work with will be asking me, why isn't your boyfriend doing these things? I'll be talking about it constantly at home because otherwise I won't have anything to talk about. I'll lose touch with football, I'll lose touch with one of the important things Dev and I have in common.

Did she change because I wasn't talking to her? Or did I stop talking to her because she changed?

If I choose this path, will it take me farther from Dev? Will he and I end up shouting over boxes in the front hall, or just quietly slipping apart? I squeeze my paws together over my chest as though there's a tiger there, and now there's no ice, no fire, just an empty aching hollow inside my ribs.

I want my tiger. I want to go home.

CHAPTER 28: PILOT ERROR (DEV)

Sunday approaches like a freight train—not barreling full-speed, but creaking its way interminably through a railroad crossing when you're sitting in the car waiting. Saturday night I don't fall asleep in the first ten minutes I'm lying in bed, so because I don't want to stay up half the night, I take a couple Ambien. The trainers gave us a small supply; the coaches don't like that, but they like tired players even less.

And I wake up Sunday feeling pretty refreshed. Lee's flying in earlyish, and after what he went through, I really want to pick him up. But he's already arranged for Hal to get him and take him to the game, and even though I want badly to hug him, I also want badly to win this game.

So I drive to the stadium, and on the way I put everything out of my mind: Brian, Lee's mom, the Pilots quote, all that shit, everything except the football game. I dress as the other guys filter in, from the outside and from the training room where the ones who need it are getting painkillers. These days, that's half the team. My ribs are a little sore, my toe is sore, but it's not at a level where I need a shot yet. So I just dress, talk with Charm, and try to relax.

Surprisingly easy. To Charm, games are very much like watching them on TV except that sometimes he gets to run out and kick. So he's not worried. Hellentown doesn't have exceptional special teams. We put the ball down, he kicks it. His casual attitude is infectious, and so by the time we get Coach's serious speech, I'm able to absorb it. Hell, I'm raring to go.

"We beat these guys already," Coach says to a quiet locker room. It feels like he turns and looks every one of us in the eye. "I'm proud of how you have all come together as a team. It hasn't been easy. There have been a lot of challenges. But you have met and conquered every one of them." Even Strike is here for this one, uncharacteristically quiet. "I don't think there's ever been a year like this one, for a lot of reasons." Here it feels like his eyes are on me. "But there's one really big reason. There's never been a year when a Firebirds team could go out and win their division on the last game of the season." Teeth flash as he looks around. "It ain't gonna be easy. They want it as bad as we do, maybe more. But if there's one thing I've learned about this team, it's that you don't give up. You go out there and you leave your best on the field, and every one of you is a winner. So let's go!" We yell. "Let's fight!" We yell louder. "Let's *win!*" We scream, we stand, we stomp. "On three, Firebirds! One, two…"

"FIREBIRDS!" The locker room and our ears ring.

And I think that's loud until we jog out of the locker room and into the deafening roar of Chevali Stadium. I try to find Lee's section and fail, until the national anthem plays, and then I see the numbers. I have no chance of finding him up there among the red and gold that looks like a Hilltown autumn. But even as I'm looking, the anthem is over, the game's getting started. If the week was moving slowly, today is speeding by.

We lose the toss and Hellentown chooses to receive the ball. Charm kicks it way downfield for them, but they have a good runback to the thirty. My helmet's on, I'm running out onto the field, and here we go.

The receiver I'm most responsible for is number eighty-three, the fox who usually lines up in the slot. On film, he demolishes one-on-one coverages like the one we use—he had an amazing run against New Kestle last week. Last game, though, I kept him pretty frustrated, so we've been looking at film to see what the Pilots might see, what changes they might make in the game plan to face us again.

On the first series, it doesn't look like much is different. He comes across the middle, I check the play. On passing plays, I stick to him. They run a few times, try going deep and miss, then get a long gain to our thirty, where the fox catches the ball once for five yards and I tackle him.

As we're getting up, he kind of shoves me away and says, "Don't mistake me for your boyfriend, homo."

A nearby fox in a Firebirds uniform laughs shortly, a kind of "ha." I think it's Vonni for a moment and start to say, "Hey, what the fuck?" when I see the number and realize it's not; it's Colin, coming in to take a couple plays while Vonni, who chased the Pilots receiver all the way down the field, catches his breath.

"Fuck off," I say, but I say it softly and I say it only in my head, so I won't get into trouble. Last thing I need in this game is to get into another fight like in Millenport. Certainly not with my own teammates.

The fox trots back to the Pilots huddle and Colin walks down to the sideline, staying in for the next play. Gerrard comes over to me. "They're gonna go to him again," he says. "What happened there?"

I tell him, briefly, and assure him I'm okay, staring at the fox. "He wasn't like that the first game."

He claps me on the shoulder. "They're gonna try to rattle you however they can. You need to stay focused."

Pike, nearby, turns his head. "Hey, Coach," he says, "We got his back."

"Don't you get distracted either," Gerrard says. "Keep your eye on that damn 98 and get around him next time."

"Yeah, yeah." Pike turns to Brick, says something in a low voice, and the two of them line up.

Gerrard points to the fox as the Pilots come back to the line. "Head in the game," he says to me.

"I'm good. You just watch that deer." The Pilots have a white-tailed deer, slippery and fast, who backs up their primary running back, and he's in on this down.

"I'm telling you, they're going to pass to eighty-three." That's the last thing Gerrard says, because the offense is set and the snap is coming.

Standing back from the line with my eye on the fox, I think, we planned for all kinds of plays they might run, formations they might change. We never planned for them to get into my head—we thought that one guy with his Jesus comment was just one guy running his mouth. It's ridiculous, anyway, that him calling me "homo" would sting after all I've already been through, but it does, a little. It makes me feel like I don't belong out here. Ironically, I guess, when I used to call someone "fag"—in college—it was a kind of inclusive insult. Because hey, you fag, get outta there, and hey, fag, you're not gonna beat me. It was something we'd call each other and so using it made you feel like part of a group. And what would Lee say about that?

Eighty-three is nothing like Lee. He's a foot taller, his tail's a different shade, the voice is lower and nastier. He's more like Colin, but even Colin has a smoother, lighter voice. Eighty-three sounds like he's been smoking his whole life, which would make him the first canid I've met with a smoking habit.

And there's no reason for me to feel excluded. My teammates are behind me, and I only have to glance up into the stands to see the signs supporting me. "DEV'S DIVAS" are still up there, and there are lots of other signs too—

All that vanishes from my mind the moment movement starts. I shadow the fox, and even though I feel like I got off a half-second slower than I should have, I'm right there when the lion at quarterback cocks his arm and throws. I reach out and feel the hard leather of the ball against my pads, and a moment later it goes tumbling to the ground and the fox keeps running to the sidelines while I pull up.

"Nice work," Gerrard says as we get back.

"Thanks," I say, but I'm thinking, I coulda had that interception. Another half-second, another six inches, and my paw closes around the ball instead of just deflecting it. They line up for the field goal and their kicker, a dappled grey horse a little smaller than Charm, knocks it through to put them up 3-0.

The missed interception bothers me all the way back to the bench, where I sit and listen to Steez tell us what we need to be doing better. We're keeping the runs down to 3-4 yards, but he wants us to get more penetration, to get some tackles in the backfield. We listen, I process what he's saying, and when he's done I look up into the stands toward Lee. I feel like he'd be disappointed that I missed the interception, but he'd be disappointed that I let that fox's remark get to me, too. And he'd say, "That's the kind of thing that you could be helping prevent."

Shit. I need to remember how much I love him, how much I want to do well for him, how much I want him to be able to come to a home playoff game here and how much I want to come home to him after that. They only got three points. We can still win this.

But Hellentown is playing pretty inspired defense, too. They double-cover Strike on pretty much every play. Jaws runs well, but when we get down to their twenty, Aston underthrows Strike in the end zone. The cheetah lunges forward, not in time to stop one of their cornerbacks from grabbing the ball out of the air. Strike tackles him immediately, but it deflates us. We were so close and now we have nothing to show for it.

I go back out onto the field with more determination, and as Pike breaks up one of their run formations, Gerrard and I bring down the white-tailed deer for a two-yard loss. On the next play, Carson tackles the tight end at the line. We rush the lion on third down, and he has to throw the ball away. So they don't get any points off the turnover, and we feel good.

The problem is that Aston is trying too hard now. He throws too fast, too long, and he doesn't look for Strike at all on the next series. Ty catches a nice pass for a ten-yard gain, but we can't get past midfield, and we have to punt it back to them.

At least we have better field position. This gives us on the defense more incentive to keep them contained, and we do, until most of the way through the second quarter. Their deer, the finesse back, slips past Brick, jukes past Gerrard. I run after him, but it's Norton who tackles him, well into our territory.

"Hold tight!" Gerrard yells at us. "Hold tight!"

That fox, eighty-three, is ready again, and I know they're going to throw to him. I'm ready, and when the play starts, I watch for him to break. I bump him at the line, throwing off his timing, and then he breaks for the sidelines. It was probably a precision play, or else the quarterback is throwing away from me, because the ball goes off the fox's outstretched paw, out of bounds to the side.

Momentum carries me into him; I put my paws out to stop myself.

Again, he growls and shoves me and says, "I told you, homo, I'm not your cocksucking boyfriend."

I can't see his face, but if I could, I feel like I'd punch it. Instead, I back up, holding my paws up, and say, "I know you're not. My boyfriend can catch."

He comes after me as I go back to the line, not physically, just trotting near me and jawing. "Maybe you should get him out there on your offense, then. You fuck all those faggots too?"

"Naw," I say. "We're just getting ready to fuck your sorry asses."

"Hey!" Pike yells, pointing at the fox. "Quit tryin' to pick up Miski and get back on your own side."

"Fuck you, seventy-three," the fox says, but picks up the pace and gets back to his huddle.

I come back to the line angry, seething, but Pike's comment makes things better, and Gerrard pats my shoulder, which helps too. Their next play doesn't go to me; it falls incomplete, and they have to try a field goal. This kick wobbles a bit and just clears the crossbar. 6-0.

Our offense goes back out with a minute and a half left. Aston's yelling as they go: "Come on, let's get something on the board!"

The Pilots have a good line, and the linebackers are pretty good—two wolves and a jaguar. I've seen them on film a little, and it's good to watch them live. The wolves are beasts against the run, and the jaguar seems to be everywhere. Time and time again, Jaws finds a hole in their defensive line and one of the wolves is right there. I'm reminded of Fisher's story about the big black wolf, Von Werner, who took out an offensive lineman in the playoffs so hard the guy never recovered.

Gerrard points out something the wolves are doing, and together we watch, and we're watching the defense so closely that we miss our offense doing something wonderful and unpredictable: they run Strike behind the line, where he takes a handoff from Aston and dashes around the end. Rodolf throws a block for him and Strike sprints down the sidelines, to their forty, thirty, and now we're watching him and cheering him on to the twenty, only their safety to beat, now to the ten and—

—and the safety trips him up, and Strike, Firebirds colors back in his fur, a flame on the back of each paw, tumbles out of bounds at the nine. The crowd goes nuts. We go nuts. Aston rushes the guys down to the line and they set up without a huddle. The Pilots' linebackers get to their spots quickly and efficiently, ready for the snap. Aston tosses the ball to Ty, quickly, on the opposite sideline. Their linebackers are ready for him, but the fox spins around one wolf before the other pushes him out at the two.

Now the crowd is frantic. I'm excited, jumping up and down, and so is Zillo behind me and Charm beside me and everyone except Gerrard, who's just staring out at the field as though he can see what's going to happen ahead of time. Forty-one seconds left, and we have a timeout, so the coaches take a chance on Jaws, but the defensive line closes up and the linebackers get a good push behind them, and he's stopped for no gain. Thirty seconds. We don't use a timeout; Aston drops back again on third down and looks for Strike, but he's doubled, and Rodolf is covered and so is Ty, and Aston tries to drop it off to the tight end but the Hellentown jaguar is right there and grabs the ball first.

We hold our breath. For a moment, my heart turns to stone and I think everyone else's does too. But then the jaguar bobbles the ball, and our tight end slaps at it, and it's on the ground, the pass is incomplete. We have one more shot.

"Go time," Charm says, and fits his helmet on as Coach Samuelson makes the hand signal for the timeout. But Coach waves Charm back as Aston comes to the sideline. "Strawberry cheesecake right," he says, calling in the play, and shows Aston and Strike and the other receivers something on his clipboard.

"No kick," I say.

"Ballsy." Charm takes his helmet off. He doesn't seem that upset to be missing the chance to kick. "They can do it."

"Damn right." I lean over to Gerrard. "The linebackers are playing better than they were last time."

"Uh-huh. More integrated." He doesn't look away from the field. "We are, too."

"Yeah." That pleases me enough that I don't want to say another word. So I look up behind me, to where Lee's sitting with Hal. He and Hal and me and Gerrard and all of us, together, watch the next play.

Our offense lines up. Aston barks out the count, his paws twitching under the center's tail. I bounce on the balls of my feet and Charm is just as fidgety. They snap the ball and Aston steps back as if to throw. I'm watching him, and then my eyes flick to the line, which freezes and then scatters to cover the receivers spreading out into the end zone. And Aston pulls the ball down, crouches and springs in a fluid motion, and leaps over the line, tumbling in a red and gold and grey blur and landing, ball in hand, squarely in the end zone.

We slap each other on the back as the stadium erupts. "TOUCHDOWN FIREBIRDS!" screams across the LED displays and the JumboTron and our ears. Aston stands up, but we only get a glimpse of him before he's mobbed by the rest of the offense. He comes back to the sidelines still clutching the ball, yelling, "You think they took notice of that? You think they took notice of that?" and Coach gives him a tight half-hug and sends him to the bench, where he stares across at the Hellentown sideline, paws gripping the ball like he wants to throw it at them.

"Bit early to keep a game ball," Gerrard says.

"He's only got three rushing touchdowns all year," I say. "Let him have it."

"If we win. There's a whole half to play."

"Yeah," I say, but I've got that feeling. We're up 7-6, and both defenses are playing pretty well. I think we've got a pretty good chance as long as we hold them to field goals. It feels impossible to me that they're going to hold Strike down for the whole game.

Coach says the same thing at the half. "It's a tough game, like we knew it would be," he says. "We're keeping 'em out of the end zone, and they're holding us down. This game is going to be won in the trenches." He points to the linemen. "You keep us in good field position and we've got a kicker who can make the difference in a game like this. We've got a game-breaker on offense and we only need one big play to put this away. You guys keep doing what you're doing and we will be here again next week."

So we're all charged up for the second half, and even though our offense goes three-and-out, we're still pumped up when we take the field. Eighty-three is out there again, and they throw to him on first down, surprising all of us. I'm there to wrap him up after a six-yard gain, and we both go down to the ground. I land on my ribs, but ignore the pain as I get up.

"Keep on chasin' me, homo," the fox says. "You ain't getting any closer to this fox tail."

Unexpectedly, Pike calls to the fox as he's getting back across the line. "Hey," he says, "You don't wanna be his boyfriend, don't flip your tail around like that."

"Yeah," Brick says, "and you smell like a girl."

One of their linemen, a solid black bear, huffs at them and says, "Least he doesn't block like a girl."

"Give him time," I yell. "He could still get that good."

We laugh; they snort, but they're getting lined up and there isn't time to retort. They get some small gains, but only across midfield, and when we think we've stopped them for a punt, they line up for a long field goal. I hurry back to the sideline next to Charm, who's laughing. "Fifty-five yards, that guy?"

"He was kicking sixty in practice."

"I kick seventy in practice." He blows a snort. "I'll bet you dinner he misses it."

"Sure." I shake just as they snap the ball. We watch the horse come up to the line, watch his foot connect cleanly, watch the ball sail through the air, straight and true through the uprights, clearing the bar by a good three yards.

"Fucker," Charm says. He turns to where the coaches are. "Hey," he calls. "Send me in for anything under seventy, I mean it."

Nine-seven, and we need another score. But the offense continues to sputter, and every series we go out there, we see that big 9 up on the scoreboard across from our 7, and we feel the pressure. Pressure's okay. Pressure we know how to handle. I think about Lee up in the stands, watching every move, making sure I get a good jump off the snap, making sure every foot lands in the right place and that I know my assignments and either cover the fox or bump one of the other receivers or get in to stuff the run. The lion QB, Buck, he's pretty good, but we break down their line a few times. Spinning away from me, he runs into Carson and gets sacked; another time, I bring him down from behind and send the football spinning to the ground. We scramble for it, but their elk, another running back, drops on it and they just punt.

They keep doubling Strike, but Aston starts to find some of the receivers on short routes, and we cheer from the side as our guys march down the field. We're in Charm's field goal range for sure.

And then one of our guys jumps early and it's a five-yard false start, our first—Hellentown's jumped twice in the game, with the help of the screaming crowd that makes it hard for the line to hear the quarterback, but the crowd knows to keep quieter when we're on offense, so this is just a mistake—and then one of those burly wolf linebackers barrels through the line and drops Aston for a fifteen-yard loss. He looks shaky when he gets up, but he stays out there and lobs a weak pass to fall incomplete.

It'd be a sixty-two yard field goal from where they are now. Charm screams, "Send me out, I can make it!" But Coach thinks otherwise; we punt and pin the Pilots back on their ten, and at the end of the third quarter we get the ball back in good position.

It's the first play of the fourth quarter, and because it's third down, the Pilots drop back to cover our receivers the way they have been all game. Only Aston hands off to Jaws, and the wolverine finds a seam and gets through the line. Only one linebacker and a safety are covering that side of the field, as Strike and Ty, the wideouts, throw really nice blocks to keep the corners away from the action. And Jaws bulls past the wolf linebacker, not quite knocking him over like that Gateway wolverine did to me, but sending him out of bounds staggering. I'm sure he'll hear it from his teammates. The safety, a lanky otter, must have seen it too, because he hesitates just a fraction of a second, and Jaws slips the tackle and goes charging into the end zone.

"TOUCHDOWN FIREBIRDS!" The crowd is on its feet, as loud as I've ever heard the stadium. We jump and laugh and slap each other on the back and watch Charm kick the point that moves the score up to 14-9.

And we all slip into that jovial victory mode. It doesn't mean we slack off. It means we bear down because we've got the lead and the clock is ticking. We know we can keep them out of the end zone, and they don't have that much time left. We just want to hold them down, out of field goal range, and we have to do it for ten minutes of game time.

No sweat. Gerrard and Carson and I are settled into the rhythm of the game, and Hellentown isn't changing things up. They seem to think that they got a couple field goals, they can get a couple more. Only we know how they're going to run their plays, and Gerrard stuffs runs up the middle, I catch the elk and drop him for a short gain, Carson sacks their lion again. Vonni and Norton and Pace keep the wide receivers well-covered, and Pike and Brick and the line mostly hold their positions, enough that we force a punt. Eighty-three mouths off to me again, but this time I ignore him because, well, look at the scoreboard.

And it's four minutes to go and we're on offense, trying to run out the clock. Jaws is punching into the line over and over, and on third and three Aston drops for a short pass over the middle, just enough to get the first down. Ty's right there, reaching out, and he has the ball and then he doesn't, he's falling, and it happens in a heartbeat, the Pilots' jaguar is right there to catch the ball and he's running around our line, down the sideline, and there's nothing we can do about it, not a thing except scream at them. The offense is running after him, but they have no chance, except…here comes Strike, of all people, a blur, but he's too far back and yet and yet…no, he tackles the jaguar, but he tackles him at the goal line and they tumble into the end zone and the jaguar still has the ball.

The stadium is still. The opposite sideline is a giddy mass of brown and gold, leaping, cheering, and we can hear them because the rest of the place is so quiet. The play's reviewed, of course, but there's no question. The ball never comes loose and the jaguar's not down outside the goal line. They line up, they kick the extra point, it's 16-14 and we have three and a half minutes to get into field goal range.

All I can do is sit on the sidelines. Our progress down the field seems maddeningly slow; as inspired as we were five minutes ago, the Pilots are now. We go three-and-out, and with 2:42 on the clock it's up to us to get the ball back to our side. I know every one of us is thinking "fumble, interception, something," and Gerrard stops us as we get out there.

"Play solid D," he says, slamming his fist into his open paw. "Solid! Don't try to be a hero. You go for a pick and miss a tackle and this game is over. You try to strip the ball and miss a tackle and this game is over. Just tackle. Fundamentals! Head in the game!"

We chorus, "Right!" and take up our positions. I look up to the stands, and think of my fox watching me, and I push away all the other stuff, all the gay activism and the nagging feeling that if I'd not been distracted in the first quarter I could've had that interception then, I could've gotten us more points or at least kept three of theirs off the board so it would only be 14-13 now and we'd be trying to hold a lead, not recapture it. None of that matters. What matters now is stopping them.

And we do it. The fox yaps at me, calls me "butt-lover" or something, but I block out the words and just focus on keeping him covered. Which is easy because they're not even throwing it, just running the elk into our line over and over. We take our last two timeouts and force them to punt just after the two-minute warning.

Back on the sidelines. Nothing I can do. "Good defense, guys," Coach says, and Steez comes over to tell us that he's proud of us too, but we're all tense. All our energy is focused on those guys out on the field.

The Pilots know we're going to throw short, but they're still afraid of Strike, and so all the short routes are open. Aston seems to have recovered from the big hit and throws a couple great passes. Ty catches one for a critical first down at the fifty, and pumps his fist on the way back to the line, his bushy red tail swishing. I pump my fist too, and Zillo, next to me, mutters, "Come on, come on." The boom of Charm's practice kicks behind us punctuates the game.

We throw it to the tight end for five, to Ty again for three, and then Aston runs it out of bounds. He thinks he's got the first down, the wolf linebacker says he doesn't, and the refs bring the ball out and the chains onto the field to measure. We hold our breath. Charm is right there next to Coach, and I can't hear them, but I know what he's saying. The special teams coach is talking too, and I'm sure our offensive coordinator is talking to Coach through the headset. Then they get the chains in place and we all look up.

The video on the big screen shows six inches of chain after the end of the ball. The referee holds up his paws six inches apart, and now Coach slaps Charm on the back. The big stallion runs out to the field, getting there before the rest of the field goal unit.

"Fifty-seven yard attempt…" The P.A. sets it up as the unit gets into place, the holder crouched, long snapper holding the ball, and the crowd is holding its breath. The play clock ticks down to five. Charm signals that he's ready, and the holder turns to the snapper. Three. Two.

The ball's snapped, the holder grabs it and puts it down. The lines crash into each other, the Pilots trying to leap into the path of the ball, and they've got a rabbit who can really jump. He leaps, but Charm is good at this too, and the ball sails inches to the left of the rabbit's outstretched paw. It clears the line, it rises in a familiar arc, tumbling end over end through the air, toward the goalposts.

It's too far to the left, I think, but my angle's weird and I can't tell. I'm holding my breath. Zillo, next to me, grabs my wrist and leans forward. The crowd is standing, the whole stadium silent for a second, two, three…and then the ball crosses the uprights, well above the crossbar.

Cheers erupt, but we're watching the two referees below the goalposts. The one on the right looks to the one on the left, and then they step forward, and they're both sweeping their arms from side to side.

No good. Wide left.

The Pilots sideline leaps and high-fives and celebrates as their offense runs out onto the field. With no timeouts left, we can't stop the clock. In a minute, the game's over.

We sleepwalk out onto the field to congratulate the Pilots. Most of them are pretty nice about it. Gerrard and I talk with the wolf linebackers (Kniss and Price) and congratulate them on their technique, and Kniss (slightly darker fur, an inch or two shorter than Price) says, "Hey, Miski, you're better than you are on film."

"You too," I say, sort of automatically. I still feel the ball sliding off my paw, the feeling that I was a half-second out of step on the pass, that I could've done better.

"You know," Price says, "some of us think Inquam is a moron who needs to keep his muzzle shut."

Inquam, it takes me a moment to remember, is the guy who made the "Jesus" comment. "Your eighty-three doesn't," I say.

Kniss waves a paw. "Fuck 'em, you know? You can play. That's what counts."

"Damn right," Gerrard says, and they slap paws. I join in, getting a little lift. Just a little. I'd rather have all the Pilots be crazy bigots and be walking out of here with a win.

There's a cheer from the crowd; we look up at the scoreboard. The Jumbotron is now showing the score of the Highbourne game: Rocs 44, Manticores 27. So Highbourne finishes with the tiebreaker over us and they get to play the worst division champion, Peco. And we go to Hellentown. "See you next week, I guess."

They grin; we don't feel like smiling. But it's worth remembering that we beat them a couple months ago, in Hellentown, no less.

"Next week'll be different," Gerrard mutters as we head back to the locker room. But those are the only words he says, at least in my hearing, all the way back into the room itself.

"Damn right." And then I go to see how Charm is doing, because I didn't see him at all at the end of the game.

He's sitting in front of his locker, holding his helmet. Everyone's going by him on their way to the trainers' room, patting him on the shoulder, saying kind words. I plop myself down next to him.

"So," I say. "Y'know, if I'd made that interception in the first quarter, we don't even need those last few points."

"I make that kick nine out of ten times," he says. "Fucking rabbit, jumping around on the line."

"So make the kick next week and the week after," I say. I flex my paws. "We're in the playoffs. Isn't that what counts?"

"Sure," he says. "Sure."

I kick the side of his massive leg. "Hey. We still gotta go out and play a game. We're in the playoffs."

It doesn't feel like it, from the attitude in the room. Gerrard's ears are still flat and he's undressing slowly. Some guys are staring into space. About half the team, though, is still joking with each other, undressing like it was just another game, what's the big deal, heading to the trainer for meds and bandaging, we'll do this again next week.

The only guy more pissed than Gerrard is Strike. He comes in and throws his helmet into his locker with a crash that makes everyone look up for a second. Then he strips, fast, and gets to the shower before anyone else.

"Just glad he's not talking," Vonni mutters nearby as he and I watch the cheetah disappear.

A minute later, Coach comes in and gathers everyone for his speech, even Strike, some soap still in his wet fur, not even bothering to reach for a towel. Which distracts people a little, because he's got these intricate dye markings of flames and wings around his chest and stomach, and he's got a sunburst dyed in bright yellow around his sheath. So I'm not the only one staring at him. Then Coach starts talking, and we give him our full attention.

"We're in the playoffs. So we have to go play a few road games. This team has never shied away from a challenge, and we're not going to give up now. The game turns on a few plays, and some days they go your way. Today, most of the breaks went to them. Next week, that's not going to be the case. So keep playing hard, because I can tell you from experience that when teams give the kind of effort you gave today, good things happen. We've got three games left and we're not going to be back here, so let's stay focused, stay hungry, and stay positive. We are the Firebirds and we are going to win a championship!"

That gets a little cheer out of us, and makes me feel a little better. But still, by the time I've gone to the trainer to check out my ribs—still sore, but doing okay—I wish I didn't have to fly to Hellentown next week.

Chapter 29: Reaching Out (Lee)

It's hard not to be deflated after a close loss, especially when the game is important. The thing to keep in mind is that it doesn't end the season. But I'm sure Dev's heard that over and over again, so I don't text it to him. I just write, *Good game. You deserved to win.*

And then Hal and I sit and wait for the crowd to disperse. We already talked about the game while it was going on, and I told him I didn't want to talk about my personal issues during the game. I don't want to start that conversation, if we're going to have it, while people are leaving all around us, so I say, "Going to Hellentown for the game next week?"

"Probably." He turns, looks at me. "You?"

"Probably." I sniff my beer. It's warm and a little flat. I set it back in the holder. "Going to bring your girl with you?"

"Don't think so." He got his beer the same time I got mine, but he drinks it anyway. "Don't know if she'd be interested."

"If she doesn't like football..."

"You know..." He looks down onto the field where the players are milling about. "Football's not really my number one sport either."

"Oh?" I flick an ear.

"It's not bad, but I like basketball more." He sets his beer down and mimes taking a shot. "Buzzer beater from the corner."

I point down to the field. "Long field goal as time expires?"

"Yeah, but...that's the kicker. He doesn't do anything else. It's not the guys who got 'em there."

"He's part of the team, too."

"Too specialized." Hal leans down, as though examining the teams on the sidelines more closely. "Kickers barely feel it when they leave the game. Maybe blow out a knee or foot."

I flop back in my seat and stretch my arms over the backs, keeping my right arm behind his seat so he doesn't think I'm trying to come on to him or something. "Again with the injuries. It doesn't happen to everyone."

"Happens to some. Then they make it worse, taking drugs to get back in the game."

"Dev's never mentioned drugs," I say. "You can print that. Anyway, you're in the wrong sport. Baseball's the one with the drugs."

"Baseball players take drugs to get an edge," Hal says. "Individual performance means a lot more. Football players take drugs just to make their body shut up when it's tellin' them they should take a break. You tellin' me Dev never got cortisone before a game? Never saw a teammate get a shot to be able to play on Sunday?"

"They're pretty stubborn," I say. "It's a tough game and it means a lot to them. They'll do anything just to stay in it."

"Don't know what's good for 'em."

Fisher's desperation stands out clearly in my mind. "Better to be part of it, even if it's hurting you, than go without it."

"Even if it hurts you the rest of your life?"

I study the intensity of his expression. "I think I liked you better when you didn't have a girlfriend and were just interested in a gay football player."

He turns and grins, and elbows me in the side. "An' I liked you better when you were a pretty lady. Can't all get what we want."

"Ow." I laugh. "Fair enough." The crowd is thinning, so I gesture. "Time to go?"

"Sure. You got somewhere to be?"

"Supposed to be a playoff celebration dinner tonight for the team. Don't think spouses or boyfriends are invited." I stand and stretch, and Hal stands, too.

"Not sure how much of a celebration it'll be anyway," he says, and looks toward the end of the stadium, to where the big flag of the States hangs. "No banner goin' up there."

I follow him along the row, my fingers trailing along the backs of the seats. "Unless they win the championship." The Firebirds are already almost all in their locker room. I saw Dev talking to the other team's linebackers; it looked civil. There was a little jawing during the game, but that's to be expected with division rivals.

"Least it was an exciting game," Hal says when we get into the stadium concourse, since I've been silent all that time.

"Yeah." I think about the miscues, the things that didn't go Chevali's way. "I hope they learn from that. There's no reason this team couldn't go to the championship this year."

"We got to beat Hellentown first."

"They did it earlier. Maybe being back there will be a lift."

The same conversations are going on all around us, all the people leaving the game in their red and gold talking about the playoffs. Hellentown primarily, but also looking ahead to Boliat and even Crystal City.

"Boxers are tough this year. Great shutdown defense, same offense that's kept them in the playoffs for years."

I hold the door for Hal. "Thought you weren't a football guy."

He walks through and holds the next door for me, his tail swishing. "Go ahead, ask me who's going to win the FBA title this year."

"Easy. The Bikers, right?"

"Nah. Keep an eye on the Mayors."

I laugh. "All right. Once the football season's over."

"Maybe I'll take you to a Whips game sometime."

"Take your girlfriend."

He nods, but looks down at the pavement. Outside, the air is warmer than in the wind-swirled stadium. A light breeze still kicks hot dog wrappers along the gutter, and tickets lie flat on the sidewalk. Ahead of us, an ermine couple—male and female—chat animatedly about the game, the boyfriend claiming the Firebirds suck while his girlfriend says, just as adamantly, that they were robbed. She's wearing a red and gold scarf; he's got on a Firebirds windbreaker.

"Things going okay with the girl?" I nudge Hal.

"Yeah, yeah. Fine."

That's a very final "fine," so I leave it be and turn my thoughts to Dev. He hasn't lost an important game in a long time—he hasn't played an important game in a long time, for that matter. Last one was the Division II quarterfinal that I went to see, and he was pretty down afterwards. I don't think he'll be as bad tonight. I mean, he's closer to this team, for one thing. For another, it's not like he's graduating and it's the last game he'll ever play with these guys. And for a third, they're still in the playoffs. They need to suck it up and go play Hellentown again next week.

"So I guess we're in for a week of 'these teams know each other well' and 'this division rivalry has taken center stage' from your colleagues, right?" I ask Hal, who's still brooding about his girl.

"Oh, probably. I'd take the angle of 'these two teams have played a close game every time they've met, so this week's is sure to be a thriller.' Makes people excited about the game without actually predicting anything."

"Don't ever want to commit, do you guys?"

He shakes his head, whiskers twitching. "Not like anyone remembers when we do. We write stupid predictions at the beginning of the season, you'll see a bunch of predictions for the playoffs, and nobody keeps track."

"You got predictions for the playoffs?"

He scratches his ear. "I think you might see Peco at Boliat for the championship. Peco had a down year, but they had some injuries and they played well the last few games once they got everyone back. And the Boxers are the Boxers. Got to be the favorites 'til they're not, right?"

"No hometown love?"

"I got plenty of hometown love. But I'm realistic, too. These boys never been to the playoffs before."

"Fisher has. Dev was in the Division II playoffs."

Hal laughs. "You got Kingston, you got Strike, and lemme see, Marvell mighta been a rookie in the last playoff year. That's what you get for bein' a career Firebird. It's a young team and they got a bright future, but this ain't the year."

"Says you."

"You think they can go all the way?"

I run down the teams in my head. I know the way you can talk yourself into things. If they exploit this matchup, if they run the ball like they can, if Dev and Gerrard and the secondary can clamp down on the line…while over there in Hellentown, their fans are thinking the same thing: if we can force turnovers, if we can get better field position…

The fact that I've met Gerrard and a lot of the players, that I know Dev, maybe skews my thinking. I don't know the guys on the other side of the ball. It's easy to imagine Dev and Gerrard getting pysched up for it. But those wolves and the jaguar will be psyched too; it's hard to imagine Buck being anything but fired up to prove he's better than he played in this game. But I don't know him. Maybe he gets depressed like Dev.

I haven't gotten a text back from Dev yet, speaking of that. So I take out the new phone and shoot him another text: *How you doing?*

Hal nods toward the phone. "How's the new gadget working out?"

"Pretty nice." I show off the new phone for a few seconds, take a picture of him to show how good the camera is, and take a picture of the late afternoon skyline of Chevali. It's a pretty town, and home for now. It could be home for a long time, but…that leads me down thoughts of my future. It's my home for the next month, until the season's over. I have to make a decision soon, but not right now.

We grab a bus back to the Golden Dunes Mall where everyone parks for games, and both of us keep quiet on the way, Hal absorbed in his thoughts and me in mine. I go back to the same problem over and over again, of whether I should just take the job in Yerba, go back to my old life of football scouting without the pressure of staying closeted, or if I should stay here and really try to make a difference.

I haven't even been to the gay neighborhood of Chevali yet, haven't explored the town apart from the places I've gone with Dev. I did a little shopping, but just wandering around the shopping district of a town is like getting to know a guy by sniffing his coat. You can only get so much from it. If I am going to stay here, I'm going to have to learn more about the city. Although if Dev does get traded, I'll move with him to the new city, start looking into the activist scene there. Or I could stay here, like some wives do when they've put down roots. I could keep his apartment here and he could stay here in the off-season.

Even as I think about all of this, though, I feel that it's just delaying a decision I've already made. And maybe the reason I'm delaying is that this decision feels like a betrayal of myself. It doesn't matter that Brian is still an asshole; he reminded me of the old me, the things that I had a passion for before I had a passion for a football player with stripes. Those old passions, they still call, they still burn when I give them room to breathe.

My phone buzzes with a message from Dev. *Doing ok. Hanging with Charm.*

Dinner later?

Team only. Sorry.

"Looks like it might be a while," I say as Hal and I get off the bus and I put the phone away. "Guess I'll maybe see you in Hellentown?"

"You going to that party?"

I shake my head. "Sounds like they're just having the team there."

He jingles his car keys in his paw. "I'm not doing anything, if you want to hang out more."

I glance over at the mall. "Why, Mister Kinnel—"

"Yes," he says, "I'm asking you out to a food court dinner. That okay? Do I have to buy you a purse after?"

"Only if you want to." I laugh. "How about that sports bar on the other side of the mall?"

●

So we sit in the sports bar and watch the recap of the game and listen to the people in the bar grouse about the Firebirds. We talk about next year, and Hal tries to educate me on basketball a little bit. I try to get him to talk about his girl, but he just dodges the questions. I return the favor when he asks about my trip home, just telling him it went badly and I'm still figuring it out.

Over barbecue chicken sandwiches, he brings up the Firebirds job, which he hasn't been able to find out anything more about. "Talked to anyone about that yet?"

"Not yet. If I decide to stay here, not go to Yerba, then it'd be nice to have real work, to have the weight of a football team behind me. But then what if Dev gets traded or signs somewhere else? What if he doesn't, and this job only lasts four months?"

"You both work in football, that's gonna happen."

I wipe my muzzle with a napkin. "I know that. Just wondering if I'll get fired for conflict of interest again if I'm talking to the gay community and Dev's in Port City or Yerba or whatever."

"Probably not from an outreach job." Hal leans back in his chair. "But I can't say for sure. That'd be something to ask them."

"Or I could just keep working with Equality Now."

His eyes measure mine. "With Brian."

I look back, then down at the table. "Uh-huh."

"Is that something you really want to do? You didn't care for him that much a couple months ago."

"We've been reliving old times," I say, curling my tail against my leg. "Remembering why we were such good friends."

"Uh-huh." There are toothpicks at the end of the table. He reaches over to take one and picks between his teeth. "Dev's okay with that?"

"As long as I don't talk about it." I sigh. "The problem's not with Brian. I mean, he's an ass, but I can handle him. The problem's with me."

Hal grins at me, his ears perked up. "*You're* an ass?"

"Ha ha," I say, although he is closer to the truth than he probably realizes. "If I want to make a difference, it's going to conflict with Dev's football. All Brian is doing is pushing that faster than it would move along anyway."

"And if Dev was happy going along with these folks, or you could convince 'em that he's never going to—if it was resolved one way or the other, that skunk wouldn't be a problem?"

"Not as much of one."

He brushes his whiskers flat and lets them spring up again. "You can't go work with some other group?"

I shake my head. "Sure. But I'll still be bringing it home, wondering why he's not more committed. I just won't have Brian to push against."

"Takin' that stress out of the equation might be a good thing."

My phone chimes. It's Dev, writing: *Angela and Gena here. Want to come? Where is it?* "Hey, apparently the team dinner is open to spouses," I say. *Grantmark Hotel.*

"Where's the Grantmark Hotel?"

Hal raises his eyebrows. "Fancy. It's over on Calderton Parkway, other side of the city." He pauses. "I could drop you off there, if you want."

I think about it. I'm full, and while I wouldn't mind hanging out with

Dev and the team, I did just have Christmas with them. But Angela and Gena are both there, so… "Sure," I say. "Thanks."

"Not a problem." As he discards the toothpick and we get up, he says, "About that Brian, though. Just be sure you're doing this for your reasons. You can't go round trying to fix friendships you shouldn't just because other parts of your life are falling apart. He was pretty shitty to you guys."

"I'm not doing that," I say automatically.

Hal's response, "Okay, good, just checking," is almost drowned out by the voice in my head that says, basically, *oh shit*, is *that what I'm doing?*

On the walk over to his car, an old Tauron, Hal stays quiet, leaving me to ask myself that question over and over until he unlocks the door and I get in. I inhale, eager for something else to occupy my mind, and sort out the scents.

You may not be able to tell a lot about a guy from smelling his coat, but smelling his car—that's something else. I sit in the passenger seat and inhale mostly Hal, Neutra-Scent, and female coyote. "Been taking your girl around?" I say. Her scent is mild and pleasant. It meshes well with his stronger fox scent.

"Some." He doesn't look at me as he pulls out of the garage.

"Car smells pretty clean. No trash in the back seat."

He hmphs. "I kept it clean anyway."

"She smells nice." I just relax in the seat, not looking like I'm sniffing her out or anything. "Glad things are going better."

He does relax then, his tail swishing behind the seat. "Something you said kinda stuck with me. Just that whole, 'let her be herself' thing. More I thought about it, the less she seemed like Cim. Beyond just the coyote thing. I mean, she doesn't like popcorn at the movies, for one. She gets the yogurt peanuts. And she talks about politics like she can actually change things, not like everyone's corrupt and it's not worth the time."

"That's how I talk about it."

"Yeah, that's fun sometimes, but it's fun to be positive, too."

"My goodness," I say. "Is my cynical scribe donning a pair of rose-colored glasses?"

He snorts and turns onto the crosstown expressway. "Things're going better, that's all I'm sayin'. At least, with me. I'm seein' her again Thursday night."

"And maybe Hellentown on Saturday?"

He wiggles his paw. "Maybe. If I can get tickets—plane and game."

"I can maybe help with the game," I say.

"Thanks." He grins.

I nudge him. "Will I get to meet her in Hellentown?"

"Maybe," he says. "Say, you know, Corcoran might be at that dinner. You could talk to him about the job."

I stretch my arm out along the armrest and watch the city go by outside the windows, faux adobe clay and yellow sandstone turned brilliant gold in the last light of sunset. "At a team dinner? He'll be with his family."

"Well, if there's time to mingle afterwards, Corky's always happy to talk business."

"One of those guys." I sit and swish my tail back and forth, glad that Dev texted to invite me over, now starting to worry if the team will feel awkward with me there. Wives are one thing, but boyfriends…still, the whole point of the equality movement is to allow me to be treated the same as a wife. So if it takes me coming to a team dinner, then that's what I'll do.

When we get to the hotel, I put a paw on the door handle and say, "Hey. Whatever's going on with your girl, it'll work out. Y'know? These things do."

"Yeah." He raises a paw. "Have fun at your dinner."

"And if they don't," I say, "then they weren't meant to and you shouldn't worry about it."

"Easy for the guy with a steady boyfriend to say."

"And look at all the shit we went through." I open the door. "Still do go through."

"Still?" He leans forward on the steering wheel, looking across at my face. "You haven't mentioned Vince King at all today."

I shake my head. Hal frowns. "You doing anything about that?"

"I really want to, but…it feels like I'm running out of options. I need to…how did Morty put it? Fish or cut bait."

"Well…" He pauses. "Keep at it, I guess. I don't know that most of what we do makes a difference. We just gotta keep doing it if it's important to us."

"Do we?" I curl my tail into my lap. "What if we have to decide between two important things? Like Cim and your career?"

"In that case," he drawls, "she kinda made that decision, not me."

"Still," I say. "You could've gone after her. You chose not to."

He taps the wheel, looks ahead through the windshield, and I think he's smiling, but it's a very faint smile. "Reckon I did. Well, you know, I figured Cim was already half gone. And journalism, that's the stuff I love. Getting at the truth. Telling your story helped some people. Telling this story about injuries, that might help people. Shine a light, right?"

"Right," I say. "It makes a lot of sense. Hey, thanks. And thanks for the ride."

He's already driving away by the time I realize I'm probably underdressed for this hotel. At least I put on a polo shirt so I have a collar, but still: everyone on staff is wearing a dark maroon suit with a bowtie, from the raccoon valet who holds the door to the concierge at his desk to the three clerks at registration. The lobby is decorated not only with art pieces, but with sculptures, and in one corner, a small fountain filling the air with soft bubbling sounds and chlorine odor. Clocks show the time in different cities around the world, there's a business lounge the size of Dev's apartment behind the front desk, and the carpet is so soft that I feel like I'm walking on someone's bed.

I rub my paws on my jeans, but nobody is rude enough to comment on my appearance. Still, I don't ask anyone; I look for the signs. There are discreet event listings—not on video screens; the hotel is too classy for that. They're on bond paper with the hotel's logo, posted in small elegant frames at either end of the lobby desk.

And I'm not the only person studying them. There's a bunch of females of assorted species clustered around them, all of them in Firebirds gear—a kangaroo rat and a coyote in oversized jerseys, a fennec in a t-shirt she's torn the bottom off of so the word "FIREBIRDS" is stretched out to twice its normal length across her chest and her tawny-furred stomach is exposed, a lioness in a two-piece bikini and nothing else but a Firebirds baseball cap, and a raccoon in a nice evening gown who would actually look like she belongs in the hotel if not for the garish Firebirds-logo earrings and the gold paint that's been not too professionally applied to her mask.

"Maybe it's the Welder's Conference," the lioness says.

"No, that room's tiny." The raccoon points to the listing. "It's got to be the Kerr-Thomas wedding. That's the only room big enough. I know. I've been to this hotel a bunch of times."

"We know, Chas, Jesus Fox already." The fennec has a southwestern drawl. "Why'n't we just go sniff around?"

"I tried that," the coyote says. "I couldn't find them. It's a big hotel an' they got some areas blocked off."

"Awright, let's wait here for them to come out."

I stand there long enough to skim the listing and see that the Firebirds' dinner isn't on it, and then I retreat to one of the plush sofas artfully arranged around a glass coffee table. I text Dev quickly asking him what room to go to, and then lean back, listen to the bubbling fountain, and pretend I really am staying here.

Across from me are two foxes, and at first I think they're a couple. But when I put my phone down and pay a little more attention, I'm pretty sure they're not. The guy is gay; I'm as sure of that as I am that I'm gay. He's slimmer than I am, wearing well-creased slacks (though worn), a silk shirt open at the chest, and a salmon ascot—no, lighter than salmon. The light makes it hard to judge color here. Pink, maybe. And he has a shiny gold ear-stud in each ear. Everything but a pride necklace. Also, I can smell his cologne more strongly than his companion's perfume.

The vixen isn't gay, though, I'm pretty sure. She's taller than he is, and dressed in a sheer red gown that looks even more appropriate to this hotel than the raccoon's. No garish earrings spoil the effect on her large chocolate ears, though. She has a jeweled stud at the base of the right one, and that's it. Though I think she has brushed some color into the fur around her eyes, it's hard to tell because I don't know her, and again, the light. She's not old enough to be his mother, so I flick a curious ear to listen to what they're talking about.

They've sort of noticed me, looking up when I sat down and then dismissing me. My polo shirt does have a Firebirds logo on the chest, but I guess that doesn't interest them so much. Their voices are low, whispers that normally I wouldn't be able to hear even this close, but the lobby echoes and magnifies them so I can catch a few words through the fountain noise and piece together others.

"…said if I saw him again he would totally take me out." The vixen has a little hope in her voice.

"And he's only, what, five years younger than you?" The gay kid smiles.

"Julie's six years older than Mike. Anyway, I'm not looking to get married or anything. I have a job."

"Be nice to have someone to take care of you, though."

She puts a paw on his knee. "You need that more than I do."

He smiles, confident. "I can take care of myself."

My phone buzzes, and I look down to make them think I'm not listening in on their conversation. Dev wrote: *Sonora Mesa Ballroom*. But the kid's confidence keeps me on the sofa for another minute, just listening.

"The tiger already has a boyfriend," his friend says, and my ears almost, almost snap forward in what would be a dead giveaway.

"I know, and his boyfriend travels with them now." The fox makes a face, and his eyes flick over to me, linger for just a second, then go back to his friend. "But he's not the only one who'll spend time with me."

"None of them will go out in public with you."

"It's not about being out in public. It's about getting to say," and he lowers his voice, but I have a pretty good idea of how that sentence ends.

"Really? I've done him too." She laughs. "I wouldn'ta thought."

"Well." The kid smirks. "A muzzle is a muzzle."

"Oh, I don't do that."

"You should try it sometime."

She sticks her tongue out. "In my *mouth*?"

"Just for a second. Then you swallow and it's gone."

"*Ew.*"

He grins at her. "To each his own. Anyway, that fox you're after was in a gay club in Yerba."

She stares at him. "He was not."

"Read the papers, dear. Miski took a bunch of them out."

"Well, I know from experience that he likes," she runs a paw down the front and side of her dress, "this."

"Maybe he likes both." The kid fiddles with his scarf again. "Doesn't matter. One of them will drink too much, will get a room here." He leans back to look at the front desk. "Just a matter of waiting."

It sounds like they're not going to talk any more gossip, or at least not name names about whom they've been with (although a fox, in a gay club in Yerba—that narrows it down to two), so I turn my phone off and stand up. That draws their attention back to me, and the kid's brown eyes narrow as he takes me in. He's sharp—so's she, for that matter—and I don't want to give him time to figure out that I know where I'm going. So I walk off quickly to the concierge, who looks at me with suspicion when I ask about the Sonora Mesa ballroom. "Do you have an invitation, sir?"

I show him my phone, with the message from my contact marked "Dev," but he doesn't seem convinced. After a little bit of negotiating, he calls his event manager, who calls Vince the press liaison, who I guess finds Dev somewhere in the banquet and then calls the event manager back, who calls the concierge, and a mere thirteen minutes later, I'm given directions to the room.

I duck around the elevator lobby and use the stairs to make sure I'm not being followed. Sometimes I like to pretend I'm in a spy movie, but in this case, I really am worried that the kid, the vixen, or some of the less subtle groupies will be following me.

Nobody does. I pad up a staircase as wide as Dev's bedroom and then down a hallway into which you could squeeze his whole apartment. It's lined with mirrors and paintings, dotted with small end tables, each of which has an intricate desert flower arrangement, and the carpet up here is a beautiful southwestern pattern of orange and blue and red and black, and oh yes, it's just as soft as the one in the lobby. Amazingly, considering how many events are apparently going on tonight, the hallway is dead silent, and the background scent is just a mélange of all the people who've walked through it, masked by Neutra-Scent in the air enough that I can't tell anything about any of them. I'd thought the coyote was a couple dominoes short of a full case when she said she couldn't find the team just by sniffing around, but as it turns out, the doors along the hallway are well-insulated against sound, and the air circulation keeps smells from collecting, and it would be impossible to find anyone without actually opening every door.

At the end of the hallway there's another staircase, this one only wide enough to fit two of our sofas across. I walk up to the third floor, at the end of which is a large pair of double doors and the sign, "Sonora Mesa Ballroom."

I hesitate—I don't want to just walk in. And then I think, I'm invited. I'm going in. So I open the door and slide into the room.

Immediately, the noise of conversation and the smells of about a hundred people greet me. I step to the left, letting the door close, and look around the room. I'd expected sedate dinners at tables, lots of eyes turned my way when I walked in, but what I've stepped into looks more like a cocktail party. There are high tables scattered around the room, but mostly people are just standing and talking to each other. Barely anyone even looked at the door as it opened and closed.

To my right, about ten clusters of people away, is a very large mass of people around what I assume is a bar, because the people working their way out of the crowd carry full drinks (mostly beer). To my left, much closer, is a large stage, empty. Beside it, next to me, an older fox and younger one, both in dark suits and Firebirds ties, confer with a weasel in a sleek grey suit and plain gold tie. Behind them, a pudgy armadillo in a badly-fit suit picks at his claws while a bobcat plays with his phone.

The older fox notices me, and says something. The weasel turns and comes over, and I recognize Vince, the press liaison. "Can I help you?" he says.

"I'm Lee," I say. "Wiley Farrell. I'm here for Dev Miski?"

"Oh!" Vince's ears come up and he smiles. "Sorry, I didn't recognize you. Come on, I think he's over here with the defense."

He leads me through the crowd. I recognize Aston, the tall wolf with a female wolf on his arm, talking to a smaller wolf whom I think is the backup quarterback. The first player I see that I really know is Pike, the huge polar bear, and when I see him, I see Kodi next to him, sipping from a beer. Then we get around them and see Charm, and Dev's with him, and Strike is there, painted up in his red and gold fur dye.

"There you go," Vince says. "Hey, Miski! Found this guy loitering around the doors."

Dev's eyes light up, and he raises the paw that isn't holding a beer to gesture me over. "Thanks, Vince," I say, momentarily second-guessing myself because we're not really on a first-name basis, but he's already hurrying back.

"It's Lee, isn't it?" Strike says, even though I just saw him four days ago. He's holding out a paw, so I shake it.

"Yep. Good to see you again. You guys played great today."

"Not great enough." Dev frowns momentarily, then recovers his spirits. "Got to do it again next week, huh?"

He lifts his beer. Charm toasts him. Strike's paws are empty. The cheetah says, while Dev and Charm are drinking, "Did you see the game?"

"Yeah." I'm not sure what else to say.

Dev lowers his beer and says, "How'd I do on my routes?"

"Uh," Strike begins, but the question's obviously meant for me, so I pre-empt whatever he was going to say.

"You were good, really crisp. Almost as good as I've seen you all year."

"'Cept once," he says.

I tilt my head. "In the third quarter? You were a little late to a tackle…"

"No," he says. "First quarter."

He doesn't elaborate, and I'm just deciding whether or not to press when Strike says, "You know a lot about football?"

"I was a pro scout for the Dragons," I say. "Looking around for a new position now." Which reminds me that I should look for Rodriguez or Corcoran. Not now, though.

"Ah. Good luck." At least he doesn't have the bad manners to ask why I got fired. That or he doesn't care enough, because he shifts topics immediately. "I know I can beat that coverage next week. I know their moves now, I'll be able to just cut past them and get open at least once or twice."

"And if they keep doubling you," I put in, "they'll have to leave one of the other guys open."

"You'd think," Charm says.

"I tried to coach those guys on how to get open," Strike says. "They don't really want to listen to me."

"Huh," I say, because everyone else is looking down at their drinks.

"Yeah, it's sometimes frustrating, you know, trying to be helpful and having people just ignore you."

"I know what you mean," I say, and then, because Dev is looking more and more grim, "Wasn't this supposed to be a dinner?" I lift my nose and can smell sautéed scallops and roasted chicken, but it's faint and there's no food in sight.

"Thought so too," Dev says. "There were appetizers."

"Were." Charm grins. "Now it's just beer." If he's suffering any from missing that kick, he's hiding it pretty well.

"Getting our playoff checks," Dev says. "Owner wants to make a big deal out of it. But I think most of us are just getting drunk."

"Don't get so drunk you can't drive," I say.

"Why d'you think I called you?" he says.

I arch an eyebrow, my ears going back a bit. "Really? Just to drive you home?"

"No," he says right away. "Not just for that."

"It's great that you're here," Strike says.

Both of us turn to him. I can't think of anything to say except, "Thanks."

Then there's an awkward silence, fortunately broken by a loud voice that cuts through the chatter around us. "Hey, guys, Mr. Corcoran is going to make a speech, and then we'll hand out your checks."

"And then we're out of here," someone behind me mutters.

Charm turns to them and says, "Not like you're not going to see us all again in twelve hours."

"Twelve?" I say to Dev.

"Well, not us." He gestures to Strike. "We're flying out to Crystal City for the commercial, but then we'll be flying directly to Hellentown after. Everyone else is flying out there tomorrow. Coach wants to practice at Hellentown all week, get used to the humidity, keep us away from distractions."

"Does that mean I shouldn't come to Hellentown?"

I was half-joking, but he looks at me and says, "I dunno. Maybe."

My ears go back. "Maybe?"

"I dunno. We can talk about it tonight."

Strike leans in. "It might be best. Supportive or not, you're a distraction that isn't about football."

"Lion Christ," Dev says, but just then the P.A. squeals with feedback and everybody turns to the stage. John Corcoran, the elder of the two foxes who'd been standing by the door when I walked in, takes the mic in one paw. The other fox, who must be his nephew, if I remember right, stands just behind him with both paws clasped behind his back. They're both a paler russet than I am, but they look a lot nicer in their suits than I do in my polo and jeans.

"Players, coaches, trainers, staff," Corcoran begins, in a raspy but firm voice, and I settle in. It's going to be one of those speeches.

He goes on about how when he bought the team, his friends made fun of him. He talks about hiring Coach Samuelson, and how some people called him a players' coach who couldn't manage games. It's all delivered in that awkward attempt at patter I'm used to hearing in speeches from guys who are not good at speaking. I'm sure when Corcoran's giving a business report he's brilliant, but there's a lot of stuff that he obviously wrote and rehearsed before coming here. Sometimes when you have a week to prepare, that can actually hurt you.

Because he's waiting for reactions and not often getting them, the speech is full of awkward pauses and seems much longer than it actually is. He talks about how long it's been since the Firebirds were in the playoffs, and he talks about what the team means to the city and the state, and he talks about the rivalry with Hellentown.

This is the only part where he gets really animated, and the team sort of wakes up, too. Charm pumps his fist and one of the offensive linemen says "Screw the Pilots," which is funny because it comes in a lull and Corcoran kind of chuckles nervously, his ears flicking over to the side. I follow them and see one or two reporters standing there taking notes. "Now, now," he says, "We, uh, don't want to give them any bulletin board, er, locker room material, you know?"

"Screw the Pilots!" Someone else says it louder, and then it becomes a chant around the room, and finally Corcoran laughs, and leans forward to the mic.

"All right, all right," he says. "Screw the Pilots!"

Big cheer, cries of "Yeah!" and laughter all around. The room relaxes. "Whatever happens from here on out," Corcoran closes with, "I am just so proud to be standing here in this room right now, and I will tell you, I have never been happier to write out checks for a total of two million dollars." And his tail wags, which is charming because for most of the speech he kept it really still.

Of course, at the mention of the two million dollars, everyone cheers, and many of them raise their drinks, and things become even more jovial. Corcoran doesn't mention the division bonus they're not getting, so at least he's that savvy. "Mark's going to hand out your checks. Come on up whenever you want and pick them up, and..." He looks down. "I guess Coach wants to say a couple words."

Another guy behind me groans softly. I turn and see Pike, and he catches my eye. "Nothin' against Coach," he says. "I don't want this to turn into one of those deals where everyone has to get up and say something."

"So go get your check, big guy," Charm says, and gestures. "They're linin' up."

I can't see over the six-foot-plus crowd, but Pike turns and says, "Hell yeah," and starts to make his way over there.

Kodi, trailing behind him, raises a paw and says hi to me, and impulsively, I walk up to him and stay alongside as he follows Pike. "Hey, how's it going?"

"Oh, good," he says. "Losing sucks, but...um. Yeah. How are you?"

"I'm good," I say. "I'm talking to the Firebirds about doing some outreach to the gay community."

"Oh?" He's interested but trying not to show it.

"Yeah. Not sure how it'll go, but one of the things I want to do is help other gay football players feel comfortable enough to come out." I keep my voice low, very low, and at first I think he doesn't hear me, because he doesn't react at all. "I'm sure there must be more out there," I add.

"Yeah," he says. "I guess. By the numbers."

We reach the back of the line, and Pike turns around. "What're you gonna spend your forty grand on?" he asks Kodi. "Me, I got my eye on this sweet gold watch."

"Oh, uh," Kodi says. "Maybe a vacation."

"How about you?" Pike grins at me. "What's Dev gonna spend it on?"

"Vacation, maybe? Savings? I don't know." I raise a paw. "I'm gonna get back to him, but...congrats, guys."

I meet Kodi's eyes, and he says, "Thanks," an echo beneath Pike's loud, booming answer. I kind of want to encourage him to contact me, but I don't want to do it with Pike watching. So I just walk back and find Dev, who's talking to Charm as they make their way with the crowd to get in line. Dev still has a bottle in his paw; Charm's hands are empty.

"Strike decided he didn't need to get his check right away," Dev says, though I didn't ask.

"So we did." Charm grins. "How you doing, Mrs. Gramps?"

"I'm good. You okay?"

"Sure," he says. "Couple beers, couple tits, couple dreams about that kick, I'll be fine. Go out next day and kick again."

"Got a girl lined up?" I return his grin. "One of the ones downstairs?"

"Nah. We came up through the side door. There's girls downstairs?"

"Yeah. Waiting for drunk players to come down and get a hotel room."

"Hmm." Charm strokes the bottom of his muzzle and looks at Dev's beer. His little ears flick around. "Maybe I need another drink."

"I'll save your spot," Dev says.

I look at Dev. "There was also one guy. A fox."

Dev shakes his head as Charm walks off. "Fucker doesn't give up."

"Oh, I don't think he's after you anymore."

"Good." He pauses and looks around. "Who is he after?"

"I couldn't tell." I step in a little closer. "So you don't want me to go to Hellentown?"

He sighs. "No, I do. I just." He runs a paw between his ears. "Are you going to be upset about the Strongwell commercial? I know I told you no to that PSA spot, but I really can't...I mean, this playoff game is huge."

Bigger than the well-being of hundreds of thousands of gay people? I push that thought down. "So if I promise not to talk about it..."

"I know it's really important to you," he says.

"It's not just me," I snap, and then I take a breath. "Yeah. It's important."

"I know," he says, and his muzzle twists up. "It's important to Brian, too."

I fold my arms and flatten my ears. "Yeah, it is," I say, lowering my voice. "Does that automatically make it invalid?"

"Are you taking his side?"

"It's not black and white. There's not one side and another."

He flicks his ears around. The players in back of us are still kind of talking, but lower, and the bear in front of us is quiet. Dev points at my chest. "You always told me to keep my mind on football."

"I did." I force my ears up. This is what I'd decided for myself, but he's being so adamant about it, and talking about Brian puts us both on edge. It's hard not to argue. "During practice and during the games. Life still goes on around your games."

"It's just four more weeks," he says. "Can't it wait? Oh, I guess not. Brian said there was something else you were supposed to ask me about."

I search his eyes in return. "We don't have to do this here."

"No, go on. Tell me."

He's angry, but not furious. A little buzzed, I think. Well, at least here in public he won't start shouting. "There's a meeting they want you to go to. With some politicians in Potomac, a week from Tuesday."

"Two days after the playoff game? No." Soft, velvet steel. "I can't. I'm not prepared, I'd be coming right from a game, and we'll probably—I can't take the time to do it."

"That's what I told them."

He narrows his eyes. "But you said they 'want' me to go to it. They still want me. So you haven't turned them down yet."

I draw in a breath. "I have until the first."

"Doc, it's no. I can't. Even if we lose." His whisper grates harsh against my ear, and there's some alcohol on his breath. "I'm not going to be in the mood to strut around some fucking politicians."

His complete refusal piques me, even though I agree with him. "Course not," I say. "It's not your place to fix the wrongs of the world. Especially not during playoff season."

The bear in front of us half-turns, ears swiveled to us, but Dev doesn't notice. "Who the fuck asks a football player to fly to Potomac in the middle of the playoffs?"

"I didn't schedule that meeting," I say.

"Was it some sort of fucking test of me, or you, that Brian set up?" His eyes glare down, challenging me.

"Yeah. Brian totally has that power over senators, but," as his ears go back and he ducks his head to his beer, "look, you know what, forget it."

His ears stay back and his tail's lashing. We shuffle forward in the line long enough for the bear to lose interest. I push all this stuff down, tell myself over and over that I'd already come to the same conclusions, that Dev and I really agree. Maybe if I repeat it enough, I'll start to feel it.

When Dev talks again, it's in a more normal low voice. "Did you talk to the guys about the Firebirds job any more?"

I shake my head. "I don't know what Rodriguez looks like. I think he's a rabbit of some sort?"

"Jackrabbit," Dev says. "I saw him up near the front."

We stand in slightly awkward silence for another few seconds, and then I curl my tail around my leg and perk my ears up. "Okay, I'll go see if I can talk to him. Here comes Charm, anyway."

The stallion's hard to miss, even if he weren't laughing loudly at someone's joke. He keeps laughing all the way back to the line, and when a coyote a couple spots behind says, "Hey, no cuts, kicker," Charm flips him off with a big toothy smile.

"Gramps was savin' my spot," he says, and wedges himself back into the line.

"You guys might as well still be in grade school." I shake my head.

Charm grins wide. "Except the girls are all grown up now."

"Thanks." Dev is still looking at me, but he smiles at Charm's comment. "Really needed that image."

"What else are friends for, eh, Gramps?" Charm lifts his beer and wraps the other arm around Dev's shoulder.

"All right," I say. "I'm going to try to find Rodriguez."

I leave with the tension of our argument still between us, trying to dismiss it as I look for a jackrabbit in a suit standing near the owner. Finally I spot a jackrabbit in a neat tan blazer and jeans standing with Coach Samuelson. They're talking, but not intently, just casually. I wait for Rodriguez—I hope—to look up, and catch his eye when he does. He flicks one of his long ears and nods at me, so I walk over.

"Dave Rodriguez," he says, holding out a paw.

"Wiley Farrell." I shake. "I talked to your assistant about the outreach position you're hiring for."

"You want a drink, Dave?" Samuelson lifts a paw. "Gonna go talk to some players on my way to the bar."

"Sure. Rum and Coke."

The wolf nods and walks off. I turn my ears to follow his progress and hear him greet a couple players before Rodriguez meets my eyes and says, "So, the outreach position. This is…for the gay community, right? Oh!" He smiles and his ears stand straighter as he points a finger at me. "You're Miski's, uh…partner."

"Right. I talked to Myrna a little while ago."

"Yeah." He folds his arms. "She sent me a note about that call. We do want to keep talking to you, but, you know, not here."

"No, no. I just wanted to introduce myself. And maybe, if you have a few minutes…"

He checks to make sure nobody's waiting to get his attention. "Sure."

"Well, we can save specifics, but I wondered if you had just a few minutes to tell me in general what you think the goals of the position would be? Like, why are you thinking of establishing it?"

He frowns. "Well, um…" He kind of looks past my shoulder and then back at me, and his ears flag a bit. "We were considering this position because we were told we had a resource in-house, or close to in-house… I'm sorry, I thought Myrna told me that you'd offered to do some outreach for us and we were trying to set up this position to accommodate that. Did you—I mean, is that still the case?"

"Oh." I frown and then rub my paw beneath my muzzle. "No, I'm definitely offering. I just thought you were establishing the position because of Dev coming out."

"We'd talked about maybe leveraging that, but I've been a little busy with the football side of things."

"Great job getting Strike on the team, by the way."

"Thanks." His smile widens and he stands straighter. "So I haven't been on all the other discussions. My time's a little more free now, but I'll be traveling to Hellentown. Do you have time on Tuesday—or are you coming to Hellentown with Miski?"

"I think I am," I say. "I'm not really sure. I might be too much of a distraction."

"Bullshit," he says, then holds up a paw. "Sorry, that's your decision. Lots of the players like to travel alone, some bring the wives along with them. But Miski's been playing better since he came out, seems like he's more comfortable being himself, and I gotta suspect you, as his partner, have something to do with that. So I say you should go along."

"Thanks." I don't know how to respond to that unexpected affirmation. "I think I'm a distraction now because, well, I used to be a pro scout, don't know if you knew that…" He shakes his head. "Anyway, one of these college players I was scouting was gay. He wrote to Dev. And then just over a month ago, he killed himself."

Rodriguez looks sympathetic but not horrified. "That's a real tragedy," he says. "I'm sorry to hear about it."

"And it looks like it was because his family was trying to get him 'help' for being gay, and he felt isolated at school…" I stop my rambling and collect myself. "Anyway, I feel like Dev could really help some of the gay kids out there, anyone who's feeling isolated and like they have nobody to look up to."

"Sure," Rodriguez says. "But he already has, right? I mean, he came out, and that was a whole circus for all of us."

I raise an eyebrow. "You got calls?"

He goes all serious. "I can't really discuss anything other teams might have talked about. But I was on the phone with the union rep and the president of the Players Association and…nothing bad, just trying to figure out what our positions and liability and all that might be, and make sure we were all on the same page. Ultimately it wasn't an issue. We made some statements to the gay rights groups and talked to a couple reporters and it blew over for us. But he's still out there, doing ads and stuff. So he's being that role model."

And of course, Rodriguez has more of an interest in Dev as a football player, which means less interest in Dev as a spokesperson for gay rights. "You're right," I say. "I'm looking at some stuff in the off-season, maybe meeting with some politicians to work on legislation, doing some spots with the equality groups."

"Hey," he says, "you two should get married. That'd be a good thing, right?"

"Uh, I guess so." My ears go all every which way.

"If you're ready for it." He laughs, kind of nervously. "I don't know how that works."

"Works the same as any marriage," I say. "We have to feel it's right, and then someone has to propose."

"Right. Well, look, about this outreach thing, I'd still like to talk to you. I think we could build a good fan base not just here in Chevali—let's be honest, there ain't much in the way of progressive thinking down here—"

"It's not that bad." I think about Brian and Paula, and the half-immigrant couples.

"—yeah, but it's not that great. Anyway, I think maybe we could build it up in Port City, in Yerba, in Crystal City even. You know, the big urban areas on the coasts. Sell some more jerseys and shirts out there. The team's behind him and it'd be nice to get some stuff out during the playoff push."

"What about in the off-season?"

The animation drops from his expression, and his long ears flag. "Yeah, obviously I can't discuss that right now." He softens. "Mostly because I don't know. I mean, anything might happen. Port City calls up and offers us Van Near and a draft pick for him, we'd have to look at that, you know? I'm not saying that's been mentioned, it's just an example."

"I don't talk to the papers." I grin. "Full disclosure: I did interview for a scouting position with Emmanuel, over at Yerba."

"Oh, yeah!" He brightens. "Good guy. I like him. They run a class organization over there. So—well, look, we can finish this up later. Myrna's got your number, right?"

He glances up over my shoulder, and I hear the coach approaching behind me. "Sure," I say. "I'm not doing much at the moment, so at your convenience."

"Thanks for coming over—Wiley?"

"I go by Lee." We shake paws, and I leave him and the coach to their conversation.

Dev and Charm are still in line for their checks, but near the front of it. It looks like the owner is handing them out personally and shaking paws and saying a few words to each player, so it might be a little while still. I scan the room for someone else I know. Pike stands out, a mass of white, Kodi still glued to his side. But there, off to the right, I spot tiger stripes, and move toward them. Gena and Fisher come into focus, talking to a coyote—I think it's Gerrard, but then I get closer and see that he's more muscular than Gerrard. Probably Dev's backup, Raef Zillar—Zillo. And actually, Fisher is talking to him. Gena's just standing there sipping a mixed drink.

When she catches my eye, she brightens, and that makes me feel good. She actually comes around the back of Fisher to say hi to me. "Thank God," she says. "They're talking about car racing. How are you doing?"

"Pretty good." It's a shorter answer than "trying to figure out why someone—probably Dev—told the Firebirds I wanted to work in gay outreach."

She lifts her glass to her lips. "Not drinking? They make a pretty good gin and tonic."

I shake my head. "I'm the designated driver."

"Lucky me. Fisher's not allowed to drink much with his medications." She grins and tosses back another swallow.

"How's he coming along?" He looks pretty good from what I can see, dressed up in a nice suit, very animated as he talks to the coyote.

"He's going with the team to Hellentown, thank God." She shakes her head. "I love him, but it's been just one thing after another. Feels like he's been in a cage and he's blaming me for it, partly."

I look across the room. Dev and Charm are still kind of in the same place, or at least, the top of Charm's head is. I can't see who's holding up the front of the line. "That can be rough. I mean, he's going to have to adjust to life after football."

She hushes me theatrically. "For God's sake," she laughs. "Don't tell him that. I tried to start, but he just got so worked up about it that I had to focus more on how he'd be back playing before the end of the season."

"Maybe in the off-season. It can be hard for people to adjust to a new kind of life."

"Mm-hmm." She looks at me over the rim of the glass as she takes another drink. "Easier when you're younger. How are you doing it?"

"Trying to rediscover my life." I smile. She looks curious, so I go on, telling her a little about wanting to do scouting again but also about my renewed interest in activism.

"Sounds nice." She swirls the drink in her glass. "Once the boys are off in college, in a couple years, I was thinking about taking up some charities. Something Fisher can get interested in, too, because he'll be home by then. I'd like to do something good and make a difference."

"Lots of people join the gay rights movement on behalf of friends." I'm not quite sure we're close enough for me to make that pitch, but she is a little tipsy, and after all, I'm not binding her to anything.

She smiles. "I wish you guys the best, but I'm not sure I'm the best person for that. I have relatives back in Chapura, and there was that chemical plant spill…"

"And the deforestation, sure." It's hard to argue that that's more or less important than the right of gay kids to feel safe, or the right of gay people to feel equal. It's certainly a worthy cause.

She nods. "Fisher has enough money saved that we could make a difference. And if they win another championship, the endorsements…"

I tilt my muzzle. "He has an agent, right? Do you do anything to manage his career?"

"A little." She wiggles her paw. "I set up local appearances, but I work with Damian on those. He sets up the endorsements and I just make sure Fisher gets to the shoots." She smiles. "Sometimes it's harder than other times, but I haven't had to worry so much about it lately."

"I'm sure it'll pick up. Maybe he and Dev can do a commercial for the playoffs. Tiger pride, or something."

She nods. "Damian's tried to work the tiger angle a couple times—he's one, too. Less of that lately, and more of building up his image through stories in the press, 'veteran at the end of his career' kind of stuff. It's been harder with the injury."

"I know a lot of Dev's teammates have been interviewed about playing with him. There was a feature on Gerrard in the Chevali paper that got picked up nationally."

"Well." She laughs. "He's got his own publicity machine. Some of the things that go on and don't get reported…"

My ears perk and then settle back. "I guess that sort of thing happens on any team."

Gena laughs. "Well, I'm not saying Fisher didn't have his own little indiscretions…" She lowers her voice, sliding her eyes back to where he's still absorbed in conversation with the coyote. "I left him once. Went to stay with a friend of mine. I told him that if he was going to fool around on the road, it better not be with other tigers or we were done, I'd take the cubs and go live with my mother." Her eyes are firm and a little moist, and her breath smells strongly of gin as she leans in toward me. "I would have. But he came back, we went to a little counseling, and he's been good since then."

How good? How can she be sure? But at least he's been discreet. "I'm glad the cubs have both of you," I say.

"I'd rather they just have one devoted parent than one parent who has to deal with the other parent constantly not being sure what his commitment is…" She stops and drains the remainder of her drink. "I'm glad he didn't go. It's easy for me to say I would've taken the cubs, but it would be so hard without him. Not just raising the cubs, but…we've been together a long time."

I nod. "My parents just split up after twenty-five years."

"I heard, from Daria." She puts a paw on my shoulder, then removes it, looking unsure. "Your father seemed okay at Christmas."

"He's dealing with it, trying to cope with it." And the phone call with Mother. I clench my fists, shouting echoing in my ears until I have to flatten them against my head, teeth gritted.

"It's hard," Gena says. "So hard." She shakes her head.

"Sometimes it's a good thing."

I'm grateful that Dev's paw lands on my shoulder then. I turn, and Gena smiles up at him. "Got your check?"

He brandishes the paper. It's got a fancy Firebirds logo on it and gold seal. "Can't wait to drop this off at the ATM."

"Can I see?" He holds out the check and I take it carefully. In computer-printed script it says, "Pay to the order of Devlin Miski," and under that, "the amount of 41,200 and 00/100 dollars." The signature, Corcoran's, looks like it's in real ink and not just a stamp. "He hand-signed it?"

"Right in front of me." Dev grins. "He said he's proud of me for my courage and happy to have me on the team."

"Did you thank him again for using the jet?"

"Oh, shit." Dev takes the check back, his ears flat. "I forgot." He half-turns.

"No, no." I laugh. "You sent him a note after. That should be enough."

"Did you get to talk to Rodriguez?"

I nod. "Yeah. He said…" I pause. Dev's on a high, our previous argument filed away, and this probably isn't the right time to confront him about whether he put the team up to hiring me. "He said we'll talk later in the week."

"Good." He drapes an arm around me. "It's pretty cool, you know. Maybe you'll be on the team too." He looks around. "I feel good with you here."

There's four beers behind that, but it's nice. And I try to enjoy it, and not to think too much about the fact that he likes being here with me when I'm not mentioning Vince King, when I'm not trying to get him to think about equality or anything but football. I try to just relax and enjoy the moment. I almost succeed.

Chapter 30: Determination (Dev)

In the end, Lee agrees to come to Hellentown on Friday, stay in a hotel through Sunday night, and then fly back to Chevali on Monday. We'll hopefully be going on to Boliat on Monday or Tuesday, but if that's the case, he'll fly up there that Friday. It's important for me to have the week to practice.

Thank God he doesn't mention the Potomac meetings or doing a TV spot again before I leave. It's bad enough that I'm worrying about him hanging out with Brian and those guys without him distracting me with what I should be thinking about if I were a good person. I'm a football player, and that's hard enough to keep in my head. He spent years getting me to focus on that, so now this departure is confusing and I'm worrying that it'll cost us another game if I keep stressing about it. God knows we don't have another one to lose, not now.

We stop for burgers on the way home. Unlike the glow from the playoff check, the beers have mostly worn off when Ogleby calls half an hour after we get home, while Lee's checking his e-mail and I'm just chilling. Ogleby's in full-on squeak mode; I have to assure him three times that I have everything I need, I am totally prepared for the commercial shoot tomorrow, I'm going to be on the plane with Strike and all the other stuff that goes with it. Finally he calms down enough to talk about the playoffs and the people who have called to ask for some time with me in the next week. Not the reporters; they all have my number and call me or text me after games now. I don't see my quotes show up all that often, which tells me I'm getting better at being bland and uninteresting, just the way Gerrard would want it.

"Women's channel wants you to call in for this roundtable show they have. I don't think it's that big a deal, probably not worth your time but I told them I'd make sure."

"Pass."

"Okay, and got a contact from some guys doing a documentary on gays in sports. They want to interview you sometime in March."

"Fine. Anything after the playoffs is fine. Until then, I'm a football player."

"That's okay, the gay people stopped calling a couple weeks ago. I told them you were concentrating on football and we'd contact them when your time freed up."

That might be the first thing Ogleby's done right in a month. "So it's just football stuff and endorsements?"

"Mostly, yeah, but Dev, we got a chance to work on some big stuff this off-season, I don't know if you saw but there's already buzz about Van Near renegotiating his contract and he's the same year you are, so—"

"Lion Christ, he was Rookie of the Year last year. Not the same situation."

"I'm just saying, it's happening, and we should start thinking about where we can shop you if Chevali doesn't renegotiate with us because your value is clearly much higher now than—"

"See," I say, interrupting, "this is exactly the kind of thing I don't need right now. I want to be a football player."

"Honey, this is a football contract, it's not a gay contract."

"It's not about the game. That's what I need to spend all my time on."

Whether he's actually getting better or just on sort of a mellow high from the million-dollar commercial, Ogleby actually settles down. I do a couple of post-game chats with two of the sports reporters, saying a lot of the same things about how disappointed I am that we didn't win the division, but I believe in our chances during the playoffs. I'm all ready to tell them that the fox calling me "homo" was no big deal, that my teammates stuck up for me, but they don't even ask. They do ask about the guy with the Jesus quote, but I just say that I didn't see him, we were never on the field together, it didn't come up. And that's it.

I feel this sense of triumph almost. They treated me like a football player. Not "that gay football player," but a linebacker, one who contributed to his team, who was affected by the loss, who shows resolve going into his first playoffs. I put the phone down and wonder if this is a corner turned, if there can be gay comments going into a game without me having to be front and center about them. It feels a little liberating.

When I come back into the living room, Lee's put his laptop away and is watching a local sports highlight show, WSN, ears still perked. "Tough round of interviews," he says.

"Just football," I say. Alongside the pride of being a football player, guilt crawls up my spine and down my tail, which curls. To distract myself, I point at the screen. "Hey, those guys called me."

"What'd you tell them?"

"The usual." I plop down beside him. "Tough game. Good team. Get 'em next week."

He doesn't put a paw on my leg. I pull the check out of my pocket and stretch it out. "So," I say. "I'm going to leave you in charge of this. You figure out what to spend it on, and whatever it is, we'll do it. Vacation to an island, ski resort, new car. Not a motorcycle, though. I don't think I'm allowed."

He turns to look at the check. "What if I want to save it?"

"Sure."

"What if I want to donate it?"

I sit and look at the TV screen. Over the highlights of our game, I can see Lee's reflection, sitting with his tail curled around his legs, watching the screen—no, he's looking at my reflection, too. Our eyes meet in the TV, and then he looks away.

I drop the check in his lap. "That'd be great. I'd love to have my money help out. Just don't publicize it 'til after the playoffs, okay?"

He takes the check, folds it up, and gets up to put it on the end table beside the TV, then sits on the couch. "Thanks," he says. "I'll think about it."

"So what happened with your mom?" I ask, and he hesitates, and then he tells me everything. It unfolds like a horror show, the escalating anger, the lock on the door and the burned things. I want to ask if his mother's possessed, if this otter is like one of those evil spirits you see in horror movies who take over the lives of otherwise ordinary people and make them do terrible things. But I know she's real, I know that people can influence other people.

So I hug him, and he says it's okay, he's dealing with it. "Hope you understand that's why I was so upset about the activism stuff yesterday," he says. "I just feel like I need to do something to balance her out."

Giving him the playoff check should at least be a sign to him that I care. Because I do. If it's just a question of money, hell, I'll take half—okay, maybe a tenth—of what I get from the Strongwell commercial too. I'll support him if he wants to be a full-time activist, as long as I don't have to talk to that fucking skunk.

I point to the check. "That'll go a long way. And look, you still have your father. You have your aunt, most of your family. You haven't talked to your mother in years anyway."

He nods. "I don't want to go back, but it feels weird to know I can't."

I don't know what to say to that, so I just put my arm around him. We sit and watch the highlights of the game on the sports channel as the anchors show stats for how long it's been since the Firebirds were in the playoffs, having fun with it: this person was president, this person wasn't born yet, this quarterback was in his last year, nobody knew what the Internet was except for people in universities, and so on.

"I am proud of you," he says. "You're doing great. The whole team is great."

"I know," I say. "It's thanks to you. You taught me to keep working at football. Gerrard's been a great mentor, but you're my motivator."

He nods. "Seems like you've been doing a good job motivating yourself these days."

"I still feel you watching me every game." When he doesn't respond, I put a paw on his leg. "I still need you."

A second goes by, then two, and he says, "I know."

"Seems to me," I say, "like I need to prove it."

That finally gets a smile out of him. He rests his paw over mine. "Stud, you don't need to prove anything to me." I start to protest, and then he says, "but if you want to, well, I'll always be glad to hear your penetrating arguments."

I lean over. "Gregory's the one who makes arguments," I say. "I'm the one who fucks you."

"Well," he says, his ear flicking with a shiver, "I certainly wouldn't want to get those two mixed up."

I know everything's not okay, but it's as okay as it can be until after the playoffs, I think. So I take him into the bedroom and prove I need him, and in the morning I prove it again until we're both satisfied.

That makes the awkwardness of leaving to film a commercial a little easier to take. It's awkward for me, at least, because I know he said he had until the first to respond to Brian about that Potomac meeting. He hasn't talked to me about it, which means one of two things. Either he's accepted that I'm not going to do it, or he's desperately hoping he can change my mind in the next two days.

I hope to God it's not the latter. We've had a really nice fall, at least when Brian wasn't trying to poison my fox's mind against me. If he just lets it go and lets me get through the playoffs, then I feel sure we can figure things out. He'll see how little it means to just wait one damn month.

And the playoffs—wow, I am actually nervous about them, getting to the airport, because I'm going in the opposite direction from my team. I know I have Coach's permission to do this commercial, but this feels wrong. I should be with the guys, because I finally proved I'm one of them, and we have to bear this pressure together. When I went to the D-II playoffs two years ago, barely anyone noticed. There was a score update on SportsCenter, and that was about it. Now, if anyone's five minutes late to a team meeting or misses curfew, there'll be articles written about what it means and whether the team is handling the pressure.

I know this because Lee told me there were articles about me and Strike filming this commercial in the middle of the playoff run, and whether it'd be a distraction, and so on. He told me not to worry about it, and I'm trying not to, but part of this media attention that I still haven't gotten used to is the enormous weight of everyone judging you. It can make you second-guess yourself even when you know you're doing the right thing. Especially when the person closest to you might not think you're doing the right thing.

Well, Strike is, if anything, more dedicated to the game than I am. Gerrard approves of that in him, and so I don't feel so bad, getting on the plane to go to Crystal City. Because he's a football player, and so am I.

And that's thanks to my fox. Maybe like that otter changed his mom for the worse, he's changed me for the better. I'm more passionate—well, no. He's focused my passion for the game. I still look for him every game, feel his eyes watching, think about how he'll analyze my performance. I love him, more than I ever thought I could love someone, much less a guy, and having him around has made all the difference in the world.

Junior year of college, I figured I was on track to work in Dad's auto shop. Maybe get a job at the high school as an assistant football coach if I were lucky. Lee changed all that. He opened the door to this life, and I'm not going to let it slip away, because that would be letting him down. I know he wants me to be more outspoken about gay rights, but this Vince King guy has nothing to do with us. My Dad used to say that he can't fix all the cars, only the ones they bring into the shop, and not even all of those. Vince King is one of those cars you feel bad for, but he's not in our shop. I have to pay attention to the things I can fix, and those are me, my fox, and my football team.

Chapter 31: Resolution (Lee)

I spend most of Sunday night thinking about Dev and the conversations I had with him and Rodriguez. It all kind of comes together for me, and I try to push it aside so I can at least see Dev off without him worrying about me, but I know he senses something. When you live with someone, you can't really hide your worries. You can only hide what they're about. Hopefully he thinks I'm just wondering what to do with that big check he gave me.

Rodriguez was upbeat and businesslike, but clearly had no idea what to do with an outreach person, no plan in place. That's fine; part of the job could be to come up with an outreach plan, and I got kind of excited about that. Except that I also realized that what that meant was that Dev must have called them to get them to hire me. And I'm sure he did it with the best of intentions, trying to get me a job. But I can't help thinking that he also did it to distract me, to keep me away from Brian, to keep me under the control of the team and not doing things that would inconvenience him.

Which are not good thoughts, and I know that with my head, but my heart sours on the whole Firebirds job. I don't want to take it just to be shuffled out of the way, and I have to remind myself that it might be a good opportunity just to talk to people in the organization and give them a good direction to go, whether I move to Yerba in February or not.

If they offer me the job, though, I have to go, don't I? Dev would probably support me whatever I do, but if the previous day has shown me anything, it's that he and Brian are oil and water. Or, like, fire and gasoline, maybe. I could keep working with Equality Now, but it would be a friction between us that wouldn't go away.

The thing is, I worry that doing anything activist on my part will cause friction. Because I still feel that he should be using his unique position to make more of a difference, and I can't see myself giving up that belief in the next month. And I know myself. I'm the guy who came out to his boss on a football team because he made vaguely gay slurs for ten minutes. Not exactly the model of restraint.

I can try to change, but it won't happen soon. It took Mother two years or more to change from a slightly standoffish but caring mother to someone who burned her son's things because they looked gay. Father accepted my life, but he hasn't really changed. Dev hasn't changed that much; he was energy in search of a direction. And Brian…Brian changed in one violent night, a sharp angle like a fracture in his life, and he's never changed back.

Or maybe he was always that way, always personally driven to get what he wanted, and with his silver spoon background, he never encountered resistance like he did that night the Forester football players beat him up. The bitterness and fear from that night is partly what drove me away from him. I thought it was gone, thought that maybe the Equality Now work had healed him. But it hasn't. I've seen it showing through the cracks in my conversations with him, and especially in his confrontation with Dev, the threats, the way he views football players—still—as the enemy. If he doesn't want to be my boyfriend specifically, then he wants me not to be Dev's. He's just smart enough to know that he can't say that out loud to me.

And no matter what else is going on in my life, I can't have that be part of it. So I'm going to have to break up with Brian, and Equality Now. I'm going to have to say good-bye to thinking about a national campaign against Families United, bringing Vince King's story to the national press, showing my mother the true nature of the company she's keeping. I can maybe help some college athletes if I sign on with the Firebirds for a month, but I'm not even sure that's a good idea right now.

Dev calls in the middle of my deep thoughts and distracts me, for which I'm grateful. He says the commercial shoot is weird, much more elaborate than he had with Ultimate Fit (who basically came to the stadium and filmed in the parking lot). He might have to go any minute, he says. He's in a studio with a catering table (he describes that to me twice) and the guy he has to put his arm around on camera is a cute wolf. Don't get attached, I say, and he laughs. I ask how Strike has been, and he says Strike's been Strike, but not intolerably so. I tell him I love him, and to let Strike be himself.

Let him be himself, I think when I hang up. I gave Hal that advice; I should take it too. Let Dev be who he is, because after all, that's the tiger I fell in love with. I can't force him to care about gay rights the way I do. He has enough trouble keeping his football life and his media presence in check (and he really needs to fire Ogleby already, but I'm not going to push him on that either). And he cares about me, that's the important part.

I'm glad I got to meet his Auntie Za and see that fire in her to *do* something, where it wasn't in the rest of his family. I wonder how she's doing, over there in Moskva, wonder if it's satisfying the activist side of her. I wonder as I call Brian if she'd understand what's eating me inside, why I have to do what I do that evening.

Brian is only too happy to meet me for dinner, tossing out a couple "it's about time" lines at me, which I ignore. I dress up nicely, put on that tie that Dev got me, and head downtown to the bistro I went to with Hal. I'm apprehensive the whole way down, because it would have been so much easier to have this conversation over the phone, and I know I'm putting myself in line for a not very fun night.

"So honored to be invited to dinner," Brian says when I arrive and sit down at the table he's already occupied. Not only is he early, he's already made his way through half a glass of wine. Red, of course. "It's always a delight to see you."

I ask for a chard and then arrange myself politely, and smile. "Well, you know," I say. "Awfully rude to break up over the phone."

His smile wavers, but doesn't disappear, though his ears do flick back, momentarily hiding the scar from my view. "Is that what you think this is?" He takes a sip of wine, and the fur around his lips glistens. Easier for him to drink red wine, with black fur all around his muzzle. When I spill red wine on my white fur, it shows all evening.

"Seemed the best comparison," I say.

"So you couldn't get your boyfriend to spare a moment of time for a good cause."

I shake my head. "Didn't try that hard, to be honest."

"Should have known a jock wouldn't ever care about *us* fags." He fixes me with his gaze, and his ears are back up, the notch now clear against the tan walls.

"It's not about that," I say.

"No. It's not." And his eyes hold mine. I don't want to be first to look away, but I am.

The waitress, a tall mare, brings my wine and takes our orders. Brian gets a steak; I get a trout fillet and a salad.

"Too bad all that focus didn't help him win the division," Brian says, after a few moments of silence.

"He played well."

"They all played well. They needed to play great. Looked like he was having some words with Jennings."

"The fox? Yeah. He didn't tell me what it was about."

He looks over his wine glass at me, eyes bright. "On TV it looked like Jennings said 'homo' a couple times."

I force myself not to rise to his bait. "Possible. Like I said, he didn't tell me."

"Media doesn't even care about it now. It's like he never came out."

"It's not like that at all."

"So what about you, Tip?"

Off-handed, casual. I lean back in my chair, trying to match his attitude even as I fiddle with my tie. "What about me? I've got a lead on another scouting job. I'm watching the college bowl games, keeping up with the league. That's my career."

"That's not your life."

Still casual, still easy with the weighty pronouncement. I flick an ear and look amused, and keep in mind my advice to Hal. Brian is who he is. "It's not *your* life," I say. "I'm really glad you've found a purpose."

He leans across the table and loses the amused look, and I hold up a paw. "Spare me the whole lecture about how activism is my life, okay?"

That shuts him up. He leans back, the gleam in his eye less friendly now. I go on. "It's still important to me, and I'm thrilled that you and Paula and all the people there are doing so much, and I hope that meeting with the senators goes great and that Derrick and Maria—"

"David," he says.

"—can live with their partners here and all that. But my life is bigger than that now. I have to weigh the things I want to do with the things I have to do."

"You don't have to do anything you don't want to." Brian signals for another glass of wine as he finishes his, and the waitress brings it over just as my salad arrives. "So all that means is what I've been telling you ever since you met him. Getting laid is more important than doing the right thing."

"First of all," I say, "reducing it to 'getting laid' is insulting. Second of all, are you getting laid?" He scowls. "Then don't knock it 'til it happens to you."

"Plenty of people in committed relationships are in Equality Now," he says as I eat my salad. "They manage to make it work. Some of their partners are executives, vice presidents in big companies, and they still contribute, still *let* their partners spend time with the dirty ol' gay activists."

I let him talk, because that's what you do in a breakup, you let the other person rant at you. By the time I'm scraping up stray pieces of lettuce through trails of Caesar dressing, he's calmed down a little and has moved on to bargaining. "You know, we can find something for you to do. Stuffing mailers, cold-calling, even working with Marilee to craft e-mails."

"I thought there wasn't anything for me to do if Dev wasn't involved."

"That was a motivational tactic." He grins at me without humor.

"*Was* it."

"Aw, Tip, you know I would love to work next to you again."

"Uh-huh." They clear the empty plate, and I take a sip of wine to complement the cheese and garlic. "Well, you know, I don't see that happening."

"Look me in the eye and tell me it's not something you'd like. Tell me you don't miss it, those FLAG days."

I stare steadily at him. "I don't want it. I miss FLAG, but not at the cost of what I have now."

He searches my eyes. "So," he says, "this really is a breakup."

"Afraid so."

"Well," he says, "nice of you to pay for dinner."

I know it's not nice, but I return his grin and say, "Oh, think of it as Dev paying for it. After all, it's his money."

He glowers, and doesn't say another word until our meals have arrived. The trout is good, meaty and flaky, and with a bit of lemon it's got a nice tang to it. Brian signals the waitress as the steak arrives. "What's the most expensive wine you have that you'd recommend with this?"

"Well." The mare looks down at the steak. "Our most expensive red is a Far Niente cabernet sauvignon, but with that steak I would prefer—"

"I'll take that one," Brian says. "Whole bottle, please."

"Yes, sir." She glances at me.

"I'm fine with the white," I say. When she's gone, I shake my head at Brian. "That's not going to be more than a couple hundred bucks."

"Might as well get my money's worth, right?" he says. "You certainly are."

"Going to drink it all here?"

He shrugs. "If you stay long enough."

I take a deliberate drink from my glass of water. "Gee, Spot, you don't have to give me more reasons to leave early."

Two bites of steak while he stews over that, then, "This isn't you."

"Jesus Fox," I say. "When you don't have someone writing your lines for you, you just say the same old shit over and over again."

"I mean it." He leans across the table. "It's not going to last. I know you think you're different now, but I can read you, Tip. I know what's going on behind those slit-pupil eyes."

"Really," I say. "Do tell."

He chews his steak and swallows. "You called me. I didn't call you. Something in you still wants this life."

"I can have both." I hope those words at least have enough force to persuade Brian.

He's unruffled. "Principles last longer than relationships. So eventually he's going to leave you, once he signs that megabucks contract he's heading

for in a year, or soon after. More gay guys will come out and he'll meet one who plays football. They'll spend more time together, they'll realize they have more in common because they understand the life. And then you'll be left alone, with nothing but the memory of all those years you wasted." He finishes off the second glass of wine. "Maybe some money. He seems like the kind of guy who'd pay you off to make himself not feel guilty."

"He's not going to leave me," I say.

"Now who's being stubborn?"

"I think I would know myself and him better than you. But you know what?" I stop for a drink of wine, sweet and sharp all at once. "I don't care. I know...I know what might happen. I know I'm making a sacrifice. And I'm making it for us."

"But, Tip," Brian says softly, looking up from his steak, "does he know? Does he appreciate it?"

"Of course," I snap, and then we have to stop because the waitress is back with Brian's expensive West Coast wine.

There isn't much more to the conversation. I pay, as I'd pretty much intended to even before he assumed it, and even the bottle of wine (at $250, it costs more than the rest of the meal combined) barely makes me blink. Maybe the forty thousand dollar check on the table at home helps. Or maybe it doesn't.

I toss my credit card down on the bill, and Brian picks up his bottle of wine. "Well, thanks for the parting gift, Tip," he says. "*I'll to my truckle-bed. This field-bed is too cold for me to sleep.* I've no doubt we'll meet again."

"It's not quite thirty pieces of silver," I say, "but I hope you get good and drunk on it. Or get someone else good and drunk. Might do you some good."

He looks sad for a moment, and it makes me a little sad too. But then he raises the bottle and says, "Have fun getting fucked by your football player." And he says it really loudly, enough that the fifteen people closest to us prick up their ears. Some turn and stare at me. The hostess starts over, but stops when Brian grins and walks out. She just stares in my direction, and of course, I can't leave until the waitress comes back with the credit card slip.

Driving back, I do wonder if Dev will ever really understand how important this is, not just to me, but to the world. I think he knows with his head, but I don't think he feels it with his heart, and I don't know how to get that through to him. Maybe if I confirm my suspicions about Kodi, maybe if Dev knows there's another gay guy on his team who's afraid to come out...maybe. Of course, then I think of Brian saying that Dev will eventually hook up with another gay football player, and I worry that he'd feel protective of shy, scared Kodi, that one night on the road, while Vonni's getting a blow job that doesn't count and Gerrard is doing whatever he's doing and that male fox groupie is sucking off some guy who doesn't want to admit he likes guys…

I grit my teeth and shake my head. That's what Brian would want, to get into my head like that. But at the same time, I can't quite shake it. And I can't talk to Dev about it, I don't want to expose stress in our relationship to Hal, and I can't talk to Father. I want to drive to a liquor store like he did, buy a good bottle of scotch, and just get quietly, miserably drunk.

Sacrifice is most worthwhile and hardest when nobody knows you're doing it. If I went to Dev and told him how much this meant to me, that I was giving it up for him, well, he'd feel terrible about it. It would pretty much screw up the whole thing. So I have to keep it tucked inside myself, and what worries me is that I have never been very good at that.

•

New Year's Eve, Dev is in Hellentown, two hours ahead of me and Chevali. He calls me right around ten o'clock—his midnight—and says he's out with the guys but wanted to wish me Happy New Year. I toast him with a glass of the scotch I bought and curl up alone on the sofa.

An hour later, I call my father for his midnight. He's doing the same thing I am: drinking at home. At least he's doing sparkling wine rather than scotch. We talk about maybe getting together for one of the playoff games if I can get an extra ticket. Otherwise it probably won't be until the off-season. I tell him Dev and I will come up and visit, and he says if it gets too cold, he might fly down to Chevali again. I say I'd like that, and that I hope his '09 is better than his '08.

And then it's ten to midnight and my phone rings with Dev's number. I'm a little drunk from the scotch already, so I just listen to him talk about practice and the excitement around the playoff game. A couple times I break in with tips for him, but otherwise I stay quiet.

He notices, and asks if I'm okay, and then what I've been up to. I tell him I've been watching college bowl games, looking for my players, but it's frustrating not having control over the film. When the TV cuts away from the player I want to see, that's it. I don't get another angle, don't get to see more.

There's a short silence, and then he says. "January first is tomorrow."

"That's what usually happens after New Year's Eve, stud."

"Did you talk to the Equality guy?"

"Brian. Yes."

Another pause. "And?"

"I told him you're not going to do it."

He exhales. "Thanks, fox."

I lean back on the couch. "Well, you weren't. It wasn't like I could lie to him."

"No, but…" He might be a little drunk himself. "You could've kept bugging me about it."

"I know better than that. You were right. I told you to focus on football and that's what you should do. No matter whether there's people out there who need to be recognized. That's their problem."

"Doc."

"Sorry." I sigh. "I might have had a little to drink."

"You can make it up to me Friday."

"I will."

"With sex."

I don't say anything. He goes on. "That's a joke. I mean, not that I don't want sex. It's…"

"It's okay," I say. "I get it."

"Did you figure out what to do with the forty grand?"

I pause. "You said you'd be okay if I donated it to Equality Now, right?"

"I…yeah. If that's what you want to do with it."

"Okay."

He knows me too well to let it go. "Is that what you did with it?"

I curl my tail around my legs and look up at the ceiling. "I'll tell you Friday. Maybe."

"Am I going to have to work it out of you?"

"You can work something out of me."

"That's my fox."

"Yes," I say.

The clock on the TV starts counting down. I count into the phone, and Dev counts with me, from twenty down to zero. Then he makes a kissing noise, and I make one back, and it's 2009, a new year, and he and I are facing it together. I imagine my arms around him, and he imagines his arms around me, and we imagine together some of the things we'll do on Friday.

When he hangs up to go get some sleep, I walk to the end table, pick up the check, and look at it. Then I set it down and go into the bedroom.

You can't break up with a principle, Brian said. Shows how much he knows. I don't want to send the check to Equality Now, because I don't want Brian helping spend the money, but I don't just want to spend it on us either. Right now I think I'm going to save half of it and give half to some gay rights cause. But I don't know what cause that'll be.

Lying in bed in the first hours of 2009, I think about searching for a cause, and that leads me to thinking about another member of my family who must have lain in bed many a night wondering what cause she could give her time to, who made a decision that—no matter what my father says—led to the dissolution of her marriage and the estrangement of her family, at least for now.

It frightens me that I feel that kinship with her. Is this the path that led her to Families United, this feeling of powerlessness and boredom and betrayal? Did that overwhelm her family instincts, lead her to throw her son out and break her marriage of twenty-five years? I want so badly to understand it, to take it apart so I can put it together in reverse, for her and then for everyone else in the country.

Mother can say she loves me and still lock my door and burn my clothes and refuse to acknowledge the person I am now. Brian is the guy who was my best friend in college, and the guy who tried to have an awkward tryst with me, and the guy who outed my boyfriend and the guy who really wants to change the world. He can be all those things at once. So I can be the activist and the boyfriend and the football scout too, find a way to balance them without letting them tear me or Dev apart. I have to. Because Brian, damn him, is right about me.

I can still work on my anger, with my father and maybe Hal. The gay activism I will have to pursue opportunistically, see if I can sacrifice a little and still remain myself. I'm just going to have to work harder at it, and remember that Dev and the love we have is the compass point to guide me through life. I wish I had more confidence in myself to follow that star.

Dev's voice still echoes in my ears, his scent is in our bed, and his imaginary paws rest on my sides. I close my eyes. It's a new year, for me and Dev, for my family and his family and his team, and if anyone can inspire me to carry on despite losing my motivation, it's the Firebirds. After all, they may have lost the division, but they're still going to the playoffs.

Cast of Characters

Chevali Firebirds (* = starters)

Gerrard Marvell	coyote	middle linebacker (Mike)*
Carson Omba	leopard	strong-side linebacker (Sam)*
Fisher Kingston	tiger	defensive end
"Brick"	black bear	defensive tackle*
Colin	fox	cornerback*
Ty Nakamura	fox	wide receiver/kick returner*
Aston	wolf	quarterback*
"Jaws"	wolverine	running back*
Norton	cheetah	cornerback*
Vonni DiCarlo	fox	cornerback*
Pace	jaguar	safety*
"Charm"	stallion	kicker*
Corey Mitchell	cougar	weak-side linebacker, started until injured, when his spot was taken by Dev
"Zillo"	coyote	linebacker (backup)
"Pike"	polar bear	defensive end (backup)*
Kodi	brown bear	defensive tackle (backup)
Jake	black bear	defensive tackle (practice squad)
Baki	cheetah	QB/WR (practice squad)
"Steez" Mikilios	cougar	linebackers coach
Vern Samuelson	wolf	head coach
John Corcoran	fox	Firebirds' owner
David Rodriguez	jackrabbit	Firebirds' general manager

Family

Mikhail	tiger	Dev's father
Duscha	tiger	Dev's mother
Gregory	tiger	Dev's brother
Marta	tiger	Gregory's wife, Dev's sister-in-law

Brenly	fox	Lee's father
Eileen	fox	Lee's mother
Carolyn	fox	Lee's aunt

Angela Marvell	coyote	Gerrard's wife
Gena Kingston	tiger	Fisher's wife
Daria DiCarlo	fox	Vonni's wife
Jaren Marvell	coyote	Gerrard's son (older)
Mike Marvell	coyote	Gerrard's son (younger)
Bradley Kingston	tiger	Fisher's son (older)
Fisher Kingston, Jr.	tiger	Fisher's son (younger)

Other

| Hal Kinnel | swift fox | reporter |
| Peter Emmanuel | fox | Yerba Whalers' GM |

About the Author

Kyell Gold took up furry erotica writing after high school, making the team at his small liberal arts college as a walk-on. He was drafted late by Sofawolf and blossomed in the professional league, earning four Ursa Major awards in his first three years as a pro for his novels and short stories. He has since won eight more Ursa Major awards, including one for "In Between," the first Dev and Lee story, one for *Out of Position*, which also won two Rainbow Awards for gay fiction, and one for *Isolation Play*, the second Dev and Lee book. At least two more Dev and Lee books are planned following *Divisions*.

His various online presences are linked from *www.kyellgold.com*, and you can follow him on Twitter at @KyellGold. In the off-season, he lives in California with his husband.

About the Artist

Blotch was one of the top-rated high school furry artist prospects of 2006 and starred in college before being made the #1 pick of Sofawolf. He's excelled in his first two years, garnering several convention GOH appearances. He has won the last three Ursa Major awards for Best Published Illustration (including a 2009 win for the cover of *Out of Position*), and in 2008, his full-color graphic novel *Dog's Days of Summer* won an Ursa Major for Best Other Literary Work. His next project is the Nordguard Adventure, a painted graphic novel to be released in three parts. *Across Thin Ice*, the first volume, has earned wide acclaim, and part two, *Under Dark Skies*, is forthcoming.

His all-ages gallery can be found at *www.blotchinc.com*. For more information on the Nordguard Adventure, please visit the official website at *www.nordguard.com*.

About Sofawolf Press

Sofawolf Press was founded in 1999 to provide a venue to showcase great writers of anthropomorphic fiction and to promote the genre to a wider audience.

Since the debut of its flagship publication, Anthrolations, a literary anthology of short stories, the Press has added to its lineup other magazine-length anthologies, novels, shared-world anthologies, and other novel-length collections, comics and graphic novels, artists' sketchbooks, and calendars. The Press continues to seek out new and creative ways of expanding its offerings of printed creations. Sofawolf's publications have won twenty Ursa Major awards, and in 2012, Ursula Vernon's *Digger* gave Sofawolf Press its first Hugo Award.

Please visit their website at *www.sofawolf.com* for a full list of titles available from Sofawolf Press. Thanks for reading!